Not long after the nation's slickest public relations wizards were brought in to refurbish the image of John D. Rockefeller, he began to have a recurrent dream in which a young man approached him and said, "Mr. Rockefeller, to what do you owe your success?" and Mr. Rockefeller replied, "Oh, pshaw, I want to tell you the truth, and the truth is that you must squeeze the other fellow before he squeezes you. And the one who squeezes best is the one who gets ahead, you know. After all, that's what made this country great."

Whenever he had this dream, Mr. Rockefeller always awoke much refreshed.

1

Richie Flynn went up to look at the synagogue the day after Fowler had spoken to him about it.

The synagogue was in the South Bronx, and Flynn drove from Manhattan in his Volkswagen over the Madison Avenue Bridge and turned into the Grand Concourse. On his right at One Hundred Fifty-second Street he passed his old high school, Cardinal Hayes. It was still the same, but that could not be said for much else.

Up the street from Cardinal Hayes was the Concourse Plaza Hotel. It was a massive structure ten stories high, with four hundred rooms, that stood on the crown of a hill, its windows on the west and south offering a spectacular view of New York City. The Concourse Plaza at one time was the centerpiece of social life in the Bronx. Assembly-line bar mitzvahs and wedding receptions paraded through it like frozen-faced mannequins on a fashion-show runway. Visiting ball clubs playing at Yankee Stadium always stayed there. During the World Series the hotel would be jammed. It had since become a welfare rattrap.

The eight-lane expanse of the Grand Concourse stretched ahead of him. In the bright April sunlight it appeared at first to fulfill its original intent as a sweeping testimonial to solid middle-class prosperity. But Flynn could not help noticing how lifeless it seemed. And at night it was completely dead. To reside one day along Grand Concourse, to stroll leisurely down it in the evening, had been the dream of many thousands of Jewish immigrants to the city. Now the elderly few who remained shivered in fear behind barred doors.

About halfway up the Grand Concourse Flynn turned right. Geographically he was in the mid-Bronx, but he still was in what was called the South Bronx. The South Bronx was a state of mind. It had once been located below One Hundred Thirty-eighth Street, then One Hundred Forty-ninth Street, then One Hundred Sixty-first Street. It had reached two-thirds of the way up the borough, and the end was not in sight. The South Bronx boasted certain distinguishing features. It was black or Spanish-speaking, and it had burned-out buildings.

Flynn drove through a maze of side streets. On nearly every block he passed houses of worship with painted signs like "Iglesia de Dios" and "Grace Baptist Church." He could tell that they had once been synagogues because of the six-pointed stars that were in the leaded stained-glass windows or chiseled into the masonry.

He skirted a park and came to the synagogue that Fowler had described. It was much larger than the other synagogues he had passed, an impressive edifice designed in the Moorish style, with smooth white concrete walls, well over a hundred feet long, about fifty feet wide and three stories high. There were two graceful arches over the main entrance steps reaching almost to the third story. Twin square towers rose above the front corners of the roof, and when Flynn stepped back, he could see their slanted red-tiled tops.

The entrance was protected by a padlocked steel fence. Two windows on one side had been shattered and would have to be replaced. Sprayed on the wall under the windows in blue letters from an aerosol paint can was the legend "The Young Sheiks," and under that another notice that said "Fuck the Young Sheiks," with a crossed-daggers signature. Let them write anything they want, Flynn thought. Fowler had said that the heating plant and the electrical system were in reasonably good shape, and that was what counted.

The synagogue had been deserted for more than a year. According to Fowler, the congregation had moved to Westchester County, to some place like Scarsdale or New Rochelle. Flynn ran a finger against the hard granular surface. It was a miracle that it was still standing. Across the street was a gutted apartment house. And in the park, fronting the entrance, rows of concrete stanchions that once held wooden benches ranged like tombstones. The last of what had been a series of steel supports for children's swings lay grotesquely bent, the others having been ripped from their foundations for their value as scrap metal. A wading pool was filled with rubble, and in the sun shards of glass glinted.

Churning with restless energy, Flynn walked for several blocks. He turned a corner. The street before him curved slightly. There was something wrong. It took him a moment to realize what it was. The street was devoid of human habitation. He walked along it for another five blocks. There was nothing, not even garbage. It was as if the street were a movie set swept bare. Here, in the middle of the Borough of the Bronx, with a population of more than a million and a half, the only sound Flynn heard was the wind.

All the buildings had been burned. They were only shells. Every fixture, every inch of copper and brass piping, was gone. Some of the buildings had metal fire shields where the windows had been. They grinned blankly at Flynn, like a skull's teeth. But most of the windows were empty holes. The City of New York used to put the shields up on every burned-out building as a safety precaution. But there had been too many fires in the South Bronx, thirty or forty a day. In the beginning slum landlords had the fires set to collect the insurance. Then the insurance companies terminated the policies, and junkies started the fires in order to sell what was left. Now the people in these buildings lit the fires so that they would not have to live in them anymore. Many experts had visited the area to try to figure out what should be done about it. One of them said that it should be flattened out and plowed under, that if people could not survive such an environment, a certain strain of hardy winter wheat might do well there.

On his way back Flynn saw smoke billowing from an ancient tenement and heard the wail of fire trucks. Adjacent to the burning building was a school yard. A group of black kids was playing basketball. A kid had just driven toward the basket from midcourt when a huge cloud of dirty smoke enveloped the yard. Then a shift in the wind blew the smoke away. The kid with the ball was now leaping up at the basket. He had never stopped dribbling through the smoke. All over America kids would halt whatever they were doing to watch a gathering of fire engines like this. Except in the South Bronx.

It was incredible to think that in the midst of this decay and deprivation the synagogue could make Flynn somebody again, and when he had returned to it, he reached out and touched it once more to reassure himself of its reality. In his reverie, he thought of his dead father, a subway motorman who had died of pulmonary tuberculosis

when Flynn was ten. His father had never been anybody;
he had never scored.

Then Richie Flynn got into his car and drove north. At
One Hundred Eighty-second Street he passed through a
strip two blocks wide and ten blocks long that had been
totally leveled. It reminded him of the scenes he used to
see on the evening news of a no-man's-land cleared around
South Vietnamese villages to prevent sneak attacks by the
Vietcong. The only evidence that it had once been a living
part of the city were some fire hydrants and no-parking
signs.

On the far side of the strip it was as though Flynn had
switched to another channel. The neighborhood was almost completely Italian. The houses, mostly two or three
stories, were painted bright blues and reds and yellows.
There was a bustling activity in the streets. Vendors
hawked vegetables at the top of their lungs. The fragrance
of fresh bread filled the air. Masons were busy laying
brick walls for a new store. Flynn parked in front of Rose
Spano's restaurant and went inside.

He sat in a booth and ordered a Goldblatt beer. Rose
herself came to greet him. She was a stout woman, with
marcelled gray hair and dark coppery skin. She looked
like a grandmother, which she was several times over. She
was also co-leader of the regular Democratic club in her
district. Her job on election day was to get out the vote,
and her faith in and dedication to the political process had
produced tangible results. One son was a city marshal, a
daughter clerked in the county courthouse and another son
acted as a no-show adviser to a legislative committee in
the State Assembly.

Flynn's quick little-boy grin drew a broad smile from
her. "Richie, how are you?" she said, embracing him.
"You never come up here no more. What can I get you?
A little pizza, like usual?"

"Just make sure the crust's extra thin, Rose. I got to
watch myself. I'm getting on, you know." His wide corn-
flower-blue eyes regarded her mischievously. Flynn was
thirty-three, and although his jawline had softened from
the drinking and he had thickened somewhat in the
middle, he was still reasonably close to his old playing
weight of one hundred seventy pounds.

"What are you talking, Richie?" she bellowed delightedly. "You look like a million!" Then her voice dropped.

"I wish I could say the same for Heinemann. You read about him?"

"Yeah," he said, "it's too bad." Heinemann was a local assemblyman who had been convicted of political bribery. He had offered a potential opponent a job if the opponent would hold off running against him until Heinemann finished another term in office.

Rose Spano glowered. "The mayor has the same problem, and he goes down to Washington and gets his problem a big federal appointment, and everybody laughs and says how smart the mayor is. Heinemann does the same thing, and he goes to jail. With that fat little ass of his, he'll last about twenty seconds in there. It isn't right, am I right? I don't know what the world's coming to."

"Rose," Flynn said, already adopting the dispassion of someone who has it made, "the world's always been that way."

"You know," she said, "you're right. What do you want on your pie? Sausage and peppers? Maybe some mushrooms?"

2

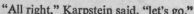

"All right," Karpstein said, "let's go."

"Sure, Albert," said Tommy Biondo, leaping up from the cracked red leather sofa as if touched by a cattle prod, his swarthy face under the fluorescent ceiling lights reflecting the greenish cast of spoiled steak. Arms askew, a too-large shirt and suit enveloping his slight frame, Biondo careened toward the front office in a herky-jerk fashion that made him look like a bit player perpetually struggling against the elements in a Buster Keaton comedy. There was a reason, at least, for Biondo's oversized jacket: the snub-nosed .38-caliber revolver he carried in a shoulder holster during business hours. "Tommy's my man," Karpstein would explain on occasion to an interested party, "a real gunsel." While Biondo had, in fact, as he artfully put it, "blown away" seven unfortunates during his twenty-seven years on earth, this sort of remark by Karpstein elicited nervous titters from his audience not so much because of any intrinsic wit on Karpstein's part, but because of Karpstein himself.

Now striding purposefully behind Biondo, Karpstein measured six feet one inch and weighed two hundred forty-three pounds. But most people experienced such an immediate rush of terror in his presence that they invariably ascribed several additional inches to his height and fifty or so pounds to his heft. Indeed, he had acquired basic law enforcement statistics of six feet five and two hundred ninety pounds after his initial booking for assault and battery (by fist) in his hometown of Hoboken, New Jersey, when a half dozen cops, clutching his brown curly hair and yanking his jacket down over his arms as a makeshift straitjacket to record a memorable mug shot, then failed to subdue him further and finally resorted to estimating his proportions.

Karpstein was thirty-eight. He had massive, sloping shoulders and an enormous torso that was supported by somewhat spindly legs. His lips had a built-in sneer, and his eyes, indeterminately dark, wavered between human and inhuman. In repose, under bushy brows, the eyes had a hooded, sleepy look. When he was angry or upset, they dilated and turned as cold and hard as chunks of anthracite. But what was ultimately so terrorizing about Karpstein was the random, totally unpredictable ferocity that emanated from him, as palpable and invisible as an electrical charge. In one instant he might appear as genial as a neighborhood shopkeeper; in the next he would be sinking his teeth into your neck.

During a lunch break at a trial in which Karpstein was charged with armed robbery, he called a bookmaker who owed him a six-hundred-dollar payment on a loan. "Bring it down to the courthouse," Karpstein said. "I could use the money."

"I ain't got it," the bookmaker said. "You get it when I got it."

"Hey, I want it today, *now,* or I'll break your chops good," Karpstein said.

"Listen, do me a favor and get off my back," the bookmaker said, and hung up in the mistaken, if reasonable, expectation that Karpstein, with a possible ten-year prison sentence in the offing, had more pressing matters on his mind.

Karpstein screamed inside the phone booth. He burst out of it so fast that the glass door shattered. He pushed his way through the crowded courthouse lobby, went down the steps, hailed a cab and took it to the saloon where the bookmaker was. When he walked in, the bookmaker was seated at the bar reaching for a stein of beer. Karpstein beat him to it. The bookmaker started to turn around indignantly, saw who was holding the stein and said, "Oh, my God!" The bookmaker also wanted to say, "I'll pay you right now," but Karpstein wasn't interested in the money anymore. He swung the stein against the side of the bookmaker's head, and as the bookmaker toppled off his barstool, Karpstein hit him a second time so hard that all he had left in his hand was the stein's handle.

The bookmaker fell to the floor with multiple fractures of his jawbone, his ear nearly severed, the blood mixed in with the beer running down his neck. Karpstein leaned over him and said, "That'll learn you some respect."

When Karpstein got back to the courtroom a half hour late, he stared up at the judge and said, "I'm sorry, Your

Honor, I had some business," and the judge coughed nervously and said, "Well, don't let it happen again."

It required twenty-three stitches to put the bookmaker's ear back in shape, and for the next two months he ate through a straw, but he never said a word in the investigation that followed his arrival at the hospital. There must have been thirty witnesses in the saloon, and they did not say anything either.

Karpstein was known by a variety of names. One was "King Kong." The newspapers, in noting his arrests or otherwise involving him in a story about the underworld, always identified him as "Albert (King Kong) Karpstein," but nobody, of course, called him that to his face. Actually, this sobriquet had another beastly antecedent when a sportswriter on the Newark *Star-Ledger* reported "Godzilla entered the ring at the Jersey Gardens last night in the form of Albert Karpstein, a young heavyweight from Hoboken," but an alliterating copy editor, who was also a veteran of Pacific action during World War II and detested anything made in Japan, switched monsters in a flush of patriotic fervor. King Kong Karpstein's boxing career was short-lived. While he clubbed three carefully selected opponents into insensibility, even his tubby patron, Joseph Iacovelli, alias Joe Hoboken or Joe Hobo, reluctantly concluded that Karpstein was too ponderous to be a contender and returned him to the street, where his talents could be better utilized. Joe Hobo was the dominant Mafia figure for that part of New Jersey within sight of the lower Manhattan skyline; he regarded Karpstein with the same sense of accomplishment and pride as someone who has managed to leash-train a pet panther, and he affectionately called him "Milky" because of Karpstein's predilection for Milky Way candy bars. But as a rule people who had any dealings with Karpstein tactfully addressed him as Albert and hoped for the best.

Joe Hobo's Mafia colleagues, especially those who gathered at the Ravens Club, had a harsher appellation for Karpstein: "the animal." The Ravens Club was on Mulberry Street in the Little Italy section of Manhattan; Joe Hobo, who had grown up in the neighborhood before prospering in New Jersey, took to visiting it with increasing frequency as he advanced into his late sixties. The club's modest exterior was painted ivy green. A discreet sign in gilded letters by the front door said, "Members

Only," although no local resident would ever dream of setting an uninvited foot inside it. And in case curious tourists were attracted by the big espresso machine barely visible through the curtained plate-glass windows, there were always two young toughs stationed on the sidewalk to advise them, "The place is private." The decorative features of the club, basically one large room, had remained untouched for years. Behind the coffee bar was a sepia photograph of a young Joe DiMaggio in uniform; a tinted reproduction of the Sacred Heart of Jesus hung over the green baize-draped archway leading to a small back room, where discussions of a confidential nature could be held; and on the wall opposite the bar were several faded portraits of Italian boxers dating from the 1920s, all with Irish ring names. Here Joe Hobo could pass a pleasant afternoon gossiping with his fraternal peers, reminiscing about the old days, sipping coffee and playing gin rummy for ten dollars a point on the polished oak tables, filled with a sense of belonging that had eluded him in New Jersey despite his rackets power. Joe Hobo, for example, controlled the private collection of garbage in two suburban counties. He could walk into any of the exclusive country clubs that dotted the area and shoot a round of golf whenever he felt like it, since the management of each club knew what the alternative was. They knew because an assistant manager at one club had approached Joe Hobo after he completed an afternoon on the course and told him that some of the members had expressed dismay at his presence.

"You mean I can't play here no more?"

"If it was up to me," the assistant manager said, "you could play all you want. But we have been getting complaints. You know how people are."

This encounter occurred near the end of June. By the Fourth of July weekend, every fly in the state seemed to be buzzing around, and the stench of uncollected garbage was so overpowering that the club's annual fireworks display had to be canceled. After the club's board of governors held two emergency meetings, the club's manager telephoned Joe Hobo directly about the garbage.

"Garbage?" Joe Hobo said. "What do I know from garbage?"

"I realize that, sir," the manager said hastily. "I was just calling to say that an unfortunate error was made a few days ago concerning the, uh, use of our facilities."

"You mean I can play?"

"Yes, sir, anytime. Be our guest."

Still in the delicate balance of human relationships with all their social, class and ethnic distinctions, Joe Hobo, for all his tangible clout, could be no more than a guest. That he did not challenge this further was partly a matter of pride, but mostly it was because in his heart he subscribed to the same precepts that barred him from membership in such places. So he repaired to the exclusivity of the Ravens Club, where he did not have to fret about who and what he was, and where the only jarring note came during lulls in the conversation when someone would needle him about Karpstein. "Hey, Joe, how's the animal? What you feeding him these days?"

Normally Joe Hobo ignored gibes like these. Once, however, upset after having lost heavily at cards, he rose passionately to Karpstein's defense. "Listen, Milky's a little crude, I grant you, but he does a job. Couple of months ago this guy comes to me for a Teamster loan, and I tell him I will see what I can arrange for ten percent, which is thirty-five hundred. I get the guy a letter of intent from the union, and I ask my commission, and this creep says the loan ain't through yet, and I tell him I done my part, that was the bargain, and I want my money, and the guy says he can't pay it. Well, to make a long story short, I call Milky and tell him the guy owes me thirty-five hundred, and the next day Milky walks in and hands me the money without a word. So I ask that kid Biondo that hangs out with Milky how he done it, and the kid says Milky went right into the guy's house. The guy's wife was there alone, and Milky pulled off her pants and sat her in a chair, and put on a rubber glove and took a glob of Vaseline and worked open her snatch and stuck a knife in it, and told her to call her husband and explain the situation, and that if he wasn't over with the money in one hour, she was going to have to get up and walk around on the knife. So OK, he's crude but, you know, efficient."

Everybody at the Ravens Club was silent when Joe Hobo had finished speaking. "You mean," one of his fellow capos finally said, "he stuck a *knife* in the broad's snatch?"

Joe Hobo's eyes darted uneasily about the room, his

pampered cheeks reddening slightly. "Goddammit, he got the money, didn't he?"

"Yeah, well, just keep that fucking animal out of the city."

☆

On the day Tommy Biondo leaped up so precipitously from the sofa in Karpstein's office, Karpstein was headed into the city at Joe Hobo's behest to make another collection for him.

"What's the particulars?" Karpstein had asked, and Joe Hobo had felt his nerve endings twitch in vague alarm. For longer than he liked to recall—more than twenty years—Karpstein had been carrying out his instructions without question, and suddenly, it seemed, Karpstein started wanting to know the particulars. Joe Hobo's antennae were a little late in picking up the warning signals. While Karpstein might have become unconsciously more self-assertive after all this time, he had for at least a decade carefully recorded and sequestered in a safe-deposit box the details of every errand his patron had sent him on, a hedge, as it were, against the unforeseen.

"The particulars," Joe Hobo said irritably, "are these two sharpshooters screwed me out of fifty grand." The two men who had kindled his fury were partners in an over-the-counter brokerage house speculating in fringe securities. Through an intermediary Joe Hobo had invested fifty thousand dollars with them in the takeover of a land development company specializing in, among other things, Arizona real estate. The thought of what could be made to bloom in the desert after the example of Nevada was a constant nettle in the psyche of mafiosi like Joe Hobo, and they endlessly brooded over the foresight of their Jewish brethren, those "fucking Christ killers" who had created a bonanza in Las Vegas that they were able to share only in the way a pack of jackals might snap up odd entrails after a big kill. And while their dreams of constructing a string of palatial casinos on a barren landscape they could call their own had been thwarted, primarily by an aggressive local press, Arizona retained its magical allure. So Joe Hobo had opted for retirement home sites, the idea being that the fabled sun and dry air of the Southwest, combined with a hard-sell mail-order campaign, would transform twenty-five dollars expended on each forlorn acre into profits a hundredfold that amount. Joe Hobo loved the concept; the suckers would come flocking in. The trouble was, however, that the two gentlemen his accountant chose to do business with had apparently diverted most of their ready cash to fend off creditors from other ill-fated ventures. They had gotten away with this many times before, but their mistake in the present instance was not knowing with whom they were dealing.

"What do you want me to do?" Karpstein said. "Throw a scare in them? Kick the shit out of them? Or what?"

"I don't give a fuck what you do," Joe Hobo said. "Just get me my money back."

If Karpstein had a regret in life, it was that he had not been born an Italian. He tried to resolve his identity crisis by often using an Italian pseudonym. "This is Johnny Rocco," he said when he made his appointment with one of the partners in the brokerage house. "I'm calling for a client that you pricks beat for fifty grand, and I'm coming in to straighten this whole thing out once and for all."

The firm had a Wall Street address and a fancy name, Cambridge Associates, Ltd. When Karpstein arrived, he found that the offices consisted of a small anteroom, with a nervous middle-aged secretary in it, and a second room, not much larger, with two desks, no view and seven telephones. He also found only the partner he had spoken to, a handsomely tailored man named Jay Landers. Karpstein noticed that he was wearing a gold watch.

"How many widows and orphans you swindled?" Karpstein asked.

"I beg your pardon," he said in a cultivated voice.

"Forget it," Karpstein said. "Where's the other guy? I told you I wanted both of you."

"I don't know," Landers said. "I spoke to him after your call, of course, but I really don't know what this is all about." The partnership, according to Landers, had been dissolved. As part of the settlement, his former colleague had taken the Arizona land promotion with him; it had been his all along anyway. Landers offered to open up the firm's ledgers as proof.

"Let's see them," Karpstein said. "I want the checkbooks, too."

After studying the records, Karpstein concluded that

Landers was basically telling the truth. "You know," Karpstein said, "you're a fucking moron. You wind up with nothing out of this deal, but you picked that guy to be with, and you have to pay. This is my decision. I'm giving you a break. I'm holding you responsible for one-third of the fifty, which is sixteen thousand six hundred and sixty-six dollars, sixty-six cents."

"My dear fellow," Landers said, "you must be joking."

Karpstein continued to speak as though Landers had not said anything. He told Landers that he wanted an immediate down payment of five thousand dollars, the check to be made out to Joe Hobo's accountant. Landers was also to open an account in the accountant's name at the First National City Bank, Forty-second Street and Sixth Avenue branch, and deposit one thousand dollars in it by noon each Monday until the principal was retired. "You could pay the six hundred and change the last week," Karpstein said.

"Why don't I just jump out the window?"

Karpstein's eyes went blank. "Be my guest," he said. "It saves me pushing you."

Landers stared into Karpstein's eyes and began to shake. "My God, where'll I get the money?"

"Hock your house," Karpstein said. "You got a beautiful house out there on Long Island, Eleven-ninety-nine Garth Drive, Great Neck." Almost as an afterthought, he added, "You got a beautiful wife, too. What's her name? Oh, yeah, Ingrid. And two kids, right? Boys, twelve and sixteen. Hey, that's nice."

Landers looked as if he were going to faint. He buzzed his secretary and told her to prepare the check for his signature. After Karpstein had pocketed it, he said, "Listen, tell that slob partner Mandelbaum you had I'm very aggravated he didn't show. That ain't respectful. You give him this number to call. You tell him I'm not Johnny Rocco, I am Albert Karpstein. Tell him to ask around what that means."

As Karpstein was leaving, he remembered something— tomorrow was Tommy Biondo's birthday. "I almost forgot," Karpstein said. "Give me the watch."

"It's a Piaget," Landers said.

"So?"

"I mean it's an expensive watch. It cost three thousand

dollars wholesale." A lot of the polish had disappeared from his voice.

"Good! I'll take it. You want your arm to go with it?"

"Please," Landers said. "It's an anniversary present from my wife. It's engraved and everything."

"Don't worry about that," Karpstein said. "Besides, I didn't charge you interest, huh?"

Tommy Biondo was delighted with the watch, although Karpstein began to rue giving it to him. Biondo kept telling him what time it was. "You sound like a fucking train announcer," Karpstein said. "I want to know what time it is, I got my own watch."

Two days after the confrontation with Landers, Karpstein received a call from a man named Lawrence Farber. "I'm an attorney," Farber said. "I represent Mr. Marvin Mandelbaum. Mr. Mandelbaum asked me to contact you. There seems to be some dispute, and perhaps I can be helpful in resolving it amicably."

"Where was that fuck?" Karpstein said. "He didn't show. That's the way he does business? The other guy took care of his end, and he wasn't even the culprit. Where the hell was Mandelbaum?"

"Well, frankly, from what I gather," Farber said, "he was afraid."

"That scumbag don't show the next time, he's got something to be afraid of. Nobody stands me up. Today is Wednesday. I am fixing a meeting for Friday at five o'clock," Karpstein said, and gave the Manhattan office address of Joe Hobo's accountant. When Karpstein got excited, his voice tended to rise. It had become quite high. "If he ain't there, I'm going hunting for him."

"Calm down," Farber said. "Can't we discuss this rationally?"

"Five o'clock!" Karpstein said, and hung up.

The appointed Friday was now at hand, and Karpstein, following Biondo to the door, was in a fouler mood than ever. A job like this, which should have been disposed of in short order, had already consumed the better part of a week. That alone was a sufficient irritant. But even worse, while Karpstein had remembered Tommy Biondo's birthday, he had forgotten in his rage at Mandelbaum that this Friday was also his seven-year-old daughter's birthday, and he had promised his wife to stop in at a party for her that afternoon. "Hon, you just have to see her in the dress I got her," his wife had said.

Karpstein briefly considered calling off the meeting with Mandelbaum. Remaining resolute, however, was vital in his line of work. There was no question in his mind that Mandelbaum would finally appear as ordered, but if Karpstein changed the hour or the date of the meeting at the last minute, he knew how a Mandelbaum would exploit this, how many cries of injured protestation and additional evasions would ensue, how much more time would be required to settle the affair.

The building from which Karpstein and Biondo were emerging was a one-story dingy white cement-block structure in the north end of Hoboken by the Hudson River. It was surrounded by an eight-foot chain-link fence topped by three strands of rusting barbed wire. A pitted asphalt driveway through a gate in the fence led to six row garages in the rear. On the front of the building was a weather-beaten sign, barely legible, that said "E-Z Trucking, Inc." The immediate neighborhood was equally underwhelming. Scattered haphazardly on grassless lots were dilapidated asbestos-shingled dwellings, machine shops, an automobile wrecking company and some warehouses and truck depots, interlaced by ancient undulating cobblestoned streets, whose dips dutifully collected and retained great pools of stagnant rainwater. Rotting deserted piers poked into the river like broken fingers, and overhead pollutants from oil refineries and factories a few miles to the west reduced the lowering sun to a washed-out wafer the size of a nickel.

The cement-block building contained one large room, thirty by forty feet. The floor was speckled black and white linoleum, and there was a pool table in the middle of it. A refrigerator and an electric hot plate occupied one far corner, a bathroom the other. In the near right corner were file cabinets and the desk at which Leo Weissberg, Karpstein's elfin bookkeeper, labored while listening to chamber music on his FM radio. On the left was the red leather sofa where Biondo lounged when he wasn't perfecting his skill at eight ball. Karpstein's own desk was at a right angle to the sofa, facing out. There was a combination safe next to it, and on the wall behind was a sign that he had made up which said, "The Secret of Success Is Secrecy." Often, while chalking his cue, Biondo would cock his head quizzically at the sign, trying to plumb its Delphic implications.

Karpstein had acquired E-Z Trucking as the result of a defaulted loan. He had variously been an enforcer and executioner, the brains behind a burglary gang, a dope dealer and a fence, but although he still engaged in these activities to one degree or another, his principal occupation, by both design and reputation, was loan-sharking. He had chosen it because there was nothing fly-by-night about lending money. It had continuity and substance, and it offered him power and control over people. Karpstein liked that. "The most important thing about the shylocking business," he confided to Biondo, "is respect."

To command a level of respect that he found acceptable, Karpstein relied on discipline. When a garment manufacturer came to him for a ten-thousand-dollar loan, Karpstein said, "Here's the money. Count it."

The manufacturer counted the bills and said that they added up to the correct amount, and then Karpstein told him the day and hour the interest would be due each week. "If you're ten minutes late," he said, "you just get a beating. If you're one day late, you don't owe me nothing because you are dead." Under these conditions the manufacturer decided that he did not want the loan. "All right," Karpstein said, "that'll cost fifty dollars for counting the money."

Among creditors and debtors in loan-sharking circles Karpstein was referred to as the Last Resort. People borrow money from loan sharks because they can't get it anywhere else, of course, because they don't have the security that banks and other legitimate lending agencies require or because they want the money for something that can't be repossessed. There is a special prayer for citizens who take money from loan sharks: "O Lord, please send me a trusting shylock with a weak heart."

Generally loan sharks will do almost anything to keep their money circulating and earning interest. A loan shark will go out at three A.M. in the middle of a blizzard to deliver funds to a client, a service bankers are not noted for. Tuesday is an especially active day for loan sharks, since that is the day bettors and bookmakers settle their accounts. M-Day is another peak period for loan sharks, particularly in working-class neighborhoods, where people put everything they had into owning a home. M-Day is the day the monthly mortgage payment comes due.

Loan sharks traditionally used strong-arm methods to collect arrears, but new federal laws have imposed harsh penalties for the use of "violence" to extort repayment, and to counter what they consider this outrageous incursion against the free-enterprise system, most loan sharks have become more selective about whom they supply cash to; if a debt cannot be paid back, a negotiated settlement is arranged where possible, and if worse comes to worst, it is written off.

King Kong Karpstein, however, clung steadfastly to the old ways. And despite his reputation, he never lacked for clients because they believed he had what they wanted—unlimited money with no questions asked. Like Americans who are the first to swallow their own propaganda, persons who flit in and around the underworld are the most gullible about their own myths, and it was an article of faith among them that Karpstein was the biggest shylock in the East, perhaps in the whole country. No amount was thought to be too much for him to handle, say, half a million dollars, at a moment's notice. The fact was that the largest loan he ever made was seventy-five thousand to a bookmaker who was caught short after the New York Jets upset Baltimore in Super Bowl III, and only because he knew the bookmaker was good for it. Karpstein, aware of his legend, carefully nurtured it. If someone came to him for a loan beyond his resources, he simply laid down such stringent requirements for it that the would-be borrower was forced to depart empty-handed, but with Karpstein's image still intact.

Normally Karpstein would not have taken over something like a trucking company, jewelry being the only item he weighed in lieu of cash. "The word gets around, you know," he told Biondo, "and people think they can dump anything on you." Talking to Biondo relaxed Karpstein. It was like talking to himself without arousing suspicions that he might be crazy.

Coincidental with the trucker's default, however, Joe Hobo had rewarded Karpstein for services rendered by giving him a piece of a Teamsters local. It was a happy arrangement all around. E-Z Trucking's main business was hauling produce into New York City. E-Z Trucking had only three small vans, but with Karpstein on the scene the produce firms agreed to hand over several of their own trucks to him and lease them back. In return they got guaranteed labor peace. Karpstein's drivers, all black or Puerto Rican, had to pay a twenty-five-dollar initiation fee to join the union, along with three dollars and fifty cents a month in dues, for which they received minimum wages and no benefits, but at least, as Karpstein pointed out, they were working. The trucking company also provided Karpstein with a convenient cover for income tax purposes. Corporate connivance with the Teamsters brought him a further advantage. For his intimidating presence should unrest break out in the local's rank and file, he got a weekly salary of one hundred and forty-seven dollars as a loading-platform foreman at a printing company in Jersey City, although he had never been near the plant in his life. The money itself meant little to Karpstein, who deposited each paycheck in a trust fund he had established for his daughter, but a no-show job like this carried great prestige among racketeers, and short of being inducted into the Mafia, forever denied him because of his ethnic origins, Karpstein was pleased to have it, much the way an ambitious customer's man who yearns for admittance to the Racquet and Tennis Club nonetheless settles for membership in the New York A.C.

Karpstein was born on New York's Lower East Side. He was an only child. His father, whose name was Solomon, was a cutter in the garment center, and his mother, Rebekah, sewed piece goods at home. On a summer Sunday when he was thirteen, his father took him and his mother on a ferryboat ride across the Hudson River to Hoboken. After admiring the massive bronze facade of the Hoboken ferry slips and watching the arrival of the famous passenger train the *Phoebe Snow* in the adjacent terminal of the Lackawanna Railroad, the Karpsteins strolled about the city. They passed a vacated tailor shop, and Solomon and Rebekah instantly had the same thought. They made inquiries. They learned that the tailor who previously occupied the premises had died a few days before and that there were no competitors within five blocks. They had saved just enough money to go into business and rent the apartment over the shop and, given the modest circumstances of the area, did well from the start. For young Albert it was another matter. The neighborhood, within the shadow of Our Lady of Grace Church, was almost exclusively Italian, and whether or not it would have made any difference, none of the sustaining richness, camaraderie and tradition usually associated with Jewish life was available to him. He was big for his age, awkward and lonely. The Italian kids called him a "mockie," a "kike," a "Jew bastard." He became a habitual truant. He fought a lot. He would take on seven or eight Italian boys at once, wreaking havoc on them. Under the sheer weight of numbers, he would eventually go down himself, but he was capable of absorbing enormous punishment and even appeared to enjoy it. He became very secretive. After a truant officer had visited his parents, he would show up, bloodied from another fight. His father would demand to know what had been going on. He would stare back sullenly, refusing to speak. Physically there was nothing his father could do. Oddly enough, his father was a small, delicately boned man, and his mother, although given to fat, was not much larger. His father would rail at him, shouting such things as "You're no son of mine!" while his mother retired to her bed, weeping inconsolably, aghast at what had happened to her *bubeleh.*

All around him, meanwhile, Karpstein perceived and envied the mystique of Italian togetherness, warm, voluble, supportive. Then, one day, to his astonishment some of the Italian youths he had been battling enlisted him in a foray against a juvenile black gang that took place on a railroad overpass along the northwest edge of the city. Karpstein went berserk with joy, tossing one of the blacks onto the tracks below just in time to be decapitated by a freight train. In due course Karpstein's bullyboy exploits attracted the interest of Joe Hobo, and shortly thereafter Karpstein started using the name Johnny Rocco. Joe Hobo became his surrogate father. It was from Joe Hobo that Karpstein developed his fixation on respect, listening to the way the Mafia capo evaluated mankind, overhearing him say, "Fuck that guy, he ain't worthy of respect," or "Gino's a man of respect, we got to honor our commitment." It was also Joe Hobo who subsequently gave his benediction to Karpstein's marriage to an Italian woman, a widow, and stood before the baptismal font as godfather to their daughter.

Not until Israel's dramatic triumph over Egypt in the Six-Day War did the first sense of Jewish pride creep into Karpstein's consciousness. He went to the Hoboken Public

Library and on the advice of an elderly lady at the desk took out *A History of Jews,* which he never returned, and bought a paperback copy of *Israel's Fight for Survival.* In addition, he purchased a gold Star of David on a chain, although he did not wear it. Along with the books, he kept it in his safe at E-Z Trucking, Inc.

☆

On the street now in front of E-Z Trucking Biondo got behind the wheel of Karpstein's dark green Buick sedan. Karpstein had selected a Buick because it was substantial without being ostentatious. "It don't pay, you know what I mean, sticking out in a crowd," Joe Hobo had once counseled him. Karpstein was carrying a black leather attaché case and had on a brown suit and navy blue topcoat, attire that he felt was appropriately sober and businesslike. As always, his shirt was white, and his tie conservatively narrow. The sole bit of sartorial fancy that he allowed himself was matching belts and shoes, usually alligator.

Biondo started the Buick and made a U-turn directly in front of a sign that said "No U-Turn." A cop was standing across the street; Karpstein stared at him. He stared back for a moment, then quickly looked away. The cop knew what had happened to a police captain in Hoboken named Delahanty, who had been on the force when Karpstein first began flexing his muscles for Joe Hobo. Delahanty found the situation highly amusing and had Karpstein hauled in on various suspicion and loitering charges, just to see, as he put it, "the Jew boy running around with the guineas."

Deeming himself unjustly harassed, Karpstein finally walked right into Delahanty's office at police headquarters and leveled him with one punch, breaking his jaw. That night Joe Hobo spirited Karpstein aboard a freighter in Port Newark bound for Cuba. Joe Hobo had an interest in a gambling casino in Havana, and he arranged to have Karpstein hired on as a "security man." Karpstein had worked there for the better part of a year when a drunken player at a blackjack table began yelling that he had been cheated. Karpstein hustled him outside and, under instructions, passed him over to the Havana police. The man, who was carrying an Argentinian passport, turned out to be a former SS officer wanted for numerous atrocities committed in German-occupied Holland. The Batista dictatorship, its hands full with the Castro uprising in the mountains, could do little for the SS man even if it had wanted to, so he was shipped back for trial, and Karpstein wound up getting a thank-you letter from the great Nazi war criminal hunter Simon Wiesenthal.

The incident meant nothing to Karpstein, but it did mean something to Joe Hobo, who told him to return forthwith to Hoboken and saw to it that he appeared in a courtroom presided over by Judge Morris A. Greenberg. Karpstein pleaded guilty to assaulting Delahanty, and Judge Greenberg noted the gravity of the offense, not to mention Karpstein's fugitive status. Where, he inquired, had Karpstein been?

"Well, Judge, to tell the truth," Karpstein said in his carefully rehearsed reply, "I knew I had to straighten myself out, so I went down to South America looking for Nazis. You probably don't know this, Judge, but they're thick as thieves down there." Karpstein's lawyer then produced the Wiesenthal letter.

In a voice choked with emotion, Judge Greenberg declared that he had rarely been witness to a nobler effort at self-rehabilitation, prophesied a fine future for the defendant and gave him a year's probation.

Delahanty got a measure of revenge, however. About six months later Karpstein received a phone call purportedly from one of Joe Hobo's minions instructing him to go to a garage where there was a job to be done. When Karpstein entered the garage, it was empty except for a truck. He looked inside the truck and found it loaded with men's suits. There was a bill of lading to Bamberger's department store in Newark, and each suit had a Bamberger label sewn into it. Moments afterward the garage was swarming with police, and Karpstein was arrested and charged with robbery, grand larceny and possession of stolen goods. He faced a jail term of up to twenty years. Everyone knew it was a setup, since the first thing even the most simpleminded fence does is cut out identifying labels from merchandise like this, thus making it next to impossible to prove that it was stolen. In addition, Delahanty produced an informant who swore that Karpstein had planned the hijacking.

Joe Hobo did everything he could to fix the case, even visiting the irate captain to suggest that enough was

enough, remarking with a world-weary shrug that personal
feelings should never interfere with business and, more to
the point, reminding Delahanty of the weekly payoff he received "regular as clockwork" from Joe Hobo's numbers
operation. The proceedings against Karpstein were further
weakened when the informant unaccountably disappeared;
he had, in fact, died peacefully in his sleep, an ice pick
thrust into his ear.

Despite it all, Karpstein was going to have to go to
prison for a while. "I'm sorry, kid," Joe Hobo told him. "I
was hoping this whole thing would blow over, but the guy
is still sore about his jaw. So you got to do some time to
make it right. Not much. A couple of years, maybe. It's a
good lesson. You got to use your head. I mean, socking a
cop, for Christ's sake!"

Karpstein served nineteen months in the state peniten-
tiary, where he diligently applied himself to improving his
long-neglected reading and writing skills. The events leading to his incarceration left an indelible impression on
him. Like some monstrous fish propelling itself through
the sea, ravaging whatever crossed its path, yet sensing
certain limitations imposed by shoreline shallows, Karpstein acknowledged, more by instinct than anything else,
the basically indistinguishable, institutionalized power on
all sides of him. It was not that he feared it, nor would he
hesitate for a second to confront any of its various
manifestations head-on if necessary. It was simply there, to
be treated with caution, taken into consideration. That was
why, old loyalties aside, Karpstein continued to maintain
relations with Joe Hobo long past his period as a protégé
and was at this moment on his way to a meeting with the
recalcitrant Marvin Mandelbaum on the mafioso's behalf.

Biondo drove north out of Hoboken, through Wee-
hawken, to the Lincoln Tunnel. Ten minutes later he
parked the car in a lot on Forty-second Street just west of
Eighth Avenue. In the gathering twilight the glitter of
Forty-second Street made the transformation from day to
night pass almost unnoticed. The smell of rancid popcorn
filled the air. Stuttering light bulbs of a movie theater identifying it as the Michelangelo featured *Ghetto Guys* along
with the pitch on its marquee, "Hard Hard Hard." Twenty
feet distant Cinema Eve presented *Nurses at Play* with
"Live Sex" on stage at three-hour intervals from noon to
midnight. The second-story Temple of Love, with flashing

red arrows pointing upward, promised "Body Rubs" at ten dollars a rub, "No Tipping." A bookstore, instead of the reproductions of pre-Columbian, Roman and Greek sculpture on sale in its Fifth Avenue counterparts, offered a life-size, blow-up doll with a *"vibrating* electric vagina." Another bookstore, equally dubious about the literary attention span of its clientele, emphasized an all-new collection of peep show films, including "Hot Animal Acts."

Pausing before a candy store that displayed upright chocolate phalluses complete with bonbon testicles, Karpstein said, "Remember when the biggest thing around was some nigger tits in the *National Geographic?*"

"Yeah," said Tommy Biondo, who had never heard of the *National Geographic.*

It was the beginning of the evening rush hour. Hundreds of suburban family heads streamed toward the West Side bus terminal while whores stationed themselves in doorways, like bears on a riverbank during a salmon run. Every so often there would be a swirl in the flow as a pickup was made, twenty minutes of relief in a hotel room between the office desk and a night at home with the wife, the kids and the television. For those who preferred other pleasures, there was a scattering of pale-faced, blank-eyed teenage boys hunched against building walls; the boys did pretty well, too.

Karpstein, attaché case in hand, marched straight against the oncoming tide, which parted instantly at his approach, Biondo weaving alongside him, a pilot fish hovering by a dorsal fin. Then a black whore wearing a blond wig, a fake fur coat and high white boots made the mistake of propositioning Karpstein. She briefly opened her coat, revealing bright red hot pants and bare thumb-shaped breasts. "Hey, big man," she said, "want a date?" Karpstein never stopped moving. With a sweep of his arm he sent the whore skidding across the sidewalk on her knees. "Motherfucker!" she screamed, still on the sidewalk. Her pimp, standing a few feet away, dressed in a pink slouch hat, pink coat and pink shoes with elevated heels, went to help her up. "Get that motherfucker!" she screamed again. "You see what he did?"

What the pimp had seen, however, was Karpstein's eyes, and he told her, "Cool it, baby."

Karpstein strode on. The incident with the whore had uncorked a new wave of anger, and the suppressed fury at this second trip into the city to collect Joe Hobo's money all because of Mandelbaum, forcing him to miss his daughter's birthday party, surged through Karpstein once more. Suddenly he was ravenous.

"Give me a Milky Way," he said to Biondo.

Biondo frantically searched his pockets, a look of anguish on his face. "Jeez, Albert," he said, "we left so fast and everything, I forgot them."

Karpstein grunted unintelligibly, handed the attaché case to Biondo and wheeled into a food shop specializing in hero sandwiches and barbecued chicken. "Give me a chicken," he told the counterman.

"To go?"

"No, I'll eat it here."

Karpstein picked up the chicken in both hands. He tore chunks of breast from each side of it with his teeth, swalloping them without seeming to chew. He broke off first one leg and then the other, sticking them into his mouth like lollipops, ingesting the meat with a soft, sucking whoosh. The whole process took possibly thirty seconds. He belched and said, "Orange juice."

The counterman started to pour a glass of juice from a quart container.

"All of it," Karpstein said, reaching for the container. He drained it in continuous gulps. He belched again. Bits of meat clung to his grease-smeared lips. He glanced to his left and saw a man gaping at him.

"Something wrong?" Karpstein said.

"Oh, no," the man said, and darted out the door, the counterman calling after him, "Hey, what about your sandwich?"

Karpstein wiped his mouth, paid the cashier and rejoined Biondo on the sidewalk. Biondo was excitedly brandishing a Milky Way. "I found one," he said. "I had it all the time!"

"I'll eat it later," Karpstein said.

The office of Joe Hobo's accountant was in a building on Forty-second Street east of Broadway. Karpstein and Biondo rode up a wheezing hydraulic-powered elevator to the fifth floor. The office was deserted except for a secretary who had been waiting for them. After she let them in, she departed. "Don't worry," Karpstein told her. "I'll lock up."

Karpstein instructed Biondo to stay by the front door.

He went into the conference room. The table, plastic imitation walnut, seated six. Karpstein sat at the far end, placed his attaché case next to him and worked his tongue on a piece of chicken lodged between molars on the upper right side of his mouth.

At six minutes after five the conference door opened, and Biondo came in, followed by Marvin Mandelbaum and another man. Mandelbaum was just under six feet tall and enormously fat, weighing around three hundred pounds. He moved with a fat man's precise, delicate gait, as though he were walking on rubber cushions. Even if Mandelbaum had lost one hundred and fifty pounds overnight, he would still have looked fat.

"You're late, Mandelbaum," Karpstein said. "You don't show respect."

"It was the elevator," he almost shrieked. "The goddamn elevator didn't come!" Mandelbaum's eyes, buried in his face like raisins in cookie dough, peered nervously at Karpstein. "I'm telling you, it was the elevator."

The man with Mandelbaum nodded vigorously. "That's right," he said, "I can attest to that." He was slender, appeared to be in his early thirties and wore a plum-colored suit, the jacket waist pinched, trousers flared. He had long sideburns and a toupee, styled modishly flat.

"Who the fuck are you?" Karpstein said.

"I'm Larry Farber," he said. "Mr. Mandelbaum's attorney. Remember, I spoke to you on the phone. I, uh, Mr. Mandelbaum thought my presence here might be useful."

Karpstein scrutinized him. "I bet you're real hot stuff with the girls," he said. "All right, sit down. You too, Mandelbaum." Karpstein's tongue probed the piece of chicken stuck between his teeth in another futile effort to remove it. Then he opened his mouth and dug at it with a fingernail, still without success. The two men at the opposite end of the table watched as though a bomb were being defused in front of them.

Finally Karpstein gave up. "Now," he said, "we are going to conduct this meeting in an orderly manner, and the first thing we are going to do is see if you fucks are wired. Tommy, frisk them."

Grinning delightedly at his onstage role, Biondo stepped forward from his position at the door and searched Mandelbaum and Farber. "They're clean, Albert," he said. "They ain't got nothing on them."

"Good," Karpstein said. "They're smarter than I thought. So let's get on with it. Mandelbaum, you're a fucking thief."

"Just a minute, Mr. Karpstein," Farber said.

"Shut up," Karpstein said. "I am the judge and the jury here. Lawyers ain't allowed to speak. I don't know what Mandelbaum brought a lawyer for anyway. What he needs is a rabbi."

There was a pencil on the table. Karpstein picked it up and fingered its sharpened point. "Mandelbaum, for two lousy cents I'd take this pencil and put it right through your eye," he said. "You think I won't do it? It don't mean a thing to me."

Marvin Mandelbaum slumped in his chair, seeming to disintegrate into a featureless blob. He tried to speak; his lips twitched, but no sound came forth.

"You've been thieving left and right," Karpstein said. "You owe my client money. You deny it?"

Mandelbaum shook his head.

"Well, ain't it time you paid up?"

"I meant to," Mandelbaum managed to squeak. "The money was tied up in other deals."

"Excuse me," Farber said, reaching into his jacket pocket. He took out an envelope and slid it toward Karpstein. "As an indication of good faith on Mr. Mandelbaum's part, here is five thousand in cash."

Karpstein opened the envelope and counted the bills. "That covers the interest," he said. "Now we got to straighten out the principal, which is two-thirds of the fifty. You got seventy-two hours."

"I can't do it," Mandelbaum whispered. "How can I do it?"

"That's your problem," Karpstein said. "What's the matter, the seventy-two hours? I tell you what. I'm a reasonable man. You got a week. Write out the check. Postdate it. Next Friday."

While Mandelbaum made out the check, Karpstein worked furiously with his tongue, trying to suck out the piece of chicken trapped maddeningly between his teeth; he still could not dislodge it. "That check better not bounce," he said, "so we are going to take out a little insurance. Sign this paper." The paper was an assignment of Mandelbaum's residence in Pelham Manor, New York, to Joe Hobo's accountant in settlement of certain debts.

"Date it the same day as the check. The check clears, I tear it up. You, what's your name? Oh, yeah, Farber. You sign as the witness. You're his lawyer. That makes it nice and legal."

After the paper had been signed, Karpstein said, "You know, Mandelbaum, this money don't mean anything to me. I ain't even getting it. But you caused me aggravation, and you're going to pay for it. I'm teaching you some respect. Take off your clothes!"

Mandelbaum remained frozen in his chair.

"Take them off!"

Mandelbaum slowly got up and stripped to a silk undershirt and voluminous drawers that almost touched his knees. Great mounds of dimpled flesh encased his upper arms. Pendulous breasts sagged from his chest, and his belly strained against the undershirt like an indoor-tennis bubble top. Then Mandelbaum sat down again, as though he were a chastened schoolboy, toes pointed inward, clutching himself, his body quivering.

"When was the last time you saw your balls?" Karpstein said. He stood, removed his coat and loosened his tie. He opened his attaché case and lifted out a length of white plastic telephone cable filled with copper wiring. It was about two feet long and an inch thick. He walked toward Mandelbaum and with a sudden backhand sweep brought the cable down on Mandelbaum's stomach.

"Oh, my God," Farber said. "I can't watch this."

"Tommy, take him outside," Karpstein said. "And listen to me, Farber. You got any ideas talking about this, forget it. I got bodies buried all over the place they'll never find. I'll reach out for you wherever I am. Don't try me."

Karpstein turned to Mandelbaum again and slammed the length of cable against a fat white calf. A red welt immediately appeared. Mandelbaum put his arms down to cover his legs. The cable whipped across his left arm just above the elbow.

Mandelbaum began to whimper. Karpstein set himself next to Mandelbaum, occasionally moving around to achieve a better angle, holding the cable at the end with both hands, like a baseball player at bat, slamming it against his legs, his arms, his back.

Mandelbaum's whimper rose to a blubbering cry. Tears streaked down his cheeks. The cable had come down on him perhaps twenty times when he slid from the chair to the floor. As he did, the cable caught him under the ear. Blood ran down his neck. At the sight of the blood Karpstein, breathing heavily, stopped at last. "All right, you fucking slob," he said, "get up, get dressed and get out. Remember, you got one week."

☆

Karpstein arrived home shortly after eight o'clock that evening. He lived in an almost exclusively Italian section of Hasbrouck Heights, a quiet middle-class community about ten miles northwest of Hoboken. Most of his neighbors were professional and business people, and Frank Sinatra had resided there when he first became famous as a singer. Karpstein had bought the house as a wedding present for his wife and had installed her in it, along with her eleven-year-old daughter by a previous marriage and her widowed mother. The house had a spacious nine rooms. Its style was split-level medieval California. Its exterior walls were dark brown shingles broken in the front by two picture windows. Its exposed foundation had a flagstone veneer that also ran up each of its corners and under the eaves of a slate roof. The main entrance, off a tiny circular driveway, featured a miniature three-quarter-round tower with a peaked top and two slotted stained-glass windows. There was a carved stone heron poised on the patch of grass in the middle of the driveway.

Karpstein's wife, Angelina, née Carpezzo, had experienced an instant flush of pride and satisfaction when she saw the house. She was two years younger than Karpstein. Her hair was dyed raven black, and she wore it in a spray-lacquered pageboy flip impervious to the fiercest wind. She was barely five feet tall. She had a pretty, somewhat petulant face with full lips. Her figure was invitingly curved, marred only by hips and legs that were disproportionately heavy.

Karpstein considered her extraordinarily beautiful and counted himself among the luckiest of men to have won her. She was a late, only child. Her father, a druggist, brought her up with puritanical zeal. When she was seventeen and had yet to see even a movie, he had arranged her marriage to the son of his best friend, a Hoboken undertaker. To all outward appearances the match was ideal and in due course produced a baby. But her husband, a preening sort who fancied himself a great lover and waited impatiently for the day he would inherit his father's establishment, soon began to belittle her innocence, beat her regularly, often did not return home until the early hours of the morning and kept her on the most stringent budget. Angelina took her revenge by refusing to sleep with him further. The marriage was abruptly terminated when he was found bedded down with another man's wife and was shot to death on the spot by the aggrieved husband.

The public scandal proved too much for Angelina's father, and he succumbed to a coronary occlusion. Under the circumstances, relations with her former in-laws were strained, to say the least, and since Angelina and her mother were ill-equipped to run the business, they sold it and were living on the diminishing proceeds when she met Karpstein.

The connection was her second cousin, a woman about her age considered "not nice" by the rest of the family. "Look," the cousin said, "you only live once," and under her auspices Angelina had started to date, to drink and smoke, although she had little interest in sex and did not become promiscuous. The cousin was going out with a member of a robbery gang headed by Karpstein, and eventually he was introduced to Angelina. Karpstein, whose previous experience with women had been limited to whores, was smitten at once. He found her not only beautiful but warm and understanding, a lady. He lavished gifts of jewelry on her. He bought her a car. He gave her a mink coat. He also got one for her mother.

At first her feelings were mixed. He was not attractive physically. She was aware of his reputation and feared it. On the other hand, he always treated her gently, and the security he offered was evident. And she secretly tingled with pleasure at the power he projected, the deference paid to him by other men, the way maître d's leaped to attention whenever he escorted her into a restaurant in Hoboken, nearby Bayonne or Jersey City. Once she took a sample of his handwriting to be analyzed. The analyst told her, "This is a dangerous man, but underneath he is very protective to those close to him. He believes that the world is corrupt, that most of those in it are no good, so he can dispense his own justice."

Finally Karpstein sought Joe Hobo's advice. "I know about that girl," Joe Hobo said. "She's had a tough time.

Her people brought her up like a bird in a gilded cage. I'll
see what I can do."

Then Karpstein was thought to have been spotted one
night driving away from a quarry where he had unloaded
the body of a dissident union man for Joe Hobo. "How
come you didn't take more care?" Joe Hobo asked.

"Well, it was late, and I wanted to see Angelina."

"All right, that does it," Joe Hobo said, and arranged to
have dinner with her. He told her that she was going to
have to swear that Karpstein had spent the entire night in
question with her and that, of course, to salvage her good
name, she would have to marry him. "Look," he said,
"let's face it, you still got your looks, but you're no spring
chicken either. And you got that kid and your mother to
think about. You got to think ahead. Don't worry, I'll
speak to the old lady myself. Believe me, this is for the
best."

He sent for Karpstein to join them. Joe Hobo bought a
bottle of champagne and lifted his glass in a toast. "I wish
you all happiness," he said. Then he left.

Angelina remained motionless for a moment before
bursting into tears and fleeing the restaurant. Karpstein sat
there for about half an hour staring at his glass. Suddenly
he knocked the glass over and stormed out after her. He
went to her apartment and pounded on the door until she
had to open it, afraid that her mother or daughter would
awaken. She cowered in a corner, certain that she would
get a beating far worse than had ever been administered to
her by her husband or her late husband. But Karpstein simply said, "What's the matter with you? Don't you understand? I love you."

They were married three days later. They moved into
the house in Hasbrouck Heights. He made few sexual demands on her. He treated her daughter as if she were his
own, even after the girl he had fathered was born. He
remembered every anniversary with an expensive ring,
necklace or brooch. The only untoward note was her
mother hissing waspishly to her now and then, "What
would Papa say? His only daughter married to a Jew!"
But Mrs. Carpezzo, quite conscious of the material advantages Karpstein had brought, remained properly cir-
cumspect in his presence.

Actually, with the passage of time Angelina began to
believe that she was in love with Karpstein. And now, as

usual, upon his return home from his meeting with Mandelbaum, she was at the front door to greet him. "Hi, hon," she said brightly, and pecked him on the cheek.

Karpstein walked into the living room. Tired balloons drooped from the ceiling. "I put the little one to bed," she said. "The party was too much for her, and she got cranky. Oh, honey, you look like you had a real rough day. Are you hungry? Mama made some lasagna. I'll heat it up."

"No, it's all right," Karpstein said. "But would you get me a toothpick? I got something stuck in my teeth."

3

Swirls of diaphanous fog were coming up from the river. On the corner, half a block away, the shimmering green neon lights of the Liffey Bar & Grill beckoned. Behind a curtained window on the deserted street a woman's sweet voice sang of Kevin Barry's hanging.

Richie Flynn allowed himself a delicious shiver in the damp night chill and drew his trench coat tighter around him, his eyes suddenly searching the dark doorways for lurking Black and Tans of the British army ready to pounce on Irish patriots. It was a testament to Flynn's fantasy life, since he stood not in Dublin, 1920, but Inwood, New York City, 1974. The fog was rising from the Harlem River, and while any danger he could reasonably expect might well be black or tan, given the temper of Inwood, it certainly was not in uniform.

Inwood encompassed the entire northern tip of Manhattan. On the west side, wild parkland dropped straight to the water, unfettered by the highways that elsewhere girdled the city. Centuries-old tulip trees and yellow poplars were rooted there, some with trunks fourteen feet or more in circumference. In the spring jack-in-the-pulpit, mayapple and star-of-Bethlehem bloomed in profusion, while thrushes, towhees, jays and orioles flashed through the woods. In a quiet cove pairs of crested wood ducks floated like fallen leaves. The rest of Inwood looked more like some river town up the Hudson than part of the city. Even the El that ran through Inwood, with its antiquated stations, the last in Manhattan, gave it an old-fashioned, other-world flavor. Immigrant Irish transit workers had settled there because it was where the subway marshaling yards and trolley barns were located. They were still in use along the Harlem River, although the trolleys, of course, had been replaced by buses. The buses were garaged in a sprawling structure that said in carved granite, "3rd Ave. R.R. Co."

This was where Richie Flynn was born and grew up, in

Good Shepherd parish, where his character was developed, his attitudes shaped. Saloon after saloon had a shamrock adorning its sign, and many were open early in the morning to catch the night-shift motormen and dispatchers, maintenance crews, drivers and conductors on their way home, to say nothing of those going to work. The remoteness of Inwood seemed a historical imperative; even the resident Algonquins refused to go along when Indians in the downtown forest sold Manhattan for twenty-four dollars, and the Dutch finally had to expel them by force.

But all the tensions of the city arrived, beginning with the completion of the Project twenty years ago. The Project was a big municipal housing complex. It was originally conceived of as a place for union members and civil service employees to raise their families, where retired transit workers, firemen and policemen and the like could live out their lives in peace and security. These tenants were also naturally conceived to be white. By then, however, the great black influx from the South was in full swing. Blacks began to push out of Harlem, and the unions, chief among them the transit workers, started to change complexion as well. Blacks moved into the Project as soon as it was finished, and after the blacks came Hispanics, many of them on welfare. "They're not Puerto Rican, so I'm told," said Dick Hoolihan, the Liffey's owner. "They're supposed to be mostly Dominicans from the Dominican Republic, but you can't really tell, don't you know, unless you have an ear for their accent."

As the aliens spread out from the Project, Inwood acquired the siege mentality of, say, Johannesburg. Longtime residents sniffed at how filthy and trash-strewn Sherman Avenue had become, how bottle-ridden the park was, giving not so much as an inch to the fact that the newcomers had little money and less hope and were systematically stripped of their self-respect in a city that was falling apart. Iron gates clanged across storefronts at day's end. At night the streets were considered unfit for decent people. Once Inwood had three movie theaters; now there were none. A combination restaurant and dance hall, a mecca for the Irish all over New York, closed its doors. Some businesses tried to make an adjustment. O'Malley, the grocer on Two Hundred Seventh Street, used to have a sign that said, "Irish/American Groceries." He put up a new one, possibly unique in the world, that said,

"Irish/American/Spanish Groceries," but even O'Malley admitted that he was just holding on until he could unload the place for something approaching reason. The number of saloons dwindled; most of the ones that remained had a buzzer under the bar that had to be pushed before the door could be opened.

The Liffey Bar & Grill was one of the few that did not have such a device. This was in part because New York's neighborhoods are measured in nearly self-sufficient blocks, and the Liffey was on one that was still securely white. The other part was Hoolihan's night bartender, Gerald Cummins, a bull-necked man with a great gap between his front teeth and crew-cut graying hair, who kept a club next to the cash register. One night two young black holdup men came in waving pistols. When one of them ventured too close to the bar, Cummins grabbed the club and clouted him over the head. The second black panicked and ran. The body of the one Cummins had knocked out was later found in the gutter. A search of the scene, together with an autopsy, revealed that he had been slain by bullets from five different guns. Manhattan North homicide detectives listed the case as unsolved, and the Liffey had yet to have another incident like it.

Men sat at the bar, beginning at eleven A.M., when the Liffey opened. They came and went during the day and evening, perched side by side, gazing into their glasses, at the bar, at the bottles behind the bar. Beer remained the popular item, but the shots of rye that once accompanied it as the day progressed had given way to the steady sipping of scotch and water or vodka and tonic. During Lent, Hoolihan, a religious man, also ran birch beer through one of his tap lines for those who had taken the pledge. Almost all the customers were regulars who knew one another. When anyone spoke, it was often to the general assemblage and was supported, debated or greeted with silence. The conversation would always come back to the latest alleged affronts to civilization committed by the "spicks and spooks," the deterioration of the area, the mass exodus from Inwood to prefabricated tract housing with community swimming pools outside the city.

"Come graduation day, thirty-nine families are to leave the parish," Moran the ironworker said. "Sister Mary Louise told me so herself. That's up from last year. Last year it was twenty-six, she said."

"Monsignor Culligan down at Our Lady of Lourdes was right," croaked Billy McKeon, the Afghan Kid, who had moved up to Inwood from the Washington Heights section of Manhattan. "We should of listened to him, the poor man running out the rectory every night telling us, 'They can't move in if you don't move out!' "

McKeon wore a green and white softball cap and a matching zippered jacket with a Holy Name Society patch over the left breast pocket and "Good Shepherd" sewn across the back. He was about the size of a jockey, and had he been born in Kentucky, he might have been one. But he was from New York, and he was a hustler. One of the things he used to hustle was fake silver fox furs. He would dress up as a uniformed delivery boy and hang around a midtown hotel, carrying two boxes both addressed to the same person presumably staying at the hotel. McKeon would sidle up to a likely prospect and say that the store had made a mistake, that he had an extra fur worth two hundred dollars to dispose of at half price and would show the prospect the bill. McKeon had a truck as well, and he would pull right next to a limousine on the East Side waiting for a light to change and make a similar pitch. He took side trips to Philadelphia and Boston and even went to Chicago. In a good week he got rid of ten or twelve furs, always in wealthy neighborhoods. The furs cost McKeon thirteen dollars each. Someone once asked him where they came from, and he said, "Some fucking goat in Afghanistan, I think," and from then on he was known as the Afghan Kid.

In the Liffey everyone nodded solemnly, as if the wraith of the late Monsignor Culligan were upon them, one after the other. "They can't move in if you don't move out, that's what *he* said," McKeon croaked again, pounding his vodka and tonic on the bar, his black eyes burning, cheeks sunken. But it was not fanaticism that gave the Afghan Kid his gaunt, feverish look. At the age of forty-five the cancer had begun to spread from his larynx, and his life expectancy was a matter of weeks.

"I'll take another," he said, extending his glass, suddenly exhausted.

☆

On the sidewalk in the fog Flynn, having ascertained the absence of any menacing Black and Tans, stepped off the curb and was immediately greeted by reality. His right knee went. The sensation was not so much one of buckling as it was a loss of control, as if the knee were going off somewhere on its own. With practiced instinct Flynn put his weight on his left leg to keep from falling, almost willing the knee back into place so he could walk again.

The knee had gone like this on countless, unexpected occasions since that stiflingly hot, absolutely windless, cloudless August day eleven years before, when Richie Flynn, a second-year running back for the New York Giants football team, faked to his left and then charged right for the last time in a preseason nutcracker drill. In this version of the nutcracker, the action took place between two large bags filled with foam rubber. A quarterback took the snap from center and handed off to one of two running backs while two offensive linemen blocked their defensive counterparts. In theory this was supposed to improve everyone's various running, blocking, tackling and reaction skills. In fact it was just a way to knock heads together at close quarters, to draw blood as a bull is baited before combat, for the drill was never used during the regular schedule, and all but a few maniacal players hated it.

The play called for Flynn to go in behind a rookie guard against a veteran tackle. In the heat, the coaches snarling obscenities, everyone was on edge. Flynn took a half stride to his left before cutting back with the ball to follow the rookie's block on the veteran. He was about to scoot clear when the veteran broke the block and grabbed and held Flynn's right leg. For a fraction of a second Flynn tried to struggle free, but that was all it took. The other defensive lineman, also a rookie and desperate for a job on the team, recovered from the fake, hurtled through the air and crashed into him shoulder high. Flynn was still being driven left by the first tackle; suddenly his whole body above the knees reversed direction under this new impact.

He actually heard the ligaments pop. The pain was instantaneous. First it was in the knee. Then it raced to his head. As he fell, he thought, This is it, it's all over. He lay on his back on the field. All at once, where there had been shouts and curses and grunts around him, there was silence. He had seen this happen to others. Some screamed. Some threw up on the spot. Flynn felt his stomach retch, and he fought the bile back and did not throw up. He stared into the glaring white sky. The grimy, sweaty, helmeted face of the veteran who had tackled him intersected the sun. "Richie," he whispered urgently in a hillbilly twang, "you going to be OK." Flynn nodded at him. The pain came in waves. It's all over, he thought again, it's all over, and tears welled in his eyes.

He was carried off the field on a stretcher. The knee was kept packed in ice to keep the swelling down. It blew up anyway. Lying in bed, he tried the knee but could not bend it more than an inch. After the ice, heat packs were applied to keep the blood circulating. One morning he awoke and was frightened to find the entire leg black and blue. Some members of the team came to see him in the infirmary of the small Connecticut college where the Giants practiced. They came into his room tentatively, as if visiting a terminally ill patient. "No problem," they would tell him in rote, "you'll be OK." He looked into their eyes and saw what they were really thinking. Not all of the team came, of course, and he understood that, too.

X-rays were taken. Doctors probed, manipulated, deliberated. Finally a decision was made to operate, to tie the ruptured ligaments and repair the torn cartilage. "What kind of chance do I have?" he asked.

"I really won't know until I get in there," the surgeon said. "It could be bad. But if you want to play again, it's your only chance."

The knee was in a cast for seven weeks. When the cast was taken off, Flynn was shocked at how the muscles had atrophied. He began the laborious process of building up the knee again, lifting progressively heavier weights with his leg. Later, throughout the winter and spring whenever the weather permitted, he would go to the stadium and run alone for hours up the aisle steps. In July he was fitted with a brace and started another training season. He worked out gingerly at first, testing the knee, avoiding contact for the time being, regaining his confidence. Then one day he ran an ordinary pass pattern in practice and turned to catch the ball, and the knee gave way just like that, nobody within twenty yards of him, and he fell to the ground and could not get up unaided, and that was the end of it.

The worst part, the part Richie Flynn could never forget, was that because of football, he had tasted what might have been, had experienced for a brief moment the mindblowing high that a city like New York can bestow on a suddenly discovered hero.

Playing football had become serious when he was able to attend Cardinal Hayes, supported by his widowed mother, who doubled as a bookkeeper for both the Liffey Bar & Grill and Ahern's Maintenance and Supply Company. He was very fast and had good moves that compensated for his lack of size, and he made the varsity his sophomore year. When he was a senior, he was picked for the citywide All-Catholic second team and through the recommendation of his coach was offered an athletic scholarship to Marquette University in Milwaukee, Wisconsin. The trouble was that he had a C-minus scholastic average, which did not meet admission standards. He immediately began serving regularly at the six o'clock morning mass in the chapel, also regularly attended by Sister Patricia of the school administration office. Sister Patricia noticed his new devotion, and one day she asked him what he planned on doing after graduation.

"Well, Sister, I was going to college."

"What college is that, Richie?"

"Marquette."

"That's wonderful!" Sister Patricia exclaimed. "I'm so glad you chose a Catholic college. So many of the boys don't these days."

"Yes, Sister. Well, I *was* going, but to tell you the truth, I wasted a lot of time, and my grades aren't good enough. I'm trying to make up for it now, but I guess it's too late." Flynn gazed at her with all the earnestness he could muster. "And, you know, I had to help Mother at home."

"Richie, it's never too late," Sister Patricia said sternly. She bit her lower lip. "What will you do then?"

"I just don't know. Get a job, I guess, or something."

The "something" hung ominously in the air between them, like Satan's sneer. Sister Patricia chewed harder on her lip. "You keep up the good work," she told him. "Our Lord does many wondrous things. I'll see you at mass tomorrow." Three weeks later, when Flynn's academic standing arrived at Marquette, he was listed as being in the upper third of his graduating class.

"What the hell, maybe it was God's will," Donny Scanlon had said on the eve of Richie's departure for Marquette. "I mean, Sister Patricia is His han'dmaiden, right?"

"Don't talk like that," Flynn said. "It's bad luck."

They were drinking beer in the Liffey. Scanlon was Flynn's best friend in Inwood. He had been a year ahead of Flynn at Cardinal Hayes before dropping out when he was a junior to work for McMullen the bookmaker.

Scanlon laughed. "All right, me bucko, down to business it is then," he said, lapsing into a theatrical brogue. "I bring ye glad tidings from McMullen himself. The good fellow has empowered me to offer twenty a week to jingle in your pocket, for he hears the girls of Milwaukee are an expensive lot. In return he asks but a wee favor, which is the general nature of the team prior to each game, injuries, that sort of thing."

"Jesus," Flynn said, "I couldn't do that."

Scanlon dropped the brogue. "Listen, Richie," he said, "nobody's asking you to throw a game. We want old Marquette to win every time. Who cares? We want the information to establish the line. Marquette ain't no Notre Dame, but it's a Jebbie school, and it gets action here. McMullen has a good line on Marquette, he don't get stuck. One hand washes the other. Things work out, you could do the basketball, too. Marquette basketball gets even bigger action."

The line Scanlon was talking about was the number of points a bettor would either give or receive relative to the final score when wagering on a specific game. Flynn thought it over and failed to find a flaw in Scanlon's logic. Besides, he could use the twenty dollars, so he said, "OK."

At Marquette Flynn did not distinguish himself until his senior year, when, because of several breakaway runs, he became the team's leading ground gainer. Still, at five feet nine and one hundred seventy pounds, he was considered too small for professional football and was passed over by team after team. Finally, on the eleventh round of the annual college player draft, the New York Giants took him, mostly on the whim of Wellington Mara, the team's president and a sentimental man, who recalled that the Giants had not had anyone resembling a home-grown back since Len Eshmont of Fordham in the late 1940s, a note of interest duly reported in the local sports pages.

Flynn would be paid thirteen thousand five hundred dollars if he made the team, and to everybody's surprise he did, the sixth of six running backs the Giants would keep during the year, although he was picked over what remained of the competition because he was from New York and Irish as much as anything. That night in celebration he went out with and finally managed to seduce and, as it turned out, impregnate Agnes McGinty, a plainly pretty, freckle-faced girl he had yearned for ever since he was in grammar school at Good Shepherd. Six weeks later they were married.

The Giants used Flynn sparingly. He performed adequately, if unspectacularly, on a number of kickoff returns, but by the last game on the schedule he had carried the ball only thirteen times from scrimmage for a grand total of twenty-three yards. Then at Yankee Stadium against the Cleveland Browns with less than two minutes left, Cleveland leading 20–17 and the Giants in possession of the ball on their own seven-yard line, Flynn was sent in as a messenger to deliver a pass play. But the Giant quarterback, looking over the defensive alignment, decided that the play was exactly what Cleveland was waiting for. On a hunch he could never truly explain to himself, although he would rationalize that he had done it because he had three more downs to go anyway and Cleveland would never suspect Flynn might get the ball, he called another play in which he started to drop back as if to pass and then handed off to Flynn.

Fortunately Flynn did not have time to think. He went in low off tackle, past onrushing linemen and a blitzing linebacker intent on reaching the quarterback. A key block protected him from the middle linebacker. Suddenly he had some running room. An animal roar began to well up in the stands. Flynn sped diagonally toward the right sideline, where a cornerback was coming up to meet him. At the last instant Flynn cut left and eluded him. The roar grew louder. Now, as defensive backs across the field frantically tried to recover from guarding decoy pass receivers, only the free safetyman near the fifty-yard line could stop him. Flynn faked right, then left, then right again. The safetyman committed himself a moment too soon and wound up clutching air. The roar from the crowd was overwhelming. From then on it was just a footrace with Flynn the easy victor, and as he returned to the bench, sixty-seven thousand people screamed themselves hoarse.

Not only did the Giants win 24–20, but Flynn's ninety-three-yard run was the longest from scrimmage in Giant history.

After the game was over, Flynn started to trot off the field with the rest of the team. Hundreds of teenage boys came at him, trying to touch him, nearly knocking him down, and it required a cordon of security guards to get him to the dressing room. Reporters crowded around him, and despite his elation, he remembered to be properly modest, crediting the blocking of his linemen for the run. He had always been popular with his teammates—he even had a nickname, Fast Richie, because of his pool-playing skills—but he sensed from them now, along with all the jokes, a new respect.

In the evening Flynn took Agnes with him to the party that one of the more publicized bachelor Giants threw after every home game. He had already been to two of them alone—along with other Giants, a number of sports buffs, and more models and stewardesses than he had ever seen together in his life. But he had felt uncomfortable and out of place, on the fringe of things. The last time he was standing alone, staring out the window at the East River, when a model with burnished black hair that hung down to her small, pointed, braless breasts came up to him and asked him what he did. He said he played for the Giants, and she asked his name, and he said, "Flynn, Richie Flynn," and she had said, "Oh," and walked away, and he had stopped going to the parties until now.

This time it was different. The moment he walked in, there was a rush toward him, and almost at once he was separated from Agnes. Someone thrust a drink into his hand, and then the model who had said, "Oh," to him materialized out of nowhere and looked into his eyes and said, "Oh, wow! Fantastic, just fantastic!" before she was shouldered aside by two men in sports jackets and turtleneck sweaters who greeted him like a lifelong friend, although he had never seen them before, and rehashed the run as if Flynn had been on another planet at the time. There were more drinks and more people, and Flynn was reduced to saying, "Yes, I went to Marquette," and, "Thank you, thank you very much," when somebody said, "Let's go to Shor's," and he found Agnes in a corner, and then they were going through the revolving doors of Toots Shor's on Fifty-second Street, where the New York sporting fraternity hung out.

Word quickly spread that he was there, and Shor himself bounded forward and hugged him and called for drinks on the house, as he should, having bet ten thousand dollars on the Giants. Flynn was ushered to a banquette, Agnes next to him. Another table was pushed up and filled with more Giants and their girl friends and people from the party whom Flynn did not know and people already in the restaurant, who just brought over chairs, while more stood packed around it, looking at him. The drinks kept coming, and Flynn soon had a half dozen glasses in front of him. Agnes said she was hungry, and could she have a chicken salad sandwich? Hands reached across the table to shake his hand, and other hands thrust forward pieces of paper for him to autograph. While Agnes was trying to eat her sandwich, a man, his face red with alcohol and sweat, pushed a paper napkin past her mouth and said to Flynn, "Sign it. My son'll get a real kick out of it. Write 'Best regards to Tony.' He'll love it."

There are a great many people in New York who believe that they will turn to stone if they stay in one place too long, and Richie and Agnes found themselves jammed into the back of a limousine, on their way to Eddie Condon's jazz club. The scotch was beginning to get to him, and as he was going out of Shor's, he had stumbled and nearly fallen, and someone had said, "It's good you weren't drinking before the game," and Flynn thought it was the funniest thing he had ever heard. At Condon's, his arrival was cheered by manicured cloak-and-suiters, accompanied by petulant blondes in scoop-front black dresses that showed off their pushed-up creamy bosoms. Mostly they were cheering the fact that Flynn's touchdown had beaten the point spread on the game. The band interrupted "Tin Roof Blues" to play a ragged version of "When Irish Eyes Are Smiling." The faces around Flynn blurred. Agnes whispered that they should go home, and Flynn said no, that he wanted a hamburger, and a complete stranger shouted, "On to P.J.'s!"

Despite the hour, the bar at P.J. Clarke's seemed impassable, but by now Flynn had self-appointed courtiers yelling, "Make way, make way for Richie Flynn!" and the crowd toasted him and reached out to pummel him as he was taken through it, and even the people lined up for a table in the back room did not protest as he went by them. It was the first time he had been to Clarke's, and the owner, Danny Lavezzo, who also had bet heavily on the game, smiled and quietly said the only sane thing he heard during the night, "That was a nice run you made today, kid."

He was plunked down at a table and was given another scotch, and in the dimly lit tumult a voice said, "This is Marlene, she loves Giants," and Marlene, blond and musky with perfume, slid into the chair next to him and entwined her fingers in his and guided his hand under the table and began rubbing the inside of his thigh, and he suddenly remembered that Agnes was not with him, and with great effort he tried to puzzle this out and decided that well, she must be somewhere. He had barely wolfed down his hamburger with his free hand before he was in a cab with Marlene, whose last name he never did catch, and another girl and two men, and then they were in Marlene's apartment. The apartment had a lot of gilded mirrors, and the walls were covered with fabric, and there was some kind of incense burning. The latest Chubby Checker record was on the stereo, and Marlene was fixing drinks when Flynn felt very tired and went into her bedroom and lay down and closed his eyes. Then hands were fiddling with his zipper, and something warm and moist was nibbling at him. He peered down and saw the blond top of Marlene's head between his legs. She looked as if she were bobbing for apples, and he suppressed a giggle at the thought of Marlene bobbing for apples. The door to the bedroom opened, and a silhouetted male figure stood there observing the scene for a moment and said, "Some pipe job, huh?"

Flynn got home about six A.M. His wife was asleep or at least was feigning sleep. He was grateful on either count. He was in no condition to talk even if he wanted to, and he took off his jacket and shoes and fell asleep on the sofa. He would later recall that his marriage was never the same after that night, but then nothing was.

The telephone woke him at eleven in the morning. It was a publicist on the Giant staff reminding him that he was the honored guest at the weekly Pro-Quarterback lunch at Mamma Leone's restaurant. Flynn jumped up from the sofa and found a note from Agnes saying that she had gone shopping with her mother, which was not an auspicious sign. He undressed to dress again and was horrified to see lipstick smeared on his shorts, and that was when bits and pieces of the night began coming back to him in some detail.

Not knowing what else to do with the shorts, he stuffed them into his overcoat pocket and left them on the floor of the cab when he got out. At the lunch he managed to down two bites of roast beef and drank six glasses of ice water. Wyszkanski, the right tackle, nudged him and whispered, "I hear you ended up with Marlene."

"So?"

"So you must be a star. Marlene only goes down on stars."

Later, while he was signing autographs, one of the sportswriters standing nearby asked him how he felt. "Are you kidding, after last night?" he said. "Give me a couple of belts, though, and I'll get the other *n* in Flynn." They laughed and wrote warm follow-up stories about the cocky young gamebreaker the Giants had been lacking for so long.

The following August, in less than a second, his professional football days were finished. He would, of course, constantly relive every nuance of the run. At first it was all he had to cling to, but as time went on, there were moments when he was almost demeaned by it, as if he had no existence without it. He never knew whether it was a life preserver or an anchor around his neck.

4

Until now.

Now the run had provided a chance to change everything. The sudden collapse of his knee once more on this foggy night in Inwood tempered his elation, reminding him that nothing was certain, but even so, the possibility *was* there, an opportunity to score again. "I can't talk on the phone," he had told Donny Scanlon. "I'll meet you at the Liffey at eight."

As always, he hesitated before going inside, wondering if it was still in place behind the bar, a photograph of Flynn at sixteen, cradling the ball in one arm, the other arm outstretched toward the camera, in his Cardinal Hayes uniform with an inscription in a round schoolboy hand that said, "Best Wishes, Richie Flynn."

But it was there, and he immediately felt much better. The picture was his private talisman. It was responsible for whatever he had been able to salvage from his knee injury. And his fear that it might be removed was not complete paranoia, for it occupied a spot that had previously featured a portrait of Franklin D. Roosevelt. If Roosevelt could go, so could he.

One day, when he was still at Cardinal Hayes, a new district supervisor for Goldblatt's Brewery had dropped by the Liffey to make the owner's acquaintance. It was a time when nationally distributed beers were beginning to mount a major assault on the New York market, and since Goldblatt was one of the few remaining local breweries in the city, the supervisor had returned a month or so later to cement relations with Hoolihan.

"Say," the supervisor exclaimed, "wasn't that Roosevelt's picture you had over there? Who you got there now?"

"Why, that's young Richie Flynn," Hollihan replied. "They say he's the finest footballer ever to come out of Inwood."

"Is that right? Well, any kid who can replace FDR I want to meet."

"In that case, if you stay put, you will. The lad should be along any minute. His mother works here Thursdays as my bookkeeper, and he picks her up on the way home."

When Richie came in, Hoolihan introduced him to the supervisor, who shook his hand, gave him his card and said, "I like your style, son. You ever want a job, call me."

Flynn had forgotten about the encounter until he became an unemployable running back, with a wife and an infant boy to support. His physical education major at Marquette had hardly prepared him for a business career, and even if he had any desire to teach or coach, it was too late in the year to do anything about it. Some of his friends thought that with his engaging manner, he might achieve success as a sports announcer. But the sad truth was that despite the run, he had not played long enough to establish himself as a name. Broadcasting executives, however, did not say this to him. Instead, they said that they would consider him after he had taken diction lessons, that his accent was "too New York." In corporate circles this is known as letting a guy hang on to his nuts.

So he telephoned the supervisor, who by then was Goldblatt's vice-president in charge of sales. To Flynn's amazement, he did not refer to the run. "Oh, yeah," he said, "I remember. You're the kid who knocked Roosevelt off the wall."

After a trial period as a trainee, Flynn was hired by Goldblatt to be an on-premise salesman servicing one hundred and twenty-five saloon and restaurant accounts. Since he was new on the job, these accounts were usually in out-of-the-way places in Nassau County on Long Island and in Westchester, north of the city. Their very smallness made him a center of attention. Most of the saloonkeepers had been watching on television when he had scored his touchdown, as had their customers, and he was peppered with questions about the Giants and pro football. If he did not know the answers, he soon learned that it was just as easy, and sometimes even better, to fabricate them. He had a film clip of his run. Upon request he would show it at various fraternal and civic father-and-son nights. Afterward he would speak gravely about how football was an ideal means of preparing for manhood and the vicissitudes of life, how it strengthened one's resolve, self-reliance and general well-being whether it was played for fun or profit.

Goldblatt's Brewery was delighted with his efforts. His first-year salary was nine thousand dollars, plus six hundred in bonuses. Now, a decade later, he was a supervisor himself, earning seventeen thousand dollars annually, the same amount he would have received from the Giants had he been capable of playing a second season with them.

Usually, when Flynn walked into the Liffey, he would stop and chat with each patron he knew, and that was practically everybody. But on this particular night he limited himself to a few cursory nods and hellos, and abstractedly clapping a couple of backs closest to him, he looked around the room for Scanlon. "Have you seen Scanlon?" he asked the bartender, Cummins. "Has he called?"

"Richie, he's been neither seen nor heard from this evening. What'll it be? Goldblatt?"

"No," Flynn said. "Scotch and water. Make it a double."

The customary Friday night crowd lined the bar. There were no women present. Most of the Irish kids left in Inwood frequented the dance halls along Fordham Road in the Bronx across the Harlem River, so Flynn was easily the youngest one there. The men finished dinner by seven, and as they rarely, if ever, drank at home, they came to the Liffey and stayed for hours until their wives were asleep. Male menopause by their mid-forties was an accepted state of being. Alcohol had replaced sex as a tranquilizing agent, and sexual high jinks of one sort or another were unabashedly described in the past tense, like an adolescent caper.

The conversation at the bar concerned Richard Nixon. Several of Nixon's closest White House aides had already been indicted in the Watergate cover-up. If the Liffey regulars had been a cross section of the nation, Nixon would have had nothing to worry about. They were traditionally working-class Democrats, but their politics had become eclectic, to say the least. The election district where the Liffey was located had gone five to one for John F. Kennedy. But when Nixon ran for reelection, he carried the district with sixty-four percent of the vote. They no longer entertained any illusions about what sociologists called upward mobility and were grimly intent on simply keeping what they had. They were convinced that the ruling councils of the party had sold them out. Richard Nixon, on the other hand, was against the giveaway programs and

welfare cheats that they blamed for rising taxes and the inflation that steadily eroded their savings. They identified
with Nixon; they believed that he was being pilloried by
an unholy conspiracy of weirdos, pinkos, fags, limousine
liberals and abortionists, who, among other things, had
subverted the press. Whether Nixon was guilty of criminal
acts was academic, since they did not believe that a crime
had been committed. He had not done anything that any
other politician had not done; he had just been caught,
that was all.

Sipping his scotch, waiting for Scanlon, Flynn could not
bear the familiar litany and went to join Cornelius J.
MacShane, seated alone at one of a half dozen tables opposite the bar. MacShane was seventy years old. His face
looked like a turtle in a Walt Disney cartoon. He had a
scrawny, wrinkled neck, a beaked nose and sparse white
hair combed straight back. Liver spots dotted his forehead.
He was thin except for a small, round belly. Pince-nez
glasses with gold rims dangled from a ribbon around his
high, starched collar, and he wore both a belt and suspen-
ders to hold up his trousers.

MacShane was a retired carnival man. Even so, he kept
his hand in. When a friend who owned a discount television store was stuck with a heavy inventory, MacShane
equipped the store's salesmen with earplugs that looked
like hearing aids, put a sign in the window that read "We
Hire the Handicapped" and had the price tags removed
from the TV sets. After a customer came in and asked
how much one of them was, a salesman would call up to
the owner on a balcony overlooking the floor. The owner
would holler back the price, and the salesman would always quote a figure that was a hundred dollars less. The
word of mouth was fantastic. Within a week's time the
store was cleaned out.

"Listen to those jackasses pissing and moaning about
Nixon," MacShane said. "They can't say I didn't warn
them, eh?" Despite his anxiety, Flynn had to laugh. It was
true. After Nixon was reelected, MacShane came into the
Liffey with a dog-eared press clipping of a net worth statement the President had released during his reelection campaign. "Look at this," he had said. "The man hasn't made
a real score in his life, except selling his apartment, and
that's no trick. There's always some fool who'll pay anything to put up a plaque saying, 'The President Slept

Here.' Mark my words, now that he's won big, he's going to make up for it. There ain't nothing wrong with that, but he's dumb and he's greedy, and that ain't good." It was MacShane's opinion that Nixon had not destroyed the damning White House tapes until it was too late because he intended to use them in negotiating for his memoirs and then to donate edited portions of them to some university for a huge tax write-off, since the law disallowing such deductions technically did not cover tapes.

"Well, it don't matter none who the President is, or the governor, or the mayor," he said to Flynn. "The ASPs run the show. They run the banks, and that means they run everything they want, and the rest of us scramble around for the leftovers."

"ASPs?" Flynn said. "Don't you mean WASPs? White Anglo-Saxon Protestants."

"ASPs is what I said, and snakes is what they are," MacShane snorted. "That's a redundancy you were using. I never heard of an Anglo-Saxon Protestant that wasn't white."

MacShane tossed down the jigger of Jack Daniel's that Flynn had offered him. He watched as Flynn drummed his fingers nervously on the table and said, "Something bothering you, Richie? You got another problem with Goldblatt?"

Flynn remembered how MacShane had helped him. Four years after he had gone to work for Goldblatt, the New York *Times* reported a list of contributors to the National Association for the Advancement of Colored People which included a twenty-five-thousand-dollar gift from a woman on Goldblatt's board of directors. Before Flynn realized what was happening, rumors spread, eagerly abetted by Goldblatt's competitors, that the contribution was from the brewery itself and had gone not to the NAACP, but to SNCC, the radical, largely black Student Nonviolent Coordinating Committee. Pretty soon the alleged amount of the contribution had soared wildly to a million, a million and a half, *two* million, depending upon where Flynn was. All over the city, led by policemen and firemen, white ethnics stopped drinking Goldblatt's "nigger beer." Because of the kind of clientele patronizing his accounts, Flynn was especially hard-hit. The saloonkeepers sympathized with him but said there was nothing they could do. Flynn finally sought out MacShane, who told him, "Richie, you're tight with the proprietors, right? You just ask them to change the knobs on their tap lines. Who the hell can tell one beer from another anyway?" Flynn tried it, and it worked. Flynn would be sitting at a bar chatting with a customer under the illusion that he was drinking Schaefer, or Pabst, or Budweiser, and Flynn would inquire, "How come you don't drink Goldblatt?" and the customer would shift uneasily on his stool, unwilling to reveal the truth, and say, "Gee, Richie, I can't put my finger on it. I get headaches from Goldblatt. My stomach gets upset. You know, sourlike." Eventually, as MacShane predicted, the whole thing blew over.

"No," Flynn now said to him, "no problems with Goldblatt." Flynn was on his third scotch and water. He debated about telling the old man what he was planning. But at that moment the debate was resolved. Donny Scanlon had come through the door, and Flynn excused himself.

"Where you been, for Christ's sake?" Flynn said.

"The relief man was late," Scanlon said. "I had to wait for the relief man. I couldn't just walk out."

It was difficult to believe that Flynn and Scanlon were only a year apart in age. Scanlon seemed ten years older; he was working on his third chin, the puffy circles under his eyes looked as though they had been smudged by a dirty eraser and the way he had arranged individual strands of hair across his crown accentuated its baldness. When McMullen the bookmaker had died, Scanlon took over the business, and for a while he did well. Then Scanlon committed a grievous error. He started betting himself. All at once he owed eighteen thousand dollars to a pair of loan sharks with whom he had a line of credit. By this time he had twenty-nine arrests—all of them were for the record, however, to make the police look good, and were regularly dismissed for insufficient evidence, since Scanlon was always scrupulous about paying off the law. The thirtieth arrest was different. A new, ambitious detective burst in on Scanlon and caught him not only on the phone in the act of taking a bet but also with a list of other bets he had booked. In return for forgetting the arrest, the detective told Scanlon that he wanted him to become an informant. Scanlon agreed and got back his betting slips. A few days later the detective came to him for information about another gambling operation, and Scanlon said, "Fuck you. I ain't no rat." The detective grabbed the fingers of Scanlon's right hand, bent them back until Scanlon thought they were going to break and advised him to take up residence in Altoona, Pennsylvania. That afternoon Scanlon decided to give up bookmaking. Through some old contacts he got a job as a dispatcher for a radio taxi company in Brooklyn. His salary was three hundred dollars a week. One hundred and fifty of this went to help settle accounts with the loan sharks. In addition, he secretly pushed money for them. The loan sharks normally charged a point and half a week, or one and a half percent of the loan. If Scanlon could arrange a two-point payback, the difference was applied to his debt. On the night he met Flynn in the Liffey, Scanlon had four thousand dollars to go before he was free and clear.

Flynn guided him to a rear table and ordered another scotch. Scanlon had a vodka and grapefruit juice. The grapefruit juice made him feel virtuous about watching his weight, and the vodka was so that the maiden aunt he lived with would not smell liquor on his breath. "All right," Scanlon said. "I'm here. You're here. What's the big deal?"

Flynn felt the excitement pump through him again. "It is a big deal, and the deal is a day-care center."

"A what?"

"A day-care center. A place mothers leave their kids while they're working."

Scanlon gestured toward Flynn's drink. "You ought to lay off that stuff," he said. "It ain't doing you no good."

"Listen to me. It's like I won the lottery, a million-dollar lottery."

"Do you mind if I have another vodka?" Scanlon said.

"I'm not kidding."

"OK. You're not kidding. So what do you know about running a day-care center? I bet you never even changed your kid's diapers."

"I don't have to know anything. I own it, I mean I own the building."

"Oh, that explains it. I was just joking about the booze before. You really have gone around the corner."

"Donny," Flynn said, "over in the South Bronx and Harlem and Bedford-Stuyvesant, all over the place, there are all these mothers with all these kids, and they are working all day as maids on Park Avenue, and somebody has to take care of their kids, and the government is throwing money into it like it was going out of style. It's part of the War on Poverty."

"Some fucking war," Scanlon said. "It's doing me a fucking lot of good, I can tell you that."

"Well, you're the wrong color and the wrong sex, and you don't have any kids." Flynn permitted himself a faint smile. "Not that I know about anyway."

"I suppose a wee fairy whispered all this in your ear."

"No, wise guy, a wee fairy didn't tell me anything. Goldblatt's got this new account down near City Hall, the Corner Tavern, and I'm there paying a courtesy call, having a beer, and there's this guy at the bar staring at me, and finally he comes over to me and says, 'Hey, aren't you Richie Flynn?' and I think, Oh, Christ, here we go again, I got to listen to the same old shit, but this guy, when I tell him, 'Yeah, you got me, pal,' this guy just raises his glass and says, 'I'm Harry Fowler. Boy, that was some run. I was there. I had ten bucks on the game. I'll never forget it. You beat the points.' And I say, 'Thank you very much,' and he shakes my hand, and that was that. Maybe a month later I'm in there again, and this Fowler guy is there, and he says, 'Hi, Richie.' Well, I'm there a few more times, and he's always there, too, so I figure he must work for the city or something, and I ask him, and he says yes, he's in the welfare, and I say, 'So you're one of the ones who's spending all my money,' and he just laughs and says, 'You know, you're right.' "

Flynn saw that Scanlon was at least listening to him now. "You want another vodka?" he asked.

"Of course I want another vodka. Does a whore suck?"

"OK. This is the payoff. The other day I'm back there, and this Fowler comes up to me, and this time he says, 'Richie, do you have a minute?' I say, 'Sure, what's on your mind?' and he says, 'Not here, let's take a walk.' So we go into that park by City Hall and sit on a bench, and he says, 'Boy, I bet you know a lot of people,' and I say, 'Well, you know, I get around,' and he says, 'No, I mean you being famous and all, you must know a lot of people with money to invest.' I nod, or something. What the hell was I going to say? The next thing I know he says he's retiring soon, and he starts talking about day-care centers, and Donny, I'm like you. I'm thinking, What am I listening to this crap for? But then he starts telling me how much money the federal government's been throwing into day-care centers, the state and city, too, but mostly it's federal money, even though the city, the Agency for Child Development, which is *his* agency, administers it on the local level. And then he tells me how people have been making a fucking fortune off these day-care centers, and how it's a shame that some more deserving people aren't in on it before the program is over, because there are noises it's being phased out, he says."

Flynn glanced around to see if anyone was within earshot and leaned toward Scanlon. "Now I'm paying real close attention to him. 'What do you mean by more deserving people?' I ask, and he looks me right in the eye and says, 'People like you.' He says there wasn't time to build new centers when the program started, so they use existing buildings. There are plenty of examples, he says, and he gives me one where this guy over in Brooklyn bought an old ballroom for twenty-six thousand down and turned it into a day-care center and leased it to the city for one hundred grand for fifteen years. That's the usual contract, fifteen years, sometimes twenty. Then Fowler says there is this abandoned synagogue up in the Bronx that the city has had to take over, so it's back on the tax rolls. I've seen it myself. It's big, and it's solid, and if it was anywhere else, it'd be worth seven-fifty, eight hundred thousand. The city is going to auction it off next week. Fowler says he's looked into it, and whoever gets it could get it for maybe fifty thousand, ten down, and end up with a fifteen-year leaseback at one hundred and twenty-five a year."

Flynn drained his scotch and water and ordered another round for himself and Scanlon. "You hear that, Donny?" he said. "One twenty-five big ones for fifteen years. That's one million eight hundred and seventy-five thousand dollars."

"I hear you," Scanlon said. "What's the guy want?"

"Twenty percent, as it comes. There's another thing. It's a net lease. The landlord don't have to pay for the heat and things like that. The agency takes care of it. All the landlord has to do is fix the place up. That's what's so good about a synagogue. All that open space. You don't have to tear down any walls or anything, just put in partitions. Then you have the fire and health and building inspectors. But that's nothing. A hundred here, a hundred there."

"You're telling me the city is going to let you have it for fifty thousand and then pay you back twice that for fifteen years?"

"That's what I asked him, and he says, 'Richie, the city doesn't know what it's doing anymore.' Right as we're speaking, he says, the city is paying forty thousand a year up in Harlem for a building to train high school dropouts, and right across the street there is this empty intermediate school the city owns which was closed down on account of a budget cutback. One department doesn't give a fuck what another department is doing, just so long as its own books look OK."

Scanlon did not respond.

"What the hell's wrong?" Flynn said. "This is business, is all. I got inside information, an edge. All those companies downtown do it. The Chase Manhattan Bank does it every day."

"Hey, Richie, that's what's wrong. You ain't the Chase Manhattan Bank."

"I know I'm not the Chase Manhattan Bank, for Christ's sake! But what am I supposed to do? This is *my* big chance. The money's just waiting for me. All I have to do is grab it. Isn't that what America's all about, getting ahead? Don't they say it in all those fucking Fourth of July speeches? The land of opportunity. Doesn't everybody say it?"

"Yeah, well, if this deal's so great, how come everybody's not in on it?"

"Because you got to know what you're doing. It isn't all that easy. It's the government. There's paperwork, all kinds of forms to fill out, red tape, regulations. It takes time, and you can get screwed good. That's what Fowler is earning his twenty percent for. He's on the inside. He'll walk all that stuff through. He figures it'll be about a month, and the rest of the money for the synagogue isn't due for sixty days. Another thing, you got to have an association, like a block association, put in a request for a day-care center, and he has some other guy who lives up there who's organized one. I don't know what they done. Threw the junkies off the block, whatever. The thing is it's legitimate. And there's something else. Nobody's thinking of the synagogue for a center because there's one operating only six blocks away, so you figure there wouldn't be a chance for another one, but Fowler says it don't mean a thing. It's the 'demonstrated need,' which is the association wanting it, that counts."

"Suppose something goes wrong. What if the guy gets sick in the middle of everything?"

"Jesus, you got any more questions? We thought of that. The law of equity says, 'That which will be done is done,' he says, so I put down the down payment, I'm the owner of record. And the first thing we get, before all the paperwork, is a letter of intent from the city. Once I got that, I can get a quick mortgage if there's a holdup. There's a lot of mortgage money floating around looking for a good deal. If I have to pay under the table for it, so what? It's chicken feed compared to what we're getting."

"So OK. You're rich already. Why bother with the likes of me?"

Flynn looked at Scanlon. "I don't have the down payment," he said. "The guy thinks I can get it, but I don't have it. Where am I going to go for that kind of money, this kind of deal? I'm like everyone else in here. I got to go to the shylocks. Donny, I'll give you a piece. I want you to put me in with Albert Karpstein."

For the first time Scanlon's tired, blank face showed some emotion. He drew the words out slowly, for maximum dramatic effect. "King Kong Karpstein?"

"Yeah," Flynn snapped. "*King Kong* Karpstein."

"Richie, you're out of your fucking mind. That Karpstein, he hopes you don't pay back. That way he can beat it out of you."

"I heard all the stories."

For a moment Scanlon thought very hard. If he put Flynn in touch with the loan sharks he was in debt to himself, he could reduce his remaining obligation considerably and perhaps even come out ahead before it was over. The idea was tempting. But suppose something did go wrong, as he had suggested, and it all turned sour? Then he would be in the middle. The two loan sharks knew he was close to Flynn. They might suspect that he was more than a go-between, and he could wind up deep in the hole again.

Scanlon decided it wasn't worth the risk. "Why not try Tony Valente?" he said. Valente was an aging soldier in the Mafia family of Frank Donato, organized crime's most powerful figure in the city, if not the nation, according to what the press said. Valente had a hidden interest in a stable of boxers, he had a numbers operation and he did some loan-sharking. He also had a small bar and restaurant in East Harlem, which had been one of Flynn's old accounts, and Flynn knew him well.

"No," Flynn said. "I ask this kind of money from a mob guy like Valente, and right away he wants to know what it's for, and all of a sudden I got a partner I don't want. Valente's worse than any of them. All he talks about is how he missed out when some guy came to him once for money to make frozen pizzas. He could have made millions, he keeps saying, how was he to know you could freeze pizzas? He's got frozen pizzas on the brain, and he'll deal himself in. A shylock like Karpstein, he doesn't care. He's only interested in the money."

Scanlon was shaking his head.

"Look," Flynn said, "I got it all worked out. I need ten for a month, but I'll ask for fifteen to cover myself, to cover the payments if something happens. Donny, I never asked you a favor before. You wanted that information when I was at Marquette, I gave it to you. I didn't say no. I could have gotten in a lot of trouble. You got to call for me. You got to do it now."

"It's Friday night, Richie. It's the weekend. Even shylocks take the weekend off."

"That's bullshit, and you know it. Donny, the auction's Tuesday. You got to do it now."

Finally Scanlon shrugged and stood up. "Got some dimes?" he said. He went to the pay telephone just inside an archway in the rear by the kitchen door. Flynn watched as he dialed, spoke briefly, hung up and made a second call.

Flynn looked toward the bar, at all the men arguing about Richard Nixon. Five tables away MacShane was staring at him. Flynn saluted him with his glass, and the old man raised his in turn. Flynn looked back at Scanlon. He was still on the phone. Then he hung up and made another call. This call was as brief as the first one. Scanlon came back and said, "Got any quarters? I got to call Jersey."

When Flynn reached into his pocket for the coins, he felt how clammy his hand had become. Scanlon returned to the phone and dialed. He spoke into it and waited. Then Flynn saw him talking again.

Scanlon hung up and walked back to the table. "OK. It's on for tomorrow night. I talked to a guy named

Biondo. He's Karpstein's guy. He'll get back to me with the details, and I'll call you."

"Jesus, Donny, you know you got a piece of this."

"No," Scanlon said. "I pass. Tell you what, Richie. When your horse comes in, you can buy me dinner at the 21 Club. I never been to the 21."

5

===== ☆ =====

After Scanlon left the Liffey, Flynn remained transfixed in his chair, like a butterfly under glass.

He suddenly felt very light-headed. But despite all the scotch he had consumed, he did not have any sensation of being drunk. On the contrary, his perceptions never seemed sharper. His mind raced with kaleidoscopic images of future well-being. He had another scotch to calm himself.

His exhilaration only mounted. He decided he had to do something. He looked at his watch. It was ten-thirty. It was the wrong hour and the wrong day, but still, he got up and went toward the telephone. To his surprise, he slipped, but it was not his knee. He fumbled for a dime, concentrated on the number of the Bourbon Street Club and dialed it. He could feel the faint stirring of an erection, simply thinking about her.

Duke Kaminsky, the manager, answered, and Flynn said, "This is Richie. Diane there? She dancing?" He was distressed to discover that his voice sounded unaccountably awkward and stilted, reflecting none of the fluid clarity of thought he was experiencing.

"Jeez, Richie," Kaminsky said, "this ain't a good time. She's off, but she's with, you know, a customer." In the background Flynn could hear the music, the babble of voices.

"Just for a second," he said. "I got to talk to her."

"Hold on. I'll see what I can do."

Her name was Diane Dare. She had picked it herself. Her real name was Diane Drahomanov. She was nineteen years old. She had started out at the Bourbon Street as a topless go-go dancer and subsequently appeared bottomless as well, for which she received two hundred and nine dollars a week. When she was not performing, she was expected to sit with a customer who asked her to join him for a drink. She got five percent of the customer's check, excluding the sales tax.

☆ 58 ☆

She was also Richie Flynn's girl friend, or rather one-seventh of her was. Soon after they met it became apparent to both of them that he could not afford her full time, and by mutual consent he saw her once a week, usually on Mondays, one of the two days she was not working. Except for occasional oblique references to trips to Miami Beach whenever she canceled a date, she did not volunteer what she did during the rest of the week, and he was in no position to ask. Once he asked her how it felt to be naked in front of so many men, and she said that she didn't feel anything, that because of the lighting, she was hardly ever aware that they were there, and even when she was, she blocked them out. This was not true. She was completely conscious of the eyes fastened on her body, and she loved it.

Flynn had met her under the most favorable auspices. He had gone to a restaurant in Little Italy to see Vincente (Vinnie the Vampire) D'Angelo. D'Angelo had got his nickname because of the remarkably bloodless way his victims disappeared during his early days as a Mafia executioner. He was now a capo in the Donato crime family, occupying roughly the same position in the New York Mafia hierarchy that Joe Hobo held in New Jersey. He controlled more than thirty establishments in Manhattan, including restaurants, topless bars, bars that specialized in homosexuals, discotheques, an after-hours club, where affluent pimps gathered to show off their finery and sniff cocaine, and a lavish nightclub featuring female impersonators that catered to the carriage trade. D'Angelo not only controlled them but kept his income as untraceable as possible through his holdings in various satellite companies that booked all the talent for his bars and clubs, placed all the advertising, supplied all the vending machines and handled all the garbage collection. Still two other of his companies, both in real estate, either owned the buildings where the businesses were located and collected rent or leased them from the actual owners and then sub-leased them to the businesses.

D'Angelo was also a key figure in some of the Little Italy street festivals, which were major tourist attractions, and Flynn had been anxious to get the festival account for Goldblatt beer. He had been invited for coffee following dinner. When he arrived, D'Angelo was extolling the virtues of his after-hours club to a heavyset man whom he did not bother to introduce. "It's beautiful," he said. "No liquor taxes. No fucking guy coming in saying you ain't got no fucking soap in the soap dish. No bullshit about fire exits. All you got to take care of is the cops. That's it."

The heavyset man departed, and Flynn brought up the festival beer account. "Gee, Vinnie," he had said, "if you could see your way clear, I'd really appreciate it."

The problem, D'Angelo explained, was that a venerable Italian, a longtime resident of Mulberry Street, had always had the account for another beer company. "You can't take it away from him now," he said. "It ain't right. But the old guy's not long for this world. He kicks off, we work something out. You got my word."

"That's good enough for me," Flynn had said. He essayed a small joke. "I mean, I wouldn't want him to get hit, or anything, over this."

D'Angelo smiled mirthlessly. Like most of his confederates, he had a sense of humor that left something to be desired. "You're some kidder, ain't you, Flynn?" he said. He was a thin-lipped, balding man who could have easily passed as an accountant. He stared at Flynn through gold-framed glasses for a moment, then smiled again. "Well, I like you anyway. You got guts. Listen, I got a new joint just opened on West Forty-eighth Street, the Bourbon Street. I want to take a look. Ride up with me. You can look at the girlies, maybe get lucky. You're a good-looking guy."

D'Angelo's green Cadillac with a cream-colored vinyl roof was parked in front of a fire hydrant. His driver, a young, muscular tough, was lounging against a lamppost. He rushed to open the door. D'Angelo offered Flynn a cigar. "It's good," he said. "Cuban." Although Flynn did not like cigars, he accepted it with thanks and lit up.

As topless bars went, the Bourbon Street was quite elaborate. A black liveried doorman was stationed outside. At their approach he mumbled automatically, "Yes, sir, gentlemens, the ladies is waiting." Then he recognized D'Angelo and sprang to full attention. "Yes, *sir*, Mr. D. Right this way!"

The inside of the club was a large, nearly square room. In the center there was a rectangular bar. Fake crystal chandeliers hung from the ceiling. Black leatherette stools ringed the bar, and red crushed-rayon-velvet banquettes lined the walls. Overhead in each corner white plaster cherubs blew soundlessly through plaster horns. "You should of seen this place before," D'Angelo said. "I got this fag decorator, he does miracles."

The girls performed on three raised circular stages set in a row down the center of the bar, so every customer had an unobstructed view. Two of the girls on stage were white, and one was black. All they had on were high-heeled shoes. They gyrated to muted rock music. The black girl was closest to the door. With her heels, Flynn thought, she must be at least six feet tall. She had long, sloping breasts that turned up magically at the last moment. The girl in the middle was short and curvaceous. There was a tiny roll of fat around her waist that jiggled when she moved. She had a lascivious grin on her face, framed by a shock of brunette ringlets, and an enormous black pubic bush. While she was dancing, she suddenly squatted and spread her knees and laughed at the applause. The third girl, the one in the rear, was slender by comparison. She had light brown, almost blond, hair that fell below her shoulders. Her skin was taut, her breasts were conical and she bent and turned with sinuous grace, her eyes half-closed.

The bar was about three-quarters filled. Many of the men wore suits and ties. There were even some couples. Duke Kaminsky led Flynn and D'Angelo to a banquette in the back. "How's it going, Duke?" D'Angelo asked.

"Good, Vinnie. Been like this all night. Busy. Nice crowd."

"You see," D'Angelo had said to Flynn, "you got a nice joint, you get nice people. Duke, you know Richie Flynn here?"

"Do I know Richie Flynn? Boy, could the Giants use him now." Kaminsky hovered over D'Angelo. He was a stout man with a bald pate and gray muttonchops. "What'll you have?"

"Scotch and water," Flynn said.

"Plain soda," D'Angelo said.

The three girls who had been dancing when Flynn came in were ending their number, and three other girls were preparing to take their places. "Where do you find them?" Flynn asked.

"You mean, where do they find *me?*" D'Angelo had said. "Duke, how many girlies you audition?"

"Gee, Vinnie, I don't know. Couple of hundred. There's a big waiting list, too."

D'Angelo glanced speculatively at Flynn, and then he said to Kaminsky, "Send over them three that just got off."

The three girls came to the table at once. They were wearing identical see-through red off-the-shoulder smocks with sashes tied around their waists. The smocks barely covered their upper thighs. They sat dutifully in front of D'Angelo, cautious, attentive smiles fixed on their faces. They addressed him as "Mr. D'Angelo." "How's it going, girls?" he said. They all spoke at the same time. Everything was wonderful, they said.

"Meet Richie Flynn here," D'Angelo said. "He was a big football star."

The tall black girl, whose name was Candy, said, "You big at anything else?" She emitted a deep-throated laugh. She had on vermilion lipstick and flashed two rows of startling white teeth.

The short brunette giggled. She said her name was Maureen.

The girl with the light brown hair did not introduce herself. "Oh, Candy," she had said to the black girl in a soft, breathless voice, "you shouldn't say things like that." Flynn thought that she had blushed slightly. She turned to him and said, "I used to be a cheerleader." He was sure that she had blushed a second time.

"Where?"

"Toledo. Toledo, Ohio."

"What's your name?" he had asked.

"Diane," she said.

Candy ordered brandy and milk. Maureen had scotch. Diane asked for a sweet daiquiri. D'Angelo stood up and said, "I got to get going. You girls keep Richie company. Duke, anything Richie wants, it's on me."

"Whooee, you must be a big man," Candy said. "The boss is buying."

"When do you finish dancing?" Flynn said to Diane.

"I am finished. That was my last turn."

"Would you like to go somewhere, have something to eat?"

"All right."

"I guess the man done made his choice," Candy said, downing her brandy and milk in a gulp and standing up.

"You making a mistake, though, mister. I may be black on the outside, but I got the pinkest pussy here." She laughed and left.

Maureen giggled again.

"You want to come with us?" Flynn said.

"No, thanks. I have a date."

"I'll change," Diane said. "I'll just be a minute."

Flynn took her to Clarke's. She was wearing black boots, a black miniskirt and a matching belted jacket, and everyone stared at her when they came in.

While they were in line waiting for a table in the back room, Frankie, the maître d', came over and said, "There's a guy who wants you to join him for a drink," and pointed to a beefy man seated with another man and two women. The beefy man waved at Flynn. This occasionally happened to him. He would come into Clarke's sometimes, and nobody would notice him, and he would stand alone, have a drink and leave. But once in a while somebody would remember him and call him over and resurrect the touchdown, usually for the benefit of friends, and Flynn would feel like a performing poodle, and would hate himself for it, but he could not resist doing it.

This time, with the girl, it was the last thing he wanted. But then he sensed that she was intrigued by the invitation, even impressed by it. The beefy man looked vaguely familiar. "Who is he?" he asked, and Frankie had said, "Some councilman from Queens. Go over. I'll have a table for you any second." So he went with her, and the councilman introduced the other man, who was a visiting politician from Utica, New York, and the two women, who turned out not to be their wives. "What a run, you should have been there," the councilman proclaimed, his arm around Flynn's shoulder, while the visiting politician from Utica kept saying, "I think I saw it. On TV."

And then Frankie told Flynn his table was ready, and he and Diane moved to it, and she said, "What's it like being famous?" and he said that he was not famous, that it had happened a long time ago, and she smiled knowingly, as if she understood and appreciated his becoming modesty.

She ordered a bacon-cheeseburger and a Coke, and when he asked her about herself, she said that her people were Ukrainian, that her father worked in a tool and die plant in Toledo and that he was under the impression that she was a model, and that this was not far from the truth, since *Penthouse* magazine had asked her to pose in the nude, but she had refused because she was afraid that friends of her father might see the pictures. At sixteen, she said, she had run off with and married a Toledo boy, three years her senior, who drove a bakery truck. Eleven months later, following the birth of a daughter, she divorced her husband. "He was just too immature," she said. After a year or so as an apprentice hairdresser in a Toledo beauty shop, she came to New York, and her mother, who knew what Diane was doing, took care of the daughter. She said that she sent home twenty-five dollars a week for the child's support and that her mother brought her daughter to New York annually for a short visit. She herself tried to get out to Toledo every six months, and to make up for her prolonged absence, she went loaded down with gifts for the little girl. The last time she had brought a baby doll that cried and wet its diapers. "Honestly," she had said, "it's the cutest thing."

She polished off her bacon-cheeseburger and asked if she could have another one, and then she said to Flynn, "What did you think of Maureen?"

"She was OK."

"She's gay."

"She's *what?*"

"Gay," Diane said. "You know, a lesbian." She was sipping the Coke through a straw as she spoke, staring up at him under arched eyebrows.

He did not know what to say at first. Finally he said, "What's she doing at the Bourbon Street?"

"That's how she gets her kicks. And the money's good. There's another girl there like her. That was her date tonight." She took a bite of her second bacon-cheeseburger and chewed it meditatively. "She wanted us to room together. She's nice, but I decided I didn't want to go that route."

In the cab, on the way to her apartment, she said, "Are you married?"

"Yes," he said. "Why?"

"It doesn't matter. I was just wondering."

She lived in a small brick building on Fifty-eighth Street, just west of Eighth Avenue. A shirt-sleeved night janitor let them in. They went up a self-service elevator to the fourth floor and down a corridor to her door. While she was putting the key into the lock, he was trying to think of the right thing to say, but he did not have to say anything. When she opened the door, she motioned to him to follow. She turned on a lamp on a bureau. It cast a dim light in the room. Through an open door he could see a tiny kitchen with dishes stacked in the sink. The bed was unmade. There were three or four stuffed animals on it. Magazines were piled on two chairs and a table, and more were scattered on the floor. Blouses, skirts, dresses and pantyhose were draped everywhere. "Sorry about the mess," she had said. "I didn't expect company. Wait for me. I'm all sweaty. I'm going to take a shower. I'll only be a minute."

She went into the bathroom. He removed his jacket and loosened his tie. He took some of the magazines from one of the chairs and put them on the table. He picked up a copy of *Glamour* and opened it to a feature on how to apply mascara. He tossed it aside and tried *Cosmopolitan*. He read a column of advice which exhorted a single girl traveling alone always to fly first class. "You will find," the column said, "the men in first class much more interesting." He could hear the shower running. A movie fan magazine by his feet headlined "The Tragedy of Jackie O's Children." He leafed through it and read a story about the secret life of a Hollywood star. He failed to learn any secrets about the star except that he preferred to keep his private life private. Flynn looked at his watch. She had been in the bathroom nearly half an hour. The water was still running. He started to doze. Perhaps ten minutes later she reappeared.

She came out of the bathroom naked, skipping on her toes, smiling. She embraced him and began unbuttoning his shirt. Her body was lightly perfumed. Her hair was piled on top of her head. Damp tendrils dangled over her ears and down her cheeks. She reminded him of the nymph in the White Rock ads, demure, spotless, virginal. Suddenly he thought he would not be able to manage an erection.

After she had unbuttoned his shirt, he finished undressing himself. He lay next to her on the bed and kissed her, and then he was certain he would not get it up. He mumbled, "I don't know what's wrong."

She sat up. "Don't worry," she said matter-of-factly. "It happens all the time. I'll fix it." She knelt over him, so he could see the curve of her back, her breasts, her round buttocks, and she settled her mouth over his flaccid penis. She pulled on it with her mouth, and again. He closed his eyes. It won't do any good, he thought. Then he felt her tongue. It was like a jolt of electricity. Her tongue moved in machine-gun bursts, flicking, darting, jabbing, circling, fluttering. After a dumbfounded moment he felt himself stiffen. There was a strange, abstract quality about it, as if his cock were not his anymore but belonged to her. It had never seemed so big or powerful. He felt as though a tree had taken root in his loins. It began to throb.

He reached down for her and drew her up to him and got on top of her. He started to go into her as gently as he could. But she was very open and wet, and he slid in easily. Later he would learn that she used a lubricating cream. At first he went in and out of her slowly, trying to maintain control. He began to pump in long, steady strokes. She came up to him, held it and then fell back. Each time she arched up with greater intensity before falling back. He could feel her muscles tighten, her stomach, hips and thighs straining against him. She moaned slightly. She pressed harder, held it longer. Her breath expelled in anguished gasps. He started to lose control.

All at once she placed her hands on his shoulders and pushed him aside. "Eat me," she said. "I can't get off unless you eat me first. After that it's all right. I don't know why."

Flynn did not like to go down on women. Once when he had drunkenly gone down on his wife, Agnes, he had found the odor offensive, the taste rancid, and he had been relieved when she pushed him away, even though he sensed that she had really liked it, that if he tried again, she would not have stopped him the second time. But to his astonishment he found the smell of Diane mysteriously delicious, and he wondered what the secret was. He actually enjoyed the taste of her. When he probed her with his tongue, she shifted her position on the bed slightly, then adjusted herself again.

"That's it," she said. "Right there."

She rotated her pelvis in tight little circles. She started to rise up against him as she had before, but with less desperation, more purposefully and rhythmically.

"Don't stop," she gasped. "Oh, God, that's so good." While she was talking to him, he could not help thinking that she was really talking to herself, and in her excitement, his own excitement mounted. Stretched out between her legs, he felt himself stiffening once more beyond hope.

"Oh, Jesus!" she cried. "Daddy, oh, Daddy, do it to me!"

He tongued her harder, faster.

"Yes!" she said. "Right now. Oh, my God! Oh, Daddy!" She came up against him in one last, prolonged effort and shuddered. She shuddered again, and then she screamed. He came himself, on the sheet. He felt the warm jism on his belly.

She thrashed about momentarily before she fell back limply, his head resting against the inside of her thigh. Then he moved up next to her, and she ran her hand down toward his crotch. "Hey," he said, "I got a little excited there. I need a minute."

She propped herself up on an elbow. "That's all right," she said. "I can wait." Her hair had tumbled down over her face. She shook it back. She had a crooked grin on her face. Her eyes had an unfocused, glazed look.

She rolled away from him and took some folded tinfoil from a table by the bed and unwrapped it. There were a half dozen marijuana cigarettes in the foil. She lit one, inhaled deeply and passed it to Flynn. He had tried a few puffs once before without much effect. He sucked in the smoke anyway, carefully aping her, holding it in his lungs as long as he could. They passed the marijuana back and forth. For perhaps five minutes he did not feel anything. Then it hit him. At first he felt slightly dizzy, and then he began to feel as though he were floating just off the bed.

He was still caught up in this marvelous sensation of floating when she bent over him and her mouth was on him again, her tongue working furiously. When he entered her this time, unconcerned about coming too fast, she matched his movements, arching higher against him until she began to writhe and then shuddered and screamed once more. He could feel her fingernails digging into his back.

She dropped back in apparent exhaustion. After a moment she opened her eyes. Her pupils were dilated, and he noticed their color for the first time. They were light gray, like a cloud-layered sky. She had the same crooked grin. "Oh, Jesus," she said. "I'm so hot."

He remained rigid, and he started to move in her again. "No," she said. "Fuck me in the ass."

"Where?"

"My ass."

All night long Flynn had been trying without success to achieve some measure of dominance over her. "Can you come that way?" he asked lamely. The truth was that he had never done it before.

"Yes," she had said. "Hurry!"

She twisted away from him and crouched at the end of the bed on her knees, buttocks up, her face pressed sideways on a pillow.

He stood behind her on the floor, his knees against the bed. She reached between her legs and grabbed his cock and rubbed it along her bottom. Her bottom was unbelievably wet and slippery. Just the touch of it excited him tremendously. She guided him to her anus, and then the head of his cock was partly in. He started to shove forward, and she cried, "Easy! Take it easy!"

She moved slowly against him, so that more of him went into her, how much he could not really tell because of all the wetness, the unreality of it all. Perspiration popped out over his entire body. She rocked against him, and he was into her farther. As he rocked back, he could feel her sphincter contracting. One of her hands was at her clitoris, massaging it frantically. She groaned and whispered, "Oh, Daddy," and then she yelled, "Give it to me!"

He thrust in her, his hands on her backside, and she grunted in pain, but she did not stop. He was drenched with sweat. He had never been more inflamed in his life. Suddenly he exploded inside her.

She did not let him go, actually held him in her, really forced him to stay semierect as she continued to grind against him, rubbing herself at the same time until at last her entire body convulsed violently and there was a final piercing scream that filled the room and she slumped forward, facedown, on the bed.

He remained where he was, looking at her. The sweat was still pouring down him. His legs shook. He had never had a sexual experience approaching this in his life. The room was absolutely silent. He asked her if she was all right, and she did not respond.

He turned and stumbled into the bathroom. The bathroom was crammed with lotions and oils and creams and conditioners and assorted cosmetic paraphernalia. In contrast with the disarray of the room he had just left, everything was neatly arranged, precisely marked. He washed himself, and when he returned, he found her curled up in the bed asleep, her mouth slightly open, clutching a small rust-colored teddy bear.

Before he departed, he wrote down her telephone number. When he called her late in the morning, she answered in her breathless baby voice. She made no reference to their night together, nor did she seem to exhibit any sign of knowing who he was. "Oh, hi," she had said in a neutral tone, and for an eerie moment he almost thought he would have to identify himself beyond his name. But when he said he wanted to see her again that night, she had said she was busy, but that the following night would be fine, that she would be working the day shift and he could pick her up at her apartment. He saw her that night, and the night after. He had asked to be with her the next night as well, and she had looked directly at him with her milky gray eyes and had said that it sounded as though he wanted her to be with him exclusively, and if that were so, there were going to be some expenses, since her salary at the Bourbon Street covered only her bare necessities, to say nothing of her daughter's support, and he had replied that he had to keep seeing her, but that for the present at least he could not arrange to see her all the time. So they had fallen into the pattern of his dating her once a week. And to maintain the illusion that he was somebody for her to be with, he always took her to restaurants frequented by sporting figures so that he could count on being recognized. Once he had been invited to join a table that included the television host Johnny Carson, and she had been beside herself with excitement. She had sat wide-eyed as Carson discussed the possibility of doing a feature on triumph and tragedy in sports and said that Richie Flynn would certainly be in it, and later she had asked Flynn, "Are you going to do it?" and he had shrugged and said, "Maybe," and she had come to him that night in bed with unequaled intensity, and when he was leaving, she got up and said that she had to write a letter to her best girl friend in Toledo, that her girl friend would never believe that she had actually met Johnny Carson.

Nearly four months had elapsed since Vincente D'Angelo had taken him to the Bourbon Street and he had met her, and now, in the Liffey Bar & Grill, leaning drunkenly against the wall, waiting for Diane to come to the phone, he wanted to tell her that it did not matter whether he appeared on a show with Johnny Carson, that his friend Scanlon had made a call for him that was going to change his life and that he no longer was going to dance to somebody else's tune, that from now on he was in control of his own destiny. He wanted to tell her all this, but when she was finally on the line, all he could say was, "Hey, I want to see you."

"I have an appointment," she said with a faint touch of annoyance. "I'm not supposed to see you till Monday."

"All right, Monday. I just thought maybe you weren't doing anything. Listen, I'll be there early. We're going to the races."

"I have to go now," she said, and hung up.

It was just as well, he thought. The euphoria he felt had evaporated, and for the first time it occurred to him that perhaps he had had too much to drink. He pushed himself away from the phone, paid his bill and walked unsteadily past the bar into the street.

He searched his pockets twice before he found his car keys. When he got behind the wheel, he reminded himself to drive carefully. Fortunately the fog had cleared. He edged into a downtown lane of the parkway along the river. Cars whizzed by him. His head whirled. He concentrated on Scanlon and Albert Karpstein and what a fine thing it would be to have a chauffeur to take him home if he happened to have a few scotches too many.

His concentration was such that he missed the exit at Ninety-sixth Street and had to go down to Seventy-third before turning off and coming back up First Avenue. He lived in an apartment building in the Yorkville section of Manhattan. Agnes had not wished to leave Inwood, but Richie had argued that it would be good for them to get out, that they could not spend their lives stagnating there. Another reason was to remove himself from the immediate presence of his mother-in-law, who had never bought the explanation that her daughter had given birth prematurely and who viewed Flynn as a direct descendant of Casanova.

At first Flynn's own mother had served as a buffer, but she died within a year after his marriage, and one of the advantages of where he now resided, on East Eighty-seventh Street near Lexington Avenue, was that there was no convenient subway link between Yorkville and Inwood for the mother-in-law to use. She complained bitterly about this, but Flynn, knowing what a snob she was, claimed with great innocence that he had made the move for the sake of *her* grandson, so that he could attend St. Ignatius Loyola, which not only was considered top-rung among parochial schools in the city but was situated close by, right on Park Avenue.

The apartment, he had to admit, was a mistake. It was in one of those glazed white brick boxes that had sprouted up during the construction boom in Manhattan during the 1960s. White was the favored color because surveys had shown that prospective tenants were drawn to it, but the glaze on the bricks had quickly cracked, and the accumulated dirt streaked down ineradicably. The glittering new interiors had become equally shabby. In their greed the developers, like mad geneticists, had created a whole new race of buildings that went directly from infancy to senility.

The boom in apartments had quickly outpaced the demand for them, and concessions had been offered in the interests of gaining middle-class occupants. When Flynn signed a long-term lease, his first four months were rent-free. But by the time the lease had expired and he had grown weary of his neighbor's stereo selections, equivalent apartments were no longer so easy to find. Flynn's rent had since climbed steadily, and he was currently paying three hundred ninety-eight dollars and twenty cents a month for a living room with a dining alcove, a small kitchen and two bedrooms.

Agnes talked about quitting the city. But suburban real estate required down payments for cooperatives, condominiums and tract houses, and Flynn had barely two thousand dollars in his savings account. All that really stood between him and some personal calamity was Goldblatt's group Blue Cross plan. That was the fucking way life was, Flynn thought. The rich took care of their own, the government took care of the poor and the people in between had to shift for themselves.

Flynn parked in a garage under the building. There was an additional charge of eighty-five dollars a month for the car, but Goldblatt picked up three-quarters of this. When he got out, he suddenly realized that he had not eaten anything all evening, and he went into a coffee shop on Lexington Avenue and ordered two hamburgers and coffee. He bought a *Daily News* on sale at the counter. The front-page headline was about another Watergate revelation. Flynn turned to the sports section. He remembered that he had a ten-dollar bet on a horse in the fifth race at Aqueduct. The horse had finished out of the money. In basketball the Knicks had defeated the Boston Celtics in overtime. Bill Bradley had led them with twenty-eight points. He wondered what it was like to be Bill Bradley, to come from a well-to-do family, have an Ivy League education, be a Rhodes scholar, a star professional athlete. There were always stories in the papers about what Bradley would do when he retired from the Knicks, how he would probably go into politics, maybe even end up in the White House. Bradley, Flynn concluded, did not have a care in the world.

It was nearly one A.M. when he let himself into the apartment. He went into the kitchen and opened a can of Goldblatt. He had one almost every night before going to sleep. He felt better after having eaten, and he slumped back on the sofa in the living room, sipping the beer. From where he sat he could look down a short hallway to the closed door of his son's room. He had named the boy Sean after his father. The boy was not much older than Flynn had been when his father had died. The funny thing, he sometimes thought, was that he did not know his own son any better than he had known his father.

In the darkened bedroom he shared with Agnes, he undressed to his shorts. He had thought she was asleep when he came in, but as he lay in the bed now, he could tell from her breathing that she was not. He decided to go to sleep anyway, without saying anything to her. After the injury to his knee, with all the future uncertainty they faced, they had decided not to have any more children for a while. Agnes had insisted on using the rhythm method, and during the first years they were together Flynn would often turn to her in desperate ardor and she would move away, saying, "No, it's the wrong time." In sex, at any time, he had always been the aggressor. Then, somehow, even that had petered out, and whenever he took her, it was not out of desire but occasional biological need. In his work for Goldblatt, it was amazing how many available women he encountered in bars and restaurants, and until he had met Diane, his sex life had become a series of one-night adventures.

He and Agnes never discussed sex. Perhaps, he thought, this happened to all married couples, this dissipation of magic and excitement. It was not that he didn't care for her, or have great affection for her, or still love her in a way, but there seemed to be nothing to grow or build on. Although she was only two months younger than he, she had not aged as well. From plainly pretty, she had become just plain. There were tired lines around her eyes. Her hips had spread, and globules of fat had begun to form on the backs of her thighs. Flynn knew this was unfair to take into account, but it was a fact.

Sometimes weeks passed without sex between them. As he lay next to her now, he could not recall the last time they had coupled. Flynn thought of Diane and Monday. Agnes stirred slightly. Then he was confounded to feel her hand slide across his belly and under his shorts. He could not believe what was happening. She pulled down his shorts and took him in her mouth. My God, he thought, has she gone crazy? It was as if she had been to some porno film.

Which, indeed, was the case. Surrounded by a world awash in sex, a world she did not comprehend, and groping for some reassurance of her own worth, she had let a girl friend talk her into seeing *Deep Throat* in an East Side movie theater. And instead of being horrified, as she had expected, she had watched with fascination as her most private fantasies, many of them only dimly perceived, were portrayed openly on the screen, and she had come out of the theater determined that if this was what it took, well, she would try it.

In her awkwardness, what she was doing was as stunning to Flynn as Diane's expertise had been, and despite himself, he responded. He lay on his back as she mounted him. She had trouble inserting his cock, and like an automaton, he helped her. She rode up and down on him in frenzied little jerks. When she came, it was with a muffled cry, and he came, too. She slipped off him and lay next to him, her head on his outstretched arm. He touched her hair with his free hand. Not a word had passed between them in the darkness.

His arm started to ache under the weight, but he was afraid to move it, afraid to do anything. Finally she was asleep, and he gently disengaged himself.

Then he fell asleep and had a dream. In the dream he was getting out of a car. There was an expanse of bright green lawn. Shade from some trees dappled the lawn in the setting sun. His son was running on the lawn, playing with a huge dog. He tousled his son's hair. There was a white house. A servant opened the door. Agnes was inside. He gave her a mink coat from a box he was carrying. She pirouetted in it, smiling joyously, and kissed him. He went to the telephone and called Diane. Diane was by the phone, waiting. She was always waiting. He went to the apartment he had rented for her. She opened the door. She was wearing the same kind of mink coat. But she told him that it had a flesh lining, and when she, too, swirled in it, the coat flew open, and he could see that she was naked underneath. She laughed and pulled him toward the bed.

Flynn woke up. It was still dark. He had an enormous, pulsing erection. He got up and went to the bathroom. When he came back to the bed, he immediately fell asleep again. It was the best dream that Richie Flynn had ever had.

6

On Saturday, the day after Flynn met with Scanlon, there had been enough of a nip in the late morning air for Hamilton Wainwright IV to keep on his warm-up jacket through two sets of tennis. Midway through the third set, however, he suddenly shed it. His body heat sprang not so much from exertion as anger. He and his partner had lost the first set 2–6 and the second 4–6, and Wainwright not only did not like to lose, but especially did not like to lose the way he was losing this morning. His doubles partner was the wife of an influential, nationally syndicated Washington columnist. She was a dumpy, thick-thighed woman, and while she hit the ball with smooth authority, her game required that the ball come to her or else she did not hit it at all.

Wainwright's wife, the former Cynthia Buchanan, slim, athletic, the photogenically blond heiress to a canned-soup fortune, was paired with the columnist. Although Mrs. Wainwright could not match her husband's strength, she was a much better player in her ball control and tactical sense. She was used to his powerful, flat serves and lobbed them time and again over the head of the columnist's wife, the ball landing with maddening precision in the alley a foot or two short of the base line. It was not a question of Wainwright's getting to the ball. Verging on thirty-five, he was in excellent shape, a lanky six feet three, with a handsome angular face, golden hair and an impish grin that caused feminine hearts to beat wildly. Men could look at him and understand why women doted on him, which was no mean accomplishment.

But the grin had disappeared in the infuriating pattern of play, and instead of patiently answering his wife's lobs with ones of his own, Wainwright began resorting to over-the-shoulder smashes on the run that more often than not wound up in the net. Whenever he started moving a bit too early in anticipation of a lob, Mrs. Wainwright would counter with smartly stroked cross-court returns, some of

☆ 75 ☆

which the columnist's wife might have cut off with a little effort. Wainwright wanted to yell at her to shake her ass, but he stifled the impulse. He was at a delicate point in his career. Fresh from a sensational courtroom conviction involving labor racketeering in the building trades unions, he had been named a special federal prosecutor to head a new crusade against organized crime in the New York area. It was a prized, highly visible post, in effect giving him his own miniature Justice Department. It was also why the columnist and his wife had been invited to the Wainwright estate for the weekend. The columnist had appraised him in print as "a sorely needed addition to today's public arena, a cool yet impassioned young man who bids fair to end cocktail-party gibes about men on white horses," and Wainwright was not eager to display any character defects at this juncture.

Wainwright's chief assistant, Nicholas Simonetta, stood nearby, watching the match in the company of a local television newscaster whose voice-of-the-people manner commanded a large and loyal audience. The newscaster had a popular Sunday evening interview show as well, and Wainwright was to be his guest the following week.

And now, against the rhythmic plop of the ball, he said to Simonetta, "What's he like to work for? I need some anecdotes."

"Well, he's tough, but it's worth it."

"Yeah, yeah, I know. So what does that mean?"

Simonetta led the newscaster away from the court and said in a low voice, "I don't think Ham wants this personal stuff to get around. It's what has to be done that's important to him, not himself, but I'll never forget one time when we were down in Washington preparing for the building trades case. It was after midnight before he finally called it quits, and we got into the car and happened to go by the union's national headquarters, and Ham looked up, and he saw the lights still on in the big guy's office on the top floor, and he said, 'If that son of a bitch can stay up all night, we can, too,' and we turned around and went right back to work."

"That's great. I'll use it in my intro," the newscaster said, and when Simonetta feigned alarm, he added, "Don't worry, I'll make it look like I dug it up on my own."

On the court Wainwright, with no help from the columnist's wife, had struggled to a 6–5 lead in the third set and was a point away from winning the deciding game. Mrs. Wainwright observed her husband's demeanor and heard his strangled curse as he faulted his first service. Besides, it was nearly time for lunch, and so on his second serve, she purposely netted her return. "Oh, sugar," she said, gesturing apologetically to the columnist and thinking to herself how amazingly simple it was to restore her husband's good spirits.

"Well, we took that one," he was saying to the columnist's wife with a satisfied smile.

"But not the match, dear boy," the columnist said, "which, in the vernacular, is where it's all at."

Wainwright's pale green eyes contemplated the columnist. "You're right," he said, "as usual."

☆

Wainwright was a prominent name in the city. Wainwright's father was the senior partner in the family's Wall Street law firm founded by his great-grandfather, who had also been a notable United States congressman.

In the family tradition Wainwright completed his undergraduate studies at Princeton and received his law degree from Yale. But bored by the prospect of corporate practice, he did not join the family firm. Instead, he settled on the prosecution of organized crime as the springboard to a political career. So far everything had gone as planned. A Senate seat two years hence was what he had in mind and, eventually, the White House. It was not that Wainwright was using organized crime purely to advance his own purpose or that he did not actually perceive it to be a sinister threat to the national well-being. It was just that organized crime as a cause dovetailed nicely with his career goals.

And in this regard he drew inspiration from, and identified with, the first Hamilton Wainwright. His firebrand great-grandfather had been the strong right arm in Congress to Thaddeus Stevens, merciless scourge of the post-Civil War South and architect of the most hated edict imposed on the defeated Confederacy—blanket suffrage for former slaves. In one of his great-grandfather's diaries, he had discovered the following entry: "To give the downtrodden Negro the right to vote is noble and just by every Christian standard; fortuitously, it will also provide us with the means to maintain a Republican majority in

the Congress." Hamilton Wainwright IV found organized
crime, as personified by the Mafia, of similar beneficence
in his quest for high office.

Some advisers cautioned that there were pitfalls to be
reckoned with, that, for instance, all the world did not
necessarily love a prosecutor, and they invariably pointed
to that premier racket buster Thomas E. Dewey, who,
despite his many acclaimed triumphs, was denied the ultimate notch in his gun by a failed haberdasher from Mis-
souri. But Wainwright rejected this notion. Reality was
what people thought, and in the age of television, where it
was mandatory to look good, not only would he look
good, but he would look best. The diminutive, mus-
tachioed Dewey had carried about him the faintly unc-
tuous aura of a headwaiter in a mediocre continental
restaurant. Wainwright would have no trouble on that
count. His media consultant had him photographed as
much as possible in rolled-up shirt sleeves, his tie pulled
down, to project a tough, tireless, no-nonsense air that
contrasted reassuringly with his patrician background. The
net effect on the public was reflected in the attitude of
Wainwright's staff. It numbered fifteen hand-picked young
attorneys. They felt signally honored to have been selected
by him. They considered themselves hard-nosed, pragmatic
idealists, and they shared an elitist sense of being among
the chosen few who had found a winner in Wainwright.
The experience was heady. Wainwright not only was
wealthy and well connected but engendered fear in all the
right places. His wealth made him incorruptible; therefore,
they were incorruptible. They liked that, and the power
and prestige that went with it.

Wainwright's media consultant had charted a course
carefully calculated to mirror the external trappings of the
Kennedys, particularly Robert Kennedy, and Wainwright
lent himself to the strategy with ease. His marriage had
been the social event of the season, and his photogenic
wife had borne him four equally photogenic children,
three girls and a boy. He was quite sure of himself and his
visible family assets and was not at all loath to be put on
display in what seemed to be the most intimate, revealing
circumstances. Members of the press were regularly invited to weekend outings at his country estate in the exclusive community of Bedford Hills in Westchester County,
where if they did not ride, they could play tennis, golf at a

nearby club or indulge in more plebeian activities like touch football, softball and volleyball in the company of Wainwright and his two older children, thirteen-year-old Deborah and ten-year-old Hamilton V, along with a gaggle of their friends and the inevitable celebrity guest in political and diplomatic circles, movies and television, sports and rock music.

These weekends had always been an integral, if minor, note in Wainwright's life-style anyway. But now they were orchestrated into full-scale productions by the media consultant—a short, pallid, moon-faced, cigar-chain-smoking wizard of the national psyche, who had long since recognized that a candidate's energetic participation in sports was tantamount to being born with a spotless soul. It was also he who had advised the hiring of all-white domestic help, so as to avoid calling attention to certain unpleasant economic opportunity truths in the nation, as well as the serving of such luncheon fare as hot dogs and hamburgers to leaven the impact of Wainwright's twenty-two-room Tudor mansion, the rolling lawns surrounding it, the tennis court and the heated swimming pool, complete with bath-house and sauna and a fully equipped soda fountain. The only carping voice to be heard was from the media consultant's pneumatic wife, a former Yugoslavian entry in the Miss World contest whom Mrs. Wainwright could not abide. "Why am I never invited?" the pneumatic wife would petulantly demand, and the media consultant, biting down hard on a big number one Montecristo cigar, would snarl, "Shut up, will you? This guy's paying three grand a month right now, and there's going to be plenty more later. I'm taking him all the way to Sixteen Hundred Pennsylvania Avenue, and that ain't Belgrade. When we get there, you'll be invited. I guarantee it."

One of the highlights for visiting press wives, having left their own children in the care of in-laws and baby-sitters, was a privileged tour of the nursery to see the newest Wainwrights, Melinda and Tracy, ages four and two. These tours, of course, aroused great envy in viewing bosoms, but they were conducted with such casual, good-natured openness, as if everybody had a nursery and nannies, that the envy was a yearning rather than rancorous one, and the Wainwrights, servants and all, more and more epitomized the American dream family.

Reporters, both male and female, meanwhile had the

chance to mix informally with the mighty, to pick up inside gossip, to wind up occasionally in the gossip columns
themselves to their secret satisfaction, to cultivate contacts
in prestigious surroundings and, not so coincidentally, to
propagate the Wainwright name. One of the problems with
organized crime was that the public's interest in it was cy-
clic, so it was important to keep up a drumbeat of stories
concerning its consummate evil. Wainwright himself selec-
tively passed on information about ongoing investigations,
grand jury probes and forthcoming indictments. Indictments were, of course, simply formal accusations, but he
manipulated leaks so well that they were in effect treated
as convictions. He was not without a philosophical ratio-
nale for his methods and was quite candid about it to
friendly reporters. "Listen," he told them in confidential
briefings, "we've got to fight fire with fire. I'm not about to
let these hyenas take a walk just because they can get the
best defence money can buy. If I know in my heart
they're guilty, I'm going after them. And that's where you
fellows are so important. The public has to be educated. If
we don't destroy them, they'll destroy us. It's that simple."

None of the reporters Wainwright confided in saw fit to
note that it was extremely difficult under the rules of evidence to cross-examine what was in the special prosecutor's heart. And in return they got scoops. One concerned
a Mafia capo, so intent on keeping it all in the family, as
it were, that he married his first cousin, a union that had
resulted in three of their seven children being grossly re-
tarded. Few people found anything untoward about this
revelation; the capo in question was widely believed to be
running a major heroin ring. But on another occasion
Wainwright quietly arranged to have a reporter fed secret
grand jury minutes, in which an informant testified that he
had overheard a lawyer telling a Mafia client that he had
a certain judge in his pocket. The story broke into print
before the grand jury had actually come to any conclusion, and in fact, it could never be established whether the
lawyer meant what he had said or was only trying to
impress a client. But from then on, a cloud of suspicion
hung over the judge. Wainwright shrugged this off without
a second's thought; at the very least it served notice on
other judges that he was keeping an eye on them, and if
the judge was in fact blameless, he was the kind of innocent casualty that unfortunately occurred in every war.

Some of the press did not cotton to Wainwright's methods, but they were considered carping spoilsports who did not appreciate the nobility of his crusade. Most reporters, especially younger ones eager to make names for themselves, argued that his was a fresh voice in the land, crying out against a chorus of tired cynicism. Besides, like his staff, they wanted to be with a winner. When Hamilton Wainwright IV got close to a reporter, he would often ask advice about a particular matter, a direction he should or should not take. The moment the flattered reporter responded, he became Wainwright's eager acolyte. It was, as his media consultant pointed out, only human nature.

☆

Having showered after the tennis match, Wainwright sat at one of the white wrought-iron tables on the flagstone terrace by the pool. He wore Gucci slip-ons, blue jeans, a blue buttoned-down shirt open at the neck and a beige cashmere sweater with a hole in the right elbow. As the jacketed butler removed a plate with the remnants of a hamburger on it, Wainwright finished his milk shake and held out his glass for a refill to go with a large slice of chocolate layer cake. "All you have to do," he was saying to a young feature writer from the *Daily News*, "is look at a Mafia boss like Frank Donato."

The seventy-two-year-old Donato was a favorite Wainwright target. His last recorded conviction had been in 1925, when he was sentenced to six months in jail for carrying a concealed weapon, a pistol. "Donato's crime family is in everything you can think of," Wainwright continued, jabbing a fork into his cake. "But when was the last time he saw the inside of a cell? I'll tell you. It was almost fifty years ago!" He paused for dramatic effect. "Is that right?" he demanded. "Is that the way it has to be? *I* don't think so."

The gathering this Saturday was modest by the usual Wainwright standards. Except for the Washington columnist and the star of a television adventure series who had been a classmate of Wainwright's at Princeton, the guests were all from the local media. It had been purposely arranged so as to give them a subtle sense of being members of an inner circle. Only the columnist was invited to the weekend's major event, a dinner dance that evening honoring the governor.

Now, at lunch, the mix was working very well. Most of the press wives had gathered delightedly around the television star. A few of the reporters were with them; others, sure of their place in the Wainwright orbit, chatted among themselves or with Simonetta. The columnist, disdaining what he deemed his journalistic inferiors, sat regaling Cynthia Wainwright with the latest scandals. Wainwright regarded him with some misgiving. Although he was as wellborn as Wainwright, he was rumored to be a closet homosexual with all the emotional instability that involved. Once Wainwright had heard him shriek drunkenly at a United States senator, "I'll destroy you with my pen!" Wainwright figured that someday the columnist could turn on him with as much venom as his current praise, but by then enough of a file would have been compiled on his sexual habits to make him think twice about it.

At the moment, however, the columnist was a decided blessing. Wainwright's wife was uncomfortable around reporters, considering them crude lowlifes, and the columnist was keeping her captivated with the real story behind the sudden announcement that a famous Texas tycoon was divorcing his wife, an extraordinarily beautiful French countess. The tycoon had already made headlines by leaving his first wife after twenty years of marriage and five children to take up with the countess. But according to the columnist, he had recently discovered that his new wife was carrying on a passionate liaison on the side—with an equally stunning Italian movie actress. The two women were supposed to have even formalized their relationship in a lesbian wedding. "It's all quite amusing, don't you agree?" the columnist said, eyes sparkling maliciously. "In the English upper classes, male homosexuality is accepted as a matter of course. In France and Italy, it's the same for female homosexuals. And all the while, we in America remain primitive nitwits."

Wainwright himself had spent most of his time with the young feature writer from the *Daily News*. It was his first visit to the Wainwrights, and although he appeared to be no more than twenty-five, Wainwright's media consultant had advised that he had an important future on the paper. He had an earnest, square-jawed face, and his wife, who was seated near the television star, looked as though she might have been a prom queen in college. "Everyone seems to think you have a great political career ahead of you," he said to Wainwright. "Doesn't it bother you that you could be antagonizing so many Italian-Americans? You know, going after the Mafia."

Wainwright stretched his arms over his head. It was exactly the kind of question he enjoyed. "First of all," he said, "I've got a job to do, and that's all I think about. Second, I don't believe any ethnic group has a lock on organized crime. But I'll get somebody better qualified to answer you." He crooked a finger at Simonetta. "Hey, Nick, come over for a minute."

Simonetta was at his side at once, and Wainwright said, "I've just been asked an interesting question. Am I too hard on Italians?"

"Yes," Simonetta said.

The young feature writer appeared startled, and then Simonetta added, "Especially on me," and the writer laughed.

Apart from all his other qualifications, Simonetta knew that Wainwright had picked him as chief assistant because he was Italian. But as Wainwright rose, so would he. And the truth was that Simonetta, the swarthy son of immigrant parents from southern Italy, took the Mafia as a personal affront. The endless snide asides, the slurs masked as little jokes that he had endured through college and law school were precisely why he believed that he had to tie himself to someone like Wainwright to be stamped clean.

Wainwright gauged the reaction of the young feature writer and leaned forward and said, "Keep this to yourself, but we've having a small party for the governor tonight. I'd like you to come. I'm sure you'll find it worth your while. The only thing is that it's black tie."

"That's no problem."

"Terrific. Eight o'clock. And of course, bring your wife."

After lunch the columnist fell into step with Wainwright. "Very nicely done. You have them eating out of your hand. I approve. You're going a long way."

Wainwright maintained an appropriately solemn expression. "I appreciate that. I value your counsel. I hope I can call on you for more of it."

"I'm at your disposal, my boy. By the way, shall we have a rematch in the morning?"

Wainwright could barely refrain from wincing at the thought of being teamed again with the columnist's wife. "I can't. I have to speak at some father-son breakfast. Who's putting it on, Nick?"

"The county police," Simonetta said.

"Splendid," the columnist said. "Keep going public. You won't mind if I pass up the opportunity to hear you?"

"You'd be certifiably committable if you didn't. Anyway, there'll be plenty of people around here for doubles."

☆

The young feature writer drew his wife to the edge of the terrace and told her about the invitation.

She blanched and said, "Oh, Lord, it's formal? What'll I wear? And my hair? What'll I do about my hair?"

"For Christ's sake, cut it out," he hissed. "This is a big chance for me. You'll just have to do something." And as he hurried along the drive to get his car, he wondered for the first time if he had married the wrong girl.

7

───── ☆ ─────

That same Saturday shortly after eleven A.M. Flynn awoke, his head aching. He put on a torn terry-cloth robe, went into the kitchen, got a cold can of Goldblatt, pressed it against the nape of his neck and then opened the can and began to drink out of it.

In the living room his son was watching an old Abbott and Costello movie on television. "Hi," Flynn said.

"Hi," the boy said without looking up.

"Where's your mother?"

The boy did not answer, his eyes still fixed on the set.

"I said, where's your mother?" Flynn's voice had risen irritably. The blood throbbed in his temples, dissipating what little relief he had obtained from the beer.

The boy stared at Flynn and blinked, as though he were seeing him for the first time. "Oh," he said, "she went shopping," and immediately returned his gaze to the television set. Flynn had once envisioned pleasant afternoons in the park tossing a football around with his son. But the boy detested football. He liked soccer, a game Flynn found boring and pointless. Oh, well, Flynn had thought, at least the kid would not have to worry about getting a bum knee in a nutcracker drill.

He went back into the kitchen and made himself a cup of instant coffee. He much preferred freshly brewed coffee but was not up to preparing it himself. The day, he decided, was getting off to a bad start. He took some aspirin. If he had remembered to take the aspirin before going to sleep, he would be feeling all right now. He did not know why, but the aspirin always seemed to work better as a preventive measure against a hangover than after the fact. The trick was in remembering to take it. Flynn had once met a man who worked in the advertising department of Bayer Aspirin, and he had suggested to him that the company get some famous drunk to do a commercial on this aspect of its product. "You'd open up a whole new market for the stuff," Flynn had said as the man from Bayer recoiled in horror at the idea.

By the time he finished showering, shaving and dressing, Agnes had returned, her arms filled with grocery bags. "Oh," she said, "you're up. You were sleeping so soundly I thought I'd be back before you woke up."

There was an unaccustomed solicitude in her voice, and then the whole scene of what had happened between them during the night flashed in his mind. How, he thought, could he have completely forgotten something like that? He must have blacked out, and he privately swore to cut down on the booze. He went to help her unpack the grocery bags. He saw her wrinkle her nose, and he knew she had smelled the beer on his breath.

"I'll fix you some bacon and eggs," she said.

The thought of food turned his stomach. "No," he said. "I already had some coffee. That's all I want."

"You need protein, Richie. You're drinking too much."

"It was only a beer."

"Well, you should eat a decent breakfast."

"Tomorrow. We'll have a big Sunday brunch tomorrow after mass." Flynn threw in the mass as a peace offering, since he rarely attended church anymore.

"You can't," she said. "You have that father-and-son breakfast up in Yonkers tomorrow morning. Detective O'Neil called about it while you were sleeping."

"Jesus, I almost forgot," Flynn said. Ever since the mix-up about Goldblatt's contributing money to SNCC, the brewery had embarked on a campaign to supply free beer to any charity event sponsored by police or fire departments in the New York metropolitan area. The campaign had been markedly successful and had spilled over to provide other services. In this instance Flynn had promised to deliver as honored guests to the father-and-son breakfast Rocky Tomaselli, the ex-middleweight boxing champion, and Frank Gifford, the former New York Giant star. Flynn was not concerned about Gifford. He was extremely reliable about his commitments, and arrangements had already been made to pick him up at his home in Westchester County not far from Yonkers. Tomaselli, however, was another matter. Flynn had said he would bring the fighter himself. He called O'Neil back to reassure him. "Tomaselli's staying at the Commodore overnight. The breakfast's at eleven, right? Don't worry, I'll be down at the hotel for him at nine."

When he was through with O'Neil, he said to Agnes, "I won't be home tonight. I've got an appointment. It's important."

"Oh," she said.

"What's the matter?"

"It's just that I thought we'd all go out to eat somewhere and see a movie. We haven't been out together, all of us, for a while."

"Look, I can't break it. It could change a lot of things for us." Flynn wanted to say more, but he was sure that she would be frightened by a deal like this and would try to argue him out of it. He was also uncomfortably aware that she had not even asked him what the appointment was about. He had lied to her so many times before and had thought nothing of it, and now, suddenly, he was telling her the truth, and he felt waves of guilt envelop him. "I'm not kidding," he said. "It's important, believe me."

All afternoon Flynn waited for Scanlon to call. Twice he went to a neighborhood bar for pops of scotch. "Anybody calls, get his number," he told Agnes each time.

Finally, late in the day, the phone rang, and it was Scanlon. "OK. Listen. You know where the Stage Delicatessen is down on Seventh Avenue? Be on the sidewalk in front of the Stage at eight-thirty. Somebody will pick you up."

"How'll I know who he is?"

"You won't. Wear a white flower in your lapel, a gardenia or something. He'll find you," Scanlon said, and hung up.

At seven o'clock Flynn could not stand it any longer and left. The Stage Delicatessen was between Fifty-third and Forty-fourth Streets, and he would kill the time by walking to it. "I'll be home as soon as I can," he said to his wife.

As he headed downtown, the jitters got to him again. He hesitated in front of another bar. He should not be drinking before the meeting with Karpstein. But then he decided that one more wouldn't hurt.

He was in front of the Stage a good half hour before Karpstein's man was supposed to come for him. The delicatessen was jammed. Directly south the lights of Times Square flickered and blinked. Across Seventh Avenue, a block down, cabs pulled up to and away from the Americana Hotel. Knots of people constantly gathered around the delicatessen's entrance, so that Flynn had to keep moving in order to have a clear view of the traffic. Three or four times cars stopped to let out or pick up patrons. Other cars appeared to slow down maddeningly and then go on.

At twenty minutes after eight he realized that he had forgotten his identifying white flower. He looked quickly around. There didn't seem to be a florist shop in sight. He cut across the avenue, ducking between cars, to the Americana but was told that the hotel did not have a florist. He rushed out of the hotel and went along Fifty-second Street to Broadway. All he saw open were record shops, hamburger joints, peep shows, a clothing store and a store selling tourist souvenirs.

He did not know what to do. Then he saw an old woman seated in a doorway with a carton of bouquets in paper cones. Most of the bouquets were red roses, but a pair of them was white. He hurried up to the old woman, digging two quarters and a dime out of his pocket. "I just need one white rose," he said. "How much?"

"You got to buy a bunch," she said. "Only bunches." The old woman was wearing a black dress and a black shawl, and she had gray whiskers.

"All right, give me a bunch. How much?"

"Three dollars."

Flynn opened his wallet. There were four ten-dollar bills in it. He gave one to the old woman.

She shook her head. "No change," she said. "You no got the right change?"

"Oh, Jesus," Flynn said. "Keep the change. Just give me the goddamn flowers." He grabbed a bouquet, pulled out a flower, dropped the rest of them on the sidewalk and scurried around the corner. All he needed now, he thought, was his knee to give way. Behind him the old woman, muttering to herself, bent down and picked up the paper cone of roses and returned it to the carton with the others.

It was eight-thirty-two when he was back in front of the delicatessen. He wondered if the person who was to meet him had already come and gone. He felt how wet his armpits were. He opened his trench coat and tried to put the white rose in his jacket lapel buttonhole. But it was sewn tight. Finally, feeling foolish, he stuck the rose in the one on his trench coat lapel and waited. Then, as he looked up the avenue, he saw a lighted florist shop diagonally across the street on the next block. The fact that it had been quite visible all the time rattled him even more. Calm down, he told himself. A passerby stared at him curiously, and Flynn realized that he had actually said it out loud.

At five to nine a black Ford sedan drew up in front of the delicatessen. There was a short beep on the horn. No one else seemed to be paying any attention to the car. Flynn stepped forward to the curb. He could barely make out the face of a man peering at him from behind the wheel. The horn beeped again, and the side window slid partly down. He went to the car, and the man inside said, "Flynn?"

"Yes."

"Get in. I'm taking you to Jersey."

The man did not introduce himself. He appeared to be about Flynn's age. He was unshaven. In the dim light Flynn could see boils on his face and the scars of old ones. He was wearing a green quilted windbreaker. He turned the car right on Fifty-third Street and then left on Ninth Avenue toward the Lincoln Tunnel. He still had not said anything more.

"Nice night," Flynn said. "Not too cold."

"Yeah."

The roar of the tunnel traffic made any further attempts at conversation impossible. Flynn stared at a cop slowly pacing the tunnel catwalk. Someone had told him that cops drew duty in the Manhattan tunnels for disciplinary reasons. It was easy to believe. Working in the tunnels, breathing the exhaust fumes from thousands of cars and trucks, must be like smoking twenty packs of cigarettes a day. He wondered what the lung cancer rate was.

He glanced at the man driving. In the lighted tunnel he could make out the boils more clearly. He did not blame the man for skipping every shave he could. One of the boils was an angry red and seemed ready to burst. Flynn was revolted by the sight of it and shifted his gaze straight ahead. Suddenly a terrible thought occurred to him. Ever since Scanlon had told him that it was all set, that the meeting with Karpstein had been arranged, Flynn had assumed that he would get the money from the loan shark. But suppose Karpstein turned him down. What would he do then? As Flynn watched the tiled walls of the tunnel rush by, he felt the wetness under his arms again.

The car emerged from the tunnel. After passing the toll booth, the man with the boils veered to the right off the circular drive that led to the New Jersey Turnpike. He proceeded through a series of dark blocks faintly lighted by old-fashioned streetlamps. The car began to shake noticeably, and it took Flynn a moment to realize that they were riding on cobblestones.

They went down an incline, over a hump in the street, and parked in front of E-Z Trucking, Inc. A naked light bulb hung by the entrance. Flynn, not knowing where he was or what he was to do, remained motionless until the man with the boils said, "This is it. I stay here."

Flynn got out, opened the chain-link fence gate and approached the building. Behind it he could see the lights of New York shimmering on the surface of the river. It was an incredible sight. The city sat low in the water, glittering like a gigantic ocean liner. To the left there was a reddish glow in the sky coming from Times Square. Overhead he saw the lights of a plane moving up the Hudson in a landing pattern for La Guardia Airport. Another set of lights followed it, and then still another. All around Flynn, except for the naked light bulb, it was pitch-black and silent. A cold breeze was coming off the river.

Flynn pushed the buzzer next to the front door of the building. The man who opened it had a cue stick in his hand. "You Flynn?" Tommy Biondo said.

"Yes."

Biondo had been very excited when he learned that Richie Flynn was coming to see Karpstein. "You know who that guy is?" he had said. "He's the guy that won a fucking big game for the Giants. He don't fuck up his knee, he'd of been a big star. Ask anybody."

"Yeah?" Karpstein had said. Except for boxing, he knew little, and cared less, about sports. He kept up with boxing, particularly heavyweights. There was no question in his mind that he would have been a champion had he been allowed to develop his skills.

When Flynn entered the room, Karpstein was seated at his desk. He was cleaning his fingernails with a file and watching a television show on a small portable Sony that was on the desk.

"This is Albert," Biondo said to Flynn.

Karpstein looked up, and Flynn felt an instant stab of fear. He had heard the stories about Karpstein, but he was totally unprepared for the reality of him. It was not his massive, menacing bulk that was so terrifying. It was his eyes. Flynn had never seen eyes like them. A pig's eyes, he thought, must look like this. He had never really known what the expression "pig eyes" meant until now.

"Sit down," Karpstein said, motioning toward the leather sofa at right angles to the desk.

Biondo, still holding the cue, walked to the pool table and took aim. Click went a ball.

"No," Karpstein said to Flynn. "Over here."

Flynn had sat at the near end of the sofa, and Karpstein was pointing at the other end by the desk. Flynn moved to the indicated spot and sank back in the cracked cushions. Now Karpstein loomed directly over him. Karpstein leaned forward and switched off the television. Then he swiveled around, still working on his nails with the file. At the pool table Biondo was racking up the balls. Flynn's knees were shaking. He wondered what he should say.

Karpstein saved him the trouble. "All right," he said, "we're all here. Tell me what you want, and don't give me any bullshit." His voice was surprisingly soft.

"I, uh, want to borrow some money."

"How much?"

Flynn was confused. Somehow he thought that all this had been taken care of when Scanlon had made his calls. He stared out into the room. He saw Biondo bring his cue forward. He heard the click of balls and then a ball dropping into a pocket and rolling through the innards of the pool table. Flynn wished his knees would stop shaking.

"Well, you know, fifteen is what I was hoping for."

"Fifteen?" Karpstein said. "You want fifteen? What do you want fifteen for?"

Flynn had not counted on this, on Karpstein's asking what the money was to be used for. He pondered how much to tell him, how much Scanlon might have said about the deal on the phone. He did not even know, as he now remembered, whether or not Scanlon had talked directly to Karpstein. His impression was that it had all been done through intermediaries. Another ball Biondo had hit dropped into a pocket.

"It's a real estate thing," Flynn said finally. "It's the down payment for this building, this property, which the city is going to lease back. The letter of intent from the city is already in the works. It's just a matter of paperwork." He hesitated over the size of the anticipated return. He wanted it to sound good, but not too good. "We look to make three, four times our investment."

For the first time Karpstein's eyes showed some expression. "We?" he said. "Who's we?"

"Uh, well, there's this guy in with me."

"What's his name?"

"He doesn't have anything to do with borrowing the money. I'm doing this myself."

A little of the softness disappeared from Karpstein's voice. "I want to know everybody in this thing. What's his name? What's he do?"

"Fowler," Flynn said. "Harry Fowler. He's with the city."

"The city, huh?"

"Yes, the Agency for Child Development. Part of the welfare. The real estate deal is a day-care center for kids." Flynn struggled to find the right words. The balls on the pool table clicked again, and another one rolled down through a pocket and smacked against the balls that had already been played. This time Flynn jumped at the noise. "The city," he said, "pays to take care of the kids so their mothers can work."

Karpstein leaned back in his chair. He picked at a nail with the file. "Oh, yeah," he said in a softer tone, "I heard something about that. Hey, you fellows stand to make a nice piece of change. You get another one like this, let me know."

Flynn was filled with relief. So he had been right about Karpstein, he thought. Karpstein was not going to cut himself in on the deal. He would just lend the money.

"You want fifteen?" Karpstein said.

"Yes."

"I want thirty in return."

Flynn's mouth went dry. He knew that the basic loanshark rate of "six for five" would not be applicable in a loan this large. "Six for five" meant that for every five dollars borrowed, six must be paid back. If a thousand dollars were lent, the return to the loan shark would be a hundred dollars a week for twelve weeks. For a loan in the amount Flynn was requesting, however, the interest would be calculated instead on a point basis, a point being one percent of the principal payable each week. The points usually ranged from one to three, again depending on the circumstances of the loan and the relationship between the borrower and lender. In some of these loans the principal also had to be reduced on a prearranged weekly schedule, although more often than not the borrower simply paid the interest until he was able to retire the principal when he wished to—or could. As in all such transactions, there were negotiable aspects, but while Flynn expected Karpstein's demands to be harsh, he never expected anything like this. He ran his tongue over his lips and said at last, "That's a little steep, isn't it?"

"What do you think it should be?"

"Well, first of all, we, I only need the money for thirty days."

"You better figure on sixty," Karpstein said. "These things sometimes don't work out so fast."

"No, thirty days is fine."

"Have it your way. So how much do you think my return should be then?"

Click went the balls. Flynn waited for a ball to drop and roll, but it did not. Biondo had missed his shot. "How about twenty?" Flynn said. The wetness under his arms was now running down the sides of his body.

"Listen," Karpstein said, "you come recommended, else you wouldn't be here in the first place. But you're high risk, know what I mean? I got to take that in account. You own a house?"

"No."

"You got a family?"

"Yes, a wife and son."

"You got insurance for them?"

"There's the company group insurance."

"That's term insurance. You can't borrow on it."

"I also have ordinary life, too," Flynn said quickly. "Twenty-five thousand."

"How much can you draw on it?"

"About thirty-five hundred."

Karpstein sneered. "That's how you look out for your own wife and kid, a lousy twenty-five thousand?" He sat up in his chair. He took the nail file and punched the point into the top of the desk. The file held, quivering. Then Karpstein pulled open a desk drawer and took out a huge wad of bills. They were hundred-dollar bills, wrapped twice with a thick rubber band. Flynn had never seen so much cash in his life. He stared at the bills hypnotically. He looked away. Biondo was standing by the pool table, chalking his cue, staring at him. Richie Flynn looked back at the money.

"That's a nice idea you had," Karpstein said, "but I'm not going for it. I'll make you a deal. You want to pay me twenty, OK. You get twelve five. That's it. I'm not here to bargain."

Karpstein removed the rubber band from the bills and started peeling them off. He did it slowly, so that Flynn could count with him. When he got to a hundred and twenty-five, he stopped and took another rubber band out of the drawer and put it around the new stack of bills and tossed the stack on the desk toward Flynn. He took the rest of the bills, riffled them once with his thumb and placed them in his pocket. "There it is," he said. "Take it or leave it."

"I'll take it," Flynn said. "Do I have to sign anything?"

"No, a handshake is good enough for me. That's the way I do business." After Karpstein had leaned over and squeezed Flynn's hand, he said, "OK. We got a deal. Now there are a couple details, and the first thing is that you are going to pay five hundred a week for the thirty days, and that is deducted from the balance at the other end. Tuesday is the day payments are made, and the business hours in this office are ten to four-thirty. I'm not here, you give the money to my bookkeeper, Weissberg. He sits over there. You be here on Tuesday by four-thirty, or you're in big trouble."

All the time Karpstein was talking, Flynn had been staring at the stack of bills. Now he looked at Karpstein, into those terrifying eyes, and swallowed and finally said, "Wait a minute. Today's Saturday. Tuesday's only a couple of days away. That isn't fair."

Karpstein giggled, almost delightedly. The giggle had an eerie, high-pitched quality. He's crazy, Flynn thought, and for a moment he considered bolting from the room, but he did not. The money was there, within his reach.

"All right, you have a point," Karpstein said. "We'll make it Thursday. Your day's Thursday. When you come in, you bring that insurance policy with a new beneficiary on it for half the twenty-five thousand. The name of the new beneficiary is Leo Weissberg, this address. Here's the card. You can change it back when you pay up. You don't look so good to me, Flynn. You look kind of white. You could have a heart attack or something. You got my money, I got to have some security. You got that?"

"Yes."

"OK. Pick it up, sucker. You just made the biggest score of your life."

When Flynn extended his hand for the money, he saw that his fingers were trembling. He tried to stop them, but he could not, and he saw that Karpstein saw them. He clenched the bills in his fist and slipped them into his inside jacket pocket.

"Just don't get any funny ideas," Karpstein said. "What's mine is mine." He opened another drawer in the desk and pulled out a revolver. The revolver had a pearl handle. "You know what this is?"

"I've seen them."

Karpstein pointed the revolver at Flynn's chest. "You're not afraid of them?" he asked.

"Yes, when they're aimed at me, I'm afraid of them."

Karpstein broke the revolver and removed the bullets from the cylinder one by one and dropped them on the desk. "See," he said, "it's loaded. It's always loaded. This is one way to collect if anybody tries to beat me out of my money. But I don't like this method. I like this." Karpstein bent over and picked up his attaché case. He unsnapped it and lifted out the length of white plastic telephone cable that he had used on Marvin Mandelbaum the day before. He flexed it with both hands, tapped it against his thigh and then slapped Flynn's left leg above the knee with it. "How does that feel?"

"It hurts."

"That's right," Karpstein said softly. "It hurts. It hurts even more when I do this." He raised the cable over his head and with a grunt slammed it against the desk. The noise reverberated around the room. The bullets on the desk bounced up and down. One of them rolled off the desk onto the floor. Karpstein shoved a pad of paper and a pencil toward Flynn. "All right, you can go. Just put down your home address and phone, the same with where you work. Where *do* you work?"

Flynn's mouth was dry again. He licked his lips before he said, "Goldblatt's Brewery. I'm a sales supervisor."

"Goldblatt, huh?" Karpstein said as though it were a

matter of great personal interest. "I drink it myself sometimes. It's not bad. Oh, yeah, and put down that other
guy's number and address too, what's his name, Fowler?"

When Flynn finished writing the information, he stood
up. The tension in his muscles had so cramped them that
for a second he was not sure whether he could walk.
"How'll I get back to the city?"

"That guy outside, Patsy, he'll take you." Karpstein
came around the desk and put his arm around Flynn's
shoulders. As they went toward the door, Flynn could feel
the weight of Karpstein's body. Karpstein dug his fingers
into Flynn's right shoulder and increased the pressure.
"You know," Karpstein said, "I like you. You got any
other deals, we'll do some more business."

Flynn was just about to leave when Biondo said, "Hey,
Flynn, you shoot pool?"

Ever since he had arrived, Richie Flynn had suffered
one humiliation after another. But he was a very good
pool player. Suddenly he saw playing pool with Biondo as
a means of somehow regaining a little of his lost dignity.
He looked at Karpstein. "Go ahead," Karpstein said.

Flynn walked to the table, working his fingers, trying to
concentrate, and selected a cue.

"Eight ball. We'll play eight ball," Biondo said.

"How much?"

"A hundred," Biondo said, and smirked. "What the hell,
you got a lot of walking-around money. I'll break."

Breaking first is an advantage and is customarily determined by seeing which player can bring the cue ball back
closest to the head of the table after hitting it against the
opposite cushion. But Flynn did not protest. He was sure
he could beat Biondo. Eight ball was the first pool game
he had learned as a boy. A player has to sink all seven of
his balls, either striped or solid-colored, and then the eight
ball. If a player accidentally sinks the eight ball before his
other balls are off the table, he automatically loses.

Biondo set up the fifteen balls in a tight triangle, the
eight ball in the middle, and broke them with the cue ball.
One of the solid balls dropped. Biondo had a run of three
more solid balls before he missed.

He's not all that good, Flynn thought. He should have
run more balls. Flynn looked at the table. Biondo had left
him a straight shot into the far corner pocket. If he drew
the cue ball back with reverse English after making the

shot, he would be perfectly positioned to run all his balls. As he was sighting the cue, he glanced to his left and saw Karpstein watching him. He shot and missed. Flynn cursed his shaking hand.

Grinning, Biondo sank one more of his balls before missing. Unnerved by his previous failure, Flynn misplayed a relatively easy bank shot. Biondo had two balls to go before he could shoot for the eight ball. The only problem he faced was that all of Flynn's balls remained on the table, blocking some angles. He made his first shot, but the cue ball scratched, and Biondo had to put back the ball that he had sunk.

Flynn forced himself to forget about Karpstein and pocketed three balls in a row. He still was not fully composed, however, and missed a difficult fourth attempt. Once again Biondo had just two balls to play before getting to the eight ball. The one he chose first was not more than an inch or so away from a pocket. But in his eagerness to win, Biondo shot too hard, and after knocking in the object ball, the cue ball spun off the cushion and bounced into one of Flynn's balls. It in turn struck the eight ball, and Flynn and Biondo stood mesmerized as the black eight ball rolled slowly across the table, teetered on the edge of a side pocket and plopped gently in. Even though Flynn had managed to sink only three balls, Biondo had lost.

"You lucky son of a bitch," he said. "Another!" And without waiting for Flynn's response, he set up the balls. Flynn, considerably more relaxed now, broke them, dropped a striped one and had a run of five more. Biondo made two shots before missing, and Flynn rammed in his last ball and then the eight ball, which he had to put, unlike the others, into a designated pocket.

"Double or nothing," Biondo snapped.

As the winner, Flynn broke again. This time Biondo never had a chance. Flynn sank all of his balls. "That's it," he said. "Four hundred bucks."

Biondo glared at him and threw the money on the table.

Flynn felt dizzy with elation. He took a deep breath. "See you," he said, and picked up his trench coat from the sofa and went out the door.

After he had left, Biondo turned to Karpstein and said, "Hey, I don't like that guy."

Karpstein was behind his desk, putting the bullets back

into the revolver. "Nobody asked you to play with him," he said. "You should know better, trying to hustle a hustler." Karpstein looked at his watch and yawned. "Get over here and see if you can find that slug that fell on the floor. And then drive me home. I'm tired."

☆

The elation ebbed from Flynn the minute he stepped outside. He felt drained and wobbly. The nightmarish experience with Karpstein came at him again. He half expected someone to club him over the head in the darkness and take the money. He patted the bills in his pocket to reassure himself that they were there.

The white rose was still in his trench coat lapel. He took it out and tossed it on the ground and got into the car. It seemed much colder to him than before, and Flynn realized that it was because he had been sweating so much. The man with the boils, Patsy, was as mute as ever. He started the car and began weaving through the bleak, unfamiliar streets once more. Not until they came out of the Lincoln Tunnel on the New York side did he speak. "You want to go back to the Stage, or what?" he said.

Flynn could not remember when he had yearned more for a drink, but he was afraid to stop anywhere carrying all that money. So he told Patsy to drop him off at the cabstand in front of the Americana. Then he went directly home.

Except for a light in the foyer, the apartment was dark when he entered. He tiptoed to his bedroom door and looked in. This time Agnes was sound asleep. He could hear her snoring slightly. He went back into the living room and removed his trench coat and jacket. He kept a bottle of scotch stashed in the hall closet. He brought it out, carried it to the living-room sofa and took a deep swig from it, and another. He felt dirty and wished he could take a shower, but he was afraid of waking Agnes. Someday soon, he thought, he would have a place with his own dressing room and bathroom.

He reached into his jacket pocket and pulled out the roll of hundred-dollar bills. He snapped off the rubber band and started counting them. There were exactly one hundred and twenty-five. He took the four crumpled bills he had won from Biondo out of another pocket in his jacket, flattened them and laughed. Then he again counted the bills that he had got from Karpstein. He counted them a third time just for the sheer pleasure of it. He could not believe that he had them. He fanned them out on the coffee table in front of the sofa. He rubbed his fingers across them. He studied the face of Benjamin Franklin. Franklin's face looked different. Then Flynn realized that he had never really examined a hundred-dollar bill before and that Franklin was not shown wearing spectacles. He saluted Franklin's portrait and wondered where to hide the money as he swigged on the bottle of scotch.

Then he had an idea. He scooped up the bills, stacked them carefully and went to the hall closet. A summer suit of his that Agnes had sent to the cleaner's the previous fall was still hanging in its plastic garment bag. He raised the bag's skirt so as not to tear it. He divided the bills roughly in half and put them in the inside pockets of the suit jacket. He patted the pockets to make certain that they did not bulge too much and smoothed down the tissue paper stuffing. He went back to the sofa, took another swallow of scotch, picked up Biondo's bills and put them in his wallet and then returned the bottle to the closet. He went into the bedroom, undressed quietly and got into bed. Agnes stirred but did not wake. Almost at once he fell asleep.

The alarm clock rang at seven-thirty in the morning. Flynn groaned, perplexed at why it had gone off so early, and reached over and turned it off. Then Agnes was nudging him. "Richie," she said, "wake up. You have that breakfast up in Yonkers."

Now Flynn blinked his eyes open, remembering that he had to pick up the former middleweight champion, Tomaselli. He groaned again.

"I'll put some coffee on," Agnes said.

"No, it's OK. Go back to sleep. I'll get something at the corner." Flynn showered and dressed. As he was going out the front door, he stopped at the hall closet and looked at the plastic garment bag containing his summer suit and the money. With his other summer wear stored there it was hardly noticeable.

After he had coffee and an English muffin, he got the Volkswagen out of the garage and drove down Lexington Avenue and parked by the Hotel Commodore. He looked at his watch. It was ten to nine. He was early, and he considered waiting a few more minutes. Then he decided to go in immediately. With Rocky Tomaselli, he thought, you never know.

Tomaselli was being paid three hundred dollars by Goldblatt to be one of the honored guests at the father-and-son breakfast, which was being sponsored by the Southern Westchester County Police Athletic Association. Tomaselli had a particular attraction. He was the last white American to reign in a sport that, aside from the heavyweight division, did not have at this moment a native-born champion of any color. His brief, flamboyant career had come to an end when his mob-connected manager, realizing that Tomaselli's personal life-style was not conducive to staying upright in the ring for very long, orchestrated a major fix, earning all the participants a great deal of cash. Tomaselli wound up with an interest in a flourishing liquor store and remained in the public eye with occasional offbeat television commercials and personal appearances such as the one Flynn had arranged. The trouble with Tomaselli was that he could blow a commitment like this as easily as he had blown his final fight.

Flynn walked across the lobby to the house phones and asked for Tomaselli. The phone rang. There was no answer. He asked the operator for Tomaselli's room number, and she said that she could not give it out.

He went to the clerk at the front desk. "I'm Mr. Flynn of Goldblatt's Brewery," he said. "We made a reservation for Mr. Tomaselli. Mr. Tomaselli doesn't seem to answer his phone. He has to make an appearance for Goldblatt this morning. He's probably asleep. What's his room number?"

The clerk started to give Flynn the same answer that the operator had given. Then he noticed the ten-dollar bill Flynn was holding in his hand and said, "Nine-oh-two."

Flynn dropped the bill on the counter and took the elevator to the ninth floor. He knocked on the door, waited and knocked again. Then a voice, Tomaselli's, said, "Who's there?"

"Flynn, Richie Flynn. Come on, Rocky, open the door."

The door opened perhaps six inches, and Tomaselli's familiar, beard-stubbled face filled the space, his black hair unruly, eyes bleary. "Go away," he said. "I can't make it. I don't feel good."

"Listen, Rocky, you're getting three hundred for this."

"Shove it up your ass," Tomaselli said, and slammed the door.

Flynn had not been able to see into the room, but from the cautious way Tomaselli had guarded the door, Flynn sensed that someone was in there with him. He returned to the lobby and telephoned Jack O'Neil, the Yonkers detective in charge of the breakfast. "We got problems," he said. "Tomaselli's in his room, and he won't come out. I think he's shacked up with a broad."

"He's *what?*"

"You heard me. I don't know what to do."

"You wait there in the lobby," O'Neil said. "I'll be right down. Don't move."

Flynn settled himself into a club chair. Even with the sparse traffic of a Sunday morning, he was sure it would take O'Neil at least three-quarters of an hour to arrive from Yonkers. O'Neil strode into the lobby in exactly twenty-nine minutes. He was ramrod straight, six feet tall, with gray hair and perpetually compressed lips. He was wearing a green felt Tyrolean hat. "What's his room number?" O'Neil snarled.

"Nine-oh-two."

Flynn knocked on the door once more and identified himself. Tomaselli yanked it open and started to say, "I told you to . . ." But O'Neil barreled into him, knocking him backward. Flynn saw a young girl on the bed grab a sheet. Tomaselli recovered his balance. He was in his shorts, going to fat, but still powerfully built. He lunged at O'Neil, then stopped. O'Neil had pulled out his off-duty revolver. The girl on the bed, the sheet drawn up to her neck, stifled a scream. She had brass-colored hair, stiff from too much spray. Flynn could see the dark roots.

"Sit down," O'Neil said to Tomaselli. Then O'Neil told the girl, "You. Out!" The girl leaped from the bed, naked. She had a skinny body with big, elongated breasts. As she bent over to pick up her panties, her breasts swung out from her chest, like melons in sacks. She wriggled into her slacks, half buttoned her blouse, grabbed her purse and coat and ran out the door, carrying her shoes.

Flynn could not believe what was happening. Neither could Tomaselli. He sat in a chair, O'Neil's gun pressed against his ear. "Listen to me, you guinea cocksucker," O'Neil said. "There are four hundred kids waiting to see you. You're getting up from this chair, you're going to shave and get dressed and you're going to be there for those kids."

Tomaselli raised his hands. "OK. Just put away the piece, will you? I was just kidding. I'll just be a minute."

To Flynn's amazement, they were only fifteen minutes late for the breakfast. The boys and the fathers all applauded when Tomaselli walked in. Frank Gifford was already seated on the dais. After they had eaten, Gifford was introduced first. The urbane Giant star, whose long career was ended by an injury suffered during a game at Yankee Stadium, graciously noted Flynn's presence in the audience. "Richie would have been a great one," Gifford said. "As you know, he hurt his knee during preseason training and didn't hear any cheers when they carried him off the field. Well, I told him, 'Don't worry, Richie, I didn't hear any either.' I was out cold."

There was laughter and applause, and Flynn felt a pleasant tingle as he took a bow. Tomaselli was presented next. He raised a fist and said, "All I can say is keep punching," and glowered down at Flynn.

The main speaker, Hamilton Wainwright IV, was introduced by the master of ceremonies as a man who had forsaken private gain for the public good, a description that Wainwright's media consultant had supplied. "Boys," Wainwright began, "I want you to look at these two great athletes and what they stand for."

Jesus, what does this guy know about anything? Flynn thought, and looked at Tomaselli, reliving the morning he had spent with him. Then he thought of the twelve thousand five hundred dollars in the suit hanging in his closet. He would, he told himself, never have to spend a Sunday morning like this again.

8

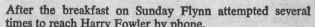

After the breakfast on Sunday Flynn attempted several times to reach Harry Fowler by phone.

He finally got him at the Agency for Child Development around ten o'clock on Monday morning.

"I told you, never call me here," Fowler said.

"Come on, Harry, I tried you at home all day yesterday. Where were you?"

"My sister-in-law's. It was her birthday. And you shouldn't call me at home either."

"What the fuck am I supposed to do," Flynn said, "use a goddamn pigeon?"

"Well, I suppose you could call me at home, but be careful, that's all."

"I just wanted to tell you the money problem is all taken care of," Flynn said.

"Problem? What problem? You never said anything about a problem."

Flynn was sitting in his apartment. He closed his eyes and saw Albert Karpstein. He opened them at once. "Forget it," he said. "There isn't any problem. That stuff doesn't grow on trees is all I'm saying. Listen, Harry, the auction's tomorrow, and we got to get going on this thing. That's what I'm trying to say."

"I can't go to the auction!"

"Jesus, Harry, I know that. But we should get together right after the papers are signed. I mean, let's not lose any time."

"There's no problem with the auction," Fowler said querulously. "I checked with a fellow in Real Estate. There have been no inquiries about the building, nothing."

"I didn't say there was. The question is, where should we meet?" He could hear Fowler breathing over the phone in the throes of a decision that was apparently beyond him. "Harry, it's not like you're deciding on open-heart surgery. What about that park by City Hall?"

"No, not there!" Fowler's voice trailed off in whispered alarm. "Somebody might see us."

"So what?" Flynn said. "OK. How about the zoo then? Right by the seals. Five o'clock?"

"Yes, all right," Fowler said. "But remember. Don't call me here anymore."

"Screw you," Flynn muttered after Fowler had hung up. All of a sudden Harry was turning into a regular nervous Nellie, and the morning had been vexing enough as it was. Flynn had waited around the apartment for more than an hour before Agnes finally departed for the basement washing machines with a load of dirty laundry. As soon as she was gone, he had hurried to the closet, carefully lifted the garment bag and taken the two wads of cash out of the suit.

He had just tucked them inside the brown and white hound's-tooth sports jacket he was wearing to take Diane to the races, resisting the impulse to count the bills once more, when his wife barged back through the door. It was as if she had been poised outside all the time, ready to pounce, to demand an explanation for his new affluence or, worse yet, to trigger some sort of ultimate confrontation over the meaning of their lives together.

He stood guiltily in the center of the room, like a defiant child. He felt as though he were holding the money in his hands, that he had actually been counting it when she came in. He braced himself for a torrent of questions, myriad accusations that had been seething within her. His face grew hot.

"Downy," she had said. "I forgot the Downy."

"The what?"

"Downy," she repeated. "The fabric softener. You have to put it in the final rinse. I forgot it."

He had watched nonplussed as she strode into the kitchen and reappeared clutching a blue plastic bottle. She paused by the door. "I thought you said you were going to the track with a customer."

"I am. I have to make a couple of calls first."

"Bet two dollars for me," she said as she went out the door again.

Flynn had slumped back on the sofa, berating himself for his near panic. The fact was that Agnes suspected nothing. It was all in his head. And what difference did it make anyway? He was getting into this day-care center deal as much for her as for himself. Why, he thought, should he care whether she saw the money or not? Righteous indignation buoyed him.

His spirits further improved as he contemplated the day ahead with Diane. Usually, when he went to the racetrack, it was for some urgent purpose, such as raising the rent money. Today he would attend for the pure pleasure of it, as a sportsman, not particularly concerned with winning or losing, and he would go in style, bankrolled by the four hundred dollars he had taken from Biondo playing pool. He had already arranged to have Jimmy Limousine chauffeur them to the track.

Jimmy Limousine's real name was James Rafferty. He had a gypsy limousine business. After a wayward youth, Rafferty had filched some W-2 tax forms, made up a social security number and rented a post office box under an alias. Then he filed an income tax return as a textile salesman working on commission, whose earnings entitled him to a rebate of two thousand three hundred ninety-one dollars and sixty-seven cents. As soon as the check arrived, Rafferty closed out the box. Eight months later notification of an impending audit of his return was sent back to the Internal Revenue Service by the post office stamped "Addressee Unknown." He invested two thousand dollars of his rebate in a used Cadillac Fleetwood sedan and began to hire out. He dealt only in cash and never filed another return.

Rafferty always took Mondays off to go to the races, so Flynn knew he could get a bargain rate from Rafferty to drive him to opening day at Monmouth Park in New Jersey, where he was taking Diane, and had instructed him to be in front of her building at eleven-thirty.

Flynn left his apartment and went to the Franklin Savings Bank around the corner on Lexington Avenue. He rented a safe-deposit box and put the twelve thousand five hundred dollars in it. He looked at the money and fingered it. He started to close the lid of the box and then stopped. He fingered the money again. Finally, at the last moment, he took five hundred dollars out of the box and added it to the four hundred already in his wallet that he had won from Biondo.

Outside on the street a wave of exhilaration enveloped him. He patted his jacket pocket where the wallet was. For the first time he really thought of the money as being his.

He could not recall feeling more secure, so unfettered by anxiety. It was not just the money; it was the sense that he could do anything he pleased with this particular nine hundred dollars, that there was no call on it. Rich people must always feel like this, he thought. That was truly the difference between the rich and everyone else, their unconcern, the fact that they did not have to care.

Flynn bought a *Daily News* and hailed a cab to go to Diane's. The big story in the paper was that President Nixon had been discovered to owe more than four hundred thousand dollars in back taxes. The second lead reported that the kidnapped heiress Patricia Hearst had announced in a tape recording that she was joining the terrorist group that had kidnapped her in order to fight for a better world and featured a photograph of Miss Hearst brandishing a gun. No doubt, he thought, it was her way of underscoring her commitment to the downtrodden.

He was about to turn to the sports pages when his eye caught a photograph of the man who had been the main speaker at the father-and-son breakfast the day before, Hamilton Wainwright IV. The accompanying interview, by the young feature writer who had been at Wainwright's over the weekend, made it plain that the special prosecutor was a long-needed scourge in the temples of the underworld and quoted him as declaring, "Organized crime is an insidious cancer in the American corpus. It must be rooted out ruthlessly wherever it festers. Too often we settle for punk hoodlums while the big ones, the powerful ones, go untouched. I pledge that my office will touch them and that they will feel and regret that touch." Chief among those listed by the feature writer as having thus far managed to thwart justice was "rackets kingpin" Frank Donato.

The story went on to cite Wainwright's family and educational background. He sounded like the kind of guy, Flynn decided, who did not know what it was like to wake up in the morning without nine hundred dollars in his wallet. And Flynn idly wondered what the Frank Donatos, the Vinnie D'Angelos, the Albert Karpsteins or even the Tony Valentes felt when they read something like this. Probably, he thought, they just yawned.

☆

When Diane opened her door, Flynn stepped back, startled. She looked like a Stone Age savage. She was naked, she had three large rollers in her hair and her face was covered with a green facial mask. She stuck her tongue out at him and said, "I'll only be a minute." There was none of the petulance that had been in her voice when he telephoned her from the Liffey the previous Friday night. She was a creature of habit. Friday had not been his day. Monday was. If Flynn had wished to reserve Fridays as well, she would have been as compliant as she was on Mondays. It was the only way she knew how to operate. At the moment Friday was given over to an elderly widowed jeweler, who would sit and watch her dance and buy champagne for her between her turns on the stage behind the bar. Depending on her hours, he would take her out afterward. The old man, who had three married sons, would often tell her, "I wish I had a daughter like you." At the end of each evening he would give her fifty dollars. Twice during the winter he had taken her to Miami Beach for the weekend and bought her whatever clothes struck her fancy. He made no advances toward her, other than holding her hand. Once he spoke of his wife, who had died four years before of bone cancer, and he cried. He never talked about his sons beyond acknowledging that he had them. She considered suggesting that he go down on her, but she was afraid it might offend him. Some people, she had long since decided, were weird.

Flynn followed her into the room. She got on a towel on the bed to resume what she had been doing when he rang, which was anointing her vagina with a Q-tip dipped in Johnson's Baby Oil. The baby oil, it had turned out, was the reason for her sweet vaginal scent. She sat with her legs spread, a small mirror propped up between them. She worked intently, oblivious of his presence, bending forward, peering into the mirror, gently manipulating the cotton swab with one hand, holding herself open with the other, her breasts moving ever so slightly, little washboard ripples in her stomach. Unlike most women, she did not mind being seen as a work in progress; she cared only about the finished product.

Flynn felt as if he were witnessing some pagan religious rite. Her green facial mask combined with her nakedness was enormously erotic. His cock stirred. This is ridiculous, he thought. "What's that stuff on your face?" he said.

"It's a clarifier," she said, still gazing into the mirror.

"Yeah? What's it for?"

"It clears your complexion. It takes away all the dead-cell layers in your skin."

"What do you need it for? You look pretty good to me."

"That's why." She reached for another Q-tip.

He could not stand the ache in his balls any longer. "Listen," he said, "I want you."

She looked at him. "Richie, it has to stay on my face for another five minutes. Besides, I'm setting my hair."

"You can get on top. I won't touch you, I swear."

"No."

Normally that would have been the end of it, but this time Flynn got up from the chair he had been sitting in and walked toward the bed. He reached for his wallet, took out a hundred-dollar bill and dropped it on the bed beside her.

She stared at the bill and then at him and back at the bill. "You didn't have to do that," she said.

"I know I didn't. It's for your kid, to buy her a present or something. Don't worry, there's plenty more where that came from."

She looked at the bill again, and then she picked it up and swung off the bed and went into the bathroom. "I'll be right out," she said.

He took off his clothes and was lying on the bed when she returned. She had removed the facial mask and the rollers. Her hair was parted in two waves over her forehead and was held up in back by a comb in a chignon. "Don't muss my hair," she said.

"I told you, I won't touch you." He was exultant. It was the first time he had ever felt in complete control of her, and it suddenly occurred to him that there could be many more like her in the future, not to seduce or charm, but to command. Who said that money did not make a difference?

She lowered herself on him, and aided by the lubricant she had applied, she eased him into her. She began moving up and down. He kept his arms alongside his body. "Look," he said with a grin, "no hands."

She nodded but did not grin back. She seemed to be fixing her gaze on some object beyond his head. There were little beads of perspiration on her upper lip. He knew that

she would not come. Oh, well, he thought, a hundred
bucks was worth a lot of orgasm. And then he came, and
she raised herself off him and disappeared once more into
the bathroom.

While he was getting dressed, he glanced toward Diane's
night table and saw what she had been gazing at. It was a
new photograph of her daughter. The little girl was in a
white party dress and black patent-leather Mary Jane
shoes. Instantly Flynn was filled with remorse. He tried to
tell himself to stop being so sentimental, that Diane, after
all, was a nude go-go dancer in a mob bar, not a recently
deflowered virgin. Still, their whole relationship had now
changed, and he felt that he had to proceed with some
caution. He retreated warily behind his *Daily News*, and
when she came out of the bathroom, he said, "Hello,"
without looking up. She did not respond.

He continued to bury himself in the paper until she finally said in a flat tone, "I'm ready."

Then he looked at her. She was wearing a cream-
colored bowler with matching pumps, a white blouse under a navy blue blazer and a white pleated skirt that
showed off her marvelous legs. It was important to say the
right thing. "Jesus," he said, "you've never been more
beautiful. I want you all over again."

After a second's hesitation she smiled. "Do you think
I'll be warm enough?"

Satisfied that he had assuaged any hurt feelings she
might have had, he said, "You'll be fine. It's really nice
out." And it was, the weather exceptionally springlike, perfect for Monmouth Park's opening, which was earlier than
usual this year. The early opening was why Flynn would
be occupying a private box, and if he had been searching
for an omen, he could not have found a better one. The
box was owned by Frank Considine, who was greatly responsible for his promotion to a sales supervisor at Goldblatt. Considine was the eighty-four-year-old patriarch of
the Considine clan, which controlled the food and bever-
age concessions at most of the ball parks and racetracks in
the East. He was a genuine American success story. He
had started out as just another peanut vendor in 1912 in
the old Polo Grounds in Manhattan. Every evening after a
ball game, he would gather up the thrown-away brown paper bags that he and the other vendors sold their peanuts
in. His wife would stay up through the night pressing the

wrinkles out of the crumpled bags with a handiron. Considine would then use them again the next day, and with the saving in his costs he was able to undercut the competition by two cents a bag. Eventually he gained control of all the peanut-vending in the Polo Grounds, and the rest, as he liked to say, was history.

Considine Enterprises was the concessionaire at a track for trotting horses in Flynn's sales area on Long Island. During World War II, when there was a shortage of malt and hops, Considine had asked Goldblatt to help him at one point with an extra delivery, and Goldblatt had refused. The old man's response was to stop dealing with Goldblatt at all. He never forgets and he never forgives, Flynn was told, but Flynn decided to try anyway. He got two friends who were sportswriters to introduce him to Considine one day at Belmont Park.

Considine was a short, pugnacious-looking man with a mottled red face and a fringe of white hair under his derby. He had on a wing collar, a diamond stickpin in his cravat, and he was chewing the stub of a cigar. A black man in a chauffeur's uniform stood by attentively, waiting for him to select his bets for the next race. Years ago, Flynn had heard, Considine sent his son to place a thousand-dollar bet for him. The horse finished out of the money, and the son said, "Don't worry, Pop, I didn't make the bet. I saw this trainer on the way to the window who told me the horse didn't have a chance. Here's your money." Considine floored his son with one punch. "I tell you to make a bet," he said, "you make it."

Considine had told Flynn that he remembered his touchdown run for the Giants and commiserated with him on his injury. "What are you doing now?" he asked.

"I'm with Goldblatt, sir. I was hoping to sell you some beer for the Nassau track. That's part of my territory."

"Goldblatt, huh?" Considine stared blankly out into space. "I don't have much to do with Goldblatt." The conversation seemed to be at an end.

Flynn tried to think of something to say. Just then two disgruntled bettors walked by. One of them was eating a Considine frankfurter. "Hey, Considine," he yelled, "your beer should be this cold."

At once Flynn grabbed the man and dragged him over. "I think you owe Mr. Considine here an apology," he said.

The man struggled briefly before he mumbled, "I was only kidding, I'm sorry," and Flynn released him.

Considine took the cigar stub out of his mouth and eyed Flynn speculatively. Finally he said, "Give me your card. I'll call you tomorrow."

Nobody at Goldblatt had believed Flynn when he said that Considine was going to call in an order. But late in the day, when he dropped by the office after visiting a number of saloon accounts, he learned that the old man himself had telephoned with an initial request for two hundred and fifty cases of beer. "That's a nice boy you have there, a real go-getter," Considine had said, and shortly thereafter Flynn was elevated to supervisory status. So when Considine's grandson left a message at Goldblatt that his grandfather was disinclined to quit the warmth of Florida, where he spent his winters, and wanted Flynn to have his box for the Monmouth opening, Flynn saw it as another unmistakable sign that his luck was changing, that everything was beginning to break his way.

Now, coming down in the elevator with Diane, Flynn felt himself tingling again with anticipation, like a craps shooter in the middle of a hot streak. In the street she said, "Where's the Volkswagen?"

"I'm not using it. We're going in that," he said, pointing to Rafferty's limousine. "I don't think I'll be using the Volkswagen much anymore."

"Fantastic," she said, clapping her hands in an abortive skip. She looked at Flynn curiously, started to say something and decided not to.

As Rafferty pulled away from the curb, he handed back a folded newspaper. "I took the liberty of getting you a Daily Racing Form."

"Oh, what's that?" Diane said.

"Miss, the Daily Racing Form is to the horseplayer what the Wall Street Journal is to an investor. It provides all the information you need to pick a winner. The rest, of course, is up to you."

"Really?"

"Yes," Rafferty said. "You have to know what you're doing at the track. Once there were these two horseplayers out at Aqueduct, and they were down to their last sawbuck. Well, they went down to the paddock to study the horses, and glory be, they spied a priest standing before the number five horse making the sign of the cross.

It's fate, they said to themselves, and they rushed to the ten-dollar window and put it all on number five's nose. Well, number five finished so far up the track, as they say, that you could hardly see him. The two fellows couldn't believe it, and then, as they were trying to figure out how to get back to the city, they saw the same priest, and they went up to him and said, 'Father, we don't understand. We saw you giving the word to that number five horse, and we bet on him and lost every cent we had.' "

Rafferty paused, and Diane, leaning forward raptly, said, "What happened? What did the priest say?"

"The priest said, 'That's the trouble with you Protestants. You don't know the difference between a blessing and extreme unction.' "

For a moment she appeared confused, and then she squealed delightedly, and pressed Flynn's hand and whispered, "Oh, Richie, where did you *find* him? I thought that was a real story, not a joke."

Flynn settled back in his seat, pleased at how well the day was going, pleased with himself. He opened the *Daily Racing Form*. It was a full-sized newspaper stuffed with racing information—charts, results, workout times, gossip and comments covering every North American thoroughbred track. If the President had been assassinated, he would do no better than page eight in the *Daily Racing Form*. Page eight was where the paper acknowledged the existence of events beyond racing, usually in a dozen or so news briefs. For many horseplayers, these news briefs were the sole way they had of knowing what was occupying the attention of most of their fellow citizens. When Flynn turned to page eight, he saw that the big story of the day in the rest of the press, Nixon's back taxes, rated one paragraph and that Patricia Hearst was not mentioned at all. This accurately reflected the peculiar myopia of the racing world. Once, while Flynn was home on vacation from Marquette, his friend Scanlon had taken him to an elegant East Side wire room where affluent players gathered to hear the results of races from around the country. In between these announcements, the loudspeaker was hooked to a local FM radio station that normally carried classical music. On this particular afternoon, however, it was broadcasting an address to the United Nations General Assembly by Ambassador Adlai Stevenson on the Cuban missile crisis. The planet had never been closer to a nuclear conflagration; millions of lives were potentially at stake. In the middle of Ambassador Stevenson's speech, a well-modulated voice broke in: "We interrupt this program to bring you an important sports bulletin. In the fourth at Hialeah, the winner is . . ."

Suddenly Rafferty was past the toll booth on the New Jersey side of the Lincoln Tunnel and went by the exit on the right that said Hoboken. Karpstein's expressionless pig eyes materialized. Flynn heard the crack of the telephone cable smashing down on the desk. He shuddered and endeavored to regain his composure. In a month, he told himself, Albert Karpstein would be nothing more than an unpleasant memory, like a bad dream.

He looked at Diane. Her skirt had slid up, exposing her young, sturdy thighs, and he reached over and patted them possessively and somehow felt reassured. This was his reality, he thought, and then he tried to concentrate on the past performance charts for the Monmouth Park entries.

The drive south took about an hour. When Rafferty drove up to the clubhouse entrance, a red-jacketed attendant leaped forward to open the car door for Diane. Flynn tipped him two dollars. He told Rafferty that they would be up in the club for the day and to check in after the sixth race. He slipped a hundred-dollar bill into Rafferty's hand and said, "If I get lucky, you keep it all. Otherwise, I got fifty coming back."

Rafferty stared past Flynn at Diane waiting on the walk, her back to them, a slight breeze pressing her skirt against her round behind. "It looks like you got lucky already."

Flynn laughed and said, "Mind your manners, James," and went to Diane and took her hand.

She was standing by a bed of pansies. There were other beds filled with crocuses and daffodils. Yellow flashes of forsythia gleamed in the sun against green hedges. Monmouth Park had a lovely, intimate country feeling about it, unlike the impersonal bigness of, say, Aqueduct; the horseplayers had the same serious, intent faces, but they seemed less raucous, more at ease with themselves. There was none of the frantic pushing and shoving and angry, impatient yells in the lines to the betting windows as post time approached.

The section of the clubhouse they were going to was called the Parterre. It was the topmost part of the track and overlooked the finish line. It had three tiers of boxes

fronted with white planters full of geraniums. Each box
also had space for lunches and entertaining. The boxes
were occupied by stable owners, track directors and
wealthy racing enthusiasts. They were usually handed
down from generation to generation within a family, and
rarely did one open up to the long waiting list of appli-
cants.

When Flynn stepped off the elevator, he was met by a
carefully coiffed receptionist. "May I help you?" she said.
Flynn could practically hear her next words start to form,
that she was sorry but this was a private area for boxhold-
ers only.

"Richie Flynn," he said. "I'm Mr. Considine's guest.
Mr. Frank Considine, Senior."

Instantly the receptionist's face was wreathed in a bright
smile. She stood up and shook Flynn's hand and said,
"Oh, yes, we've been expecting you. I'll ring for someone
to show you to Mr. Considine's box." Diane had come out
of the elevator behind Flynn and was standing several feet
away. The receptionist's eyes narrowed slightly. "Is the,
ah, young lady with you?"

"Yes."

"Well, all right then, if you'll just sign in here for both
of you."

Diane whispered, "What's with her?" and Flynn said,
"Forget it." A Parterre attendant led them to the box and
handed Flynn two programs for the day's races. Flynn
tipped him five dollars. Then they wandered through the
third tier, where the Considine box was located. The talk
around them was muted. There were murmured greetings
between people who had not seen each other over the winter, references to yearling sales, how awful the weather
had been in Palm Beach. Many of the women were deeply
tanned. The uniform of the day seemed to be Chanel suits
in various pastel shades. Diane was, by far, the youngest
female present. The other women gazed at her with undisguised hostility. Her response was to unbutton her blazer
so that her nipples could be seen straining against her
blouse. This immediately produced the desired result. Every man in sight fastened his eyes on her.

They ordered steak sandwiches. Flynn got a double
scotch and water, and Diane had a Coke. Sitting slightly
sideways, she hiked up the hem of her skirt and crossed
her legs, bringing more stares from every passing male.

"Why not take all your clothes off?" Flynn said.

"I just want to give it back to those old bitches," she said. "Did you see the looks they were giving me?"

While they were eating, Considine's grandson, Frank III, the heir apparent to the business, came into the box. He was about Flynn's age and had a sleek, well-fed face. Young Considine did not like him because of Flynn's special relationship with his grandfather. It was why Flynn had rejected any notion of going to work for Considine Enterprises. As soon as the old man went to his reward, and it could happen any minute, Flynn knew he would be out on his ass.

"I'm down a few boxes with some friends," Considine said. "Grandpop wanted me to make sure that you had everything you wanted." All the time he was talking, he was staring greedily at Diane. She was obviously the reason for his solicitude. When Flynn introduced her, Considine said, "Well, you certainly add a great deal to opening day here, Miss Dare."

He sounded as if he had a mouthful of marshmallows, Flynn thought. It was difficult to believe that the grandson had any connection with his feisty forebear, and he savored the prospect of being able, in another month or so, to tell this stuffed turkey to fuck off.

Considine appeared to be in no hurry to leave, so Flynn said, "Thanks, Frank. If there's anything we need, I'll let you know."

Considine's face reddened at the dismissal. "Anyway, nice to meet you, Miss Dare. Perhaps I'll have the pleasure again some time. See *you* around, Richie."

"You weren't very friendly," Diane said after Considine had departed.

Flynn grunted and reached for his *Daily Racing Form*. Betting on horses was like buying stock. It gave the player the satisfying illusion that he was not really gambling, that by the dint of arduous study and analysis, calculation and insight, he would emerge an inevitable winner. Flynn had a favored system. In handicapping horses, he awarded point values according to where they had finished in the money during the past year and divided the sum into their total earnings. This enabled him to compare their average purse with the purse of the race he was betting on. Having thus rated the horses, he considered whether they were moving up in class, how long it had been since they had raced and what their last workout times were.

He tried to explain to Diane the code that was used to detail a horse's performance in a particular race. But when he saw her eyes begin to glaze over, he gave up. They had arrived too late for the first race. He made his selection for the second one and got up to go to the betting windows in the Parterre. Diane looked at him uncertainly. He gave her a hundred dollars. "Here's your stake," he said. "Have fun."

Flynn bought a hundred-dollar win ticket. He had never bet that much on a horse before. The horse came up lame and finished out of the money. It did not bother him. He felt a strange elation in losing a hundred dollars just like that and not caring about it. He looked at Diane's disconsolate expression and knew that she had also lost.

He decided to skip the third race.

"Why?" Diane asked.

"It's a race for three-year-old maidens."

"What's that?"

"Maidens are horses that haven't won yet. You can't tell anything about them. You might as well buy a lottery ticket."

Diane said she would bet anyway. She lost. In the fourth race, Flynn could not make up his mind between two entries. His system showed them to be evenly matched. He flipped a coin and bet another hundred on heads. Heads finished second.

Before the fifth race, Flynn ordered a bottle of champagne and told Diane that he was going to take a stroll through the grandstand. On the lower grandstand level he spied Nicky Kazan. Kazan was a reverse racing snob. His father, a Greek immigrant who had made a fortune in New York real estate, had left him and his two sisters several million dollars each. After his father's death he had made racing a full-time obsession. But despite his money, Kazan always preferred to remain in the general admissions area of whatever track he was frequenting. "I want to be with the people," he would say. In deference to the amounts he wagered, however, he was provided with a stool near the fifty-dollar windows in front of one of the closed-circuit television sets that had become a standard feature at all tracks. And while he liked to think of himself as a man of the people, Kazan disdained standing in line with them, so he had a runner, Pedro from Panama, make his bets. Pedro's father had sent him to the United States to study medicine at Tulane University. On the way in from the airport, Pedro from Panama had stopped off at the Fair Grounds in New Orleans and never made it to medical school. For a time, until he became too heavy, he was an apprentice jockey. He continued to hang around tracks nonetheless and one day bumped into Kazan, who paid him a hundred dollars a week and a percentage of his winnings.

Besides making bets for him, Pedro would bring Kazan an occasional beer and hot dog from a Considine refreshment stand. Kazan would also send Pedro from Panama down to the walking ring to observe the horses firsthand before every race. Kazan spent countless hours charting horses, but it did not mean a thing if they turned out to have bandages on their forelegs. For Kazan, regardless of what his charts said, the bandages indicated some fatal defect, and if Pedro, who had trouble mastering the nuances of English, came back with a report that a horse Kazan had picked was wearing "Band-Aids," Kazan would not bet. It did not make any difference to him that Forego, one of the greatest geldings in racing history, wore the cursed bandages. If Kazan abandoned his theory, it would have been a far greater defeat than any race. Napoleon must have felt the same way en route to Moscow.

Kazan was so immersed in his calculations that Flynn had to tap him on the shoulder. "Hey, Nicky, what do you like in the fifth?"

"Richie, how are you? Ball of Fire, that's all I see."

When he returned to the box, he found Diane drinking the champagne with a chubby, pink-cheeked man with blond hair. "Richie," she said, "this is Mr. Philip Turner. Mr. Turner gave me a tip on the next race. And he's got his own investment house on Wall Street, can you imagine?"

"Hope you don't mind, Mr. Flynn. Gosh, your name has a familiar ring."

"Richie played football with the New York Giants," Diane said.

"That's it!" Turner exclaimed. "I knew the name was familiar. What are you up to these days?"

"I've just started a little investment firm myself." It was the first time Flynn had ever said anything like that. He liked the sound of it, and the resentment he had experienced when he discovered Turner in the box immediately vanished.

"Really? Anything special?"

"Real estate. You know, speculative stuff."

"Risky business, that." Turner said. "Still, if you're on to what you're doing, you can make a killing. Well, I've got to be off. Nice meeting you, Miss Dare. Mr. Flynn, I apologize for the intrusion."

"No problem," Flynn said. "By the way, what was the tip?"

"Ball of Fire."

According to Flynn's system, there was another filly in the race that rated at least three points better. But the spread between a tieless, baggy-trousered Kazan in the grandstand and the hand-tailored Turner here in the Parterre could not be bigger, Flynn thought, and at the mutuel window, seconds before post time, he switched his bet to Ball of Fire, which finished fourth. The filly that Flynn had originally handicapped to win came in first, paying nine dollars and twenty cents on a two-dollar bet. Flynn drank the last of the champagne and ordered another double scotch.

The sixth race offered nothing very attractive. He bet ten dollars simply for the action. When the race was over, Flynn sourly reflected that he might as well have fashioned a paper plane with the bill and sent it fluttering down on the crowd below. Little tendrils of annoyance began to creep through him. An attendant advised Flynn that his driver was at the Parterre reception desk. Flynn tipped the attendant a dollar and sent a message back to Rafferty to be outside the clubhouse entrance after the seventh race.

Flynn's irritability grew. By now he had less than three hundred of the nine hundred dollars he had started with. His best bet of the day was in the seventh race, another test for fillies. The horse's name was Evening Star. The odds on her were four to one. If she won, he would recoup most of his stake, and he could still count the day as the pleasant outing he had envisioned, relaxed, completely carefree, a taste of what was to come. But he had lost his confidence. He tried to tell himself that the money did not matter, although he regretted dipping into the cash he had borrowed from Karpstein. What did matter was the euphoria draining out of him, the sense of riding high, that he could do no wrong.

Diane had disappeared into the women's lounge. Flynn was just getting up to place his bet when she rushed breathlessly back into the box. "Richie, please, I don't have any more money. Please give me fifty dollars." She tugged at his arm. "Please, Richie, please!"

He had never seen her so excited. He hesitated, but he knew that he really had no choice. "Don't spend it all at once," he said as he handed her the money. Then he bet a hundred dollars on Evening Star.

The race was six furlongs, three-quarters of a mile. He expected Evening Star to break in front, and she did. She was a speed horse, and everything Flynn had noted about her showed that she was rounding into peak form. She continued to set the pace, and going into the turn, she was a good four lengths in the lead. At the head of the stretch she was still well out in front of the field, but because of the angle, Flynn could not determine exactly how far. The crowd began to roar, and Flynn could not hear the track announcer. He was yelling himself now, urging Evening Star on, vaguely aware of Diane next to him, also screaming. It was the most thrilling moment of a race for him, the horses charging toward him almost as if they were in slow motion. He was certain that Evening Star had the race wrapped up.

Then, with a sixteenth of a mile to go, a horse slipped through the pack along the rail and started closing the gap. Flynn kept on yelling, waving his rolled-up program in a clenched fist. But it was no use. At the wire the number nine horse flashed past Evening Star to win by a head. Flynn could not even remember number nine's name. "Shit," he said.

"I won! I won!" Diane shrieked. She was jumping up and down crazily. She threw her arms around Flynn's neck and kissed him. Her bowler fell off. Her hair tumbled down. Flynn stared dumbly at her. Her lipstick was smeared. The top button of her blouse had come loose. She grabbed him again. "I won! Richie, I won!" she shrieked once more. "Ivan's Girl won!"

Slowly the realization of what had happened dawned on him. He looked at his program. The name of the number nine horse was Ivan's Girl. Lights blinked on the parimutuel board. Ivan's Girl had gone off at seventy to one. Flynn had not even considered her, nor apparently had very many other people. She paid one hundred forty-four dollars and sixty cents.

"You bet the whole fifty?" he asked.

"Yes, all of it."

"But why? The horse didn't have a chance."

"Ivan's Girl," she said. "That's my dad's name. Ivan! Ivan Drahomanov. I told you I was Ukrainian. I was putting on some lipstick in the lounge and there was this program and I picked it up and I just saw it."

Flynn thought of how he had been worrying about his luck a few minutes ago. Then he started to laugh and said, "Baby, you are some handicapper." He hugged her and swung her around in the box until they both nearly lost their balance. Suddenly Flynn said, "The ticket. Where's the ticket?"

"The ticket?" she said, her eyes widening. "Oh, the ticket." She opened her palm. "Here it is."

He took the crumpled piece of paper and smoothed it out. There it was, indelibly printed, a win ticket for the seventh race. Number nine.

"You cash it," she said. "It was your money. I have to fix my face."

Flynn went to a pay window. The cashier looked at the ticket and said, "You sure know how to pick them," and counted out thirty-six one-hundred dollar bills, a ten and a five.

He waited in the box for Diane. When she returned, she was laughing. "The top button on my blouse is gone," she said. "Do you think anybody'll notice?" She laughed again.

Flynn peeled off eighteen of the bills and gave them to her. "We split," he said. "Half and half."

"I can't believe it," she said. "Wow!"

Flynn called the waiter who had been serving them and asked for the check. The waiter replied that it had been taken care of, that Mr. Considine had left express instructions about this.

"There's one other thing," Flynn said. "We have a little celebrating to do on the way home. Can you get me a bottle of champagne to go and a couple of glasses?"

"I'm sorry, sir. It's against the rules."

"It was only an idea," Flynn said, and handed him twenty dollars. "Thanks for your trouble."

The waiter shifted his feet and said, "I'll see what I can do," and came back with a brown paper bag. "The glasses are plastic. I hope that's all right."

Rafferty had the limousine ready. As Diane got into the rear seat, Flynn said to him, "You can keep the other fifty."

Flynn popped the cork on the champagne. It foamed down the sides of the bottle. Diane held the glasses while he poured. They toasted each other. She nestled against him. "Oh, Richie," she whispered, "this was the best time I ever had." He drew her closer to him. Out of the corner of his eye he could see the sensuous swell of her left breast.

They had left the New Jersey Turnpike, the Manhattan skyscrapers ahead of them, when she turned toward him and nibbled on his earlobe and said, "Honey, can I ask you something?"

"Sure, why not?"

"It's just that, well, things seem different. Like you told that man at the track you were in investments now. I know it's none of my business, but you know what I mean, this limo and everything."

"You're right. Things are different. I am into investments. I can't go into the details yet, is all." He cupped her partially uncovered breast with his hand and tweaked her nipple.

She smiled and pushed his hand away playfully. "Stop, honey," she said. "Not in the car. Later." She paused. "You know, I was thinking. I wish I could see more of you."

"Don't worry, you will."

"Maybe I should get a bigger place. I was thinking of bringing my little girl here, too. I miss her an awful lot. You'd really like her."

"Yeah," he said neutrally.

"Where to?" Rafferty asked.

"Where you picked us up," Flynn said. When Rafferty stopped in front of Diane's building, Flynn told her to go on ahead, that he would join her in a minute. Then he made a deal with Rafferty for another twenty dollars to wait for them.

"How long?" Rafferty asked.

"An hour. Whatever."

"I'll grab a bite then."

After Diane had let him into the apartment, he said, "I told the driver he could go get something to eat."

She had already undressed. "Lie down," she said. "You're what I'm going to eat."

She took off his jacket, and when he was stretched out on the bed, she removed his tie, shoes and socks. She pulled off his pants and shorts and traced her finger under his testicles. She unbuttoned his shirt and hung it carefully over a chair. "You should leave some extra clothes here," she said.

When she knelt over him, she devoured him ferociously. He came in her mouth with a gasp of incredible ecstasy and relief. He had not realized how uptight he had been.

She drew a bath for him and sponged his back and kneaded his neck and blew in his ear. "Feel good?" she asked.

"You've got to be kidding," he said. "I'm staying in here forever."

"No, you're not. I have to take a bath, too. Someday we'll have a tub for two. Oh, Richie, I'm so happy with you."

She said that she wanted to go to the nightclub owned by Vinnie D'Angelo that presented female impersonators. The food was great, she said, and he would love the current revue, which had come all the way from Paris, France. She called and asked to speak to the maître d', whom she appeared to know. He heard her say that she would be with a good friend of Mr. D'Angelo's.

She was wearing a black silk blouse and culottes. "How do I look?"

"Terrific, except I can't see your legs."

She stepped back and said, "Use your imagination, silly."

D'Angelo's club was called The Fallen Angel. When Rafferty pulled up, there were a half dozen Cadillacs and Lincolns parked in front, along with a Rolls-Royce. "That's it for the night, pal," Flynn told Rafferty.

The inside of the club was the same rococo style as the Bourbon Street, except that the predominant colors were blue and white, and instead of cherubs, devilish imps were in evidence.

Diane preceded him to a thickset, swarthy man, standing by a reservation desk, bursting out of his tuxedo. "Hi, Chickie," she said. "Do you know Mr. Flynn? Mr. Richie Flynn."

"I don't believe I've had the pleasure."

Flynn included ten dollars with his handshake, and he and Diane were led to a table bordering a tiny dance floor in front of a stage.

He asked for a scotch, and Diane had a sweet daiquiri. He let her order, and they ended up with lobster Thermidor, which Flynn did not especially like but ate anyway in deference to her desire for the exotic. "You don't get this in Toledo," she said.

"You want some more champagne?" he asked.

She reached for his hand. "Can we?"

The revue was much like any nightclub featuring girls, except that they were men and formerly men. Diane had told him that while most of them were transvestites, there were also some actual transsexuals. "You can't believe what goes on in the dressing room," she said. "They're all so catty. It makes the Bourbon Street sound like a convent."

The last number of the first act was a striptease solo. The dancer was introduced as Amazonia. "That's one that had an operation," Diane whispered.

Flynn looked at the raven hair, the pouty red lips, the jutting breasts. "I don't believe it."

"It's true," Diane said. "Look at its knees. Women's knees are round. Men's aren't." She tried to suppress a giggle. "They can operate on its you-know-what, but they can't do anything about its knees."

Near the end of the second act Vincente D'Angelo arrived. He sat at a small rear table between the bar and the dining area that was always held for him and any close associates who might drop in unexpectedly. D'Angelo never ceased to be amazed at how packed with people The Fallen Angel was night after night, goggling at and applauding the antics of what he perceived to be a bunch of freaks. And high-class people, he thought, a lot of them real society. Not that he was complaining. He had acquired a long-term lease on the property two years before, and it had been a consistent failure until now. First he had opened a restaurant which had done well enough at lunch because of all the nearby office buildings, but these same buildings left the surrounding neighborhood deserted at night. Next he had started a discotheque, but the premises were not big enough to make it successful. D'Angelo's decorator was the one who had suggested turning it into a cabaret with its new entertainment policy, and it had been an instant hit. He could not fathom why. It must be a sign of the times, he finally decided. "The whole country is falling apart," he had confided to his wife one night. "These kids with long hair running around, spitting on the flag and everything."

When the show was over and the lights had gone from dark to dim, he beckoned Chickie, the maître d'. "Anybody here I should know about it?"

"No, boss, nothing special. Wait. There's a guy named Flynn come in with one of the girls from the Bourbon Street. Cute. Semipro. She said he knows you. He duked me ten."

"Flynn, huh? Where?"

"There. Table eight."

D'Angelo stood up, looked past Chickie's pointing finger and saw Richie, slumped back in his chair, and Diane. He also saw the champagne bucket on the table.

"What's his tab?"

Chickie snapped his fingers at a waiter. "Mario, what's the check on table eight?" When Mario came scurrying back, he whispered to Chickie. Mario would never dream of addressing D'Angelo directly.

"One fifty-seven and still counting, boss."

D'Angelo sucked in his lower lip. "Send over another bottle," he said. "Compliments of me."

He waited until the champagne had been brought to the table and uncorked. He saw the girl peer around, and then he made his way toward her and Flynn.

"Hi, Mr. D'Angelo," Diane said, smiling radiantly. "Gee, thanks."

"Hello, doll," he said. "Don't get up. Hey, Richie."

Flynn tried to focus. He had been drinking most of the champagne. He was aware that a new bottle had been placed on the table, but he was not quite certain how it had happened. His head swam. He looked up and saw D'Angelo's gold-framed spectacles glittering in the light from the table lamp. He squinted and recognized the mafioso at last. "Hey, Vinnie," he shouted, and struggled to rise.

"Please," D'Angelo said, a hand on Flynn's shoulder. D'Angelo pulled back his lips, revealing his teeth, which was the closest he ever came to grinning. "Looks like I started something here. You two kids look like you're having a swell time." D'Angelo kept his hand on Flynn's shoulder. "Hey, Richie, what'd you do? Strike oil?"

Flynn labored to pull himself together. "Not exactly, Vinnie," he said, "but I'm into a deal that's OK."

"Good, eh?"

"Real good, Vinnie."

"Well, keep in touch. I'm always looking around, you know."

"Sure, Vinnie, will do." Flynn slumped back in his chair again, waving a hand vaguely in the air. D'Angelo squeezed Flynn's shoulder and left. He watched Flynn stagger out of the club after Diane and made a mental note to keep an eye on him. In this business, he reminded himself, you never know what might be around the corner.

In Diane's apartment, Flynn flopped on the bed. "You all right, honey?" she asked, stepping out of her culottes.

"Come here," he said. Then he passed out. When he awoke, he was still lying there in his clothes, except for his shoes. He looked at his watch. It was six A.M. He looked at Diane. She was curled up, a thumb against her mouth. It was the first time he had spent an entire night away from Agnes. He found his shoes on the floor by the bed and hurried out to find a taxi.

He arrived home shortly after seven o'clock. Agnes was in a robe, fixing breakfast for their son. "Where's Sean?" he asked.

"In the bathroom, brushing his teeth."

"Listen, I'm sorry, I met old man Considine at the track. He offered me a job better than Goldblatt. We went back to his place on Central Park South, and I don't know, I drank too much. That's all."

Agnes bent over the stove, scrambling eggs. She did not turn around. His head was pounding. It was that fucking champagne, he thought. He swore he would never drink it again.

"I made the bet for you," he said.

She did not say anything.

"I'm not kidding. Look. A seventy-to-one shot. It paid one forty-four, sixty cents." He counted out the money and laid it on the kitchen counter. "You can look it up in the paper," he said. "Ivan's Girl."

Then he went into the bedroom and undressed and fell asleep again, remembering this time to take two aspirin.

9

═══ ☆ ═══

As with a cancer-ridden patient, attempts were made peri-odically to excise the malignant growths that spread block by block through the City of New York. Each month, for instance, there was a public auction of "surplus city-owned properties." "Surplus" was a euphemism for "abandoned." The city took over these properties, generally small apart-ment buildings or single-family residences that had been subdivided, and tried to auction them off for a fraction of their original cost on the theory that this would revitalize them and return them to the tax rolls. The properties, naturally, were not located on the fashionable East Side of Manhattan. They were in the rotting, rat-infested old ghet-tos of the South Bronx, Harlem and Bedford-Stuyvesant and in such newly disintegrating sections as Inwood, Jamaica in Queens and Bushwick and Bay Ridge in Brooklyn. Most of the purchasers were black or Hispanic and poor. When they had managed to scrape together a few dollars to buy, as the promotional literature put it, "a piece of America," they immediately discovered that they were unable to obtain building loans or mortgages from a bank, or even insurance, because of the very locations they were supposedly helping to revitalize.

The auction Richie Flynn attended was in a large room on the mezzanine of the Statler Hilton Hotel. He arrived a few minutes after two P.M., when the afternoon session, devoted to the sale of parcels in the Borough of the Bronx, was scheduled to commence. About three hundred people were there, seated in rows of folding chairs. Flynn was among a handful of whites present. He sat down next to one of them, an elderly man with a flowing bow tie and bushy white eyebrows. The man was on the aisle, and he nodded without speaking as he shifted his legs to let Flynn slip past him.

Flynn had awakened at eleven-thirty that morning, his hangover gone. He had a Goldblatt anyway. Agnes, as usual after a domestic scene, had left a note that she was

☆ 127 ☆

with her mother. But she had not run off in such a fury as
to neglect taking the money he had dropped on the
kitchen counter, and he was certain that by evening she
would be in a better humor.

He flipped through the auction brochure. The cover had
red, white and blue stripes on it, along with an exhortation
that said "An Investment in New York City Is an Investment in Your Country." Approximately two hundred
pieces of property were being offered in the Bronx. A
number of them had "upset" or minimum prices of only
twenty-five and fifty dollars. There were also a number of
photographs that showed bleak, graffiti-covered structures
with cracked windows that reflected the hopelessness of
the streets they were on. At least, Flynn thought, the brochure pictures did not attempt to disguise the truth, or perhaps the truth couldn't be avoided.

The synagogue was about a third of the way down the
list, without a photograph. It had, however, one of the
highest upset figures—fifty thousand dollars, which, as
Fowler said, required a down payment of ten thousand.
"Next month," Fowler had predicted, "the price will probably be reduced to forty. But what the hell, let's strike
while the iron's hot. You can't tell what could happen."

Flynn patted the inside breast pocket of his jacket. Before coming to the auction, he had converted ten thousand
dollars of the money from Karpstein into certified bank
checks and kept the remainder in cash.

The auctioneer was saying, "We have here a parcel
three feet by a hundred. Perfect for motorcycles. Who
owns a motorcycle?"

The auctioneer was aided by three gimlet-eyed, shirt-
sleeved aisle men. They all wore trousers that were belted
high on their paunches, which made them appear strangely
disproportionate. They scuttled around the floor, heads
thrust slightly forward, like pointers. When bidding began
on a piece of property, an aisle man would rush to the
side of a bidder, stare at him intently and dramatically
shout out the bid as though he were bidding himself.
Sometimes a single aisle man would wind up handling two
competing bidders, throwing himself into the cause of first
one, then the other, until he finally became aware of this
unseemly conflict of interest and relinquished one of the
bidders to a colleague.

"Fifty dollars, anyone?" the auctioneer said, moving on

briskly. "Speak up. It's a corner parcel, for God's sake! How can anyone go wrong? I don't care where it is."

Flynn looked more closely at the people in the room. Many of them were families, with children in tow. They were dressed in their best clothes, as if this attested to their determination and worth. Rarely did the bidding encompass more than three or four people. Obviously each was there to acquire a particular house. How deep ran the instinct to own property, he thought, no matter who a person was.

He looked at the man with the flowing bow tie next to him and extended his hand and said, "Flynn, Richie Flynn. You here to get something?"

"Roger Martin's my name. Pleased to make your acquaintance, Mr. Flynn. No. I used to be a broker. Retired now. I just come to these things to keep a hand in, so to speak. Watch the city go down the drain."

There had been some spirited bidding for a house between two black women, an aisle man poised by each of them barking out new offers. Then a commotion erupted. "Ladies," the auctioneer cried, "please calm down, and I'll help you out."

One of the women, with a figure like a fire hydrant, in a purple dress and a hat that had a garland of flowers around it, stood up and said, "Help me, shit!" She glared at the woman who was bidding against her. "I'm buying this for my grandson," she said. "Three thousand is all I got. You top three, I cut you, sister. I cut you good."

"Ladies, please," the auctioneer admonished.

"See what I mean?" Martin snapped. "City's going to hell because of rent control. Landlord can't make a decent profit, he walks away and these animals come in. Mark my words, pretty soon the whole city's going to be up for auction, if it doesn't burn first."

Flynn did not say anything. He knew that his mother could not have survived without rent control. If life was unfair, why shouldn't it be as unfair to the landlord as to the tenant? The system was what was wrong, he thought. The system said to look out for yourself. Nobody was worrying about Richie Flynn, except Richie Flynn. That's why he was here, sitting in this chair with twelve thousand five hundred dollars of Albert Karpstein's money in his pocket.

The auctioneer was selling a three-story dwelling.

"Come on," he said, "it's brick, isn't it? Two hundred dollars. Any advance? There! The man in the green hat. He has saved the day," the auctioneer said as the crowd tittered appreciatively. The house finally went for one thousand nine hundred and thirty dollars.

The synagogue was next. Flynn straightened up in his chair. "Item three-sixteen," the auctioneer said. "We start at fifty thousand, that's what it says here, so it must be worth it. Do I hear fifty thousand? Another beautiful corner parcel."

Before the auctioneer could further extol the synagogue's attributes, Flynn raised his hand, waving the brochure. An aisle man twenty feet away spotted the wave at once and hurried toward Flynn. "Fifty thousand," the aisle man shouted.

"Well, there's a sport if I ever saw one," the auctioneer said. He did not bother trying to raise the ante. "Going once," he said, raising his gavel.

"Fifty thousand five hundred!"

Flynn felt a weird rushing in his head. He nodded automatically, and the aisle man yelled, "Fifty-one thousand."

"Fifty-one five!"

At first Flynn could not pinpoint who was making the competing bid. Then he spotted another aisle man taking up a position five or six rows in front of him. The aisle man was standing alongside a black man who was wearing a hat like a fez, only flatter, and a loose-fitting African tunic. It had a funny name; Flynn could not remember what it was. The black man was looking back at Flynn, grinning broadly, flashing a huge expanse of teeth, one of which was gold.

This is insane, Flynn thought wildly. There had to be some mistake.

"Do I hear fifty-two?" the auctioneer cried.

Flynn nodded dumbly, and his aisle man called it out. The black man was still grinning back at him. He had never seen anything more malevolent. The other aisle man shouted, "Fifty-two thousand five hundred!" The people in the room fell silent. There was a tangible excitement in the air.

Flynn raised his bid five hundred dollars. Then he turned in desperation to the retired real estate broker next to him and whispered, "Mr. Martin, do me a favor. There's something screwy here. Could you find out what that guy's doing? It's important. I'll make it worth your while."

"Glad to, young fellow," Martin said, "and for free. I'm curious myself. I just hope you know what *you're* doing."

As Martin reached the black man's side, the other aisle man called, "Fifty-three five!"

Flynn watched Martin and the black man talking. The black man was gesturing. Once he jabbed a finger in Flynn's direction. "Any advance?" the auctioneer demanded. "This is a prime parcel, a steal! Do I hear fifty-four?" He paused. "All right, then, last call."

Flynn nodded to his aisle man.

Martin, crouching low, came back and sat beside Flynn. As he did, the black man made another bid. This time, however, he jumped his offer a hundred dollars, instead of five hundred.

"That's his sign of good faith," Martin snorted.

"What the fuck is he *doing?*" Flynn asked.

"He said, 'That honky want that parcel real bad, pay that kind of money. He want it so bad, he pay me two hundred, I stops.' That's a direct quote, Mr. Flynn."

"You mean he doesn't want it himself?"

"That's right," Martin said.

"Going once, going twice," the auctioneer said.

Flynn pulled himself together and raised a finger, one finger. "But he can't do that."

"Oh, yes, he can," Martin said. "When he goes out to complete all the paperwork, he'll say he made a mistake, didn't understand the price. By then, of course, it'll be too late to auction it off today. The city will just put it up next month. That's my advice. Wait till next month."

"I can't. You don't understand."

Martin shrugged. The black man bid a hundred dollars more, forcing Flynn to do the same. Hate cascaded through him. Flynn would have given anything to see the grin of this black man's face transformed into screams of unbearable agony as he was being flayed alive.

The black man bid an additional hundred.

Flynn yanked out his wallet, fumbled for two hundred-dollar bills and handed them to Martin. "Here. Give it to him."

When the black man received the money, he turned toward Flynn, brought the bills to his lips, kissed them and bowed elaborately.

Flynn slumped back, his fury mixed with relief that it was over. But suddenly he realized it was not. The auctioneer was about to bring down his gavel for the third time following the black man's last, unanswered bid. The aisle man standing by Flynn leaned forward, reddish eyes set in sharp-nosed albino face, and snapped, "You letting that nigger beat you out."

Flynn shook his head.

"Fifty-four six," the aisle man announced triumphantly.

The auctioneer, sensing that the bidding had ended, repeated the figure and matter-of-factly intoned, "Last call, and final warning. Once. Twice. Sold!"

"I don't know how to thank you," Flynn said to Martin. "You really helped me out. Can't I buy you a drink at least?"

"I hope I did. No. I'm not only a retired broker but a retired drunk. Anyway, up the Irish! And good luck to you."

There was a room off the auction room where the processing for each sale was done. Flynn got in line, still shaken by what had happened. A black couple was in front of him. He remembered that they had bought the house for one thousand nine hundred and thirty dollars before the synagogue went on the block. The man was a muscular giant, yet he had a peculiar gentleness about him. The woman held his hand. She was tiny by comparison, delicately featured, her skin the color of coffee laced with cream against his purple darkness. She led him to a table when their turn came. They sat down. The woman opened her purse and started taking out crumpled bills. Flynn could see they were all tens and twenties. The woman counted them and pushed them toward a clerk on the other side of the table. The clerk had a fish-belly countenance that coordinated beautifully with his neon-green double-knit suit. He re-counted the money and pushed it back. Heads came together in conference. The woman took more crumpled bills out of her purse. The clerk counted them again. "You're still twenty dollars short," he said loudly. "Plus twenty-five for the auctioneer's fee."

"I told you we thought it was ten percent down, not twenty," the woman said.

"Lady, it's right there in black and white," the clerk said in exasperation, pointing at the brochure. "Didn't you read it?"

The black couple stared at the money, as though by sheer force of will it could be made to multiply. The woman was on the verge of tears. The black man's enormous arms hung helplessly at his sides. He glanced around and saw Flynn. "Mister," he pleaded, "you lend me forty-five dollars? I give you my name, address. I got a job. Mercury Moving Company. Wife here, she got a job, too."

Ordinarily Flynn would have been touched by the request. But not this time, not now, not after what the grinning man in the African tunic had done to him. "Sorry," he said, looking away.

"Mister, I swear I'm good for it. We just didn't know it was twenty percent down, you know."

"You're holding up the line," the clerk said to the couple. "You'll have to step aside. You get the money by four-thirty, you can have the parcel."

Go find a grinning, fucking brother with a gold tooth, Flynn thought.

"Can you believe these people?" the clerk sniffed when Flynn sat down. "Let me tell you, it happens all the time. I wish they'd all go back to Africa."

Flynn gave him the bank checks and the extra cash he now had to fork over. The municipal bureaucracy was out in majestic force at the auction, and he had to go to four more tables to complete the necessary forms. At the last table he was told that he had sixty days before the rest of the purchase price was due.

Then Flynn went to a bar across the street from the hotel and had two shots of scotch in quick succession with a Goldblatt chaser. He took out a pad of paper and a pencil and started to figure. Ten thousand nine hundred twenty dollars for the synagogue. Two hundred more to buy the nigger off. And a hundred the auctioneer got for a sale of this size. Which left him a thousand two-eighty of Karpstein's loan. Add to this the roughly fifteen hundred dollars he still had from winning on Ivan's Girl, and there was barely enough to cover the interest payments to Karpstein. Flynn wondered what he would have done if Diane did not have a father named Ivan. He shivered involuntarily and ordered a third scotch.

☆

At a quarter to five in the afternoon, waiting for Harry Fowler, Flynn leaned against the railing around the pool where the seals were kept in the Central Park Zoo. The water was a glassy, opaque green. Every so often the seals would surface with a snort and dive out of sight again. When they did, cigarette butts, balled-up cellophane bags and empty Cracker Jack boxes bobbed up and down in their wake. A boy about eleven in a blue blazer and gray flannel pants tossed a candy-bar wrapper into the water. "Alexander," a well-dressed woman admonished, "how many times do I have to tell you to use a litter basket?"

The boy looked at her and said, "The world is my litter basket."

Flynn moved restlessly away from the railing. Nearby was a clock tower over an arched passage that led out of the zoo to the rest of the park. The tower contained a carillon. Every half hour a series of bronze fairy-tale animals clutching musical instruments paraded around the tower while chimes played. As Flynn approached it, perhaps thirty or forty children, most of them with uniformed nursemaids, stood waiting expectantly. Five o'clock came and went. There was no sound from the carillon. The bronze hippo and elephant, the bear, the two kangaroos and the rest of the figures remained frozen in place. A minute passed. Then a little girl began to cry. A blue-caped nanny stopped a park employee. "What's wrong?" the nanny asked.

"Lady, it's broke."

"But when will it be fixed?"

The park employee shrugged. "A week, a month, who knows?"

It's the same all over the city, Flynn thought. Up in the Bronx the poor kids could not go wading because they'd cut their feet to ribbons on shards of glass. Here in the Central Park Zoo right off Fifth Avenue rich kids cried because the carillon did not work. Nothing worked. Nothing could be fixed.

Flynn went back to the railing where the seals were. He looked up, and for a crazy moment he thought that all Fifth Avenue as far as he could see was on fire. But it was just scores of luxurious apartment-house windows glinting in the rays of the sun setting over the New Jersey Palisades.

Then Harry Fowler came up beside him, so quietly that

Flynn did not realize he was there until he felt Fowler's hand on his arm.

"Hello, Richie," he said, his eyes instinctively taking in the same fiery spectacle that Flynn was watching. "Unbelievable. They say those co-ops go for three, four hundred thousand. You wouldn't think so many people had that much money."

Fowler's face was the color of putty. It was crosshatched by hundreds of tiny wrinkles, like overlaid spider webs. He was fifty-nine years old, a bulky man with deliberate movements of hand and body. His job in the Agency for Child Development was to evaluate both the site and the sponsoring group of proposed day-care centers.

"Jesus, Harry," Flynn said. "You don't know what happened at the auction. A fucking nigger tried to rip me off. Wait'll you hear about it. Besides the ten thousand, I had to pay another nine-twenty for the synagogue, plus two bills to the nigger. We almost lost it, I ain't kidding."

"Not here," Fowler said, glancing at the people lined against the railing like so many Ahabs waiting for the seals to surface again.

They walked under the clock tower out of the zoo and along a winding path. Finally Fowler selected a bench he deemed safe, and they sat down. Flynn started to tell him what had occurred at the auction, but Fowler, staring straight ahead in the gathering dusk, paid no attention and began to talk. Flynn got the eerie feeling that Fowler was actually talking to himself. "More than thirty years I've been in social work," he said. "And for what? To make some people rich so they can live over there, that's what!" Fowler jerked a thumb over his shoulder toward Fifth Avenue. "Last week I inspected a center downtown. There were so many rats running around the basement nursery the kids couldn't use it. I saw with my own eyes little kids with rat bites—in a day-care center! I close it up, so what? The landlord had an ironclad lease with the city that has eleven years to go. He gets a hundred and ten thousand a year for eleven more years no matter what. There's a budget cutback, it doesn't hurt him. Just the children, and who gives a fuck about them?"

That was the most amazing aspect of the day-care center program, as Flynn had already learned from Fowler. When the federal government had made hundreds of millions of dollars available for day care in the latter half of the 1960s, political powerbrokers in the city quickly realized that they had a bonanza on their hands. It was suddenly decided that the nonprofit community and church-affiliated organizations that traditionally ran these centers were not moving fast enough to utilize the new money, so an alternative system was devised whereby the city would pay rents directly to private landlords and developers who submitted plans for their own centers. A select cabal of public officeholders, real estate speculators, bankers and lawyers—the kind of solid citizens who could be found at cocktail parties fulminating about "welfare cheats"—was in on the scheme from the beginning. They had become the dominant force in day-care centers, and the city, according to the terms of their leases, paid not only the rents but the utility bills and real estate taxes as well, all the money coming out of allocations that were supposedly devoted to caring for children while their mothers worked. These long-term leases were written in such a way that if a building ceased to be a day-care center for some reason, the landlord still got paid the full amount. Landlords also made an immediate windfall profit because mortgages within the cabal were obtained on the basis of a lease's net worth, which was always far greater than any construction, rehabilitation or acquisition costs.

Fowler sat on the bench, palms planted on his knees. "I was looking at some figures the other day," he said. "Eight landlords—count them, eight—got seventy-three day-care leases. One bunch owns twenty-two leases with a payoff of thirty-four million. Another has fourteen leases worth thirty-seven million. Vultures. They're all vultures!"

Flynn tried to cope with the staggering sums that Fowler had just rattled off. Well, he thought, the million eight hundred and seventy-five thousand their synagogue would spin off wasn't so bad either.

Fowler turned to Flynn, as if at last acknowledging his presence. "I'll tell you one thing, Richie," he said, his voice constricted with emotion, "that synagogue is going to be a decent center. There won't be any rats biting little kids."

"That's for sure, Harry," Flynn replied, his mind still fixed on the million eight hundred and seventy-five thousand dollars. "I mean, Jesus, who wants that?"

Darkness was falling rapidly, and from where he was on

the bench, Flynn could see the lighted midtown skyline bordering the south side of the park. It reminded him of the view of the city outside Karpstein's office in Hoboken. Once or twice he had considered telling Fowler about Karpstein, but he had been unable to bring himself to do it. At first it had been a question of ego as much as anything. Fowler perceived him as a famous sports personality who knew everyone. Flynn liked that and had not wanted to disillusion him. Then he had hesitated to reveal the loan shark's role because he was afraid that this might cause Fowler to drop the whole idea or, worse, to find somebody else. Finally he had rationalized that what Fowler didn't know would not hurt him. It would all work out. Was it not the bold, he remembered hearing somewhere, that seized the day?

There were three basic ways to launch a day-care center. One was for a bona fide community group to seek a license for a rent-free facility, usually in a church, a settlement house or a public housing project. The procedure was stupefyingly complex. The instruction book alone, listing rules and regulations, steps to be taken and specifications to be met, weighed more than a pound. A group could count itself extraordinarily blessed if it got approval in a year's time; most groups simply gave up. A speculator with the right connections, however, could march in and sign a lease for a center directly with the Department of Real Estate acting on behalf of the city, and the Agency for Child Development had to scramble around to find a suitable organization to operate it. If sufficient muscle was brought to bear, it did not matter whether the agency or even community leaders objected to the site; it still went through.

Not wishing to appear unduly piggish, with all the unwelcome publicity that might ensue, the powerbrokers also allowed a less well-connected landlord access to a direct lease if a neighborhood group picked a building that the landlord happened to own. Not that they made it easy. Months of negotiations, replete with kickbacks, were required. But occasionally it did occur, and it provided somebody like Fowler with the opening he needed. He would give a rave review to the block association that he had lined up to sponsor the synagogue's conversion to a day-care center, as well as to the physical layout and location of the synagogue itself. As a ringwise veteran in the agency he knew how to maneuver the application through its maze of divisions and special offices, and with both the association and the synagogue getting such high marks, the Department of Real Estate, according to Fowler, would acquiesce swiftly, indeed gratefully, to preserve a facade of fairness in granting leases. "It's a little like jujitsu," he told Flynn. "You use the other fellow's strength to beat him at his own game. Or in this case, ride along with him."

"It'll take a month, right?" Flynn said now in the park.

"Don't worry. You have sixty days before the balance has to be paid on the synagogue. Believe me, everything will be done by then."

"Hey, Harry, you said a month. One month, Harry. *Remember?*"

"A month, two months. What difference does it make?"

"Goddammit, it makes a lot of difference. These friends that gave me the money, I promised them it'd only be for a month. They did me a real favor, and I got to honor it. Don't you read the fucking newspapers, for Christ's sake? Money's never been tighter. Double-digit inflation, all that shit. They could of done a lot of other things with the money besides doing me this favor, like they did."

"Look," Fowler said, "if worse comes to worst, I'll see the association gets a letter of intent from the agency that it's backing the synagogue for a center. It's as good as gold. You should be able to get a short-term loan just like that."

"How long does the letter take?"

"I don't know. A couple of weeks."

"You're positive?"

"Richie, I want this to go through as fast as you do."

"Yeah, but you don't have the responsibility about the money."

"You think I'm not taking risks?" Fowler's voice had a brusque, challenging tone. "Maybe we ought to forget about this right now."

Flynn thought about the nearly two million dollars at stake. "Harry," he said, "I only wanted to know where we are, is all."

Fowler seemed mollified. He handed Flynn a manila envelope. "Just sign these forms where I made a check mark. I'll fill in the rest. Can you see? You have enough light from that lamp over there?"

"Yeah," Flynn said. "What are they?"

"They show you're now the owner of record for the synagogue and that it's available for a center. They go in with the application and the incorporation papers from the block association."

After Flynn had signed the forms, Fowler said, "There's one more thing. We have to do something for Willie."

"Who's Willie?"

"Willie Townsend. He's the secretary for the association. He's my boy. The association's driving spirit, as we say. We must present him with a token of our esteem. Keep him interested."

"What would interest him?"

"I'd say a thousand."

"No way, Harry. I tried to tell you before. A nigger ripped me off at the auction bidding on the synagogue. It probably was Willie. Between him boosting the price and me buying him off, it cost more than a thousand right there. Willie's going to have to get his at the other end."

"Well, he has to get something."

"Two-fifty. That's all. The rest he gets later."

Fowler sighed and said, "So be it. I'll explain to Willie that he can expect further enrichment."

"You do that, Harry." Flynn gave him the cash as they walked out of the park together and said good night.

"I'll be in touch," Fowler said. "Remember. Don't call me at the office. And stop worrying. You worry too much."

That's funny, Flynn thought. Only yesterday he was thinking the same thing about Fowler.

When Flynn returned home, he found that Agnes had prepared one of his favorite meals—baked ham with macaroni and cheese. She fluttered solicitously around him. Finally she said, "How do you like it?"

"You know I like it."

"Not the dinner, silly. This!" She pointed at the blue sweater and skirt she was wearing. "Honestly, you never notice anything. The sweater's cashmere. It was on sale. I bought it with the track money. Well?"

"It looks great," Flynn said, his mouth full of ham. Then, as soon as their son had returned to the television set, he told her, "Listen, I'm sorry about last night. There wasn't anything I could do."

"It's all right," she said. "I know. Business is business."

10

⋆

Flynn spent the following day checking some neglected accounts. In the afternoon he was at the Café Rhinelander, an old German-American restaurant near Grand Central Terminal, having a beer with the owner, when it happened. "Jesus, Hans," he had just said, "this is one nice place you have."

"I don't know how long I can hold on to it, Richie," the owner replied, "with these fast-food joints springing up. All the overhead. Only yesterday I had to pay my insurance. You don't know what it costs these days."

Flynn started to choke on his beer. In twenty-four hours he had to make his first payment to Karpstein, and he had forgotten completely about the change in his life insurance policy that Karpstein had demanded as security for the loan. Karpstein had given him a card with the new beneficiary's name on it. Then he remembered. It was Weissberg. Leo Weissberg.

"I got to make a call," Flynn told the owner, and rushed to the telephone. Flynn's insurance broker was Brian Madden. He had gone to school with Madden at Cardinal Hayes. Insurance brokers had it made, Flynn once concluded. All they had to do was to go to school and they had a built-in clientele. Every graduating class in America must have contained at least one embryonic insurance broker.

"Richie, how are you? How's Agnes? The boy?" Madden's voice boomed so heartily over the phone that Flynn had to hold the receiver away from his ear.

My God, Flynn thought, the dumb son of a bitch was probably figuring that he had called to take out more insurance. "Listen, Brian," he said, "I want to add a beneficiary to my policy, for half. What do I have to do? Is it a big hassle, or what?"

Madden's voice lost some of its cheeriness. "No, it's easy enough. All you have to do is sign an amended form with the name and relationship of the co-beneficiary."

"But suppose he isn't related to me. Suppose he's just a friend."

"That's the relationship then. A friend. Richie, it's none of my business, but are you sure you know what you're doing? Actually, I've been meaning to call you. What you should be doing is taking out additional coverage. I mean, you do want to protect Agnes and the boy, don't you?"

Flynn suddenly pictured Madden and Agnes hunched over cups of coffee, discussing the change in the policy.

"Brian, I do know what I'm doing. It's part of a deal I'm in. I can't go into the details. But, uh, the thing is that in a month or so I was intending to increase my insurance substantially. I'm glad you mentioned it."

Madden's voice became warm, understanding. "That's wonderful, Richie. It's the right thing. Shall we set a date?"

"I can't now. You call me a month from today. At the office."

"I will, Richie. And in the meantime, I'll mail you an amended form for you to sign."

"No," Flynn said, "I can't wait. I'll come over to your place right now. I sign it, and that's it, right?"

"Well, it's not quite that simple. It has to go to the company headquarters up in Connecticut, in Hartford, to be endorsed. Put in the computer and all that before it's valid."

Flynn felt his stomach turn over. "Brian," he said, "this really has got to be done fast. I'll be right over."

☆

At three P.M. on the Thursday after he had met Karpstein, Flynn parked his Volkswagen in front of E-Z Trucking, Inc. He was astonished to see how commonplace the building looked in the daylight after the terrifying night he had experienced during his first visit to it. When he rang the buzzer, the door was opened by a diminutive bald-headed man who was wearing black cotton sleeve protectors. Flynn judged him to be in his fifties.

"Is Mr. Karpstein in?" Flynn asked.

"Who wants to know?"

"Richie Flynn. I'm supposed to see him today."

"Oh, yes, come in," the little man said in a squeaky voice. "Albert's not here. He had to go out." The man extended his hand and said, "Weissberg." He led Flynn to a desk opposite the one Karpstein had occupied. A radio on the desk was playing music. Weissberg hummed along with it. Flynn could make out the sounds of a cello and a flute, but he did not know the music.

He glanced at the pool table where he had played Biondo. "I brought something for Mr. Karpstein," he said. "I guess I can leave it with you."

"Oh, yes," Weissberg said in the same squeaky voice.

It seemed incongruous that he would be working for Karpstein. Weissberg, in fact, had been doing time in prison as a child molester when Karpstein first met him. But he was very good at keeping coded account books and was closemouthed, and that was all Karpstein cared about. It had been Karpstein's wife, Angelina, who had objected to Weissberg. "Honey, how can you have someone around you who did what he did?" she had asked, and Karpstein said, "How's a man going to straighten out if he don't have a job?"

Flynn stood by Weissberg and said, "Five hundred, right?"

"Yes," Weissberg replied, reaching for a ledger, opening it and making some notations. He was still humming. "Beautiful, isn't it?"

"What?" Flynn said.

"That's the *Brandenburg Concerto,* number two. In F major. Ah, Bach. What a man he was. Did you know that he sired twenty children?"

"Is that a fact?"

"Oh, yes," Weissberg said. He took the five hundred dollars, counted the bills and put them in a strongbox that was on the desk next to the radio. When he raised the top of the box, Flynn could see that it was filled with cash.

Weissberg cocked his head expectantly at Flynn.

"Uh, listen, will you explain something to Mr. Karpstein for me?" Flynn said. "I was supposed to bring my insurance policy here with you as a beneficiary. I already started it, but it takes time. It's got to be mailed to Hartford, up in Connecticut, first, that's where the company is, to get an OK. Will you please explain that to Mr. Karpstein?"

Weissberg studied him with mournful eyes. "Oh, yes," he said, "I'll tell him."

"Tell him I'm real sorry and that they promised I'd

have it in a few days." Flynn felt the sweat start to form under his arms again. "Well, so long." As he turned to go, he looked at all the cash in the strongbox and wondered how Karpstein could leave it there like that with only Weissberg to guard it. Then he heard a toilet flush, and a door in the rear of the room opened, and the man with the boils, Patsy, who had picked Flynn up at the Stage Delicatessen, stepped out. He was holding a magazine in his hand. He was coatless and had on a shoulder holster with a pistol in it. He stared at Flynn without a flicker of recognition, as if Flynn were just another anonymous insect that had ventured in.

☆

The following day, Friday, Flynn attended a conference of Goldblatt sales supervisors. The big national breweries, Schlitz, Anheuser-Busch and Miller, were mounting aggressive new promotional campaigns in a struggle among themselves for a larger share of the market. "We're the little guys," the executive vice-president was saying, "so we've got to be on our toes more than ever." In 1965, he pointed out, there were one hundred and eighteen breweries operating in the country. Now there were only fifty-four. To protect itself, Goldblatt was about to introduce a new eight-ounce bottle. It was going to be called the Quick Quencher. "We're going to push it on TV, radio and in the papers," the executive vice-president said. "But we can't compete with the big guys dollar for dollar. That means we all have to work harder. We're going to have to go out into the supermarkets, the taverns, the restaurants—and press the flesh!"

The conference lasted until late afternoon, and when Flynn got back to his desk, the secretary who took messages for him said, "Gee, Mr. Flynn, I hope I did the right thing."

"What's that, Roselyn?" he said absently, going through some marketing reports on his desk.

"This man has been calling you. He said his name was Albert. That's all he would say. He said he wanted to talk to you, and I told him that you were tied up in a meeting and couldn't be disturbed, and the last time he called he said that if you didn't talk to him, he would come down here and disturb you good. So I hung up on him. He sounded like some kind of a nut, but he didn't sound very nice either, Mr. Flynn. I hope nothing's wrong."

The reports had slipped out of Flynn's hands. He closed his eyes and inhaled deeply, trying to compose himself, and then he said, "No, it's OK. Don't worry about it." He stood up, holding himself very straight. "Listen, I have to go out for a second. I'll be back in about twenty minutes."

Flynn walked stiffly to the elevators. At the newsstand in the lobby he bought a package of gum with a five-dollar bill and asked for the change in coins. He wanted a drink, but he was afraid that Karpstein meant what he had said to the secretary and might already be on his way. He went to a telephone booth on the corner, took out the card that Karpstein had given him with Weissberg's name and the address and number of E-Z Trucking.

"Yeah?" a voice said.

Flynn recognized it as belonging to the loan shark himself. "Mr. Karpstein," he said, "this is Richie Flynn. Is something wrong?"

Karpstein's voice immediately rose. "You bet your fucking ass there is. Flynn, you ain't showing respect."

"I don't understand."

"We had an agreement, Flynn. I told you to bring that fucking policy with you when you came in. I tell you to do something, you do it."

"But I told Mr. Weissberg that the change in the beneficiary had to be mailed to Hartford, to the company, to be, you know, validated. Didn't he tell you? You know what the mail's like."

"Fuck the mail!" Karpstein screamed. "You crippled? You can't drive? You can't drive up to Hartford, so you can honor your agreement? Hartford's on the fucking moon, or something?"

"I'm sorry, Mr. Karpstein. They said I'd have it by Thursday. I'll bring it on Thursday, I swear."

"You better, Flynn. You don't, your fucking ass is in a sling."

Karpstein slammed down the phone. Flynn listened to the reverberation. He held the receiver for a moment before hanging it up. It was then that he began to wish that he had never met Harry Fowler or ever heard of a daycare center. But it was too late now.

He put a dime into the slot and dialed the number of his insurance agent. "Is Mr. Madden in?"

"No," the secretary said. "He's gone for the weekend. Can I help you?"

"Well, this is Richie Flynn. Remember I was in on Wednesday to make a change in my policy? I was just wondering if it went out and everything."

"Yes, Mr. Flynn, I believe it was mailed on Thursday morning."

"Thank God," he blurted. "Listen, will you tell Brian I called, and I'll call him Monday."

After Flynn hung up again, he did not return to the office. Instead, he drove uptown to the Liffey Bar & Grill in Inwood, hoping to bump into his friend Scanlon, or the old man MacShane, or somebody from his past. But when he walked in, he did not recognize anyone. Cummins the bartender told him that all the regulars were at the hospital visiting Billy McKeon, the Afghan Kid. "Billy's taken a terrible turn for the worse. I think his time has come. Have a drink."

Flynn and Cummins drank to Billy McKeon. Flynn had four more scotches. By the fifth drink, as he brooded over the conversation with Karpstein, he began to get indignant. It was not his fault that the insurance company had these regulations, and he would tell that to Karpstein, to his face, when he saw him.

But all of Flynn's drunken bravado disappeared when he arrived home and Agnes said to him, "A man named Albert called here two or three times today. I asked him Albert who? And he said you would know. He said he had been looking everywhere for you and to call him right away."

"It's all right," Flynn said in a thin voice. "He got me at the office."

"But what does he want? He said something funny. He said he knew we had a boy, and he asked how Sean was. Why would he say something like that?"

"I don't know," Flynn said. He suddenly felt very tired. "I meet these crazies all the times. He wanted to know how I thought the Giants would do this fall, that's all."

11

═══☆═══

The New York office of the Federal Bureau of Investigation occupied the top nine floors of a converted warehouse on Third Avenue between Sixty-ninth and Seventieth streets in Manhattan. As if to disguise this, the building's ground floor featured a shoe emporium and a discount drugstore. Another tenant in the building was the New York Telephone Company, which presented an irony of sorts, since the FBI office included its Surveillance Technical Room, where most locally implanted wiretaps and electronic listening devices, both legal and illegal, were monitored. The room looked like the work area of a shop that sold stereo and hi-fi equipment, but it was the most sacrosanct part of the office, actually a room within a room within a room, like Chinese nesting boxes. No one but special personnel was allowed entry to it.

And on this same Friday afternoon the room, at least tangentially, was the subject of a discussion between an assistant director of the FBI, who was also the head of the New York office, and the special agent in charge of the Organized Crime Division. The assistant director was Kevin McGrath. He was sixty-one years old and had been in the FBI for his entire professional life. Behind his back he was called Cement Head by his subordinates. This had nothing to do with his innate intelligence, for he was widely regarded as a canny and resourceful administrator. He had got the nickname in the 1930s, when he was still an energetic FBI recruit. It was a time when J. Edgar Hoover, intent on creating a national reputation, was constantly photographed personally arresting the country's most wanted gangsters. These arrests were, of course, carefully orchestrated in advance. But once, when Hoover flew in from Washington to apprehend a leading bank robber who was holed up in a Midwestern boarding house, the robber obstinately refused to come out. Hoover was warned that the man might have a gun, and he was quite annoyed. At that moment young McGrath lowered his head and used it as a battering ram to knock down the door. A few minutes later, blood trickling down the side of his face, he beckoned Hoover inside, and the director shortly thereafter emerged, amid popping flashbulbs, clutching the robber by the collar. As it turned out, the bank robber did not have a gun. With all the commotion, he had been afraid that he would be mowed down as soon as he showed his face. Hoover immediately recognized that McGrath was a man to be valued, not because of his bravery in knocking down the door, but for his good sense in not reappearing with the robber in tow, and from that point on McGrath's star rose steadily in the ranks of the FBI until he had reached his current status in the New York office, which was the most important post that an agent could aspire to outside of SOG, or the Seat of Government, as Washington was referred to in FBI memos.

An inscribed portrait of Hoover, framed in sterling silver, stared balefully at McGrath and his Organized Crime Division chief, Barney Barnett. If the old man had still been alive, they would not be having this conversation, and both of them knew it.

Several years before, Barnett had been assigned to squire Hoover's public relations man around preparatory to a speech the director was to deliver at the Waldorf-Astoria Hotel. After a long session with the hotel engineer trying to figure out the proper amount of air conditioning needed to maintain a temperature of seventy-two degrees, which the director insisted upon, in a grand ballroom with eleven hundred bodies in attendance, the public relations man had said, "OK. I guess that's it. Let's have a drink." Suddenly he said, "Oh, Christ, I forgot the television. The director's got this thing about television. The sound *and* the picture have to go on at the same time."

The set in Hoover's suite, as it happened, was black and white, so the audio and visual portions came up almost simultaneously, and the public relations man breathed a sigh of relief. Later, after his third drink, he told Barnett that the president of a big television manufacturer had once given Hoover the company's newest color console model. It had been wheeled into the director's office. He tried the automatic control. The sound came on at once, but it took twenty-six seconds for the picture to appear. The set was sent down to the FBI's electronics laboratory, possibly the most advanced in the world, where for nearly three weeks it was labored over. The best the technicians could do was reduce the time lag to nine seconds. That was not good enough. Finally a rheostat was inserted into the system to cut the current sufficiently to make it seem as though the set were off, but when Hoover pushed his remote-control button, image and sound leaped in obedient tandem to his eye and ear. The only trouble, the public relations man said, was that since the set was in fact running all the time, agents periodically had to sneak into the director's office at night to replace the high-voltage tubes.

When Barnett repeated the story to McGrath, they both treated it not in jest but in genuine awe of a man who could command such power without a moment's hesitation. And it was precisely the absence of this power that had landed them in their present quandary. The newly appointed special federal prosecutor in New York, Hamilton Wainwright IV, had requested that a listening device be placed in the Ravens Club, the Mafia social retreat on Mulberry Street. Prior to Hoover's demise, this kind of thing was routinely dispatched to Washington for the director's approval or, far more likely, his disapproval. Although the FBI was nominally part of the Department of Justice and Hoover himself theoretically under the attorney general, the director liked to conduct his own technical surveillance without anyone outside his domain knowing about it. Sometimes the existence of a particular device was never revealed, the information gathered from it squirreled away for whatever purposes Hoover deemed useful.

But Hoover was gone now, and the FBI was in considerable disarray. The new acting director was demonstrably weak, and a fierce struggle was already under way to see who would succeed him. For that matter the entire Nixon administration was wobbling toward extinction. And there were even some, including McGrath, who suspected that the mysterious source of so many leaks to the press about the Watergate break-in and cover-up was a high FBI official jockeying for position. Kevin McGrath coveted the directorship, and he had begun to think that it was within his reach if he played his cards correctly.

"What's with this Wainwright?" he said to Barnett. "What kind of a guy calls himself Ham anyway?"

"I guess he wants to be one of the boys," Barnett said. "All I know is they say he has a lot of clout, and politically he's going a long way. He's gung ho, that's for sure. You ought to see his office. He's got charts all over the walls with the mob families on them. And right behind his desk is the Donato family, with old Frank up on top. So help me, he has Frank's picture circled in red, and he's really pushing hard on the Ravens Club. Nothing in writing, of course."

"What do you think, Barney?"

"Well, first I told him, what the hell, the Ravens is a social club, and all they do there is sit around bullshitting about this and that, nothing of consequence. And then I said you put a bug in one of the tables in that big room, you're just going to get a whole lot of voices, nothing clear, and you got to put a booster someplace close outside in a firebox or like that, and because it's on a radio frequency, you have to have your recording equipment nearby, and how are you going to pull it off in a neighborhood like Mulberry Street without somebody spotting you?"

"Barney," McGrath said, "I didn't ask you what you told him. I asked you what you think."

"Is this official?"

"Barney, for Christ's sake!"

"All right, I think we ought to do something to show Wainwright we're cooperating. There's a little room in the back of the Ravens for private sit-downs, and a phone is in there. The phone is only for outgoing calls. The members don't even know what the number is, and they're very cagey when they call out. My people tell me there's a new gizmo you can put in the box the line goes through that looks just like part of the regular equipment, that a guy from the telephone company couldn't tell the difference. The beauty of it is that it picks up what's said in the room, and it goes out on the wire, so we can take it down right here, but if somebody picks up the receiver to make a call, we can always swear there wasn't a tap because it doesn't transmit the other end of the conversation."

"That's good," McGrath said. The law never quite caught up with technology. Under existing regulations a federal wiretap had to be authorized by a judge. A listening device, on the other hand, required nothing more than the director's approval and authorization from the attorney general. In Hoover's day, more often than not, the latter step was skipped, and the information that the device pro-

duced was ascribed to an informant "known to be reliable
in the past."

"Wainwright doesn't care whether it's legal," Barnett
said. "He just wants the intelligence. The problem is getting inside. Nobody's ever cracked the Ravens. Somebody's almost always around, but we think we've licked
that. They're so cocksure they haven't changed the alarm
system in twenty years. You have ten seconds or so before
it goes off, just enough to turn it off. You want to hear the
plan?"

"No," McGrath said, glancing sideways at the portrait
of the late director. "I'll take your word for it. You tell
Wainwright personally that we're doing him this favor,
and I expect to be remembered for it."

☆

At six A.M. on the Monday after the meeting between
McGrath and Barnett, a blue van with a sign that said
Acme Delivery pulled up by a garage adjacent to the
Ravens Club. Three FBI agents disguised as truckers
hopped out, unloaded several large cartons labeled "Auto
Parts" on the sidewalk and then left in the van.

One of the cartons had been placed directly in front of
the darkened entrance to the club. A hand reached out
through a moveable flap on the side of the carton closest to
the door and took wax impressions of the door's two locks.

Fifteen minutes later the van reappeared. At this hour
Mulberry Street was deserted except for other trucks and
vans making early-morning deliveries to the various
specialty shops, markets and restaurants that lined it.
There were also private carting trucks collecting refuse
from these businesses, and to the casual observer it was
difficult to distinguish between what was being delivered
and what was being picked up.

The carton with the agent hidden inside was quickly re-
loaded along with the other cartons, and the blue van
drove off once more in the dim dawn light.

12

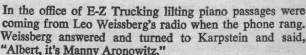

In the office of E-Z Trucking lilting piano passages were coming from Leo Weissberg's radio when the phone rang. Weissberg answered and turned to Karpstein and said, "Albert, it's Manny Aronowitz."

Aronowitz was Joe Hobo's accountant. Karpstein took the call. As he listened, his eyes began to dilate. After a moment he said, "What about that other guy, Landers?" and then, "Well, that's something anyway. Thanks for nothing, Manny. I'll take care of it."

Karpstein slammed down the receiver and summoned Tommy Biondo from the hot plate where he was making coffee. "All I get is aggravation," he said. "That fat fuck Mandelbaum, his check bounced."

Biondo ran his tongue nervously over his lips, as if he were somehow going to be blamed. "Jeez, Albert, you did everything you could. I mean, you certainly gave him the message you weren't kidding."

"Some people," Karpstein said, "you stick their heads in a bucket of water, they don't think they're drowning because their feet ain't wet." He paused, as though savoring the image of Mandelbaum thus immersed.

"Jeez," Biondo said, "what do we do now?"

"We whack him out, that's what," Karpstein said. "We are going to bury that dirty scumbag once and for all. I am through fucking with him."

"But the money, Albert. How you going to get the money then? You can't squeeze blood out of a stone."

"The house, stupid. He signed over the house, didn't he? His own lawyer witnessed it. That shyster pissant ain't going to fuck with me, he knows what's good for him. What's his name? Leo, give me that paper that Mandelbaum signed."

"Oh, yes, Albert," Weissberg said, digging into a folder, extracting a piece of paper and scurrying over to Karpstein with it.

Karpstein looked at it and said, "Yeah, Lawrence Farber. OK. Tommy, here's the address of Mandelbaum's house in Pelham Manor. You get over there now and scout around. Get the lay of the land and call me back."

After Biondo had left, Karpstein leaned back, relaxed, his eyes hooded. "Hey, Leo, what's that you got on the radio?" he said. "It's nice."

"That's Beethoven's *Sonata in C Minor*, Albert. Opus ten. Number one. He was twenty-six when he wrote it. Only twenty-six and already a genius."

An hour and a half later Biondo telephoned excitedly. "Albert, Mandelbaum flew the coop. There's a real estate sign and everything on the lawn that says the house is for sale."

"You got the number?"

"I got it right here," Biondo said. "I knew you'd want it."

Karpstein grunted, hung up and then called the real estate office. "This is Mr. Rocco," he said. "I'm interested in that Mandelbaum house you got on the market in Pelham Manor. What's he asking for it?"

"Let's see," the broker replied. "Yes, here it is. One hundred twenty-five thousand. Nine rooms, full basement, two-car garage. Would you like to make an appointment to inspect it?"

"No," Karpstein said. "I already been in it. I'm acquainted with Mr. Mandelbaum. When can him and me get together?"

"I'm afraid that's impossible. Mrs. Mandelbaum and their daughter are on a European tour, and Mr. Mandelbaum's off on a business trip for several weeks. Mr. Mandelbaum's attorney has been empowered to act for him."

"That wouldn't be Farber?"

"Yes, that's right. Do you know Mr. Farber?"

"No, but I heard Mandelbaum talk about him. I'll get back to you in a couple of days, and we'll set something up."

"I wouldn't put it off," the broker said. "We've gotten quite a few nibbles."

"I can believe it," Karpstein said.

Karpstein was chewing thoughtfully on a Milky Way when Biondo returned. "Listen," Karpstein said, "that's bullshit about Mandelbaum being away. I don't know about his old lady, but he's got to be around. He's got too many deals going. This Farber's the connection. Tommy, you take Patsy and go into the city and hang around Farber's office until Mandelbaum shows up. Then tail him. Find out his movements, where he's staying."

"Where's Farber's office?"

"How should I know? He's a fucking lawyer, ain't he? Look him up in the phone book."

"Right, Albert. I'll call you."

Karpstein had no doubt that he would locate Mandelbaum. If not today, tomorrow, the day after tomorrow. He had been vaguely surprised when Joe Hobo's accountant told him that the check had bounced. He had thought that the beating he had administered would be enough. But it had not been, and that was that. Others in Karpstein's position might have tried to contact Mandelbaum again, threatened him once more. And Mandelbaum would have endless excuses. He would say that he was selling his house to pay off the debt. Karpstein, however, no longer cared what Mandelbaum said. All his mindless predatory instincts, like those of a great shark homing in gape-mouthed on its quarry, had been set into motion. If Mandelbaum had walked into Karpstein's office at that moment with the money, it would have been too late. Mandelbaum had not shown respect.

"That fat bastard is dead," Karpstein muttered.

"I beg your pardon, Albert?" Weissberg said.

Karpstein shook his head and blinked. "Forget it," he said. He got up from his desk and walked restlessly around the room. "Leo, let's go over the books."

At eight o'clock in the evening Biondo telephoned Karpstein at home. "Jeez, Albert, you'll never guess where we are."

"What is this, Twenty Questions?"

"Hey, Albert, that's pretty good. Anyway, where we are is Huntington Station, Long Island. You were right. Mandelbaum showed at the lawyer's about four o'clock. He was in there maybe twenty minutes, and he come out, and he went to this garage and got in his car. It's a good thing Patsy was in our car, else I would of lost him. We followed him out on the Long Island Expressway. It's only thirty, forty miles, but it took two hours almost. Jeez, you should of seen the traffic. He's in this house. His old lady is with him. Also the kid. She's about sixteen. Nice knockers. You want me and Patsy should go in and whack him now?"

"No. Check into a motel, and pick him up in the morning and see what he does."

"Uh, Albert, Roosevelt Raceway ain't so far from here. You know, trotters. We could catch the last four or five races. Is it OK if me and Patsy go?"

"I don't care what you do," Karpstein said. "Just pick that fuck up in the morning."

☆

All through the weekend, after Karpstein's tirade over the insurance policy, Richie Flynn's anxiety mounted, and on Monday morning he called his insurance broker, Brian Madden. "Listen, Brian, I know the amendment to the policy went out already, but you know what the mail's like. I need that form. If I went up to Hartford, I could get it myself, couldn't I? I mean, they'd give it to me, right? You could make a call or something."

"Richie, I wouldn't know who to call. I've only been up there once myself for a seminar. That place is like the Pentagon. They must have five thousand people working there. I can't understand what your problem is. You signed the form, and I witnessed it. That's all you need. If something, ah, untimely happened to you before we received the endorsement, I'm positive the company would honor the change. You can tell the new beneficiary I said so."

Flynn tried to imagine himself standing before Albert Karpstein, invoking Madden. "Brian," he said, "if I did go up, where would I go when I got there?"

"I honestly don't know. The legal department, I suppose. Or the benefits department. Probably the benefits department."

After he hung up, Flynn decided that Madden was right, that it was ridiculous to go to Hartford for the form. During the day, however, the specter of Karpstein remained with him, and in the afternoon, having visited a half dozen retail outlets on behalf of Goldblatt's Quick Quencher, he knew that he would go after all. He telephoned Diane and canceled their date for the evening. "It's because of this deal I was telling you about," he said. "I have to go out of the city."

"Oh, honey, I miss you so much. I was counting on seeing you."

"Me too," he said. "Listen, when this thing is over, we'll have all the time we want. Believe me."

Then he got in touch with Agnes and told her that he would be in Hartford for the night, and she said incredulously, "Hartford?"

"It's the new bottle Goldblatt's pushing," he said. "They want me up there because one of the local TV stations carries all the Giant games. I'll call you."

It was dark when he reached the outskirts of Hartford and stopped at a motel. He telephoned Agnes, making the call collect, so that when she asked where it was coming from, the operator would confirm his presence in Hartford.

In the morning he parked near the headquarters of the insurance company and watched as hundreds of employees, most of them young women, streamed through its colonnaded portals. He followed them across a great hall with a marble floor and at the reception desk asked to see someone from the benefits department.

"If you're interested in a policy," the receptionist said, "you should see one of our authorized agents. They're listed in the yellow pages."

"I have a policy. That's why I want to see somebody from the benefits department."

"Well, in that case, if there's a problem, you should see your own broker."

"Lady," Flynn said, "that's why I'm here. I have a particular problem, and my broker suggested that I come here and personally talk to somebody in the benefits department."

"Did he give you the name of anyone in the department?"

"No, he didn't." Flynn tried to keep his irritation from showing. Out of the corner of his eye, he saw a uniformed security guard staring at him. "He just said somebody. I mean, *somebody's* up there, right?"

"Please take a seat."

Flynn walked over to a bench, which reminded him of the pew he used to squirm in as a little boy at Good Shepherd Church. A big circular bronze plaque was set into the marble floor. In raised letters around the perimeter of the plaque was the company's slogan, "People Are Our Business," and in the center was its familiar emblem of two disembodied, clasping hands.

After half an hour he saw a slender man wearing tortoiseshell glasses and a gray suit emerge from an elevator and go to the receptionist. The receptionist pointed at Flynn, and the man in the gray suit approached him.

"My name's Sturgis," he said. "I'm in the benefits department. Can I help you?"

Flynn introduced himself and gave his policy number and explained why he was there. "I need a copy of the endorsed change of beneficiary real bad," he said.

"But, Mr. Flynn, it's really not necessary as long as you signed the form and your broker witnessed it. The company will certainly meet its responsibility to the co-beneficiary if, ah—"

"I know that," Flynn interrupted. "It's just that I have to have a copy of it. It's part of this deal I'm in."

"If the form was mailed from New York when you said it was, I would imagine it's being processed right now."

"So I can get it?"

"No, that's the trouble. Thousands of these things come in every day. We service the entire country. The form could be at any one of a hundred, a hundred and fifty desks, even as we speak." Sturgis took off his glasses and wiped them nervously. "You don't know what it's like up there."

"You mean you can't find me? I don't exist here?"

"Of course you exist. You're in our computer banks in the files department."

"But, Jesus, what do you do when someone like me comes in?" Flynn said. "Your commercials all say you're in the people business. I'm people, aren't I?"

Sturgis adjusted his glasses. "Mr. Flynn," he said, "I've been with the company for nine years, five in the benefits department, and to my knowledge you are the first person ever to make this kind of request. We're simply not geared for it."

"But this is a matter of life and death."

"Most of our policies are," Sturgis said.

"Look, could you just find out if it's already gone through? Could you please do that for me?"

Sturgis sighed and said, "All right, I'll see what I can do."

Another hour went by before the receptionist summoned Flynn and handed him her phone, and Sturgis said, "Mr. Flynn, I'm sorry. We haven't been able to track it down. It's in the systems flow, as I explained. Perhaps if you returned tomorrow."

"I can't," Flynn blurted. "I'm in the middle of a new sales campaign, and I have to get back to New York."

"Really, I think that's best. A great deal of effort has

gone into our programming to make it as efficient as possible, I assure you."

"Yeah," Flynn said, "we don't want to upset any of the robots, do we? The hell with people."

"Good day, Mr. Flynn," Sturgis said, and hung up.

☆

In the New York office of the FBI, duplicate keys to the Ravens Club had been fashioned from the wax impressions that were taken of the club's door locks, and it was decided to go ahead with the actual installation of a listening device, using the same procedure that had been successful in obtaining the impressions two days earlier.

So just before sunrise on Wednesday special agent Peter Doyle, posing as a vagrant, walked to a pay phone off Mulberry Street and reported that the Ravens Club had shut down for the night. Ten minutes later a blue van once again stopped by the garage next to the club. This time, however, after unloading the cartons as before, the agents dressed as workmen lolled against the van, ostensibly taking a coffee break, in case something went wrong.

An agent inside the carton that had been set down in front of the club's door inserted keys in both locks and turned them. Then Doyle came back down Mulberry Street, still an apparent vagrant wandering aimlessly along the sidewalk. When Doyle got to the carton with the agent inside, he ducked quickly past it and pushed open the door. The alarm in the Ravens Club was an old-fashioned kind that many shopkeepers in the area used; unlike more modern alarms that sent a silent signal to a security office, it had a siren that did not sound until approximately ten seconds after the door was opened, which enabled a shopkeeper to enter and switch it off before rousing the whole neighborhood. The trick for someone breaking in, of course, was to know where the switch was.

According to an FBI informant, the alarm switch in the Ravens Club was behind the counter under the big espresso coffee machine, and guided by his penlight, Doyle found it without difficulty and flipped it off.

Then he hurried into the club's back room, located the connecting block on a baseboard where the cable from the telephone went and removed it. Inside was a gray plastic housing that contained the phone's circuitry. Doyle unscrewed the housing and replaced it with one that seemed identical, except that it was also a powerful miniature microphone with two pinholes invisible to the eye. It used the telephone's wiring to transmit conversations, and it was impervious to any detection methods known to be on the market. The microphone was a product of space-age technology; every time Doyle watched a rocket launch on television, he wondered not what secrets of the universe might be uncovered, but what new, even more sophisticated listening devices would result.

When he finished, Doyle slipped outside and continued shuffling down Mulberry Street. The agent inside the carton relocked the door. The other agents put all the cartons back into the van and departed. The entire operation had taken less than half an hour, and from then on any verbal exchanges that occurred in the rear of the Ravens Club went over a leased line directly to the Surveillance Technical Room in the FBI field office at Third Avenue and Sixty-ninth Street.

☆

That same morning Karpstein was driven to Huntington Station by Tommy Biondo. The day before, Biondo reported, Mandelbaum had left the house he was staying in at about ten-thirty A.M. and taken the Long Island Expressway into New York. His movements in the city had been erratic. He had not remained in any one place after garaging his car.

Karpstein liked to track a victim before striking. It was an aspect of the hunt that he particularly enjoyed, which was why he was journeying to Long Island at such an early hour. Mandelbaum's new residence was on a tree-lined street featuring ranch houses, and after looking it over, Karpstein decided that it was not a suitable spot for an execution. There were too many picture windows around, too many chances that somebody might glance out of one of them at the wrong moment.

Mandelbaum walked out of his house and got into his car at precisely ten-thirty. Parked forty yards away, sitting next to Biondo, Karpstein felt a surge of pleasure wash over him as he observed the unsuspecting fat man with his dainty steps.

Mandelbaum went down a road with a number of stoplights and turned toward the expressway, Karpstein's Buick behind him. The morning rush-hour traffic had tapered off. The access lane ran along the expressway up an incline. Near the brow of the hill Mandelbaum's car, a gleaming white Lincoln Continental, gathered speed and moved onto the expressway proper. Off to the right was an embankment. Karpstein noted this and continued to survey the terrain as Mandelbaum headed for New York, driving fast, aggressively weaving in and out of the traffic. Once in the city, Karpstein instructed Biondo to keep tailing Mandelbaum and took a taxi to Hoboken.

The next morning Karpstein again traveled to Huntington Station with Biondo, this time in a Chevrolet that Biondo had stolen at his order during the night. Mandelbaum retraced his route toward the city, and as he started up the access to the expressway, Karpstein directed Biondo to pull out immediately onto the adjacent through lane. There was a squeal of tires as a driver coming along the expressway put on his brakes. "Fuck you," Biondo muttered.

Now Biondo was abreast of Mandelbaum. "Stay with him," Karpstein said, holding a .38-caliber automatic in his right hand, shifting his bulk so that he was facing Mandelbaum's car.

Mandelbaum increased his speed, trying to beat Biondo to the point where the access lane merged into the expressway. Finally, indignantly, Marvin Mandelbaum turned his head to see who was racing alongside him, impeding his way.

That was what Karpstein wanted. Karpstein wanted Mandelbaum to know what was about to happen to him. And for a fraction of a second their eyes met. Mandelbaum's mouth opened. Then Karpstein squeezed the trigger. Blood spurted from Mandelbaum's forehead. The Lincoln bounced off the guardrail, whipped around, jumped over the railing and careened down the embankment.

Biondo automatically pressed the accelerator. "Stop the car!" Karpstein shouted, and Biondo obediently swerved to a halt on the expressway shoulder, jerking them both forward. Karpstein got out of the stolen Chevrolet, stepped over the guardrail and peered down at Mandelbaum's car. It was about seventy feet below him, upright in a field.

Karpstein had hoped it might burst into flames, but apparently that occurred only in the movies.

He strode toward the Lincoln. Unlike most killers, he was concerned not with getting away but with making certain that the job had been done, that Mandelbaum was dead. Karpstein feared nothing, and his instinct was always to do the unexpected, to keep everyone off balance.

When Karpstein got to the car, he saw Mandelbaum drooping sideways behind the wheel, held by his safety belt. Mandelbaum's eyes were open, staring sightlessly at the dashboard. The blood from the bullet hole in his forehead had already begun to congeal. Karpstein forced the door and leaned inside. He shoved a fist into Mandelbaum's body. It flopped inertly. Satisfied that Mandelbaum was dead, Karpstein spit in his face.

Karpstein shut the door. He looked up toward the expressway. Several motorists, having stopped their automobiles after Mandelbaum's Lincoln had jumped the guardrail, were gazing down at Karpstein in admiration of someone who had rushed to the aid of a fellow human in distress. Karpstein raised his hands at them, palms up, and shrugged, and trudged back to where Biondo was parked.

"Jeez, Albert, how'd it go?" Biondo asked.

"It went good. That fuck has gone." In the distance a siren could be heard. "Let's get out of here," Karpstein said. He reached into his pocket for a Milky Way, unwrapped it and began to chew on the candy bar. "Hey, Tommy, you want one?"

"Thanks, Albert. No, thanks." It was the first time Karpstein had ever offered him a Milky Way. Biondo glanced at Karpstein and saw that he was smiling. It was also the first time that Biondo could ever remember Karpstein smiling.

☆

Three times on Thursday morning Richie Flynn called his insurance broker to see if a copy of the amended beneficiary form had arrived from Hartford. Each time the secretary had said, "I'm sorry."

At noon Flynn gave up. He got into his Volkswagen and drove to Hoboken. He stood in terror outside the office of E-Z Trucking.

He rehearsed his excuses once more and rang the buzzer.

Leo Weissberg opened the door.

"Uh," Flynn said, "is Mr. Karpstein here?"

"Come in," Weissberg said. "No, Albert isn't here. He had some business, but he should be back soon."

"Well, I came with the payment, you know. It's Thursday, right? The trouble is, though, that the form didn't come yet from the insurance company. I even drove up to Hartford to get it, but it was still being processed, they said. It was still going through the, uh, computers, or whatever. Could you please explain to Mr. Karpstein that I did everything I could?"

Weissberg clucked sympathetically. "It's better you should tell Albert yourself," he said.

Flynn sat on the sofa by Karpstein's desk. He rubbed his hand nervously on his chin. He could feel the sweat bead under his arms. He watched Weissberg across the room, bent over his ledger, humming softly to violin music on his radio. Patsy, sporting a new set of angry boils, sat reading a newspaper on the other side of the pool table, his chair tilted against the wall.

An hour passed. Suddenly Karpstein burst into the room, Biondo behind him. Flynn immediately leaped to his feet. "Mr. Karpstein!" he said.

"Oh, yeah, Flynn," Karpstein said. He seemed surprised to find Flynn there. He had a sleepy-eyed look, as if he had just polished off an enormous meal. He actually appeared amiable, Flynn thought.

Flynn handed Karpstein five hundred dollars. "Listen," he said, "I've got to tell you something. I don't have the insurance form. I went to Hartford, like you said. But I couldn't get it. They said it was in the mail. It's signed and all. I waited all morning, but it didn't come."

Flynn flinched as Karpstein clapped his on the shoulder. "Don't worry about it," Karpstein said. "The mail's a mess. You'll bring it in the next time. The thing is you showed respect. There's a fat fuck I know wished he'd showed some respect."

Then Flynn left Karpstein's office. He did not know whether to laugh or cry.

13

When the FBI's Barney Barnett informed the new special federal prosecutor that a bug had been placed in the Ravens Club, Wainwright leaned back in his chair and said, "That's nice."

Barnett waited for something more. But nothing was forthcoming. Barnett coughed nervously. Finally, not knowing what else to do, he got up to go. At the door he said, "I'll see you get the transcripts."

It was then that Wainwright flashed a disarming smile. "Tell Kevin," he said, "that I appreciate his cooperation."

After Barnett had left, Wainwright stretched his arms over his head and yawned complacently, thinking how things had changed. When Hoover was around, FBI officials like McGrath and Barnett would not have given him the time of day, but now that Big Daddy was dead, they did not know which way to turn.

He got up from his desk and stared out the window across the plaza at his cupolated arena, the United States Court House for the Southern District of New York.

He moved away from the window, picked up a feathered dart and hurled it at the dart board that his staff had given him the day before. In the bull's-eye was pasted the face of Frank Donato. The next ring featured the reputed heads of the four other Mafia crime families operating in the city, and the outer rings were dotted with various princelings, among them Vincente D'Angelo. As it happened, while aiming for Donato, Wainwright hit D'Angelo. His second attempt struck nobody. On his third throw, however, he pierced Donato's left cheek, and with a satisfied grunt he returned to his desk.

The dart board had been tendered to Wainwright during a surprise office party celebrating his thirty-fifth birthday. Much merriment had accompanied its unveiling. Glasses of scotch and white wine were raised and clinked, and Wainwright, sipping a Tab, had been smiling and joking along with everyone else when he suddenly stood up on a chair, and although his manner remained easygoing and affable, his voice had an edge to it. "I know that this dart board was meant as a gag, and I think it's terrific, and I thank you," he said. "But I think it's going to be more than a gag for us. It's going to be a measurement of our success, a success that won't be complete until each of the faces on this board has a dart in it delivered by a jury in court." He paused and smiled and then said, "A dart provided by us."

Wainwright's staff had fallen immediately silent when he began to speak. "Hear, hear," one of them called out after he had finished. It had all gone very well, he thought.

And now in his office, after Barnett had departed, Wainwright summoned Simonetta and told him that the bug was operating in the Ravens Club. "I still don't see what you expect to get out of it," Simonetta replied.

"I don't expect anything," he said. "It's a fishing expedition, if you like. That's all. But you can't tell what might turn up. The main thing, though, is to get McGrath and Barnett in the habit of doing what we want. Pavlov didn't use a dog, you know. Actually, it was an FBI agent."

Simonetta laughed. He glanced at the dart board on the wall. "I see you've been playing," he said. "Who hit Donato? You or Barnett?"

"As a matter of fact, I did, Nick, all by myself."

☆

The funny thing about Frank Donato was that he did not view being the head of a Mafia family as the high point of his career. He much preferred to think of himself as a sportsman, by which he meant a personage of serious business interests who had been successful enough to indulge in a number of leisure activities that were sporting in nature, such as betting large sums on baseball and football games, prizefights and horse races. He made these bets and played cards with close associates almost every afternoon in an apartment he had obtained for his mistress on Fifth Avenue with a splendid view of the Central Park Lake, the model boat basin, the Bethesda Fountain and the Sheep Meadow. Donato's mistress was a Scottish woman named Caroline McIlhenny, whom he affectionately called "Mac." She was fifty-five and had been his mistress for thirty-four years. He had met her, a vivacious redhead, during the 1939 New York World's Fair, where she worked as a guide in the British Pavilion. She then elected to remain in America because of the confluence of Donato in her life and the outbreak of war in Europe. She had two children by him, a boy and a girl, all of whose financial needs he had seen to and who, in their childhood, knew him as "Uncle Frank."

Despite his profound attachment to Caroline, Donato believed in the sanctity of a contract, and there was not a night when he was in the city that he did not at some hour return to the apartment, albeit to a separate bedroom, which he shared with his wife, Anna, on Central Park West. In this nightly act of contrition there was also a tinge of pity for the barren, unhappy Anna, who had been imported for him as a young bride from his ancestral Calabria nearly a half century ago, when such a union seemed of great importance, and who, even now, after all this time, had only the most halting command of English. He gave her a weekly allowance of seven hundred and fifty dollars in cash, most of which she forwarded to successive *parroci* of the church in her native village to dispense with in her name as they saw fit. Donato had often urged her to take a trip back there, but she always declined, pleading continual ill health.

The two apartments were directly opposite each other, a half mile apart, across the park. Once, years before, suspecting Caroline McIlhenny of infidelity, Donato bought a high-powered telescope and under the guise of a sudden interest in astronomy spied on her for nearly a week. His suspicions proved unfounded, and filled with remorse, he presented her with a ten-carat diamond ring and swore to himself never to allow such puerile behavior to get the better of him again.

Citizens all over the country, of course, bet on the outcome of football games. Frank Donato, however, seated in Caroline's apartment in his favorite overstuffed easy chair of green velvet, would wager on any number of them, not only on the final result but on what the various scores might be at the end of each quarter. It might appear paradoxical that a man who derived so much of his income from gambling, both legal and illegal, would gamble so heavily himself. But he loved the "action," as he put it, was quite good at it, being privy to an insider's information, and considered it a proper diversion for any gentleman who could afford it.

A lack of paradox, in fact, would have been the ultimate Donatoan contradiction. In a world where vendettas, with their attendant emotions, were the norm, he operated with utter dispassion. He had got into the entrepreneurial end of gambling around 1930, when he assumed citywide control of slot machines in New York. But Mayor Fiorello La Guardia, in a burst of fiery reformist zeal, had the machines banished from the city. Ironically, Donato had been one of La Guardia's earliest, although necessarily silent, backers, mostly out of ethnic pride at a time when the Irish dominated New York politics. When someone later reminded him of La Guardia's stab in the back, Donato just shrugged, drew thoughtfully on a cigarette and said, "Well, La Guardia wasn't so good for me. But what the hell, there's seven, eight million people in the city, and he was good for them. I think he's the best mayor the city ever had."

As it turned out, both Donato and his machines were almost immediately welcomed in Louisiana by the state's political boss, the Kingfish himself, Senator Huey Long. Many scholarly works tracing Long's career have focused on the sudden arrival on the scene of the notorious racketeer, more than once hinting that Donato was the conduit for the huge resources of an organized underworld which had decided that Long was its man.

But in a rare moment of reminiscence, celebrating their tenth year together, Donato told Caroline McIlhenny what had really happened. He had met Long, then Louisiana's governor, in the latter days of Prohibition at a private club on Long Island near where Donato's boats unloaded shipments of bootleg whiskey. Long had gone to the men's room and, taken by strong waters, accidentally sprayed Donato's close friend Matty (Mad Dog) Lanza, who was standing at the adjoining urinal. Long failed to apologize, and Lanza butted him against the tiled wall. Hearing the commotion, Long's own bodyguard, a Louisiana state trooper stationed outside the door, charged in to aid the Kingfish. Fortunately the men's room attendant located Donato in time; he succeeded in smoothing things over, and he and Long spent the rest of the evening swapping stories.

The two men continued to stay in sporadic contact, and

one day Donato received a call from Long, by then a United States senator with eyes on the presidency, requesting a great favor. He had, he said, been dallying on and off with a show girl in New York who accused him of fathering her unborn child and was threatening a paternity suit that would seriously jeopardize his national ambitions. He explained that he had tried to contact the girl himself, but to no avail, that her mother had claimed her pregnancy made her too sick even to come to the phone, and he wanted to know if Donato could be of any assistance. The same afternoon Donato paid a visit to the mother, sketched out some harsh truths and as an alternative offered five thousand dollars, which the mother promptly accepted.

The grateful Long invited Donato to visit him. The two men met in the senator's suite atop the Roosevelt Hotel in downtown New Orleans. After some cordial chitchat, Long beckoned Donato to an open window that offered a sweeping vista of the city and its environs. Donato approached cautiously, reflecting that possibly among those present only he and Long knew about the girl. "When I got to him," he said to Caroline, "I put my arm around him, you know, tight. I figured if I was going to take a fall, I'd take him with me." But Long just waved a grandiose hand, telling Donato that as far as he could see, whatever he wanted, wherever he wanted it, was his for the asking. This occurred shortly after Donato's run-in with La Guardia, and he confessed to Long that he had a lot of surplus slot machines which he would like to place.

The deal was concluded at once. Later, the realities of business being what they are, payoffs were funneled to Long. And following Long's assassination, when Donato negotiated terms with his political heirs, the cost mounted, but so did the profits. Eventually, during World War II, Donato launched a lavish gambling establishment outside New Orleans, which he called Club Caroline. Its success enabled him to perceive at once that his Jewish cohorts, for whom he had great respect, were right about the potential of Las Vegas, and he was one of a handful of mafiosi with the wit to invest in the desert from the start, taking a twenty percent interest in a casino. The return came to him in cash, skimmed in the counting room off the top, and the Internal Revenue Service was beside itself trying to skewer him for tax fraud. Treasury agents were convinced that the money was going to a numbered account in Switzerland. Donato did not discourage the idea, since the cash actually went to a bank account in Mexico City that he maintained under the name of CarCorp, an arrangement which not only made it readily accessible for certain real estate ventures in and around New York but paid twelve to fourteen percent per annum. The rate was available to any foreigner with dollars to deposit. There was a risk involved, however. A depositor could walk into the bank and ask to withdraw his account, and a teller would say, "What account?" This, of course, never happened to Frank Donato.

He was five feet five inches tall, a small fact which was discovered only by standing next to him, and in profile his face resembled the Indian on the old nickel, but the physical characteristics that made him the country's most famous racketeer, and thus dear to Hamilton Wainwright's heart, were his hands and voice. When he had been called before a Senate committee investigating the possible existence of a national crime syndicate, Donato's lawyer had objected to his client being televised, so the cameras, in an inspired directorial moment, were trained on his hands, which were expressive, to say the least, and a huge television audience watched spellbound while the hands clenched, darted and writhed for the better part of three days in counterpoint to his hoarse, rasping voice. The voice added a sinister dimension to the surrealistic dance of his hands, emerging, as it did, laced with syntactical touches of the street, in a throaty growl that became the standard for endless gangster portrayals in the movies. An attempted mob strangulation was alleged to have caused his speech impairment. The truth was that in the early 1930s some polyps were found on his vocal cords, and Donato was advised that he could either have them removed surgically or take advantage of the relatively new technique of burning them off. Having a natural aversion for the knife, he chose burning, and the cords wound up permanently scorched. As he explained to Caroline with a philosophical shrug, "I went with the wrong doctor."

When his televised appearance was over, Donato had become a household word, a name mothers from coast to coast invoked to cow their children. In all probability, none of this would have occurred if he had exercised his constitutional rights and sought monosyllabic refuge behind the Fifth Amendment. He did not, however, so as to have the chance to deny under oath in a public forum that he was in any way involved in narcotics, a persistently whispered charge that had long rankled him. It was really a matter of vanity. Unlike his fellow mafiosi, skirting the shadows, holed up in Mulberry Street social clubs, Donato was a smartly dressed, highly visible figure in midtown Manhattan, eating in fashionable East Side restaurants, attending Broadway musical opening nights, sitting at ringside for important fights, holding a box at the Metropolitan Opera; as a man of substance he even set time aside for charitable works and was an energetic fund-raiser for the Salvation Army, and the idea that someone might nudge a dinner companion as he passed by and murmur, "There goes Frank Donato, the dope peddler," was abhorrent to him.

But by not taking the Fifth, he left himself unprotected against a torrent of allegations regarding his past bootlegging and present gambling interests, two activities that Donato considered eminently legitimate business enterprises. He tried to convey his feelings as forthrightly as he could. "Laws against gambling," he had testified, "is just like Prohibition was. Passing a law isn't enough. There's always an angle, you know, on how to skin a cat. There is no way to wash the spots off a leopard. If a man's gamble-minded, he'll find some trick to do it, believe me."

Unhappily, his inquisitors did not share this Olympian view. Also unhappily, they dredged up a succession of gangland murders which, as they were recited, seemed as remote to Donato as a series of minute flashes on the ground would be to a bombardier who had just pressed a button thirty thousand feet up. He saw himself as a peaceful man whose precept was that things could be worked out, negotiated, but still, there had always been those inescapable moments when with a wave of his hand, a slight nod, he had signaled his assent to what had to be done. Yes, he admitted, he had known some of the deceased. No, he had replied, he was not familiar with the circumstances of their demises.

Most startling of all, however, had been a selective reading of the guest list at the last fund-raising dinner Donato had put on for the Salvation Army. Each of those present had bought a hundred-dollar ticket, and many had taken tables of ten. Among them were twelve underworld chieftains plus assorted associates, along with six New York State Supreme Court judges, three criminal court magistrates, two congressmen, a former mayor of New York, the borough presidents of Manhattan and Brooklyn, an ex-heavyweight champion, the board chairman of one of the largest department stores in the city, the city's two biggest realtors, the president of a supermarket chain and the heads of the most powerful Teamsters and longshoremen's locals on the East Coast. How was it, the committee's chief counsel demanded, that Frank Donato, a man whose sole reported income came from being a sales representative for a building contractor—how was it that he could bring such an imposing group together? "Well," Donato rasped modestly, as a delicious shudder coursed up the collective spine of a national television audience, "you go here and there, you know, and you meet people. At the racetrack. And whatnot."

The chief counsel, lingering momentarily on Donato's employment with the contracting firm, noted that he was paid sixty thousand dollars a year and asked what he did for his salary, and Donato replied, "I solicit business wherever I am, at Toots Shor's restaurant or the Colony, anywhere where I have dinner, or lunch, or something. Anybody looking for a contractor, I would recommend the firm. It's a good firm, does good work. No chunks of concrete falling out. Nothing like that."

"And you think your services, as you describe them, are worth sixty thousand annually to your employers?"

"Well," said Donato, who actually was the company's principal owner, "*they* think so."

After the laughter in the committee room had subsided, Donato added, "And also I give them some advice."

The chief counsel, flushing slightly, was preparing to move on to another area of inquiry when the senior senator from North Dakota interrupted him. The senator had been delighted to be on the committee, since he did not often get the opportunity for such national television exposure. He had intended to question Donato about the extent of organized crime in Bismarck, the state's capital city, certain that Donato had never heard of it, thus demonstrating, on the one hand, that America's heartland, as exemplified by Bismarck, was free of the Mafia's perfidious, alien influence and, on the other hand, showing the folks back home that he was ever alert to its possible infiltration. But instead, he decided to pick up on Donato's last remark. "What do you mean by advice?" he had asked.

Donato stared at the senator, at his round, owlish face, a resemblance heightened by his pursed lips and rimless glasses. "Senator," he said finally, "let me explain it to you this way. In the contracting business you deal with developers. Now a developer is a born hustler, he's an optimist. He's always looking ahead, he has to, and sometimes he gets overextended or whatever, and he is late paying his bills. Well, anyway, the firm I work for put up these houses for this developer in good faith, I think there were thirty-eight of them, and he sold three of them and the people have moved in already, and he has commitments on most of the rest of them, but he hasn't paid us, the firm, what we got coming. He says he has a cash-flow problem, and he'll pay us when all the mortgages go through. Then it turns out the developer has another problem. In the houses where the people have moved in, the chimneys don't work. They light a fire, and the whole house is full of smoke, and the word gets around, and the developer can't get rid of the other houses. He's going crazy. He can't understand it. He looks up every chimney, and all he sees is blue sky. So he came to me, and I told him if he gives me a certified bank check for what he owes the firm, I will personally guarantee all the chimneys will be working the next day. And he gave the check, he had no choice, and I told the foreman on the job to go ahead and break the glass."

"Break the glass?"

"Yes. When the chimneys were built, a pane of glass was set across each of them inside, about halfway up." Donato paused. "You see, Senator, that was my advice."

Both *Time* and *Newsweek* ran cover stories on him, calling him the "Prime Minister of Organized Crime," the "Prince Metternich of the Mafia." He asked one of his lawyers who Metternich was and was flattered when he found out.

Naturally, he could have done without the Mafia part, but the description fit. He was a diplomat. As a Calabrian, a minority member in an organization dominated by Sicilians and Neapolitans, he had to be. It had been that way in the beginning, as a kid growing up in a stinking Manhattan tenement, when he belonged to the East One Hundred and Fourth Street gang, which was completely Sicilian except for him—and, of course, one other Calabrian, Matty Lanza. Ah, Matty, he often thought, if Mad Dog Matty had not existed, he would have had to invent him. And if necessary, he would have, which was always his next thought.

The gang had been loaded with talent. Of those who survived shoot-outs with police and battles with rival street gangs, four had gone on to become family bosses. And even then Matty Lanza had enabled Donato to be recognized as a nonviolent figure of authority in a violent world, a peerless skinner of cats. The equation was simple: To cross him was to cross Lanza, and no one was prepared to do that. Donato sometimes envied the lack of ambiguity in Matty. When he was confronted with a problem, Lanza's solution was to kill without preamble, with a knife, the garrote, usually a gun. He seemed to enjoy it, which made him all the more dreaded.

He adored Donato. Besides their common heritage, their immigrant fathers had worked on the same garbage scow. But while Donato had been born in America, days after his parents had passed through Ellis Island, Lanza's family had not quit the Calabrian mountains until he was twelve. He was squat and pockmarked, a year older than Donato, and an inch shorter. He had been put into the first grade, with children five and six years his senior, when he started school. At the end of his first week a teacher had mocked him about his English, and he never returned. He swore to Donato that he was going to cut the teacher's throat. "No, you're not," Donato had replied. "I'll teach you what you got to know."

So instead, Matty committed his first murder when he was fourteen, gunning down a night watchman who had come unexpectedly upon the gang during a fur-warehouse robbery that Donato had planned. Later, in the 1920s, Lanza was indicted on first-degree murder charges three times. Twice he was acquitted because of the sudden reticence of witnesses to testify against him. Finally, however, he was convicted and actually spent nine days in the death house before he won a new trial on a technicality, but it never took place. This time Donato arranged to have the witnesses permanently disappear. "They're gone," a voice on the phone said. That was all Donato knew, and all he cared to know. Afterward he had a heart-to-heart chat with Lanza. "Listen to me, Matty," he had said. "You're a big boy now. You got to stop doing that stuff yourself."

By then Frank Donato was a man of considerable stature, mixing easily with such other rising mobsters as Lucky Luciano and Meyer Lansky. The turning point had come for him when he was barely twenty with the arrival in the United States of Ignazio Lupo, the Sicilian don who had departed his native habitat partly because of Mussolini's marauding Fascist police but mostly because, as Lupo liked to say in his pastoral wisdom, the sheep were fatter across the Atlantic. Lupo's intent was to build a new, transplanted Mafia that would be powerful enough to topple the Irish and Jewish racketeers then dominating the scene. A key element in his grand design was the East One Hundred and Fourth Street gang, which necessarily included Donato. "Forget he's young. Forget he's Calabrese," Lupo was told. "The kid is smart. He graduated eighth grade. He's smart, like a hebe."

Despite Lupo's early misgivings, Donato quickly became his most valued counselor, advising him on the American ways, what could be done and what couldn't. Although the Prohibition era was well under way, bootlegging was still in a state of flux. Much of the alcohol being sold illegally was coming from raids on the vast stores of liquor that had been stashed in warehouses for "medicinal" purposes before Prohibition went into effect, but as these supplies dwindled, hijacking became an everyday event. It was during these unsettled times that Donato was arrested and convicted for carrying a revolver. He realized at once the stupidity of his act and resolved never to pack a gun again. After all, he thought, what did he need a weapon for with Matty Lanza around? And to seal that alliance for good, he took as his wife one of Matty's cousins, orphaned in Calabria at sixteen by a typhus epidemic. That Anna would have been much happier in a convent was unfortunate; for Donato, however, the essence of a successful marriage was not sex or romantic notions of love, but business, and the success of this particular liaison was validated when Lanza embraced him and said, "Frank, I'll never forget what you done."

Besides, at that moment he had a far more pressing problem. It was obvious that reliable overseas sources of liquor had to be developed. Donato's solution was to become the bootlegger's bootlegger—that is, to bring over the whiskey, specifically scotch, to beach it and sell it on the spot, letting others take it from there, leaving them the task of thwarting hijackers and federal agents, of setting up and guarding facilities to cut it and rebottle it and distribute it locally. A case of scotch for export was about nine dollars. Once the case landed in the United States, the price was one hundred and thirty dollars. In diluted form in a speakeasy the same case was worth between four and five hundred dollars. But along with this came the endless payrolls and payoffs and all the accompanying bloodbaths. Donato's plan avoided such unpleasantness, together with future recriminations. Ignazio Lupo bought the idea, and Donato traveled personally to Glasgow to make the deal. At first the only bribes involved small-town police forces along the south shore of Long Island, where the skiffs slipped in with scotch that had been unloaded from freighters anchored outside the three-mile limit. But then a modernized Coast Guard began intercepting these clandestine shipments, an annoyance Donato eliminated by paying a thousand dollars a week to the officer in charge of dispatching patrol boats so that they were directed elsewhere when one of his freighters hove to. Donato, of course, passed on the added cost to his customers, who accepted it without complaint, since he had the foresight to tie up a brand of scotch called Black Feather that had an especially heavy, smoky flavor, making it ideal for cutting.

While Ignazio Lupo—"Don Ignazio," as he preferred to be called—had listened to Donato about bootlegging, he did not heed his repeated warnings that America was not Sicily and that it was impossible for a single ethnic group to control all organized crime in the United States. As a result, Don Ignazio suddenly found himself facedown in a plate of linguine, the three bullet holes in his head instantly transforming the white clam sauce into one more closely resembling marinara. The coup, with Donato's acquiescence, had been engineered by Lucky Luciano, who went on to lead the Italian section of the underworld in more sophisticated fashion, although he utilized the paramilitary family structure that Lupo had envisioned with its array of capos, caporegimes and *soldati*.

Donato in the new setup was nominally in Luciano's family, but in reality he went his own way, content to let Luciano have the limelight, and after Lupo's murder, he ran the bootlegging operation himself. Anticipating the repeal of Prohibition, he arranged an exclusive national distributorship for the Black Feather label that he had been importing illegally and promptly relinquished it to two respected businessmen. The transaction was unusual in that there was no exchange of capital. In return for the franchise, Donato was to receive one dollar and twenty-five cents per case sold. The agreement was oral, and the money was paid to him in cash. Donato liked cash. He had never written a check in his life, which made it difficult for the Internal Revenue Service to gather evidence against him that would stand up in court. It was also Frank Donato's belief that while a lot of people drank, a lot more gambled, and with his profits from whiskey he financed the largest bookmaking ring in the country's history, and even more money rolled in. When two partners in a contracting firm were unable to meet their debts, he took over the firm, kept the two partners on and had them hire him as a consultant to provide some explanation for his livelihood.

He might have continued in this manner until the end of his days had it not been for two unexpected developments. One was the jailing and eventual deportation of Luciano on white-slavery charges. The other was the incarceration of Luciano's successor, Vito Genovese, for trafficking in narcotics. Both men, he was sure, had been framed. While he was sorry about Luciano, whom he considered a wily, if overly ambitious, compatriot, he felt nothing but contempt for Genovese, a crude braggart who brought everything he touched into ill repute and who had got precisely what he deserved. Beyond that he did not give the fate of either one of them another thought. But Donato's uncanny ability to make money had reached legendary proportions in the underworld, earning him enormous respect, and in the ensuing power vacuum the Mafia high commission requested that he assume command of the leaderless crime family before the situation swirled out of control. And for once Donato had no options. To decline was to invite disaster. However ambivalent he was about the organization and most of its sophomoric mumbo jumbo, he did not delude himself about either its capacity or its will to exact any retribution it deemed necessary. It was something he was stuck with and could never escape.

He conducted the family affairs with benign neglect, allowing the six capos under him to do pretty much as they pleased, dealing with them when he had to primarily through Vincente D'Angelo, who appeared to be the most businesslike of the bunch. He was adamant on only one point: The family was to stay out of drugs. No member who was picked up for handling narcotics could expect aid in the way of a defense lawyer or support for a wife and children if he was convicted and sent to prison. For Donato, it was not entirely a matter of morality. Heroin was a volatile issue. The public got exercised about it, and that could lead to pressures on other, less visible rackets. But he had few illusions about the effectiveness of his edict. The lust for a fast buck was too great, and he could imagine the *soldati* and even some of the capos muttering that it was easy enough for Frank Donato to take this stand, that he, after all, had it made. Nor would the threat of no help in the event of an arrest or jail sentence have significant impact. Despite the myths, a family member in trouble was usually on his own anyway. What kept him in line was not the promise of help, but fear. Still, Donato railed about "junk dealers" as openly as he could, especially over phone lines he suspected were tapped, in the hope of persuading his eavesdroppers that they could best direct their efforts against more fruitful targets, and in the main his strategy worked until his vainglorious appearance before the Senate investigating committee transformed him into a national celebrity.

He tried to use the unwelcome notoriety as an excuse to step down as head of the family, so that he could retire once more to his private interests. But the commission, after its customarily pompous deliberations—Donato had begun to think its members had seen too many movies—demurred. The old Luciano family was too big, conditions in it too unstable to permit a sudden change in leadership. It would literally trigger an internal free-for-all that could not be countenanced. Donato would have to stay on, at least until an orderly succession could be arranged. The real reason, he knew, was that the eleven family bosses who formed the high commission, besides being intensely suspicious of each other, had held onto power far too long, and any break in their aging ranks might set off a chain reaction toppling them as well. Even Matty Lanza, who had risen to control of the family that ran the New York waterfront, where his strong-arm methods were still in vogue, attempted to argue him out of it. "Listen, Frank," Matty had said. "You know what these people are like. You don't go along, you're dead."

So he accepted the decision. And in time much of the furor following his televised interrogatories subsided, although his name and face recognition remained as high as ever, his entry into one of his favored haunts, like the King Cole Bar in the St. Regis Hotel, causing a stir in the crowd as if he were a sort of living historical monument to be recalled and savored. The truth was that he rather enjoyed it. Up to the advent of Hamilton Wainwright IV.

Sitting in Caroline McIlhenny's apartment one afternoon, alone for a change, Donato was amusing himself with a game of solitaire when the doorbell buzzed. It was the elevator boy bringing up the early edition of the New York *Post*. The front page trumpeted a new series on organized crime, inspired by Wainwright. The series was titled "When Will Justice Triumph?" The first article featured Frank Donato.

After Caroline returned from shopping, she glanced at the paper lying on a table in the foyer and saw the headline. "Did you read it?" she asked.

"No," he replied. "It'll only upset my stomach."

14

Karpstein let a week go by following the death of Marvin Mandelbaum before he called Mandelbaum's attorney, Larry Farber.

The first published report of the shooting was in the Long Island daily *Newsday* the day after it had happened. The story listed Mandelbaum's address as still being in Pelham Manor and said that the Suffolk County police were at a loss for clues. There was some speculation that the murder might be the work of a random sniper, but as one official commented, a .38-caliber revolver was hardly the kind of weapon a sniper would use.

The next day *Newsday* printed a follow-up story with the local-angle revelation that the victim had recently moved from Pelham Manor to Huntington Station. By then more information had been unearthed about Mandelbaum, including the fact that he had been twice indicted but not convicted for stock-market frauds, and the story hinted that he had a multitude of enemies, although Mrs. Mandelbaum was quoted as saying that her husband had left for work that morning "without a care in the world."

Also on Saturday the New York *Daily News* carried a short piece about the mystery murder on the Long Island Expressway, pointing out that it had all the earmarks of a gangland killing. The *News* further noted with some outrage that there had not been a successful prosecution of a homicide involving organized crime in New York since the sentencing and subsequent electrocution of the famous chairman of the board of Murder, Incorporated, Louis (Lepke) Buchalter, a month before the Japanese attacked Pearl Harbor.

Farber himself first thought that Karpstein might be behind the slaying, but when he heard nothing more in the days after it had taken place, he began to entertain the fantasy that any number of people Mandelbaum had flim-flammed could have been responsible, even quite possibly someone he had never heard of. The more he considered this, the better it sounded. And suppose it had been Karpstein, what did it have to do with him?

He looked at his digital desk clock. He had another hour until his next appointment. It was out of the office, and he awaited it eagerly. The client was a Harvard Business School graduate, three years younger than Farber, who had used a small trust fund set up by his father to open what was advertised as a leisure spa on Manhattan's East Side called Bora-Bora. Farber had to hand it to the guy. The handbills for Bora-Bora promised a "lush, timeless, Polynesian atmosphere," a "luxurious, tropical-paradise lounge with drinks on the house," a "pool-size, communal Jacuzzi" and a bevy of "lovely attendants in beautifully appointed private rooms." Actually the guy had crammed the whole enterprise into what had previously been a hardware store and engineered it for a fast turnover. A South Seas touch was provided by some plastic palm trees. The circular lounge was barely twelve feet in diameter, and if anybody wanted to pause there for a drink, he got Hawaiian Punch with a dollop of rum in it; the pool was a square oversized sunken bathtub that at best could accommodate three bodies, and in the diffused lighting every girl looked good. The private rooms were six-by-eight-foot cubicles equipped with the kind of examining tables doctors use, but the place was clean, in a neighborhood where no one had to worry about muggings, and most innovative of all, "major credit cards" were honored, so a customer could get jacked off, blown or laid and write it off as a business expense.

It was, as Farber enviously observed, a license to steal. Farber's client had made only one mistake. He had allowed an undercover cop investigating police corruption to secretly tape him discussing the two-hundred-dollar weekly payoff he made to the local precinct house. Since this admission would effectively put him out of business, he had decided to fight it. Farber figured that with the various delaying motions that were available, he could string the case out for at least two years while the guy continued to operate, and in the end he was almost certain that the type of body recorder that had been used would fail an audibility test.

Farber also figured his fee could run to about thirty thousand dollars. And there were other benefits. After each conference with his client at Bora-Bora he was offered a girl. The last time, however, had been a nerve-racking experience. He had gone into the Jacuzzi with his giggling companion when she suddenly got on top of him. Just as Farber was having an orgasm, his head slipped under the water, and he came up frantically clutching his toupee. Although it was guaranteed to stay in place even while immersed, he had always been paranoid about the possibility of its somehow becoming unglued in public.

So, seated at his desk, contemplating the delights that lay ahead, Farber resolved to stick to less exotic sex on one of the cubicle examining tables. Then his intercom buzzed, and his secretary told him that a Mr. Rocco was on the phone. It took Farber a moment to recall who Mr. Rocco was, and the erection that had begun to form immediately disappeared.

"Uh, yes?" he said.

"Farber?"

"Yes."

"This is Johnny Rocco. Remember me?"

"Yes."

"Good, Farber. You got a good memory. You heard about Mandelbaum, right?"

"Yes."

"You're handling the estate, right?"

"Well, I—"

"It don't matter," Karpstein interrupted. "I'm holding you responsible, regardless. I got a piece of paper on Mandelbaum's house. You witnessed it, Farber, all nice and legal. You sell that house yet, Farber?"

"It's just being sold."

"Good. I want the money."

"But the paper was signed under duress. It won't stand up in court."

"Hey, Farber."

"Yes?" Farber said, instantly regretting the lawyer in him, shuddering at the vision of Karpstein standing over Mandelbaum, the telephone cable slamming into Mandelbaum's stomach.

"Mandelbaum went fast, Farber. Keep this up, you won't be so lucky. You want to talk about this a couple of days hanging from a meat hook?"

"Listen," Farber said quickly. "The will has to be probated. It takes time."

"That's the ticket, Farber. That's what I want to hear.

You stay with it. Move it along. You got the accountant's name the money goes to. You keep in touch with him. Keep him informed. You got that?"

"Yes," Farber whispered. As he hung up, he felt the rush of warm wetness in his crotch and looked down in horror at the dark stain spreading across his trouser front. The suit he was wearing was a very light brown spring fabric, and he knew that even after it dried, the telltale stain would remain. He buzzed his secretary and said, "Gloria, cancel that Bora-Bora meeting. Tell him something came up. Make another date for tomorrow."

☆

In the office of E-Z Trucking, after talking to Farber, Karpstein unwrapped a Milky Way and stuffed the whole bar into his mouth. "We got anything else today, Leo?" he asked.

"Oh, yes, Albert," Weissberg said. "There's Mr. Flynn. He should be here by now. He usually comes in quite early. Do you want me to take care of him?"

"No," Karpstein said, still chewing. "I'll wait. That fuck better not be late, he knows what's good for him."

15

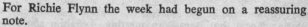

For Richie Flynn the week had begun on a reassuring note.

Brian Madden's secretary reached him on Monday morning at Goldblatt with news that the form confirming the beneficiary change in his insurance policy had finally arrived. The secretary said that she would forward it to him at home, but Flynn told her not to, that he would stop by to pick it up. The fact that the secretary called first was in itself a cause for celebration. Agnes had a habit of indiscriminately opening mail that came to the apartment, especially if she thought there was any possibility that an envelope contained a check. He had once protested this invasion of privacy. She countered by demanding to know what he had to hide, and he had responded wearily, "Nothing. Forget it."

On Tuesday, despite Harry Fowler's injunction not to call him, Flynn was about to call anyway when Fowler called Flynn instead.

"For Christ's sake, what's happening?" Flynn said.

"Richie, I keep telling you, not on the phone."

They met that evening at Neary's Pub. Neary's was an anomaly, an old-fashioned Irish saloon tucked in among expensive high rises around Sutton Place that was frequented by investment counselors and advertising executives residing in the area, none of whom would be interested in a conversation about a Bronx day-care center.

When Flynn got there, he found Fowler at a rear corner table ordering a refill of Stolichnaya vodka on the rocks. "You ought to try it," Fowler said.

"No," Flynn said. "I don't drink Commie booze."

"What are you, the last of the patriots?"

"It's just the way I feel."

"Take it easy," Fowler said. "No offense intended." After Flynn's scotch was served, Fowler raised his glass and said, "Well, here's to."

"Here's to what?" Flynn said. "That's what I'd like to know."

"To us, Richie. To success. I told you not to worry."

Flynn had never seen Fowler in such an expansive mood. He leaned forward curiously. He wondered how much Fowler had drunk. "So tell me again," Flynn said. "I'm all ears."

Fowler rolled the vodka around in his mouth before swallowing. "It's all set, practically, is what," he said. "I've approved the site physically and demographically. Ideal for conversion into a day-care center. Great need for it in the neighborhood. A thorough investigation. Three visits. All the papers backdated, signed, sealed and delivered. Also the sponsoring group that's going to run it. You recall Willie Townsend and the block association, don't you? Excellent people. First-rate. A credit to the grass-roots community spirit that is this country's backbone. By the way, Willie was a little unhappy with the financial arrangements. I told him he could count on a substantial bonus. I take it you have no objection."

"No."

"Good," Fowler said. "Now I've also verified your preliminary renovation plans, the copious square footage you intend to provide the disenfranchised tots of our town, the dandy play area, both inside and out, that they can romp in, the extraordinary plumbing you are going to install, chrome-finished, of course, where exposed, and the spotless stainless-steel kitchen that will cook up piping hot meals for tiny mouths to consume, the numerous toilets available to evacuate same, the leakproof roof and sun-drenched windows you envision, not to mention your protective floor covering!"

Fowler poked a finger at the ice in his vodka. "Did you know, Richie, that the Agency for Child Development requires day-care center floors to be of vinyl or vinyl asbestos tile at least an eighth of an inch thick with a matching resilient base, but that your plans call for a base a full quarter inch thick, so as to better cushion the fall of little bodies? I bet you didn't know that, did you?"

"I know one thing, Harry. You're off your rocker. What the hell are you talking about? What plans?"

"Your plans, Richie. They're just preliminary ones, as I said, and not really necessary for the letter of intent. But I thought it'd be a nice touch. To show your seriousness of purpose, I took the liberty of borrowing the specifications for a model center, improving on them a bit here and there. Theoretically, you're supposed to have a full set of plans after the Department of Real Estate signs the lease, but we'll use one of the contractors the big boys use, and there won't be any problem. Those fellows are the salt of the earth. For example, they always install baseboard electric heating because it's the cheapest to put in. It's also the most expensive to operate. But who cares? The city pays all the utility bills."

"I think I'll have another drink," Flynn said.

"A capital idea. I'll join you."

Flynn sipped his scotch, stared at Fowler and said, "Harry, just tell me in plain English what's next, could you please do that?"

"What's next is that the papers I've been talking about are in the office of the agency's general counsel. They get approved, and the letter of intent goes out. You use it to get the money from a mortgage outfit. Have you found one yet?"

"Yes. It's called Concourse Funding."

"Well, make sure you only make a short-term deal with them to cover what you need to pay back your friends. As soon as the lease is signed, we want to go straight to a commercial bank and mortgage out. That's how the insiders do it. The synagogue, where it is, isn't worth pissing on, but the lease is worth plenty. So a bank will fall all over itself to give us a mortgage of maybe three or four hundred thousand over what it cost to buy the synagogue and fix it up, which is immediate profit for us. That's what mortgaging out is. Plus we also have the rental income coming in every year from the city."

"Jesus Christ," Flynn said. "It's hard to believe."

"You better believe it," Fowler said. "A fellow is mayor or something, and he wants to get reelected, and he needs financing for his campaign or to keep his organization together, and this is a way for him to get it. It's a regular daisy chain—developers, landlords, contractors, lawyers, insurance men and bankers, all in line to give because they're getting more."

"Hey, Harry," Flynn said, suddenly giddy, "we could use some of the profits to start another center."

"Possible, but not probable. Right now, Richie, as I'm talking to you, the city is almost four hundred fucking million dollars into these day-care leases, and it can't last forever. We're lucky we're sliding in behind these people, even if it's the end of the game. They never figured someone in the agency, a dumb social worker, would get smart. I'd go out to one of those leased sites and protest conditions, and they'd say, 'There's old Harry. How you doing, Harry? Harry, here's two-fifty, three hundred, go buy yourself a hat.' And you know what, Richie? I'd take it. What difference did it make? I couldn't close anything down. Well, fuck them!"

"When do you think that letter will go out?" Flynn said. "Boy, I'd like to have it by Thursday. I could really use it. Not just for the mortgage people. There's, uh, some other guy I have to see."

"Tomorrow."

"You're kidding. Tomorrow? Jesus, Harry," he said, holding out his glass, "Here's to us is right."

☆

Flynn had been steered to Concourse Funding for a mortgage loan by Jack Hennessy, the Inwood branch manager of Metropolitan Trust. Most of the big banks were still pursuing a policy of keeping neighborhood branch managers in one place for extended stays so that they could develop close community ties, and in the twenty-one years Hennessy had been at the helm of the Inwood branch he had done just that, actively participating in the local affairs of the Elks, the Lions, the Rotary, the United Way, the Chamber of Commerce, the Knights of Columbus and the Holy Name Society. Hennessy liked to leave the bank early on Tuesdays and Thursdays to play golf at the Winged Foot Club in Westchester, but he worked late on Wednesdays because of another community tie he had developed. Every Wednesday afternoon the Marinello brothers, who controlled much of the numbers racket in northern Manhattan and the West Bronx, brought in all the quarters, half dollars and dollars that had been bet with them during the previous week. In return for exchanging the money into more manageable hundred-dollar bills, with no questions asked, Hennessy received a cash stipend of three hundred dollars as soon as each transaction was completed. He had been doing this without qualms for nine years. Gambling, in Hennessy's view, was a harmless diversion, and besides, if he had not entered into this arrangement with the Marinellos, he was sure that somebody else, probably Sol Katz, that smug circumcised prick at Second National, would have grabbed the deal for himself. And as the black and Hispanic influence spread in Inwood, Hennessy quickly adapted to the new circumstances and entered into a similar monetary exchange on Mondays with a gentleman of color, Ernest (Cokey) Jones. This time Hennessy did not dwell on the source of the money. Jones was once publicized as being a leading narcotics distributor with a home address in Inwood. When Hennessy's wife expressed shock at somebody like that living nearby, he had replied, "You can't believe everything you read in the papers, dear. Look at all the lies they're printing about President Nixon."

Hennessy also had discretionary powers to grant local lines of credit, and he had paid special attention to private mortgage companies in his area. Mortgage companies occupied a shadowy position between outright loan sharks and established financial institutions that found certain ventures too chancy to pass their lending review boards or apt to present awkward collection problems. By law mortgage companies were permitted to charge eighteen and a half percent annually on loans to individuals and twenty-four percent to corporate borrowers, but they were otherwise unregulated and invariably tacked on an under-the-table service fee of ten to fifteen percent.

Hennessy's favorite mortgage company was Concourse Funding. It had the kind of people behind it that he played golf with at Winged Foot, and so far as he could determine, no mob money was being fed into it, which was the trouble with a number of mortgage companies that were here one day and gone the next. Concourse Funding was operated by Ed Whittleby, who owned a large paint and hardware store just across the Harlem River on Fordham Road. That was what Hennessy liked best about Whittleby. He was "local." Hostility always surged through Hennessy whenever he thought of "downtown," a domain he considered under the thumb of rich Jews and snotty Protestants, to the nation's detriment.

So he had allowed Concourse Funding a credit line of one hundred thousand dollars on Whittleby's signature alone and never regretted it for a moment. Whittleby paid four points above the bank's prime rate. The difference between that and the legal rate Concourse Funding charged its own customers was usually around ten or twelve percent, half of which immediately went back to Hennessy. Hennessy also got a five percent finder's fee for any business he was responsible for whether the bank's credit line was used or not. He always went through one of the two brokers Whittleby employed to scout new prospects. The brokers in turn earned a five percent commission on every loan they brought in that was approved, and they showed their gratitude to Hennessy by keeping him informed about what was going on in the company.

Richie Flynn had gone to see Hennessy as soon as Fowler had assured him that all the papers for the day-care center were in the works. He tried to be as matter-of-fact as he could. He told Hennessy that he was on the verge of becoming a day-care center landlord, that the income over the length of the fifteen-year lease would be one million eight hundred and seventy-five thousand dollars, that a letter of intent from the city was expected shortly, that a signed lease from the Department of Real Estate would be ready in a couple of months, possibly sooner, and that while all this was happening, he required an interim loan on the property.

Hennessy had a heavy-lidded look. He tilted back in his chair, hands folded over a round stomach. Jesus, Flynn thought, he's like a lizard on a rock waiting for a fly to go by. "Mr. Hennessy," he said, "I'd appreciate anything you could do."

Jack Hennessy elected to play it safe while he pondered what he had just heard. "Oh, that sounds grand, Richie," he said, "it does, indeed." He did not doubt the truth of what Flynn had told him, or at least the truth as Flynn saw it. Nothing surprised Hennessy anymore. He had known Flynn for—what was it, eleven, twelve years? They had first met when Hennessy had been president of the Inwood Boosters Club and the club had given Flynn a lunch following that run he had made for the Giants. Then the poor fellow had hurt his knee. What had he done after that? Hennessy tried to think. Yes, he seemed to remember, Flynn had gone to work for Goldblatt's Brewery.

"You're with Goldblatt, aren't you?" he asked.

"Yes, sir. Sales supervisor. Special events."

"Grand," Hennessy said, pleased with his memory. "Grand company. Grand brew." Well, he thought, it was entirely possible that Flynn had the connections to bring off a project like this. Flynn had been all over the sports pages at the time, and who knew what that meant *downtown?* My God, he suddenly recalled, they still had the boy's picture up behind the Liffey Bar right down the block. Hennessy had picked up talk about the lucrative day-care centers, but he was not familiar with the details. Then what was it that was so bothersome to him about this? City leases of the sort Flynn had described were unbreakable, and a letter of intent in anticipation of one was not to be sneezed at. Yes, that was it! Why didn't Flynn simply wait until the lease was signed before getting a mortgage? Someone, or something, must be putting the squeeze on Flynn, and he was caught in a bind.

Shafts of sunlight shot through the slatted blinds on the bank windows, striking Hennessy's face. He closed his eyes and basked in the pleasant warmth.

He decided that there would be no loan from him based on a letter of intent, but he wanted to hear more. "What figure did you have in mind, Richie?"

Flynn fought to remain calm. There was the twenty due Karpstein, less two thousand when the final weekly payment was made. And another forty-odd thousand to finish buying the synagogue in case the lease was somehow delayed. Flynn watched Hennessy's fingertips touch; he looked like a prelate in repose. "Sixty, sixty-five," Flynn said as offhandedly as he could.

The sun rays moved from Hennessy's face and started across the floor, a cloud of luminous dust particles billowing through them. Hennessy opened his eyes and saw the dust. He reminded himself to speak to the cleaning people. My God, he thought, I've been breathing that stuff all day. He wished he were out on the golf course. He looked at Flynn. "Why don't you wait until the lease is signed?" he asked.

Flynn's heart sank. For a second he had allowed himself to believe, the way Hennessy had been talking, that he would get the loan then and there. Now he knew he would not. "I, uh, well, I have some commitments I have to take care of," he said. "I'm a little"—Flynn searched for the proper word—"uh, overextended."

So I was right, Hennessy thought. He wondered what the commitments were. But there was a kind of panic in Flynn's eyes that Hennessy, seated behind this same desk, had seen many times before, and he resolved not to inquire further. He might not want to hear the answer.

Flynn fumbled through some papers he had extracted from a manila envelope and thrust one of them forward for Hennessy's inspection. "Look right here," he said. "The city's guidelines for setting up a day-care center say a letter of intent should be sufficient to get a loan."

Hennessy raised a restraining hand, then let it flop back on his stomach. "I know," he said, "I know. But these are unusual times, trying times. There is a great credit crunch. President Johnson got us into it, and President Nixon has been trying to get us out of it as best he can. A loan like this would have to be reviewed thoroughly by the bank, Richie, and I sense that time is of the essence for you. Am I correct?"

"Yes, sir, it is."

"Tell me. What makes you so certain you'll be getting this letter of intent? And the lease?"

Flynn's hopes soared again. "Well, I have got an interested party in with me who has inside connections."

Ah, that's more like it, Hennessy thought. That's what I want to hear. Flynn might be building a house of cards, but at least it was not based wholly on air. Best to let Concourse Funding look this one over. The house of cards might come tumbling down. On the other hand, it might not. Stranger things had happened. And if a guaranteed lease like this came through for a mortgage, the boys downtown would be very impressed. They'd know that Jack Hennessy up in Inwood was on the ball. There had been rumors that all the big banks were thinking of adopting a new policy regarding branch managers, of switching them around every year or so, that developing close community ties had not been such a good idea. Hennessy had four years to go with Metropolitan Trust before retirement. He did not wish to spend them removed from the Marinello brothers, Cokey Jones and Concourse Funding.

"Richie," he said, "I have a suggestion for you. Write this name down. Eamon McDonough. He's a broker, with a mortgage company, Concourse Funding. Here's his number. He's a grand fellow. Tell him I told you to call. His people are in a much better position to meet your immediate needs, if you catch my drift." Hennessy fished in his coat pocket for a handkerchief and coughed into it lightly, patting his lips. "And, Richie, of course, when the lease is signed, I would expect you to come back to me regarding a long-term arrangement with the bank."

Flynn reached over and shook Hennessy's hand. "You have my word on that, sir," he said.

"Grand, Richie. That's grand. As a matter of fact, I'll ring Eamon myself, let him know you'll be in touch."

☆

Flynn felt even better when he met McDonough.

McDonough was fifty-six. He was a portly man with a florid face. His suits tended to flamboyant checks, and he sported a white carnation boutonniere. His hair was dyed dark brown and had orange highlights. It was combed straight back, like Jimmy Cagney's in his early movie roles. He had been a promoter of one sort or another all of his adult life, and his job was always to make people feel good, at least in the beginning.

After Flynn had told him about the synagogue's prospective conversion into a day-care center, McDonough said, "Oh, that looks very doable, yes, sir. I don't think you have anything to worry about."

They were sitting in a coffee shop. When McDonough raised his cup, his hand trembled so much that some of the coffee slopped into the saucer. He looked at Flynn and laughed. "Jesus Christ, what a night, last night. Tell me, how's your knee? Mr. Hennessy reminded me who you are, as if anybody had to remind me. I was there, you made that swell run. I used to go all the time in those days. Never missed a game."

"It's fine," Flynn had said. "You think this is doable, huh?"

"Oh, no question. I don't see any problems."

"Really?"

"It looks like a good package. Everybody can do good off it, know what I mean? You get the papers together, you'll have a commitment right away, don't worry."

"I already have a description and appraisal of the property. What else do I need?"

"A projected financial statement. Your collateral. The letter of intent. Incorporated ownership. The insurance and title is taken care of at the closing."

"Collateral?"

"You know, security for the loan."

"Uh, that's the letter of intent. The rent the city's going to pay."

"Oh, right."

"I'm not incorporated," Flynn said.

"Well, you should be," McDonough said, appalled at the thought of losing the five and a half percentage points of interest if Flynn borrowed as an individual. "That's a must. Just for the sake of your own personal liability. I'll look into it. Maybe our lawyer can handle it for you."

"I'd appreciate that."

"Think nothing of it. That's what I'm here for, to be of service."

"I'll call you as soon as I get the letter."

"Swell," McDonough had said.

☆

Fowler telephoned Flynn on Wednesday afternoon and said that he wanted to see him at Neary's Pub again at six P.M.

This time Flynn was early, nervously working on his second scotch when Fowler walked in. "You got the letter?" Flynn asked before Fowler could say anything.

"There's been a slight hitch."

I knew it, Flynn thought, the way he sounded on the phone. "What hitch?"

"Take it easy. It's nothing. A minor irritation, is all. But you're so jumpy about everything, I thought I'd better tell you so you don't go off the deep end. There's this new assistant counsel in the counsel's office. A girl. Right out of law school and a real pain in the ass. Women's libber, all that. To tell you the truth, I think she's a little funny in the sex department."

"Harry, what's the *hitch?*"

"Stolichnaya on the rocks," Fowler said to the waitress. "Richie, I'm telling you, nothing really. It's just that the counsel was out when the papers went in, and so this broad got ahold of them, and she's new and she goes by the book, and Willie Townsend, in the application from the block association, made a couple of mistakes."

"I knew it! I knew he'd fuck it up."

"Listen to me, it's all chickenshit. All he did was to forget to cross some *t*'s, dot some *i*'s. I even didn't notice them myself. Anybody but her would have let them by.

Look here at her memo. Look at what she wrote: 'The reference to specific age in article 3 (a) should be deleted.' Willie had put in that the center was for children between two and a half and twelve years old, when he should have said 'preschool' and 'school.' When he put down where the center is going to be, he just said the Bronx, and she says the city and the state have to be listed. He also had only nine directors on the board, when the rules say there has to be at least eleven. It's all things like that. Can you believe it?"

"Sure I can believe it," Flynn said. "I'm looking at it, aren't I? You think she thinks something's fishy?"

"No way. How could she? I went in there, and I said, 'Listen, there are a lot of poor people counting on this center,' and she said, 'I'm sorry, but I didn't write the rules. It's better to have everything in order now, so they won't have to worry later.' There wasn't anything I could say."

"What's next?"

"We'll have to revise the application. I'll get to work on it with Willie tonight."

"How long will it take to go through?"

"I don't know. A couple, three days."

"Do you think tomorrow?"

"I'll try. Listen, I always figured that we had until the lease was signed by Real Estate. Then you start with all this pressure, and you blame it on your friends. What kind of friends do you have anyway?"

The sarcasm in his voice infuriated Flynn. He wondered what Fowler's face would look like with Albert Karpstein looming over him. He felt the flush in his cheeks. "Harry," he said finally, "let's just get on with it, all right?"

The same sense of humiliation dogged Flynn the next day. He put off going to see Karpstein as long as he could, irrationally hoping for a call from Fowler, giving Fowler five more minutes and yet another five, like a betrayed lover pacing on a street corner. At a quarter to four he could not postpone leaving anymore. He had already delayed too long. The horn-blowing evening exodus from the city had begun, and as he inched his car toward the Lincoln Tunnel, he cursed himself for his foolishness.

He knew that he was going to have to ask Karpstein for a month's extension on the loan, and he had wanted the letter of intent in hand as additional moral armament. At least he had the insurance policy. This would be the third payment to Karpstein, with the fourth and final one due the following Thursday, and what he most detested about extending the loan was being forced to do business with him for another four weeks. He was sure that Karpstein would agree to the extension. If there was anything a shylock liked more than money, it was more money, and running the interest on a loan until the principal was retired was considered icing on the cake by all of them. But Flynn did not delude himself into thinking that someone with Karpstein's sadistic impulses could resist coming up with a wrinkle or two. He tried to figure out what Karpstein might do. Possibly double the weekly payments to a thousand dollars. More likely, he would keep it at five hundred and stop deducting it from the total amount that was owed. Stuck now in the creeping tunnel traffic, Flynn wished he had the letter; somehow, he thought, it would have buttressed his bargaining position, left him psychologically less naked.

It was almost four-thirty by the time he parked in front of E-Z Trucking. Weissberg opened the door. When Flynn stepped inside, he saw Biondo bent over the pool table. Karpstein was seated behind his desk, glaring at him. "You're late," he said.

"I'm sorry. I got caught in the traffic."

Karpstein pounded on the desk top. "I got caught in the traffic," he mimicked, his voice rising. "What the fuck is that, you got caught in the traffic? You don't know there's traffic? You don't make allowances for it? You keep me waiting because of fucking traffic?"

"I'm sorry," Flynn whispered. He felt very shaky, and he sat down on the leather sofa by Karpstein's desk.

"Who told you to sit down?" Karpstein said.

Flynn sprang to his feet. He watched a muscle twitching on the right side of Karpstein's jaw. Something dark seemed to be dribbling out of the corner of his mouth. For a moment Flynn thought that it was blood. Then he saw the Milky Way wrapper on the desk and realized that it was chocolate.

"Sit down," Karpstein said.

Flynn swayed slightly. He gritted his teeth, trying to steady himself. He turned toward the sofa and sat on it again, hunched forward.

Karpstein stared at him. "You have something for me?"

Flynn reached into his pocket and took out five one-hundred-dollar bills and gave them to Karpstein. Then he gave him the envelope containing the insurance policy. "Here's the policy made out to Mr. Weissberg," he said. "Just like you wanted it."

Karpstein accepted the envelope without comment. He tossed it on the desk without opening it. He picked up a nail file and pressed a finger against the point. He began scraping under a nail with the file. "The balance is due next week," he said to Flynn. "Leo, what's the balance?"

"Oh, yes, Albert," Weissberg said. "Minus the payments made to date, the balance is eighteen thousand five hundred." Flynn noticed that Weissberg, seated at his own desk, his back toward them, did not turn around.

"You hear that, Flynn?" Karpstein said. "Eighteen five. Next Thursday."

"Uh, Mr. Karpstein."

"What?"

"Well, the deal, you know, for the day-care center is coming along good. I should be getting the letter of intent from the city any time."

"So?"

"It's just that even though it's coming, there's a lot of red tape. And you were right. I should of gone for sixty days instead of thirty days on the loan. I'd like, uh, thirty days more."

"No."

It took a second for Karpstein's refusal to sink in. Flynn closed his eyes. Then he opened them and looked vacantly around the room. Weissberg was still at his desk, scribbling something. The radio was playing, but it was tuned so low that Flynn could barely hear the music. Biondo was lining up a shot, seemingly oblivious to his presence. "I wouldn't care if the other payments weren't deductible," Flynn said. He tried to keep the desperation out of his voice.

"No."

"We could make them a thousand instead of five hundred."

"No."

"Mr. Karpstein, please," Flynn said. "I need more time."

"*No!* You and that fuck Farber are the same. I am through screwing around with both of you."

Farber, Flynn thought, who's Farber? What's he talking about? Has he gone completely nuts? "Farber?" he said.

"Yeah, Farber. I just finished with him. Flynn and Farber. *F* for fuck-offs."

Flynn remained frozen on the sofa, his body rigid with tension. He tried to speak, but he could not.

The nail file Karpstein held glinted under the fluorescent lights. "Put your hand out," he said.

Flynn extended his left hand. The sweat was running down his torso. This is some kind of crazy test, he thought, before he gives me another month.

"Palm up," Karpstein said.

Flynn did as he was told.

Karpstein jabbed down with the file.

The pain was not great. It was more like a sting than anything. Flynn gazed in shock at his hand as first one, then a second drop of blood emerged. The blood oozed along the lines of his palm.

"You know what that means?" Karpstein said.

Flynn shook his head.

"It means we are blood brothers," Karpstein said. "It means that I absolve you for anything I do." He giggled. "Did you get that, Flynn?" He giggled again. "Now get out of here."

Yes, Flynn thought, I must get out. He struggled to his feet, took a step and tottered, his bad knee suddenly buckling, and sprawled on the floor. He lay there, motionless.

"Get up," Karpstein said. "I ain't even touched you yet."

Tears filled Flynn's eyes. "It's my knee," he said. "The knee goes sometimes."

"Yeah? Well, you don't bring the balance next week, you got another knee to go with it."

Flynn slowly pushed himself up from the floor, gingerly putting weight on the errant leg. He saw Biondo grinning at him.

"Hey, Flynn," Biondo said. "Ready for a rematch?"

16

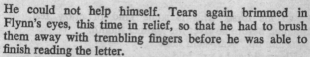

He could not help himself. Tears again brimmed in Flynn's eyes, this time in relief, so that he had to brush them away with trembling fingers before he was able to finish reading the letter.

He had been out in the field servicing some accounts on the Monday following the horror with Karpstein, and the letter was waiting for him at the Goldblatt reception desk. The accompanying note said, "As promised, Harry."

The letter was a Xerox copy of one that had been addressed to Mr. Willie Townsend, executive secretary of the East Crotona Day Care Center. The municipal seal was in the upper left corner, and the letterhead said, "Agency for Child Development."

The letter began, "This will confirm our discussions with you and your organization regarding day care at the above location in Bronx County for ninety school-age and thirty preschool-age children."

The second paragraph had triggered Flynn's tears. "It is the intention of the Agency for Child Development to enter into an agreement with your organization to operate this center in accordance with the regulations of the Agency for Child Development. We look forward to working with you to provide additional day-care services in your community."

Funding for the center, the letter added, was subject to final state approval of its incorporation papers, as well as compliance with various building, fire and health code requirements and observance of other "pertinent city, state and federal statutes."

But all Flynn cared about was the second paragraph, and he stood in front of the reception desk reading it over and over. The receptionist noticed his glistening eyes. "Is there something wrong, Mr. Flynn?"

Flynn, startled, looked up from the letter. "No," he said, "everything's wonderful."

An electric sign on the wall flashed "Quick Quencher."

Above it was a huge color portrait of a beaming Miss Goldblatt, which reminded him that he was going to see Diane in the evening. The brewery had specified that every Miss Goldblatt had to look like "the girl next door," and Diane, with her virginal face, would have been ideal. Why was it, he thought, that nothing was ever what it seemed?

All weekend Flynn had played a desperate money game trying to figure out how to raise enough cash to buy more time from Karpstein, and he had planned to ask, if necessary beg, Diane to lend him the eighteen hundred dollars she had won at the track. Now he would just fuck her silly.

Flynn hurried to his desk and telephoned Eamon McDonough. "I've got it," he said. "It came in, the letter of intent."

"Oh, that's swell," McDonough said.

"What should I do?" Flynn said as calmly as he could.

"Well, lad, the best thing to do is to drop it off, so our people can have a look at it. And tomorrow, say around three, we'll be wanting to get together to settle the details."

"I'm on my way," Flynn said.

At Concourse Funding the secretary told him that McDonough had been suddenly called to a meeting out of the office and Flynn was to leave any papers he had with her, but he was almost positive that he heard snatches of the broker's voice coming from somewhere in the rear. It did not make any sense.

He was still puzzling over this when he arrived at Diane's apartment. He forgot about it, however, as soon as the door opened and she threw her arms around him and said, "Oh, Richie, you'll never guess what I did. I found a new place. On the East Side. On Fifty-second Street. Three fantastic rooms. It's five hundred a month, but it's so cute. I had to pay a month's rent in advance and a month's security. I used the money I won at the races." She hugged him again. "See, honey, you're changing my whole life!"

"Uh, you don't have anything around here to drink, do you?" he said weakly.

☆

The next day promptly at three P.M. Flynn returned to Concourse Funding and was brought into McDonough's cubicle. Five minutes later his face was mottled in fear and anger. "What do you mean," he said, "a couple, three days, maybe a week? What is this? You said right away."

"Listen, 'right away' doesn't mean overnight." Christ, McDonough thought, he's going to fall apart right in front of me. He had told Ed Whittleby this would happen, and Whittleby had just shrugged. If Whittleby's mother wanted a loan, he'd ask her what her collateral was.

"Stall him," Whittleby had said yesterday afternoon following Flynn's call. "When he comes in with the letter, don't see him, and don't get involved in any discussions. We have to think this one over. He wants sixty for a year? Well, sixty don't exactly grow on trees. I called around, and I hear they're putting the cork on this thing. Five years they been running these leases through like shit after bad oysters. Now the money's drying up, plus I also hear there are some newspaper guys nosing around, and there could be a big stink, and that letter wouldn't be worth wiping your ass with."

Christ, McDonough had thought, I wonder if he gets all his ideas on the toilet. I'll bet he's a fucking Lutheran.

"You told me no problem," Flynn said to McDonough. "Nothing to worry about, you said."

"OK. It looked OK to me. But it's not my money. I'm only the go-between. And don't get me wrong, I'm not saying it won't go through. We just have to check everything out."

"I'd feel a lot better if there was some collateral," Whittleby had said. "I'd feel a lot better if this letter was from Real Estate, not the fucking social workers. Why is this Flynn in such a hurry? You say Hennessy sent him over? Why is Hennessy laying him off on us, this is so good?"

McDonough, seeing his commission slip away, had made a stab at retrieving it. "Hennessy said it looked good to him, except the guy needs the cash now and he couldn't move that fast with the bank. You know how these things are. Hennessy said, I already told you, Flynn has an inside connection. And the lease is worth a million eight seventy-five, guaranteed."

"Yes, when it's signed, it is. Hennessy wants me to take all the risks for the droppings, and if it works out, he comes up smelling like a rose."

"Still," McDonough had persisted, "it's a nice piece of change, however you look at it."

"Maybe so," Whittleby had said, "but I'm going to sit on it for a while."

Now Flynn stared at McDonough, the color completely drained from his face. "I'll go somewhere else," he said.

McDonough shook his head. "No good. The word gets around, don't you know? We don't touch it, nobody else touches it." He fiddled with his boutonniere. "Listen, do you have any collateral at all to put up? A house, something?"

"The letter," Flynn said. "I have the letter."

"That's the trouble. That letter don't get too specific, you know, about the lease, how long it runs and everything. I mean it's a commitment, all right, but with conditions. You got some 'pursuants' in there could be trouble."

"We've been talking sixty," Flynn said. "I'll take twenty. How about twenty?"

Good, McDonough thought, that's the way we get out of this. "Oh, that's a swell idea," he said. "Maybe I could work on that. I'll speak to the boss about it."

"Could we see him now?" Flynn pleaded, his fingers locked together like embracing thighs.

"No, he ain't here," McDonough said hastily. "I'll get to him soon as I can and get back to you. You can count on it." McDonough stood up and guided Flynn out of the cubicle, poking him playfully in the shoulder. "I'm telling you, don't worry. It'll all work out."

☆

It was practically predestined, Flynn would later reflect. He did not even have to go out of his way on his return from the Bronx after leaving McDonough. He drove robotlike down the Grand Concourse, crossed the Third Avenue Bridge into Manhattan, followed the traffic flow onto the East River Drive and veered off it, seemingly without conscious effort, at One Hundred Sixteenth Street. Almost at once he was on a side street off Pleasant Avenue in East Harlem, parking opposite the restaurant owned by Tony Valente, veteran soldier in the Frank Donato family.

Pleasant Avenue was the last redoubt for what had been one of the largest Italian settlements in the city. Donato had grown up in the neighborhood, along with such other notables as Tommy (Three-finger Brown) Lucchese, Peter

(The Clutching Hand) Morello and Ciro Terranova, the Artichoke King. The avenue was only six blocks long, and although it hugged Harlem proper, all the people walking by Flynn's Volkswagen were white. Very few blacks were ever seen around Pleasant Avenue.

Valente himself had been born in East Harlem and rarely strayed from Pleasant Avenue except to sleep in the house he had purchased for his wife in Fort Lee, New Jersey, just across the Hudson River. The city, his wife had insisted, was no place to bring up their son. Valente subsequently enrolled him in a military prep school in Pennsylvania. The boy then joined the army and was now a colonel. As he rose in rank, it became clear that he considered his father an embarrassment, and Valente had not seen him in years. Every Christmas Valente's wife would visit their son wherever he was stationed, and on Christmas Eve Valente would get drunk and send for a whore to service him in a small apartment he maintained above the restaurant. Valente had an intense dislike for "the coloreds," as he called them, but on Christmas Eve he always specified a black whore. Later he would open his wallet and peer at the photograph of his grandchildren that his wife had brought back the previous Christmas, have another drink and finally fall asleep.

The exterior of the restaurant was bright blue. The sole indication that it was a place of business was the small handpainted white lettering on the blue facade that said, "Valente's." Many myths have been written about the Mafia, but it was true that its membership enjoyed eating well, and racketeers from all over the city came to savor various Valente specialties like slivered scungilli, baked clams with oregano and veal piccata. Valente himself was an enthusiastic cook and could often be found in the kitchen with his chef tending a veal chop or stirring a cauldron of escarole soup.

Valente also conducted his modest loan-sharking and numbers operations there, the money counted and passed out over a large chopping block that had an array of knives and meat cleavers within easy reach. A corridor to the left led to the bar and dining area, which seated about forty persons.

Valente was sixty-five. He had been in what was now the Donato family since the turbulent post-Prohibition era, when the modern mob was being put together. From the first he had been a chronic complainer, smarting under imagined slights, quick to demand "sit-downs" to iron out alleged grievances, "a real ballbuster," as his immediate superior, Vincente D'Angelo, had observed. His behavior was tolerated, however, because Valente's cautious, suspicious nature made him an ideal hit man, and in his heyday as an underworld executioner he had been responsible for thirty-one homicides, all of which, in police department files, still bore the notation "Case Open."

His last such involvement had occurred a decade ago, shortly after the restaurant opened. The victim, who had been fooling around with a mob chieftain's daughter, was strangled in Valente's kitchen. The body, wired to concrete blocks, was then dumped into the East River a block away. Some time afterward Valente was watching an underwater adventure show on television, and that night he had a dream in which a scuba diver was seen slowly swimming in the murky river depths, wending his way through a forest of long-forgotten corpses that twisted and turned in the current. Ever on the alert for new economic opportunities, Valente thought it would make a wonderful opening scene for a movie, but he never could figure out what would happen next.

The restaurant enabled Valente to pick up the latest underworld gossip. He would listen, and then he would brood. He brooded about the unfairness of life upon hearing that some member of the Mafia years his junior had achieved recognition and success. He brooded over the general lowering of traditional values, which he believed to be the reason why his son had turned against him and also why many current mob murders were being carried out so sloppily. "Look at this," he would say to his bartender, Augie, brandishing a copy of the *Daily News* as evidence, "look how they leave bodies laying around in the streets." Most of all he brooded about Vincente D'Angelo, cursing the evolutionary changes in the Donato family that had made D'Angelo his particular capo. He had despised D'Angelo ever since D'Angelo had decreed that one of the fighters whom Valente backed from time to time had to take a dive. "The kid could of been a contender," Valente would tell Augie, the bartender, "but he was never no good after that. It broke his heart. Mine, too." The only bright spot Valente found in being assigned to D'Angelo's regime was that D'Angelo and the rest of his soldiers operated in midtown Manhattan, in Greenwich Village and in Little Italy, far from the environs of Pleasant Avenue. "That's how come I stick up here," Valente liked to say. "Who wants to run with them dogs anyway?"

Sitting in his Volkswagen, Flynn watched as Valente strolled around the corner, carrying a brown paper bag overflowing with links of sausage, and went down some steps into the restaurant. An hour had passed since Flynn had been with McDonough at the Concourse Funding Company.

Richie Flynn knew that what he was about to do was insane. He also knew that he would do anything now to keep Albert Karpstein at bay. Flynn sat in his car for another five minutes, planning his words. Then he followed Valente into the restaurant.

Valente was in the kitchen, gesturing at the bag of sausages and talking to the cook in a guttural Neapolitan dialect that eliminated all the terminal vowels. As soon as he saw Flynn, Valente smiled broadly. He was a stocky man with iron-gray crew-cut hair. His face looked as if it had been hammered out of unpolished agate, and the smile threatened to crack it.

"Gee, Richie, long time no see," he said. "What's with the beer business? Hey, how's for some sausages, fresh from the shop? I just got them. Look, nothing but the best. Sausages and peppers, what say, Richie?"

"It's too early for me, Tony," Flynn said. He glanced at the cook. "Listen, there's something I want to talk to you about. You got a minute?"

"For you, Richie, anytime. Guido, make me up a sausage plate and peppers. I'll be in the bar." As they went out of the kitchen, Valente said, "It's funny, I was just thinking about you. That friend of yours Scanlon that used to make book was in the other night. He says you're doing real good. And you know what else he said? He leans over to me and he says, 'Hey, Tony, you know any good nigger hookers around here?' I'll bet you didn't know that, Richie. Your friend Scanlon likes dark meat."

"Really?"

"Hey, Richie," Valente said, moving behind the bar, "would I kid you? What's your pleasure?"

"Scotch and water." I should have listened to Scanlon in the beginning, Flynn thought.

Valente poured two glasses and carefully wiped the bar. "So?"

Flynn took a drink of the scotch, set the glass down and stared at Valente. "Tony," he said finally, "you remember you told me about how you missed out with the frozen pizzas?"

Valente scowled. "Hey, do I remember?" he said. "I'll never forget it. Every time I'm in a supermarket, I see all them fucking pizzas, I go crazy. It was right after the war, and I'm through with gas stamps and I'm starting in the jukebox business, and a guy says to me, 'Hey, Tony, let's get into frozen pizzas, I know this guy who knows how to do it,' and I say, 'Who wants frozen pizza?' I mean, gee, how the fuck could I know? I didn't make it past the third fucking grade."

"Tony, I got a deal for you could make up a lot of that." Flynn reached into his jacket pocket and drew out a copy of the letter from the Agency for Child Development and handed it across the bar to Valente. "Read this."

Valente peered at the letter, holding it at arm's length. He swore to himself and took out a pair of rimless glasses that slipped down his nose, giving him an oddly benign appearance. When he finished reading the letter, he looked over the glasses at Flynn and said, "So?"

Flynn took another swallow of the scotch. "You know what it is?"

"You tell me."

My God, Flynn thought, that gorilla in Jersey is waiting to break every bone in my body, and I'm sitting here talking to this guinea hood like he's Humphrey Bogart. "It's a letter of intent from the city that says they're going to put a day-care center in that building, which is an old synagogue, up in the Bronx."

"So?"

"Tony, I own the building. When the city signs the lease, it's for one hundred twenty-five big ones a year. For fifteen years, guaranteed."

Guido, the cook, brought in the sausages and peppers and left the plate on the bar. Valente speared one of the sausages with his fork, held it up and examined it, the marinara sauce dripping, and bit off an end. "Gee, you're missing a treat, Richie," he said. He bit into the sausage again, and then he said, "I didn't see nothing in there about no one twenty-five Gs."

"That's next. First you have to have the commitment before you get the lease."

"OK. So you got it. So?"

"So the thing is I got the building, but I got to keep up the payments until the lease comes through. Which is around a month. And I'm a little short."

"How much?"

"Twenty. I need twenty."

Valente put down his fork. "Hey, Richie, what you think, I'm a fucking bank? I got some money circulating in the street. A guy wants a thousand here, a thousand there, OK. But I ain't got no twenty in one basket."

"Listen to me, Tony, this is the chance of a lifetime. It's why Scanlon said things are going good for me. We're talking close to two million. You put in twenty, you get twenty percent of the action."

Valente studied Flynn over his glasses. "I couldn't do better than ten," he said. "And I'd want in for a third."

Sweet Jesus, I've got him, Flynn thought. Just don't be too anxious. I'm too anxious, he's going to get nervous. He'll want more time to think about it. "Tony, I can't go for that," he said. "I already got plenty in it myself. I can't throw it away, Tony. Twenty and twenty."

"Ten Gs is all," Valente said. There was an air of finality about it. He dug into another sausage.

"When could I have it?"

"You could have it right now," Valente said, his mouth full.

Take it, Flynn told himself. Make a deal with Karpstein. The ten will cool him off. Time was the important thing, time for the lease to go through. Still, he had to be careful to keep up a front. "Tony, for ten I couldn't deal you in more than ten percent. Nobody ever made you a deal like this."

"You're wearing me out, Flynn. Twenty percent. Plus three points on the ten Gs until I get it back. The first payment is due a week from today."

Suddenly it was "Flynn" instead of "Richie."

"You have it here?"

"Yeah, you're lucky. I just got some payments come in."

"It's a deal," Flynn said.

Valente left the bar and went down the corridor toward the kitchen. When he returned, he was carrying an envelope. He walked behind the bar and dropped the envelope next to the letter of intent. "You don't have to count it," he said. "It's all there."

Flynn forced a smile. "Hey, come on, Tony. I can't trust you, I can't trust anybody, right?"

Valente took off his glasses and looked at Flynn. All at once he did not seem so benign anymore. "Richie, do yourself a favor," he said. "Don't fuck up."

17

Flynn shifted once again into a new position on the leather sofa by Karpstein's desk. It was a few minutes past eight P.M.

He had been on the sofa for more than three hours now. He had called and told Leo Weissberg he wanted to come a day ahead of schedule, that he had something for Karpstein. Weissberg had come back on the line and said, "Oh, yes, Albert says five o'clock would be fine."

He was half an hour early when he pulled up in front of E-Z Trucking, and he sat in the car and waited, the envelope with Valente's ten thousand dollars in it pressed against his heart.

At five minutes to five, he rang the buzzer, and Weissberg had opened the door and said, "Oh, Mr. Flynn, come in. Albert's been delayed on business." Weissberg ushered him inside and had pointed to the sofa and said, "Please take a seat," and then finally had come over and said, "I'm sure he won't be too long," and switched on the portable Sony TV set on Karpstein's desk.

Patsy, his boils festering worse than ever, sat across the room, on the other side of the pool table, leafing through girlie magazines. Weissberg remained bent over his ledgers. The phone rang several times, but Flynn could not hear what Weissberg was saying over the sound of the Sony.

Flynn wondered if Karpstein had forgotten that he was coming. He wanted to find out if there was someplace the loan shark could be reached, but he was afraid to ask.

He watched a Bugs Bunny cartoon hour on the Sony. Then the news and a word-game quiz show. On the quiz show, as Flynn looked on, hands clenched, a young Japanese stenotypist from Los Angeles won twenty-five thousand dollars. At eight o'clock a New York Mets baseball game started, and Patsy brought his chair over to look at it. He did not say anything to Flynn.

Right after the ball game began, Karpstein strode into

the room, Biondo with him. Flynn jumped up. Karpstein went by him without a word. Flynn stood uncertainly for a moment and then sat down, perched tensely on the edge of the sofa.

Karpstein snapped off the Sony. There were a number of white envelopes stacked on the desk. Karpstein glanced at the notations on the envelopes and opened them one after another, extracting cash from each of them, checking the amounts against a list on a sheet of paper. He rearranged all the bills according to their denominations, wrapped a rubber band around the bundle and put it into his pocket. He still had paid no attention to Flynn. "Leo," he said, "anything else?"

Weissberg swiveled around toward Karpstein. "Oh, yes, Albert," he said. "I almost forgot. Manny Aronowitz called. Manny says Mr. Mandelbaum's attorney, Farber, called him and said he just found out that the house was in Mrs. Mandelbaum's name all the time, so it isn't part of the estate, and Mrs. Mandelbaum doesn't care what Mr. Mandelbaum signed. Manny says Farber said to tell you he was sorry. Manny says also Mr. Hobo called about the money from his investment. When is he going to get the rest of it? Manny says he figures you'd want to know."

Karpstein seemed to expand in front of Flynn's eyes, like a balloon being blown up. He rose from behind the desk, his neck engorged, arms apart, his chest straining forward. "He said *what?*"

Even Weissberg appeared to be taken aback. "Uh, Manny said you'd want to know."

"I don't mean Manny!" Karpstein screamed. "I mean Farber. What did he say Farber said?"

"That he was sorry. Those were Manny's exact words, Albert."

The sound that Karpstein emitted was difficult for Flynn to decipher. It was not so much a moan as it was an unintelligible whine, all the more frightening because of its massive source. Farber again, he thought. Jesus, who's Farber?

Karpstein braced himself against the desk, hands balled into fists. He brought his left arm across his chest and swung out with it. The Sony flew off the desk and crashed on the floor. No one spoke.

Flynn started for the door.

"You," Karpstein said, "where the fuck are you going?"

"I was just thinking maybe I should come back tomorrow."

"That's your trouble, Flynn. You're not smart. You think too much."

Richie Flynn felt his legs quivering once more and the sweat under his arms. "Listen," he said, "I really mean it. I don't want to interrupt anything. I could come tomorrow, like usual. No trouble."

Karpstein's dilated eyes had gone blank, as if he were sightless. His breathing sounded loudly in the room. "You waited," he said, "because the last time you made me wait. Now give me what you got."

Flynn knew he had no choice. The whole desperate plan he had hatched, the idea of coming to see Karpstein a day ahead of time to demonstrate good faith, offering respect, giving him the money, explaining why it was not all the money, asking for and receiving additional time for the deal to go through—it had all seemed so reasonable, and it was, every bit of it, falling apart. Because of someone called Farber! The abstraction of Farber was the only reality Flynn had now. All the words that he had so carefully prepared and rehearsed remained frozen in his larynx, and he silently handed Karpstein the envelope with the ten thousand dollars in it.

He sat there watching while Karpstein took the envelope, opened it and started counting the money. Suddenly he remembered his friend Scanlon telling him before this nightmare began that Karpstein hoped you couldn't pay him back because then he could beat it out of you, and Flynn felt his mouth fill with saliva and he fought to keep from vomiting.

"You're short," Karpstein said. "Leo, what was the balance?"

"Eighteen five, Albert. Eighteen five."

Some signs of life returned to Karpstein's eyes as he focused them on Flynn. "That's right, eighteen five. See you only got ten here, so you're still short eight five," he said, addressing Flynn as though he were a backward child. "You got to tomorrow to come up with it. Leo, the balance is due tomorrow, am I right?"

"Oh, yes, Albert, tomorrow. Thursday."

"Flynn, you catch that?"

"Mr. Karpstein," Flynn finally croaked, "give me a break. The ten is all I could get. The day-care deal is going through." He reached into his pocket and pulled out the letter of intent. "Look, I'm not kidding. Here's the go-ahead from the city. It's just a matter of time."

"Tomorrow."

"It's why I came out today. To show you respect, so you'll know I'm serious. I'm not asking for a handout. I'll pay the points. Just give me an extension is all I'm asking."

"Tomorrow."

"Why don't you give me a break?"

Karpstein stared at him, the eyes dilating again.

Oh, Jesus, Flynn thought, don't look at me like that.

"Because you are a schemer and a swindler and a fucking four-flusher, and I am tired of being jerked around by people like you. You come to me and want me to bail you out. You make a bargain, and you shake hands on it, and right away you want to change the bargain." Karpstein's voice started to rise. "Well, you ain't changing this one."

"What can I do?" Flynn blurted.

"How should I know! Go rob a fucking bank. I got confidence in you. You want I should cash in your policy?"

"A week. Just one lousy week."

"Tomorrow."

Flynn turned and fled. He left blindly, moving with such haste that his left shoulder slammed into the side of the doorway as he tried to pass through, and he bounced off it, grunting in surprise, momentarily staggering before he recovered and went out.

☆

Biondo started to snicker at the way Flynn had run out. But he stopped short when he saw that Karpstein was not laughing along with him.

Karpstein sat behind his desk, staring vacantly into space, clutching the money Flynn had given him. Then he blinked, as if he had just awakened.

"Patsy," he said, "pick up the fucking television and get a broom. Leo, call Paulie Swag first thing in the morning and find out has he got another Sony in that drop of his. And Leo, put the price on Farber's account. He owes for it."

"Oh, yes, Albert."

"Tommy," Karpstein said, "I'm tired. Drive me home."

During the trip Biondo said, "You think that Flynn'll take off?"

"Where to?" Karpstein said.

After that Biondo did not say anything.

When Karpstein's wife, Angelina, opened the front door of the house in Hasbrouck Heights, she kissed him on the cheek and said, "Hon, you're late. I was so worried. You should call."

"I know," he said. He brushed by her into the living room. His mother-in-law sat in a chair in the corner, crocheting. She nodded at him.

Angelina trailed after him. "Sweetheart," she said, taking his hand, "you didn't even kiss me back. You all right?"

"Yeah," he said. "Listen, do we have any scotch in the house, or something?"

Now there was no question in her mind that there was a problem. Karpstein drank sparingly, and practically never at home. "Yes," she said. "You wash up, and I'll fix it for you."

As soon as he was gone, she told her mother to go to her own room.

"Perchè?" the old lady demanded, her eyes glittering in anticipation of a domestic crisis.

"Mama!" Angelina said, and her mother, muttering to herself, gathered up her needle and yarn and shuffled out.

When Karpstein returned, Angelina had a bottle of scotch and a shot glass ready. She kept the scotch on hand to entertain her girl friends, who were the only adult visitors to the house.

She balanced herself on the arm of the easy chair Karpstein was seated in. She poured him a drink. He downed it in a gulp and held out his glass. She poured another and put the bottle aside. She rubbed his free hand. "Honey," she said, "what's wrong?"

"Deadbeats," he said. "All day long I got to deal with deadbeats. I should get out of the business of helping people. I should go in some other business."

She continued to stroke his hand. "I know," she said. "It's terrible. I tell you what. You sit here and have another drink, and I'll fix you a nice steak and some nice spaghetti."

After he had eaten, Karpstein went to bed. Angelina did the dishes, and when she entered the bedroom, she sighed and switched off the night-light and undressed in the dark. She slipped into bed without wearing her nightgown. Karpstein's back was toward her. She pressed her soft, ample breasts against him and reached over and unbuttoned the top of his shorts.

He stirred and turned around and held her, moving a hand across her breasts, her belly, her vulva. She had been terrified of him the first time they coupled, but his penis was surprisingly small.

"You're so big," she had whispered. "Be careful. Don't hurt me."

He did not speak, taking her in rapid, little movements. Even though it was dark, she closed her eyes, his great bulk on her. Then he groaned slightly, and she knew it was finished.

He rolled away from her. She ran a finger down his back. His breathing deepened. "That's right, baby," she said. "Go to sleep. You'll feel better in the morning." She waited another minute or so before she got up and went into the bathroom to douche.

☆

"You mean," Tony Valente said, "you gave *my* money to that fucking ape?" Valente jerked his head, like a terrier with a bone.

Flynn sat across the table from him. His brain seemed to swell against his skull. His ears rang painfully. He held the edge of the table. Since leaving Hoboken, he had driven twice around the parkways encircling Manhattan, trying to decide what to do. The clock on the wall of Valente's restaurant showed five minutes to midnight. They were alone in the dining area.

"I told you I had to, why I had to," Flynn said. "I figured he'd give me the time. For the deal to go through."

"*My* money?"

"Tony, that's why I'm here. Karpstein goes after me, I'm dead and you're out the ten thousand. I can't pay it if I'm dead, can I?"

"My fucking money," Valente repeated, as if he could not believe what he was saying.

"Listen to me," Flynn said. "The deal goes through, you're rich. I spoke to the guy handling it on the inside.

It's only a few days off, he says. Only I got to get Karpstein off my back."

"Cocksucker!" Valente said. "All right, I'll do what I can do."

"Tomorrow, Tony. Tomorrow is all I got."

Valente reached over and gripped Flynn's wrist. "You better come through this time, Richie," he said. "I don't get satisfaction, forget Karpstein. I'll whack you out myself."

18

It was the best morning Vincente D'Angelo ever had—until his bodyguard came into the office and said that Tony Valente was outside.

"I'm not here."

"Boss, he says he was downstairs watching for you when you come in, and he says not to say you ain't here."

"Shit!" D'Angelo said, grinding out a Romeo y Julietta panatela, an act he instantly regretted, having lit it only moments before. "All right. Say I'll see him in a couple of minutes. I knew nothing could stay this good."

D'Angelo had just learned that he was about to make two million dollars. Directly opposite his Bourbon Street Club was the entrance to the new, gleaming block-square forty-three-story headquarters of International Ventures, Limited, a multinational conglomerate that was the dominant economic power in a half dozen dictatorships in the Caribbean, Latin America and Africa and that in this country had a broad spectrum of holdings, including a supermarket chain, a missile-component manufacturer, a grain-shipping fleet, an amusement park, two United States senators and three congressmen.

The building, with its fountained plaza and gallery of elegant boutiques, was hailed for its architectural daring, and International Ventures was widely applauded for the renaissance spirit it had displayed in upgrading an area so close to Times Square. All of this greatly pleased IVL's chairman and chief executive officer, Thomas F. Easton, who also was a vestryman in his Episcopal church and the driving force behind a major golf tournament the conglomerate sponsored each year.

Then, within days after the building's dedication, the Bourbon Street opened its doors, and Easton was not amused. He would arrive in his limousine each morning and stare grimly across the way at the provocative blow-ups of the girls being featured in the club. Upon reentering the limousine each evening, he would be greeted by the club's now garishly blinking lights, rock music blaring outside and the liveried black doorman loudly hustling customers.

The club, at his prompting, was closed down by the police. D'Angelo's lawyer immediately had it reopened with a barrage of First Amendment motions. Easton's next step was to have the State Liquor Authority revoke the Bourbon Street license to serve alcoholic beverages, an order that was also placed in limbo pending an appeal. "Hey, what's going on?" D'Angelo said, secure in the knowledge that whiskey was not the club's main attraction. "So I'll serve grape juice, I have to. Five bucks a pop."

Easton began buying up the block fronting his headquarters, using a series of straw men. By then D'Angelo had learned from his own real estate people what was happening, and he declined an offer of four hundred thousand dollars to buy out the ten-year lease he had on the Bourbon Street and an adjacent unused structure. He subsequently refused a million dollars. "I'm thinking of closing down anyway for some renovations," he told Easton's representatives, explaining that he planned to turn the empty building next to the Bourbon Street into a pornographic movie theater with live sex shows on stage between screenings. "I mean, you got to give the public what they want, right?"

The day Easton's attorneys gathered to advise him of the situation, the New York *Times* reported that a Latin American military junta, backed by International Ventures to safeguard its mining interests, had incarcerated twenty thousand dissident citizens in a football stadium, where many of them were being systematically tortured and killed. Thomas F. Easton did not care about the story or the hapless dissidents. All he cared about was the Bourbon Street Club. "What kind of country do we have," he demanded of the subdued attorneys in his conference room, "that lets a Mafia thug get away with something like this?"

So D'Angelo had settled for the two million, which was far more than he had expected, and not even Valente, he reflected, could spoil the morning for him.

At first, as Valente related his woes, D'Angelo's memory leaped back to the night he had seen Flynn and the dancer—he couldn't recall her name—at The Fallen Angel, and he wondered, stifling a laugh, whose money Flynn had been spending—Karpstein's or Valente's? When Valente had finished talking, D'Angelo said, "OK. You were stupid enough to shylock the money. What do you want from me?"

"Justice," Valente said. "That animal ain't supposed to be working in New York. It ain't his territory. He is with Joe Hobo, which is Jersey. I want he don't touch Flynn until I get my ten Gs back, plus the points."

"Hey, come on, what's this, territories? This is 1974, for Christ's sake."

Valente's jaw jutted. "It's our rule," he said stubbornly. "And he ain't even a member. It's Joe Hobo's responsibility to put things right. You talk to Joe Hobo, else I want a sit-down. I'll go to Mattei on this. What would F. D. say, he knew about this?"

Mattei was the aging *consigliere* of the Frank Donato family. His favorite pastime was to gather the capos together for long, boring meals while he reminisced in flowery fashion about the good old days. But he had direct access to Donato, and this was just the sort of thing he would delight in hashing over. D'Angelo was certain that Donato himself would not care about Valente's problem. Or almost certain. That was the trouble with Donato, he thought irritably. Nobody ever really knew what was going on in Donato's head at any given moment. Although D'Angelo spoke to him more than the other family capos, their conversations were always at Donato's instigation and occurred at best three or four times a year. Valente's problem, however, did involve another family, and it was technically a clear-cut violation of interfamily relationships if anyone wanted to make an issue of it. And so maybe Donato might involve himself after all. He surely was aware of the complaints that he did not concern himself enough with the family's affairs and general well-being. This might be a perfect way for him to squelch such talk. Then D'Angelo was seized by another, unsettling thought. What if Donato learned about his two-million-dollar score and decided to grab part of it by fining him for not protecting the rights of his men?

D'Angelo swore under his breath and gazed at Valente with undisguised hostility. Valente stared back at him, his jaw still set. "I'll look into it," D'Angelo said.

"How'll I know?"

"You'll know when you know," D'Angelo said, pleased with the line. It was exactly the kind of pronouncement Mattei would make, leaving his listener to ponder its meaning. But to D'Angelo's surprise, the answer seemed to satisfy Valente. Christ, D'Angelo thought, these old geezers must operate on some crazy wavelength of their own.

"Today," Valente said, "it has to be today," and got up and went out the door.

After a minute D'Angelo summoned his bodyguard and said, "Find me Joe Hobo."

☆

They met that afternoon in the Ravens Club. Although D'Angelo often passed it on Mulberry Street, he seldom went in. The pace was too leisurely for him. He found the conversation desultory, he did not play cards and, because of a flighty stomach, he limited himself to one cup of espresso a day, and only after he had eaten.

As usual, two muscular punks were stationed on each side of the club's entrance, like the lions in front of the public library. When he arrived, he saw that Joe Hobo was already there, in the middle of a gin game. D'Angelo went over to the bar where the espresso machine was and ordered mineral water. There were a dozen or so men present. Joe Hobo had yet to acknowledge him. D'Angelo watched as he scrutinized the hand he held. Most of the men were playing cards. Except for Brancusi the numbers king, only D'Angelo and Joe Hobo had on suits. Everyone else sported open-necked, short-sleeved shirts. They could have easily fit into any small-town Kiwanis social room.

The moon-faced Brancusi, seated alone in a corner, hauled himself up and advanced toward D'Angelo, carrying an empty espresso cup. "Vinnie, how's it going?" he said.

"Good, Aldo. You?"

"Eh," Brancusi said, waving a hand. "You coming to my Maria's wedding, right? At the Plaza. Grand Ballroom."

D'Angelo remembered. Brancusi's daughter was getting married in the summer. "Hey, I wouldn't miss it."

"You know what her favorite flowers is?" Brancusi said.

"Daisies. You can't get them here in August. I got to fly them in special from California. Thousands of them. A whole plane."

D'Angelo shook his head in commiseration. Ordinarily he would have been expected to put five hundred dollars into his wedding-present envelope. Brancusi was telling him to double it.

As he and Brancusi talked, D'Angelo kept an eye on Joe Hobo. Although they both held equivalent ranks in their respective families, Joe Hobo was at least twenty years his senior, and D'Angelo was uncertain as to the best way to approach him regarding the Valente matter. The thing was to get it over with as soon as possible. Joe Hobo had continued to ignore him. But now the gin game was over, and he finally looked up at D'Angelo and nodded.

D'Angelo strolled over to the table.

"You were late," Job Hobo said. "Or maybe I was early."

Oh, shit, D'Angelo thought, do we have to go through this? "It was me," he said. "I was late. I got tied up."

Joe Hobo smiled and said, "It's nothing. Forget it." He indicated an empty chair by the table.

"No," D'Angelo said. "In the back, you don't mind."

"My pleasure."

After they had stepped through the curtained archway, D'Angelo decided to skip the niceties and come right to the point. "That fucking animal you got, Karpstein," he began, "is off his leash where he don't belong."

When D'Angelo had finished the story, Joe Hobo raised a hand. "Listen, Milky goes to the bathroom himself, you know."

"Milky?"

"Yeah, Milky. You know, Albert. That's his name he goes by."

"I don't give a fuck what he goes by. He's off his leash, is what, and you got to put him back on."

"Hey, if Milky did this, what you say, he did it on his own. I didn't have anything to do with it. I never heard of this before. It's all news to me."

"I'm not saying you did, but he's your guy, and he's fucking one of our people, which is Valente." D'Angelo paused for dramatic effect. "Leastways, I'm telling you, that's how Mr. F.D. feels about it. You don't want this to go further. Let's settle it ourselves. The bosses get into it, who the hell knows what'll happen."

"You're telling me F.D. is in this?"

"I'm telling you he wants it straightened out."

Joe Hobo studied D'Angelo. He could not believe that Donato was involved. Yet he couldn't afford not to. D'Angelo had come on very strong with him, exhibiting none of the deference due his years. The correct approach would have been for D'Angelo to ease into the discussion, sketch out the details of the problem and then ask his advice about how best to resolve it. But D'Angelo had not done any of this. Joe Hobo considered the possibilities. Finally he shrugged and said, "So what am I supposed to do?"

"Tell him to lay off Flynn till Valente gets his money."

"I'll ask him about it."

"No, you tell him that's our decision. Karpstein's big, but he ain't bigger than us. Right?"

Joe Hobo's face reddened slightly. "I'll speak to him."

"Good," D'Angelo said. "I knew we could straighten this out."

☆

Flynn was at home when the call from Karpstein came about eight P.M. "You're a dead man!" Karpstein yelled. "I'm cashing in that policy. You don't come over here tomorrow with the money, I'm coming in and I'm cutting your fucking balls off. You think you're so fucking smart, you'll beg to die when I'm finished with you."

"Please, Mr. Karpstein," Flynn said, "I told you I just need some time. I thought it was all arranged."

"I don't know nothing about no arrangements. You get over here with the fucking money, or I'm coming in."

After Karpstein hung up, Flynn frantically dialed Valente's restaurant. "Tony," he said, "Karpstein just called me. He said I don't pay him, he's coming in after me."

"Don't worry about it. He's only bluffing you. That Jew boy ain't coming in here. It ain't allowed."

"You're sure?"

"I'm telling you, don't worry. It's been taken care of. Just concentrate on the deal. That's all you got to worry about it. The pig calls you again, you tell him to call me, Tony Valente, personal. You tell him to call Vinnie

D'Angelo, he wants to. And, Richie, keep in touch, you know what I mean."

Flynn put down the receiver. It was incredible, he thought. He was going to make it after all. Not as good as before. But still, he would make it.

19

Every day Flynn badgered Fowler about the status of the lease at the Department of Real Estate, and then Fowler told him that the head of the leasing section wanted three thousand dollars to give the lease application priority handling, and Flynn had yelled in desperation at Fowler, reminding him of his promise that Real Estate would fall all over itself to dress up its insider deals by approving a daycare center so highly recommended by the Agency for Child Development, and Fowler retorted that yes, he had said that, but that these people were so used to receiving something for signing anything—a "gratuity" was the exact word Fowler employed—that they could not break the habit, and Flynn said that it was out of the question and to tell the guy that they would pay him off *after* the lease went through, and Fowler had said that he had tried this, even doubling the amount, and then Flynn finally told Fowler just where the money for the synagogue had come from and how much trouble he was in—that *they* were in—and Fowler had shriveled audibly, as if he had known all the time.

And then, all at once, ten days later, it was finished, and Flynn's frantic scrambling did not mean a thing anymore. The federal government announced that it was cutting back on its funding for child development, and the state and the city, facing a financial crisis, immediately decided to follow suit. The city, in a burst of economic righteousness, also announced that it was closing down some of the centers, slashing food allowances, laying off counselors and rearranging the income and employment qualifications of mothers so as to reduce the number of children eligible for day care. The city, of course, did not announce that it would continue to pay rent to the politically connected landlords, that about a quarter of the money still being allocated to day care would go to them whether their centers were functioning or not.

The scandal erupted into the open when an angry

Puerto Rican woman named Flora Sanchez revealed that a nonprofit group she had put together for a day-care center in Brooklyn had been turned down because the site was too close to an elevated subway line but that a few months later the city had signed a twenty-year lease for the same site with a private developer at an annual rental of one hundred and eight thousand dollars.

This prompted the city to announce that it was placing an immediate freeze on all new direct leases for day-care centers.

Flynn read about it in the papers, watched it on television, listened to it on the radio and cursed Flora Sanchez. He called Fowler, who said, "Listen, Richie, it's not certain if this covers the leases already in the hopper," and in his heart Flynn knew it was over.

He called Tony Valente, and Valente said, "I got nothing more to do with it, Richie. I'm out of it. I'm out of the picture."

"Listen to me, Tony," Flynn said. "I just talked to my guy on the inside, and he said that the other deals are off, but ours maybe isn't because it's being processed already. It's the new deals that are being stopped."

"Hey, there's nothing I can do. I talked to Vinnie, and Vinnie says that all you have to do is read the paper and see nothing's going to happen in the future, and we can't hold off Albert anymore. Albert's getting very impatient about being held back."

"Can't you hold him off a little longer?"

"Well, could you get me my ten Gs right away?"

"I'm telling you the deal should break any day."

"That way," Valente said, "maybe things could be straightened out."

"Tony, everything I got is in the deal already."

There was a pause on the line, and then Valente said, "I'm sorry. I done what I could. It's between you and Karpstein now. He's been told he can make the collection."

"What did he say?"

"I imagine you'll be hearing from him soon enough yourself one way or the other," Valente said, and hung up.

Flynn stared at the receiver. There was something wrong. Then he realized what it was. Valente should have been raging at him about the ten-thousand-dollar loan, but he had made just a passing reference to it, his voice calm, almost resigned. It could mean only that when Karpstein was given the go-ahead, he would be acting for Valente as well as himself, that some division of the spoils must have been agreed upon, and the sole available spoil was Flynn's life insurance policy.

Flynn had called Valente from his desk at Goldblatt. It was six P.M. The rest of the office was deserted. He gazed at the rows of empty desks. He wondered what the people who had sat behind them that day were doing at this moment. Probably jammed into subways and buses. Snarled in evening traffic tie-ups. Indistinguishable from the hordes that poured out of every office building at the end of the day. Caught in a mindless, repetitive cycle, spinning out their lives. For what? He had tried to stick his head above the crowd, and his head was about to be chopped off. Fear pierced his bowels, as if he were a lost child. He did not know what to do, so he went home.

Agnes was in the kitchen cleaning up after supper with their son. She seemed surprised to see him. And then he remembered that it was Monday and that he had not been coming home recently on Monday nights. Monday was for Diane, but she had slipped completely from his mind. All he could think about was Karpstein. "Has anybody called?" he asked.

"No," she said, looking at him oddly. "Why?"

"Nothing."

"Have you eaten?"

"I'm not hungry." He went into the living room. "Where's Sean?"

"In his room, studying. He has a test tomorrow."

Flynn opened the door to his son's room. "How's it going?"

"Fine."

"What's the test?"

"Math."

"Oh, brother. That was my worst subject."

"I know. You told me."

The boy, bent over his desk, was in his pajamas. Flynn was seized by a sudden impulse to sweep him up in his arms, to hold him close. But what would he say? Who, he thought despairingly, would be comforting whom?

After an indecisive moment he went back into the living room. He sat on the sofa and pulled nervously at his hair. He stared at the phone. He wanted to go out again, for a walk, a drink in a bar, but he was afraid to, afraid that the phone would ring and Agnes would answer and it would be Karpstein.

She came out of the kitchen, rubbing her hands with a lotion that she always used after washing dishes. "We had pot roast," she said. "I can heat it up for you."

"I told you. I'm not hungry."

She went into the hallway toward their bedroom. A few minutes later he heard the bath running. He got up from the sofa, went to the closet by the front door and took out the bottle of scotch he had sequestered on a shelf. He held it up to the light and was relieved to find it a third full. He put it on the coffee table and went into the kitchen for a glass, water and some ice.

He returned to the sofa and made himself a drink. He stared at the phone once more and wondered why it did not ring. What kind of game was Karpstein playing with him?

Agnes reappeared in a peach-colored negligee he had not seen before, her usually mousy brown hair lustrous from a shampoo and brushing. He raised his glass defiantly toward her. She looked at him and at the bottle of scotch and said, "Well, *I'm* going to watch television."

"Be my guest," he said.

She tuned in a syndicated talk show. A stand-up comedian was doing his act. "My parents couldn't afford me," the comedian was saying, "so my neighbors had me." Agnes giggled. Flynn could not keep his eyes off the still-silent telephone. "You're sure nobody called?" he said, knowing how inane the question sounded.

She turned to him. "Of course I'm sure. What's wrong?"

"Nothing," he said.

He took a drink of the scotch, and then the thought occurred to him that if Karpstein had not called, maybe he was coming to the apartment. Flynn jumped up from the sofa and went to the door and attached the chain lock. He returned to the sofa and began to bite into a knuckle. Agnes turned to him again, and after a moment she reached out and touched his other hand. "Richie," she said, "something *is* wrong. What is it?"

He looked at her, and for an instant her shining hair and freshly scrubbed face reminded him of the girl he had seduced in Good Shepherd parish, and he felt himself crumbling inside.

"Please, Richie, tell me," she said. And then he did, all of it.

☆

She looked at him for a long time when he had finished, and finally she said, "Oh, Richie, why?"

"Because I wanted to be somebody." He tried to keep his voice from breaking as he realized that he had used the past tense.

She buried her face in her hands. Her shoulders began to shake. "You wanted to be somebody," she sobbed. "Is that what you've been doing all these nights you weren't home—trying to be somebody?"

He closed his eyes, unable to look at her. "You don't understand."

"You're right," she mumbled through her hands. "I don't understand. I don't understand anything."

"Look," he said, "I'm sorry. I didn't do anything illegal, you know, anything that a lot of other people haven't done."

Her hands came away from her face, and she gazed at him. "I don't give a fuck what they did!" she shouted. "What are you going to do now?"

He could not believe that she had used the word. He had never heard her say anything like that before. He stared back at her, speechless. "I don't know," he said at last.

"You just sit there and do nothing, waiting for this, this man, to come here? What about us? What about me? What about your own son? For God's sake, call the police! Do something!"

The police? He knew at least fifty detectives and cops that he had joked and caroused with. There wasn't one he would trust with this.

"Call the FBI!"

"The FBI?" he said.

On the television the late evening news had started. What could he do at this hour? All his life he had operated on the premise that you had to know somebody. That's how the smart guys did it. How could he possibly call out of the blue and say he needed help? How would he begin to explain? Who would he ask for?

"Yes," she said, "the FBI. If you won't, *I* will." She

jumped up and went to the phone and dialed information and asked for the New York office number.

He watched her dumbly. He had never felt more impotent. Then he remembered an FBI agent named Tim Crotty he had met around some of the midtown places like Gallagher's and Mike Manuche's and Clarke's, even coming out of 21. He took the phone from Agnes just as the switchboard operator was saying, "FBI."

"Agent Crotty," he said. "I mean I want to speak to Agent Crotty. It's an emergency."

"Who is this, please?"

"Richie Flynn. If you can reach him, tell him it's Richie Flynn who used to play for the New York Giants."

"Does he have your number, Mr. Flynn?"

"Uh, I don't think so."

"May I have it?"

After Flynn had given it to her, she said, "Hold on, please."

Tim Crotty was fifty-three, and for nearly a decade he had had an enviable assignment. While most of his fellow agents were having sandwiches and coffee in cafeterias, Crotty every day stopped by for drinks and elaborate lunches at selected Manhattan restaurants that were patronized by sports and entertainment personalities and important figures in business and politics. He made no secret of the fact that he was with the FBI, but he was so affable and so familiar a face that while people knew who he was, at the same time they seemed to ignore it. And at the end of each week Crotty would type a report about all the gossip he had picked up—about imminent boardroom deals, the whispered sexual proclivities or problems of well-known people, the latest political maneuverings. Knowing how much J. Edgar Hoover valued such information, Kevin McGrath, as head of the New York office, would then recast it in a personal memo to Hoover in Washington with the notation "Director's Eyes Only."

After Hoover died, McGrath did not quite know what to do with Crotty but finally resolved to keep him where he was. If this sort of stuff was good enough for Hoover, he reasoned, he might find a use for it himself, especially since he coveted the directorship.

One of the fringe benefits of Crotty's assignment was that he rarely had to pay for his meals. Wherever he was, he waited at the bar until inevitably someone or some group came along and asked him to join a table. He would, of course, submit weekly expenses anyway, and over the years the cash had comfortably added up.

On this particular day he had been standing alone at the bar in 21 when a partner in a Wall Street investment house invited him to lunch with two other men. It was an extremely pleasant day, and after coffee they all decided to spend the rest of the afternoon golfing at the Westchester Country Club. Moments like these tended to make Crotty forget that he was an FBI agent, but as it turned out, he did gain some interesting intelligence. While the foursome played the course, Crotty's host mentioned that his firm was putting together a package to finance a gambling casino in eastern Long Island, in the Montauk area, once the state made it legal. McGrath would love to know about this, he thought. With gambling casinos, the mob couldn't be far behind.

Crotty stayed on at the club for dinner and several rounds of drinks. And groggy from all the alcohol and sun, he was fast asleep in his house in suburban Rockland County when the FBI operator rang him about Flynn.

"Flynn?" he mumbled.

"Yes, Richie Flynn. He said he played for the New York Giants."

Crotty struggled through layers of consciousness. "Flynn? Richie Flynn? Oh, yeah."

"He said it was urgent. Do you want me to put him through, or do you want his number?"

Crotty blinked wider awake. "Put him through," he said, and when Flynn came on the line, Crotty told him, "This better be good, this time of night."

"I'm sorry," Flynn said. "I'm in real trouble."

"What trouble?"

Flynn did not know where to start. Then he said, "Karpstein. You ever hear of a shylock called Karpstein?"

"King Kong Karpstein?"

"Yes, that's him. Well, it's a long story, but I'm into him, and he's after me. I've been warned. He could be coming any second, and I don't know what to do."

Crotty looked at his watch and groaned inwardly. "Where are you?"

"I'm home."

"Where's home?"

"In the city."

"An apartment building?"

"Yes."

Crotty's temples throbbed mercilessly, his throat so dry that he could barely swallow. "Hold on a minute, will you?" he said, and got out of bed and went into the bathroom and made himself a Bromo Seltzer. When he returned, he glanced enviously at the large mound in the adjoining bed that was his wife. She had not so much as twitched, a clear testament to the advantage of having grown up in a house that fronted on the Jamaica Avenue El in the Borough of Queens.

He retrieved the phone, stifling a belch, and said, "Listen, Richie, is there a doorman, a night man, downstairs?"

"Yes."

"OK. Now, Richie, I know these people, how they operate. Karpstein hasn't come by now, he isn't coming. Believe me, these people act for their own convenience. He doesn't have to come in the middle of the night."

"You're sure?"

"Of course. I know these people, I told you. That's my job. Just to be on the safe side, Richie, double-lock the door, and tell the night man if anyone comes looking for you to tell them you're away on vacation or something. You got that?"

"Jesus, I don't know."

"Richie, get ahold of yourself. This is the best way. And tomorrow morning you come in and we'll take care of this. Eight-thirty sharp. You know the address?"

"No."

"Two-oh-one East Sixty-ninth Street. Write it down, Richie. And take it easy. You all right?"

"I guess so."

"Good, Richie, good," Crotty said, and thought what a swell coup it would be for him to bring in King Kong Karpstein, and went back to sleep.

☆

Karpstein, as it happened, had been otherwise occupied throughout most of the evening.

Because of Flynn, he had temporarily neglected Lawrence Farber. But that afternoon, when he called Farber, Farber's secretary said that the lawyer was sick and unavailable, and Karpstein stopped thinking about anything else. He finally obtained Farber's unlisted home number and address in northern New Jersey from Mandelbaum's old partner, Jay Landers, who was immensely grateful that nothing more was being demanded of him.

"I have the flu, a hundred and three temperature," Farber had said on the phone, and Karpstein said, "I don't care if you have to crawl on your hands and knees, get here to my office." Then the feverish Farber made the mistake of hanging up.

Karpstein went home to have dinner with Angelina. Biondo picked him up afterward, and around eleven P.M. he rang the bell at the Farber residence. Mrs. Farber opened the door, and Karpstein barged in, and before she really got the scream started, he said, "Shut up."

He asked her where her husband was, and she whispered, "Upstairs."

Farber thought that he was hallucinating when Karpstein walked into the bedroom. "So you weren't fooling," Karpstein said. "I thought you was faking, like usual."

"The doctor says this could turn into pneumonia. I could be in the hospital."

"How'd you like to be there permanently?"

Farber shrank back in the bed as Karpstein approached him. But all Karpstein did was take a tablet of writing paper from the night table and drop it on Farber's stomach. "Write down what I tell you," he said, "and date it today. It's a note on your house."

"I can't do that."

Karpstein bent very close to him. "You don't have a choice."

Farber's body began to jerk. He reached for a pen and started to write. The note stated that if Farber did not meet certain obligations to Karpstein within thirty days, he would sell the house to him for forty thousand dollars.

"But I paid a hundred for it."

"I'm doing you a favor," Karpstein said. "This way the two-thirds of the fifty thousand that Mandelbaum owed my client will be covered, plus five for my time and trouble, and it still leaves you a couple of thousand as a down payment for a new place. Or you could talk some sense to Mandelbaum's old lady about her husband's obligations. Work things out with her. I don't care." Karpstein continued to stare at Farber. "That reminds me. Get your wife in here. I want her to sign, too."

Mrs. Farber was a thin, pallid woman in her late twenties. She had long black hair and tremulous black eyes. As she edged into the bedroom, Karpstein stepped back deferentially. "I'm sorry I scared you," he said. "You know how some things are."

Farber held out the paper to her. "Sign this."

"What is it?"

"Just sign it. I'll explain later."

When she left, Karpstein said, "See, I was a gentleman. I didn't do anything or say anything in front of her." He seemed almost jovial.

"What do you want," Farber said, clutching his blanket, "the Mr. Nice Guy award?"

Karpstein walked over to a bureau in the corner. There was a jewelry box on top of it. He opened the box and examined the contents and flung them across the room. "You cheap creep," he said. "Is this the kind of crap you buy your own wife?" Then he took the note that the Farbers had signed and went out the door.

In the car on the way home Karpstein suddenly said, "Let's get the whole fucking thing over with."

"What's that, Albert?" Biondo said.

"Flynn," Karpstein said, digging into a pocket for the address Weissberg had given him. "Yeah, this is it."

Jimenez, the night man in Flynn's apartment building, was swabbing the lobby floor when Karpstein, Biondo beside him, banged on the locked glass door. Jimenez was still marveling at his unexpected good fortune upon receiving a twenty-dollar bill from Flynn an hour earlier, and he did not hear Karpstein at first. Jimenez had already decided that five dollars would go on the nose of a horse in the fifth race at Belmont Park the next day. A dollar would be invested in the state lottery, and fifty cents on the numbers. There had been a radio report of an armored-truck holdup in which five hundred and sixteen thousand dollars had been stolen, so Jimenez would make 516 his pick. Now he was trying to figure out what to do with the rest of the money.

Karpstein banged harder, and Jimenez came out of his reverie. He went to the door and opened it slightly. "Yes?"

"Flynn," Karpstein said. "He's expecting us."

"Not here," Jimenez said. "On vacation." He started to close the door, but Karpstein shoved against it so abruptly that the night man was thrown off balance.

"Watch him," Karpstein said to Biondo. Then he went to the intercom that listed the building's tenants, found Flynn's apartment number and buzzed it. Jimenez liked Flynn—Flynn always tipped him a dollar when he came in late and the door had to be opened for him—but he was afraid to repeat what Flynn had told him to say if anyone asked for him, afraid of what these men might do if Flynn answered on the intercom.

"I'm going up to see for myself," Karpstein said to Biondo. "Stay with this spick."

Flynn had finally begun to doze off in his bed when the intercom shattered the silence in the apartment. He bolted upright and wondered what to do. Maybe, he thought, it was the night man trying to warn him about something. Agnes came awake alongside him. "What is it?" she said, and he put a finger against her lips. Flynn strained to listen in the darkness. He heard the elevator stop in the corridor outside and then the bell ring.

"Get into Sean's room," he whispered to Agnes. "Keep him quiet." Flynn crept down the hall in his shorts toward the front door. The bell rang again, and again. A fist pounded on the door. The blows sounded thunderous. Flynn closed his eyes and started to pray. "Hail Mary, full of grace, the Lord is with thee, blessed art thou among women . . ."

"Flynn, you hear me? You in there, Flynn?"

". . . and blessed is the fruit of thy womb, Jesus."

The whole apartment seemed to shake under Karpstein's pounding. Flynn slipped helplessly to his knees. He was certain that the door would give way any second. Then there was a commotion outside, other doors were opening and a voice said, "Hey, what do you want?" and Karpstein responded, "I'm looking for Flynn." Somebody said, "I haven't seen him," and someone else said, "Gladys, call the police," and then the pounding stopped and Flynn heard the elevator door shut, and everything was silent once more.

Agnes found him in the hall, still on his knees. "Are you all right?" she whispered.

"Yes. I think he's gone. What about Sean?"

"He never woke up."

"Go back to bed," he said. "I'll be there in a little while." He groped his way into the living room, not daring to turn on a light. He sat on the sofa and started drinking the last of the scotch out of the bottle. He fell asleep where he was just as the night gave way to the first pale streaks of dawn.

═══════ ☆ ═══════

20

Agnes awakened him shortly after seven A.M. In the bathroom mirror he stared at the puffy blue circles under his eyes. His head ached. He cut himself twice while shaving. When he came out and Agnes asked him what they were to do, Flynn told her to go with the boy to her mother's, that he would call her later.

As they left the apartment, he dreaded bumping into someone who lived on the same floor, but they did not encounter any of the other tenants. He put his wife and son into a cab. Then he went to the New York office of the FBI and told the guard at the security desk that he was waiting for an agent.

Crotty bustled in a few minutes before nine o'clock and said to Flynn, "Boy, you look terrible."

"Karpstein came last night," Flynn said.

"He what?"

"He came last night."

"What happened?"

"I did what you told me. I gave the night man a twenty and told him to say I was away. Karpstein came up anyway and tried to get in, but I didn't answer, and he left."

"See," Crotty said exuberantly. "I told you there was nothing to worry about."

Flynn looked at Crotty and remembered how Karpstein pounded on his door, but he did not say anything. He followed Crotty into one of the elevators. They got off on a floor that had a long counter facing the elevator bank. Above the counter was the FBI insignia—blind Justice holding a scale and a sword. There were also a number of plaques commemorating FBI agents who had been killed in action.

Several clerks were settling down to work behind the counter. Crotty had Flynn logged in and then took him into an interrogation room on another floor that the Criminal Division and the Organized Crime Division shared.

Crotty asked Flynn if he wanted some coffee, and when

Flynn said yes, Crotty went out to get it. He returned with two cups. "I forgot to ask you," he said. "I put cream and sugar in yours. Is that all right?"

"Yes," Flynn said.

"OK. Now, Richie, there are just a couple of things to go over to make sure we have the right jurisdiction here. Am I correct in assuming the amount of money involved in this extortion is more than a hundred dollars?"

"Yes, I borrowed twelve thousand five hundred from Karpstein and another ten from Tony Valente."

"Valente? The old mob guy who has that restaurant in East Harlem? He's in this, too?"

"Yes."

"Oh, boy, Richie, that's wonderful. Now tell me something. Karpstein works out of New Jersey. Did you ever go over there, you know, cross a state line, to borrow the money, or pay an installment, or talk to him on the phone about it from here?"

"Yes, all of that."

"Wonderful, Richie, wonderful," Crotty said, and activated the tape recorder. "Start from the beginning. Tell me everything."

Crotty normally would have written a report of his interview, but this was too good to keep. For budgetary purposes, Crotty had been assigned to Barney Barnett's Organized Crime Division, and Crotty knew that ever since Hoover died, Barnett had been trying to transfer him out of the division. If that happened, he might end up being moved entirely out of the New York office to someplace like Butte, Montana.

"You wait here," he told Flynn, and barely able to contain himself, he went out and marched down the aisle toward Barnett's office past an array of desks occupied by his fellow agents.

The office had a glass partition through which Barnett could monitor the men under him. He saw Crotty coming and winced. Crotty was precisely the kind of agent that had to be purged if the FBI was ever to regain its fabled disciplined efficiency, but so far he had been too shrewd to be caught in some administrative transgression that would allow Barnett to take action against him.

As Crotty talked, Barnett listened impassively and thought, Christ, I'm never going to get rid of him now.

"Where'd you pick this up," Barnett said when Crotty was through, "at the bar in 21?"

"Hey, come on, boss," Crotty said triumphantly, "I've been on it for a couple of weeks. And on my own time."

"Have you written it up?"

"No, soon as everything broke, I wanted to tell you right away."

I'll bet, Barnett thought. "Well, do it, and have it on my desk this morning."

Crotty hesitated, waiting for an accolade. When he realized that he was not going to get one, he turned to leave. But before he was past the door, he was already softly whistling "The Sidewalks of New York." Crotty knew that he did not have to worry anymore about being transferred.

Barnett watched him sourly for a moment through the glass partition and then called Kevin McGrath. "Can you spare a minute?" he said. "I think we have something for our friend Wainwright."

☆

Hamilton Wainwright had been at the Department of Justice in Washington most of the day arguing that his special unit deserved a bigger budget. When he returned to New York in the late afternoon, Simonetta followed him into his office and asked, "How did it go?"

Wainwright angrily tossed his jacket on a chair. "It didn't. 'Wait and see,' they said. 'Make some good cases and we'll see.' They're paralyzed down there. All they have on their mind is Nixon. They know he's through one way or another, and they're terrified they're going to be involved in the cover-up for not pushing the investigation in the beginning."

"Well, I've got something to cheer you up. How does Albert Karpstein grab you?"

"The loan shark?"

"The one and only."

"What's it all about?"

"The first thing this morning in walked one Lawrence Farber. Farber's a hotshot lawyer with a less than class clientele. He kept saying he was sick from the flu, but what he's really sick about is King Kong Karpstein. Anyway, Farber represented a Marvin Mandelbaum—the *late*

Marvin Mandelbaum. Mandelbaum and a partner he had, named Jay Landers, hustled stocks, one of which was in an Arizona land company that cost an investor fifty thousand dollars. According to Farber, they never knew the actual identity of the investor, but he must have had some pretty good connections because Karpstein showed up to collect on his behalf. Apparently Landers made an arrangement that satisfied Karpstein. Mr. Mandelbaum, however, didn't hop to fast enough, and Karpstein beat the hell out of him. Farber says he was present at the beating. Then Mandelbaum was murdered. We've checked this out. Approximately five weeks ago Mandelbaum's body was found in a car off the Long Island Expressway. One bullet in the head. No witnesses. Farber says he's sure Karpstein did it."

"How come he was so quick to tell us?"

"We asked him that. Farber claims that he really didn't know until last night when Karpstein walked right into his bedroom and told him he was responsible for the money Mandelbaum owed his client and forced him to sign a note on his house."

"Where does Landers stand in this?"

"We've already contacted him. Right now he's insisting that he doesn't know anything about anything. He's scared shitless, and in a way I don't blame him." Simonetta took a sheaf of papers from a folder. "Here's Karpstein's record. Besides looking like an ape, he is one. Half a dozen assaults by fist. Three robbery-and-assaults by pistol. Fugitive from justice. Hijacking and possession of stolen goods. Material witness for murder, twice. Extortion and felonious assault. Conspiracy to extort. He obviously figures he can do what he wants. Hell, once he even broke a police captain's jaw. He operates on his own, but he's considered a close associate of Joseph Iacovelli, a/k/a Joe Hobo, the Mafia boss in Hoboken. Maybe he was collecting for Joe Hobo. What do you want to do? There's no point in handing him over to the state. They'll never get a murder conviction. But the extortion looks good, especially if we can crack Landers. We've got the jurisdiction. And Karpstein's not a bad fish to land." Simonetta paused, smiled faintly and said, "Even if he isn't Italian."

"Let me think about it," Wainwright said. "Where's Farber now?"

"Back home. I was only kidding. He does have the flu."

"Was that wise?"

"He'll be OK. He has thirty days to come up with the money. Karpstein won't try anything until we make a move."

"Anything else?" Wainwright said. "Is that everything?"

"No. I've saved the best for last. This one's even sexier. Does the name Richie Flynn ring a bell?"

"No. Yes. I think so, but I can't remember why."

"He played for the Giants ten or eleven years ago and made a sensational touchdown run in his rookie year. I'll never forget it myself. But then he got hurt and never played again. You sure you don't remember?"

"Vaguely, but that's not why. Go on."

"Flynn arrived this afternoon courtesy of McGrath and Barnett, and McGrath will undoubtedly be calling to remind you what a terrific favor he did. Anyway, after Flynn's football career was over, he was just another guy until a couple of months ago, when he was approached with a proposition that he thought would put him back in the big time. The proposition involved getting one of those direct-lease day-care centers from the city, the kind that's been all over the papers recently. Flynn's part was to come up with the front money, but since he didn't have it, he went to Karpstein, thinking he would pay him after the lease went through. Naturally, nothing went right, and guess what? If you can believe it, when Karpstein started squeezing him, Flynn went to Tony Valente for the money to stave off Karpstein. Only he neglected to let Valente in on the secret."

"Who's Valente?"

"A small-time semiretired hood who, you'll be happy to know, is listed as a member of the Donato family. As a matter of fact, he's right up there on the FBI's Donato chart you have on the wall behind you. He's near the bottom, but he's there."

Wainwright swung his legs off his desk and swiveled around to study the chart. "Is that so?"

"Yes, and there's more," Simonetta said. "Flynn's little ploy worked for a while, but it seems that Karpstein's been let loose again. He not only visited Farber last night, but he tried to knock down Flynn's door, too. We should call this Albert Karpstein Day. Flynn's outside even as we speak, ready to collapse. You want to see him?"

Wainwright was out of his chair. "Yes," he said, "but

there's something else. I just can't put my finger on it. Wait a minute! Have you been reading those transcripts from the Ravens Club?"

"Not lately, to tell you the truth. It's been mostly bull-shit stuff. They sound like a bunch of old ladies. There must be a hundred pages alone of Brancusi complaining about how much his daughter's wedding is going to cost, about how he has to fly a planeload of daisies in from California. I've had one of the assistants checking it when it comes in, but he hasn't reported anything that means much."

"Well, I looked over a copy I got a week or so ago," Wainwright said, "and I have a funny feeling that's why I remember Flynn. And now that I think about it, Valente as well. Get me all the transcripts for the week before last."

Wainwright thumbed through them and finally found the meeting between Vincente D'Angelo and Joe Hobo that had been triggered by Valente. "Ah," he said to Simonetta, "right on the money. How is it your peerless leader has to do everything himself? OK. Bring in Flynn. I want to have a little chat with him."

Simonetta could not recall having seen Wainwright in such good humor.

☆

Richie Flynn was alone in the men's room, examining himself in a mirror, when Simonetta came for him. Because of his hasty shave that morning, Flynn's face had a dark, uneven stubble of beard. He ran his hands along both cheeks, and the stubble grated under his fingertips like fine sandpaper. It made him feel uncomfortably scruffy. The pouches under his eyes were worse. His hair was unkempt, and he tried to comb it down. A coffee stain was on his shirt, and he straightened his tie and buttoned his jacket to cover it. His hands trembled. He had been given endless cups of coffee at the FBI and here at the special prosecutor's office, which had only increased his jumpiness. He had managed to swallow half a ham sand-ᵃh someone had brought him, and that was all he had He wished that he could have a drink—in fact, ʳinks.

ᵃ had learned that he was going to be placed in

Wainwright's hands, his first thought was whether the special prosecutor would remember him from the father-and-son breakfast. That at least would provide a bond of sorts, a starting point to make things easier. They would chat for a few minutes, and perhaps he would tell Wainwright about the troubles he had had with the fighter Tomaselli, and they would have some chuckles over that before getting down to business. It was, he decided, a perfect way to break the ice, and upon being introduced to Wainwright, Flynn stepped forward with renewed confidence and extended his hand. But Wainwright did not move. He remained seated behind his desk, his chair tilted back, arms folded across his chest, gazing at him with his pale green, almost colorless eyes.

Flynn's confusion was instantaneous. All day FBI agents and assistant U.S. attorneys had been clapping him effusively on the back, treating him as if he were some kind of celebrity, telling him what an important contribution to law enforcement he was making, even how courageous he was. And now the man who would control his immediate destiny sat there contemplating him with evident distaste, if not outright hostility, and without the slightest sign of recognition.

Flynn dropped his hand uncertainly to his side.

Then Wainwright said, "Sit down."

It was not a request.

My God, Flynn thought, he says it the same way Karpstein said it, and the sweat began under his arms.

Wainwright picked up a pencil and tapped it on the desk top. "Flynn, you're some piece of work," he said at last.

The indignation Flynn felt was actually a relief. "What's that supposed to mean?" he said. "I haven't done anything illegal. What did I do that anybody else hasn't tried to do?"

"Can it," Wainwright said. "You're a goddamn disgrace. I remember you, standing up at that breakfast taking a bow in front of all those kids. How'd you like them to see you now? What would you tell them? 'Hey, just follow me!' That you found a new way to score? Is that what you'd say?"

Flynn looked wildly at Simonetta, who had been so warm and friendly to him barely an hour before. But Simonetta's face was expressionless, and Flynn turned back in desperation to Wainwright. "Listen, I can help you. I can deliver Karpstein."

"No, *you* listen," Wainwright said. "This may come as a shock to you, Flynn, but you need me a hell of a lot more than I need you. I don't need you to put Karpstein away. If you don't believe me, you're welcome to walk right out of here. You're free to go. Unescorted, of course."

"I don't understand."

"What don't you understand? You speak English, don't you?"

"I don't understand what you want from me. You know I can't just walk out of here with him out there somewhere."

"That's your problem. You want me to help you, you have to give me some real help. We have to go all the way on this. Is that clear enough?"

Flynn felt his stomach turn over. "Yes," he said, like a schoolboy eager to please his teacher. "Tell me. What?"

"Have you heard of Frank Donato?"

"Sure. Who hasn't?"

"Did you know that Tony Valente is a soldier in the Donato family?"

"Well, I knew he was mobbed up."

"It's a fact, Flynn."

"OK. It's a fact. Valente is with Donato."

"Very good," Wainwright said. "Now, according to what you've told the FBI and this office, you tried to stall Karpstein with the money you got from Valente, and when that didn't work, Valente said he would take care of Karpstein until the day-care lease went through."

"Right."

"You don't believe for a minute that Valente's big enough to take on somebody like Karpstein?"

"If you say so."

"Let's get this straight. *I'm* not saying so. *You* have to say it."

"Yeah, right," Flynn said, shifting uneasily in his chair, filled with a sense of foreboding that he could not quite put his finger on.

"Do you know who Vincente D'Angelo is?"

"Yes. He has a lot of topless joints around and stuff."

"That's correct," Wainwright said. "And he's also Valente's capo, and Valente would have to go to him on a matter like this. Are you following me?"

"Uh, yeah."

"Good," Wainwright said, "because that's what happened. But there's another link in this, which is the key to it all. Karpstein is closely associated with a capo in a Mafia family in New Jersey. And even D'Angelo couldn't handle this alone. It was too big. This was something the bosses had to decide, so D'Angelo had to go to Donato himself. When you think about it, you'll see that the only person who could stop Karpstein from tearing you apart was Frank Donato."

Flynn sat dumbfounded as the realization of what Wainwright was really after sank in. Wainwright had not been fooling. He did not care about Karpstein at all. Wainwright wanted Flynn to deliver Donato, and Richie Flynn knew that he would have to deliver. He was out of options. "Yeah," he said woodenly, "I see what you mean."

"Valente probably spelled this all out more or less."

"Right," Flynn said. "I guess maybe he did."

Wainwright smiled for the first time. He got up and walked around the desk and shook Flynn's hand. "You've had a rough day, Richie. You look tired. Have you had anything to eat?"

"What I'd really like," Flynn said, "is a drink."

"Don't worry, we'll see to that," Wainwright said, and turned to Simonetta. "Nick, does Richie have a family?"

"A wife and son. They're at his mother-in-law's."

"Have someone call and tell them that Richie is safe in our hands and that he'll be in touch with them shortly. I want U.S. marshals guarding him and his family beginning tomorrow. Tonight Richie goes to a first-class hotel. And, oh, yes, send somebody up to his apartment for some clean clothes and anything else he may need."

Wainwright gripped Flynn's shoulder. "Richie," he said, "when you go to the hotel, take a hot bath, call your wife and feel free to order up whatever you want. I'd like you to refresh your recollection about what we've discussed, and tomorrow we'll have another little talk. All you have to do is your part, and we'll do ours."

When Simonetta returned to Wainwright's office after shepherding Flynn out, he said, "Don't you think we're stretching things?"

"Certainly not. Look at the transcript. D'Angelo and Joe Hobo meet, and D'Angelo says to him, 'I'm telling you, that's how Mr. F.D. feels about it.' There it is, in black and white and on tape."

"But we can't use the tape in court."

"That's where Flynn comes in. He's our live bug."

"How do you know D'Angelo wasn't just bluffing?"

A testy edge crept into Wainwright's voice. "I don't know. It's not my job to figure out what anyone was thinking, and it's not yours either. It's what was said that counts."

"I still think it's awfully thin."

"You're wrong, Nick," Wainwright said. "With King Kong Karpstein as a co-defendant in an extortion conspiracy, even Jesus of Nazareth wouldn't stand a chance in front of a jury."

He walked over to the dart board that his staff had given him on his birthday, pulled out the dart that had landed in Frank Donato's face and jammed it back in. "And you're wrong about this being Karpstein's day. It's Frank Donato's."

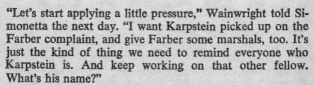

21

"Let's start applying a little pressure," Wainwright told Simonetta the next day. "I want Karpstein picked up on the Farber complaint, and give Farber some marshals, too. It's just the kind of thing we need to remind everyone who Karpstein is. And keep working on that other fellow. What's his name?"

"Landers. Jay Landers."

"Yes, well, when you talk to him again, don't forget to remind him how we take care of witnesses who cooperate with us and what could happen to a witness who doesn't."

Six FBI agents were detailed to arrest Karpstein. They arrived at his home at eight o'clock in the morning. Two of the agents went to the rear of the house and drew revolvers. The others remained in front, their jackets unbuttoned to provide quick access to their own guns, all of them acutely aware of Karpstein's reputation.

One of the agents knocked on the door, and Angelina Karpstein said, "Who is it?"

"The FBI. Is Albert there?"

"Yes, he's in the kitchen having breakfast."

"Well, will you tell him it's the FBI and to please come out?"

After a moment Karpstein's voice came through the door. "What's this all about?"

"I don't know, Albert," the agent said. "All I know is I have a warrant to bring you in."

"Is this nice," Karpstein said, "coming to a man's house like this? You couldn't call first? You couldn't do this at my office?"

"Listen, I'm just doing a job," the agent said.

"I'll come in tomorrow," Karpstein said through the door. "I have a lot of business today."

"Shit, Albert, stop fucking around. Put on your coat, and come out."

"No, I'm not going with you now. And watch your language. There's a lady present."

The agent swore under his breath. He looked at the other agents. They were silent. One of the agents who had gone to the rear of the house came around the corner and asked, "What's going on?"

"He won't come out," the first agent said.

"Oh, shit."

"Watch your language," the first agent said, and called to Karpstein, "I told you we have a warrant, Albert, and it's got to be honored."

"Is Corrigan with you?"

"No, Agent Corrigan isn't here."

"I didn't think so. He took me in once on a hijacking. He was nice about it. He called first. You get him here, I'll go in with him. Nobody else."

The agent who had come from the rear of the house said, "The hell with this. Let's go in after him."

"Are you crazy?" the first agent whispered. "The guy's a psycho. You want a shoot-out or something?" He tried Karpstein again. "Albert?" But this time there was no answer, and the first agent said, "Morrison, call the office, and tell them we need Corrigan. Say I'll explain later. And then go get some coffee. We're going to be here for a while."

☆

Karpstein was arraigned before a United States magistrate.

He stood there sleepy-eyed, surrounded by court officers and FBI agents. Once Karpstein raised his hand to muffle a cough, and all the guards and agents immediately edged toward him. Shackles had already been brought to the clerk's office, to be rushed in if they were required.

Simonetta himself appeared at the proceedings to impress the magistrate with the seriousness of the case. After Simonetta had given the particulars, the magistrate said to Karpstein, "Where's your lawyer?"

"I don't have one," Karpstein said. "I didn't have time."

"You have the right to counsel, you know."

"I'll get him when I need him. I don't need him for this chickenshit."

"Well, I can assure you that this is a serious matter and you should have counsel," the magistrate said. "If you want one, I'll get you one." When Karpstein did not respond, the magistrate directed that a lawyer from the Legal Aid Society be summoned. The Legal Aid attorney was a tall, thin young man with light brown hair in disarray. He walked with a slight stoop, as if embarrassed by his height. He requested a few minutes to consult with his client, but Karpstein refused to speak to him.

Then Simonetta argued that Karpstein be held without bail. "This man is a menace to society," he said. "He is prone to great violence, Your Honor. He *is* a violent man, and all you have to do is look at his record."

The young Legal Aid lawyer stepped forward and said, "I object, Your Honor. In this country we do not have, nor do we subscribe to, preventive detention."

The magistrate looked at Simonetta. "What do you say to that, Mr. Special Prosecutor's Office?" The magistrate had been a prosecutor himself and loved nothing better than to bait those in his former calling.

"Your Honor," Simonetta said, "you have the defendant's record in front of you. The well-being, even the lives of potential witnesses would be placed in great jeopardy were he allowed to roam at will."

"I—" the Legal Aid man started to say.

"Save your breath," the magistrate said, cutting him off and turning to Simonetta. "You haven't made a sufficient showing of danger to witnesses just because of a general propensity for violent behavior on the defendant's part. The only issue on bail is assuring the presence of the defendant for the processes of this court. Can you give me anything on that?"

"Well, look at his record. He was a fugitive once."

"Where? Oh, I see. But that was many years ago, when he was quite young, and he returned voluntarily to stand trial. All right, that's the end of this. What kind of bail do you want?"

"Because of the gravity of this case and the circumstances surrounding it, which I have tried to explain—two hundred thousand dollars."

"Fifty!"

"Your Honor," the Legal Aid lawyer protested, "even that's—"

"I told you, save your breath," the magistrate said, bringing down his gavel. "Will the clerk please call the next case?"

☆

After his arraignment and release on bail, Karpstein dispatched Biondo to check on Farber. As he expected, Biondo reported, "There're a couple of guys with him everywhere he goes. They look like cops." Then Biondo reported a surprise: Flynn had similar company.

Seated behind his desk at E-Z Trucking, chewing Milky Ways, Karpstein brooded about Flynn and Farber—and Joe Hobo. Despite all the publicity that attended his arrest, Joe Hobo had made no effort to contact him. And almost three weeks had passed since he had received the first of two cryptic hand-delivered notes from the mafioso. The first had said, "Lay off Flynn." The second, about ten days later, suddenly advised, "Do what you want with Flynn." Beyond that, there had been no calls, no meetings, no explanations. Nothing.

How was Joe Hobo mixed up with Flynn? Or even knew about him? Karpstein's instinct was to have a confrontation at once. But he had decided against it. That was not the way the Italians, Joe Hobo, operated. They sniffed around and connived and plotted, and only then did they act. So would he. The vibrations around him were bad, but he would wait for more decipherable signals. Sooner or later, he figured, Joe Hobo would have to come to him, and that's when he would find out what was going on. And on his terms, not Joe Hobo's.

Farber was his immediate concern, and rage coursed through him as he recalled the indignity of his arrest, of Angelina sobbing, "What will the neighbors think?" One day he would even scores with that pissant. He tried to imagine what sort of case could be made against him with Farber alone. Then he remembered Jay Landers. He called Joe Hobo's accountant and asked if Landers was still making his weekly payments. "Like clockwork," the accountant said.

Nonetheless he sent Biondo to observe Landers. "I'm telling you," Biondo said on his return, "there's nobody with him. He goes to the office, is all. He goes to eat. He gets in his car and goes home. That's it." Biondo got up from the sofa and started chalking a cue. "Oh, yeah, I almost forgot. He went once to a building across from the courthouse."

"*What* building?"

"It said, 'Federal Building,' on it. I think it's full of feds."

Karpstein glared at Biondo. "You asshole."

Biondo hesitated. "Jeez, Albert, what's the matter? It ain't full of feds?"

"Never mind. How long was he there?"

"An hour, maybe."

"He come out alone?"

"Yeah. I told you."

"All right. Listen to me, and listen good."

Late the next afternoon, when Landers left his office, Biondo trailed him again. Landers walked four blocks to a parking lot. There was a shanty by the entrance covered with signs that announced the various parking rates. People would pay the attendant, collect their keys, go to their cars and drive out an exit about forty yards distant. A number of people were gathered around the shanty when Landers got there, and Biondo slipped in among them.

Landers retrieved his key and walked toward his car, Biondo a few steps behind. Landers could be forgiven for not noticing him. He had plenty on his mind. The day before, at a meeting with Simonetta, he had continued to insist that he had never heard of anyone called Karpstein, and Simonetta had told him what would happen if he failed to cooperate. "You don't want to cooperate," Simonetta had said, "it's up to you. To me it's all the same. I'm going to subpoena you anyway, and when you walk out of the grand jury, I'm going to be right with you, and in front of all those reporters who are going to be there, I'm going to pat you on the shoulder and shake your hand and thank you profusely for everything you've done, and then you can explain that to Mr. Karpstein. You'll be back to see me. I guarantee it."

Landers had stared at Simonetta in disbelief and said that he wanted time to think it over. "You do that," Simonetta had said, certain that Landers was on the verge of cracking.

Now, in the parking lot, as Landers was inserting the key into his car door lock, he glanced idly at Biondo, who appeared to be doing the same thing on the near side of an adjoining automobile. Landers opened the door and bent forward to get in. At that moment Biondo turned, a revolver with a silencer in his hand. He pushed Landers facedown on the seat and fired into the base of his skull.

Biondo looked around the lot. Everyone was busy getting into a car and driving away. He rolled Landers onto the car floor beneath the dashboard, closed the door and sauntered off.

The body was discovered later in the evening by a parking-lot attendant. Simonetta called Wainwright at home with the news.

"Bring in Karpstein right away, and get his bail revoked," Wainwright said. "I don't care if you have to roust that magistrate out of bed. And make sure the press gets it. I want a story in the papers about how he refused to lock up a killer."

Then Simonetta found out that Albert Karpstein was already in jail.

☆

Early that morning Karpstein had gone to see a local, politically connected attorney. After he explained the purpose of his visit, the attorney said, "What in the world do you want to do that for?"

"Never mind," Karpstein said. "Can you fix it for today?"

"Yes."

"So fix it."

At two P.M. Karpstein was standing in front of a municipal judge pleading guilty to a reduced charge of assaulting a bookmaker in a saloon and nearly severing his ear with a broken beer stein.

"But according to the record, this incident occurred several years ago," the judge said, addressing Karpstein's attorney, "and no arrest was ever made. Why is the defendant making this plea now?"

"Your Honor," the attorney said, "it's been on my client's conscience. He's a decent man, a family man, and he can't sleep at night thinking about what he did. He wants to make restitution as best he can, pay his debt to society, so to speak."

"What do you have to say?" the judge said to Karpstein.

"Your Honor, like he said, I want to make restitution, do some time. I want to hold up my head, you know, high."

"Very commendable," the judge said, and sentenced Karpstein to sixty days in jail.

He was brought to the jail at five o'clock in the afternoon, just as Biondo was stalking Landers in the parking lot. Karpstein had not been in the receiving room for more than a minute before Herman Mueller, the warden, sent for him.

"Hello, Warden," Karpstein said.

"Good to see you, Albert," Mueller said. "I heard you were coming."

Mueller was a deceptively mild-looking man in his middle fifties, almost prissy in manner. He had in fact been a sergeant with the vice squad and on the side had handled the bets that members of the police department put on the numbers. When the local political boss, who had ruled that part of the state unchallenged for more than four decades, died at the age of seventy-six, there was a wild scramble among his self-anointed heirs to succeed him. Mueller helped back one of them with some of the graft he had accumulated through the years and also mobilized all the contacts he had developed as a cop in support of his candidate. Mueller's man won, and in return Mueller was named warden.

The job offered many opportunities for someone of his vision. Besides the usual cellblocks, there were dormitories in the jail for prisoners requiring minimum security. Mueller equipped two of them with television sets, refrigerators and stoves, and any inmate who could afford the privileges was allowed to take advantage of them. If an inmate needed a telephone, he could use one in the warden's suite of offices. And if he desired female companionship—his wife, a girl friend or prostitute—that could be arranged as well. Such assignations generally took place in the jail's counsel rooms, where prisoners were supposed to meet with their lawyers, but if there was an overflow, Mueller would press the chapel into service.

Mueller was known as Hard-dollar Herman. He made it a practice not to set a price for special treatment, so that he could honestly swear that he never had asked for money. When an inmate seeking favors came into Mueller's office, he would palm his bribe and handshake it over to the warden before making his request. If Mueller deemed the amount insufficient, he would pocket the cash anyway and murmur, "No, not now. Perhaps another time."

Mueller was a man of normally fastidious habit, and he always received his petitioners on Sunday after he and his wife attended mass, where they both prayed for the safety of their daughter, a missionary nun laboring among the Aymara Indians of Peru. But he recognized that Karpstein was an exceptional case.

"I see you're going to be with us for sixty days, Albert," he said. "Is there anything we can do?"

"I don't want to mix with the population," Karpstein said. "There's some wise guys in here, and they could be trouble for me."

Mueller looked at Karpstein and barely managed to conceal a shudder. "I can't imagine you being worried about that, Albert."

"Yeah, but you could use it for why you have to isolate me."

"That's a point."

"I want a room by myself," Karpstein said. He took out a piece of paper and read from it. "And an icebox, hot plate, TV, a table and two chairs and my own phone."

"Well, there's a storeroom next to the chapel that ought to do nicely. We won't be able to get it ready until tomorrow, though."

"That's all right. I'll stay in one of them dorms tonight. What about the bathroom?"

"The bathroom?"

"Yeah, bathroom. I got to go to the bathroom."

"Ah, yes. Let's see, there is a facility for members of the clergy. You couldn't use it during mass and so forth, of course."

"When I have visitors," Karpstein said, "I don't want them signing the book, you know what I mean?"

Mueller waved his hand as if it were a matter of no consequence, and Karpstein said, "I figure the tab is six hundred a week. Here's a month in advance."

"I trust you'll find everything to your liking," the warden said.

☆

"So he just happened to be in jail when Landers got his head blown off?" Wainwright said to Simonetta.

"That's about the size of it. It's a weird alibi, though. You wouldn't think he'd go so far."

"No," Wainwright said, "he was very cute. He knew we'd have a hell of a shot at revoking his bail, and he'd rather be where he is than with us. I hear that warden runs quite an establishment. And there's no way we can get our hands on him except for court appearances, is there, Nick?"

"Not for sixty days."

"Well, at least he isn't going anywhere," Wainwright said. "And we still have Flynn."

22

The whipped look on Flynn's face disappeared with the news of Karpstein's jailing. "I can't believe it," he said to Simonetta. "You put him away. In the goddamn slammer! He used to talk about this Farber guy all the time, and I didn't know what he was talking about. And I still don't understand it all."

"Don't worry about it," Simonetta said. "We just decided to keep him on ice so he can't do any harm. The boss told you. You do your part, we'll do ours."

It was true, Flynn thought. Wainwright had even arranged for him to stay on at Goldblatt. And he had done it in his presence. Wainwright had telephoned the brewery's president, and Flynn remembered how they had chatted for a few moments, and then Wainwright said, "I'm grateful for your kind words, but one man can't do the job alone, and that's why I'm calling you," and he went on to explain that Flynn was performing a vital law enforcement service for his country which might entail his being absent from work from time to time, and after a pause, he smiled again, winking across the desk at Flynn, and thanked the president for his patriotic cooperation.

Flynn's confidence was further bolstered by the meetings he had with two of Wainwright's youthful assistant U.S. attorneys, often with Simonetta sitting in. They were held three afternoons a week and covered most of the specifics of the case—how Larry Fowler had approached him, how in turn Flynn met with Scanlon at the Liffey, then the phone call to New Jersey that Scanlon had made on his behalf, his original trip to Hoboken to borrow the money from Karpstein, his subsequent trips to pay the weekly installments, his odyssey to Connecticut regarding the beneficiary change in his life insurance policy, the various interstate phone calls between Karpstein or Leo Weissberg and himself, his last desperate trip to E-Z Trucking with the money from Valente to buy more time and the threats that Karpstein had voiced, culminating in Karpstein's night visitation to his apartment.

He had entered these interrogatories with some trepidation, but both assistants were unfailingly supportive and courteous—addressing him in the early sessions as "Mr. Flynn" before gradually sliding into the camaraderie of "Richie." Once, when he had difficulty pinpointing the exact date of his trip to Hartford and then discovered that he had lost his motel receipt, no one snapped at him or evidenced the slightest irritation.

"Can you remember the name of the motel?" one assistant asked.

He could not. "I, uh, it was on that road that goes into Hartford," he said, growing more flustered. "There're a lot of them. I just pulled into one." His voice dropped. "I think it was painted white."

"Say," the other assistant quietly interjected, "didn't you mention that you called your wife collect from there?"

"Yes."

The assistant smiled reassuringly. "No problem, Richie. We'll just backtrack from the phone company records."

Flynn felt enormously relieved. They had made him feel as though he were on a team again, that they were all in this together, with the same stakes and goals, and he had not let them down.

Then, having been so tenderly cultivated, he was brought in to see Wainwright. Only one element in the case, the Donato connection, had been left untouched by the assistants, an omission Wainwright would rectify now with Flynn alone. This time Wainwright did all the talking. About Valente and D'Angelo. And the shadowy role a "Mr. F.D." had played in the conspiracy to extort money from Flynn. "We know this for a fact," Wainwright said, and Flynn had agreed that yes, that was how it was, that it all fit.

Afterward a lengthy statement was prepared for Flynn's signature. The last section of the statement dealt with the ten thousand dollars he had borrowed from Valente to pay Karpstein. In it Flynn declared that he had been told by Valente that D'Angelo was involved in the loan, that D'Angelo had assured Valente that there was nothing to worry about regarding Karpstein because the old man—Mr. F.D.—had decreed that Karpstein was not allowed to operate in New York and that Valente was first in line to be paid off or otherwise to share in the profits of the day-care center deal. Flynn signed the statement, attesting that he had made it of his own free will, and then Wainwright patted him on the back and said, "That's fine, Richie."

As usual, when Flynn departed, two marshals were with him. The marshals worked in shifts. During his rounds for Goldblatt they were explained away as sales trainees for the brewery. The marshals came from all over the country—from places like Clarksdale, Mississippi, and Lake City, Minnesota. Most of them had never been to New York before. They seemed in awe of the city and continually commented about how huge it was and how many people swarmed through its streets and also how dirty it was. At first this made Flynn exceedingly nervous, and he asked Simonetta why he could not have marshals from New York, and Simonetta had told him that Washington controlled the assignment of marshals. Later he discovered that being appointed a marshal was part of the political patronage system and that expense-account travel was one of the rewards of the job.

Still, they carried pistols and appeared to know how to use them, and they treated Flynn as a person of importance. With one marshal routinely at the wheel, the other seated next to Flynn in the rear of a car, he started to enjoy the attention, and as the image of Karpstein receded in his mind, he began to think of them more and more as *his* personal staff, *his* chauffeur and bodyguard.

To top it off, his son began to look at him with new respect. Sean, of course, had immediately wanted to know who the marshals were and why they were always around, and after an awkward pause, Flynn replied that he was doing some important work for the government that required their presence. "Gee, *what*, Dad?" the boy had asked, wide-eyed, and Flynn said that he couldn't tell him right now, that it was secret stuff, and stared at Agnes, daring her to contradict him. She stared back and started to say something, but then she turned away.

The marshals were also with him when he visited Diane in her new apartment. The first visit was promptly reported to Simonetta.

"Who is she?" Simonetta said.

"Just a girl. Young. Real good-looking. I think he's been seeing her for a while."

"What did they do?"

"He wanted to take her to dinner, but I told him I'd have to check with you, so they sent out for some Chinese food."

"Anything else?"

"Well, they went into the bedroom, and I guess he humped her." The marshal, who was from Elkhart, Indiana, colored slightly. "I mean, I didn't go in there with them."

Simonetta sighed and said, "OK. Anything to keep him happy."

That he had been able to think about Diane at all amazed Flynn. But in the aftermath of his first tense sessions in Wainwright's office, he could think of little else. And at home, in bed, when he finally fell asleep, there had been the memory of her pale breasts rising toward him. He saw her nipples harden, and he watched himself suck them. For the first time since he had been in college, he had a wet dream, and waking abruptly, his heart thumping, he looked to make sure Agnes was still sleeping, and then, feeling the sticky wetness on his stomach, gave silent thanks that he had been on his back so the sheet would not carry a telltale stain.

Each time he was with Diane, one marshal remained in the car outside the building and the other stayed in the living room while Flynn took her in the bedroom. The presence of the marshal in the adjoining room seemed, if anything, to heighten her sexual excitement. Flynn told her that he needed the men to guard and drive him because of the investment deal he had spoken to her about, that the deal had now become so big that certain people would stop at nothing to prevent it from going through, and she had looked at him with the same wide-eyed wonder he had seen on his son's face.

☆

Three weeks after Flynn had gone to the FBI he was called before the federal grand jury that had been impaneled to hear the special prosecutor's cases.

There were twenty-three grand jurors in all, eighteen of whom constituted a quorum. They sat on two tiers in leather swivel chairs in a mahogany-walled room. In front of them was a long table. Wainwright and Simonetta and the two assistants involved in questioning Flynn were at one end of the table. The grand jury foreman was seated at the other end. In the middle, facing the jurors, was a witness chair. A court reporter was off to one side. No judge was present at a grand jury proceeding. Theoretically a prosecutor like Wainwright was the grand jury's counsel and adviser. In fact he was its ringmaster, and it was rare that a grand jury did not do what a prosecutor desired.

Wainwright noted with satisfaction that only one juror was absent. He nodded at the double-tiered rank and then to the foreman opposite him. The foreman eagerly nodded back. He was a rotund public relations executive for an oil company. He wore a miniature American flag in his lapel, and he had told Wainwright that it was an honor to be working with him.

Wainwright motioned to the court reporter to hold off recording the minutes. "Ladies and gentlemen," he said, "it's a pleasure to see you again. When we first met, if you'll recall, I asked you whether it wasn't time for at least one grand jury to stand up and say enough of organized crime and its horrible influence on civilized society. You are to be commended for your response to that challenge. And now, this morning, we have before us our most significant case thus far, one that reaches into the highest echelons of organized crime, and I have no doubt that you will continue to do your duty."

He signaled the reporter to start stenotyping, cleared his throat and said, "Ladies and gentlemen of the grand jury, we are here this morning to consider crimes of conspiracy and extortion in violation of Title Eighteen of the United States Code. The pertinent citations will be entered in the record and discussed at length later. Suffice to say for the moment, the type of extortion we are dealing with is the extortionate extension of credit, commonly known as loansharking, in which it is understood that the delay or failure to make repayment could result in the use of violence and other criminal means to cause harm to the person, reputation or property of any person."

Wainwright had decided that in addition to Flynn, he would need only two other witnesses: Karpstein's accountant, Leo Weissberg, and the FBI's Barney Barnett. He led off with Barnett, and after introducing him as the head of the Organized Crime Division in the New York field office of the Federal Bureau of Investigation, Wainwright asked him, "Mr. Barnett, can you tell us about one Anthony Valente?"

"According to our intelligence files, Valente is a soldier in the Frank Donato crime family. In 1927, when he was nineteen, he was sentenced to three years for burglary. In 1955 he was sentenced to five years for conspiracy to violate federal narcotics laws. He is known to be active in loan-sharking and the numbers racket."

"Just what is a soldier?"

"A soldier is the lowest level in what is popularly called the Mafia, although we in the bureau refer to it as the LCN—La Cosa Nostra."

"Does the name Vincente D'Angelo mean anything to you?"

"Vincente D'Angelo, also known as Vinnie the Vampire, is a lieutenant in the Donato family. He is heavily engaged in pornography and the infiltration of legitimate businesses. In 1935 he was convicted of armed robbery. In 1944, during World War II, he received a two-year sentence for dealing in counterfeit meat- and sugar-ration stamps."

"Mr. Barnett, would you explain what a lieutenant is?"

"Yes, sir. In every LCN family there are a number of regimes, or companies, like in the army, each of which is run by a lieutenant."

"Is there any relationship between D'Angelo and Valente?"

"Yes. Valente is a soldier in D'Angelo's regime."

"I see. Now who exactly is Frank Donato?"

"Well, as I have already indicated, he is the family boss. He sits on the national commission of La Cosa Nostra. According to our information, he is the most powerful of the family bosses, although he has only one conviction—in the 1920s for carrying a concealed weapon."

"How can that be?"

"Well, as someone advances in the power structure, he becomes insulated. There are layers and layers between him and the commission of a crime, and it becomes almost impossible to get a conviction."

"At any rate, there is a direct link, a direct chain of command, from Donato to D'Angelo to Valente?"

"That is correct."

"Is Donato generally known by any other name?"

"Yes. By his initials. Mr. F.D."

"All right. I direct your attention to Albert Karpstein, alias King Kong Karpstein and Johnny Rocco."

"He is reputed to be one of the biggest loan sharks in the country. He is a mob enforcer. He has a long record of armed robberies and assaults. He is considered extremely dangerous. He is a close associate of Joseph Iacovelli, also known as Joe Hoboken and Joe Hobo."

"Who is Joe Hobo?"

"He is a lieutenant in the New Jersey family. Like D'Angelo with Donato."

"So Karpstein would be subject to the wishes of La Cosa Nostra?"

"Absolutely."

"And D'Angelo and Joe Hobo have links, do they not?"

"They have been observed together many times."

"All these men we have spoken about, therefore, are associated. They have regular channels of communication with one another, either directly or indirectly, in the normal course of events."

"Yes, sir."

"Thank you very much, Mr. Barnett."

Wainwright turned to the foreman and asked if he had any questions. The foreman shook his head. Then one of the grand jurors, a retired schoolteacher, lifted her hand hesitantly. "I was just wondering. Is this Mr. Karpstein the terrible man who was in the newspapers recently for another extortion that involved a murder in a parking lot?"

Wainwright quickly glanced down at a list that had a précis of each juror's background. "That, of course, is not germane to this case, Mrs. Treleaven," he said, the barest flicker of a smile on his lips, as if they were sharing an intimate secret. "But, yes, now that you mention it, he *is* the same person."

☆

Flynn testified for less than an hour. Wainwright touched on just enough highlights to establish his case without going into the details. The one name he did not raise in questioning Flynn was Joe Hobo. Since it was unlikely that Flynn would have known about the New Jersey mafioso, Wainwright decided not to include him because it might lead to an embarrassing inquiry about illegal listening devices. "I still haven't given up on the Farber thing," he told Simonetta, "and we can get him later." As a further precaution, the day before the grand jury convened, the bug in the Ravens Club was removed by the same FBI squad that had installed it.

Leo Weissberg, subpoenaed as a material witness, served another purpose. Wainwright knew that he would refuse to answer questions on the grounds of self-incrimination. Weissberg was immediately hauled before a judge, and when he was granted immunity and still would not talk, he was found in contempt and remanded to the federal detention center in lower Manhattan until he "purged" himself. It struck exactly the right note of conspiratorial defiance.

In the afternoon, following a lunch break and a summation by Wainwright, the grand jury handed down the indictments he wanted. An hour later Flynn arrived home, pulsating with excitement, like an engine racing madly out of clutch. He had invited the two marshals to come up for a beer. Agnes was sitting with Sean while he ate his supper. When Flynn burst through the door, she looked at him but did not say anything. They hardly spoke to each other anymore, and Flynn let it go. He uncapped bottles of Goldblatt for the marshals and one for himself and paced the room, gesturing with it. "Boy," he said, "that Wainwright's something else. He got those indictments wham, wham! Just like that!" What Flynn could not get out of his head was the way Wainwright had handled the synagogue deal. He had made it sound like an ordinary business venture, with Flynn a helpless entrepreneur, strapped for cash, victimized by insatiable monsters. "Thank you for coming forward, Mr. Flynn," Wainwright had said in front of the grand jury. "If it were not for citizens like you, we could do nothing."

And the pristine thought kept drumming through him that he would actually come out of this whole, even better than whole; he was a hero, he really had done something for his country. Hadn't Wainwright said so? Standing in the middle of the room, swigging on his Goldblatt, Flynn exclaimed, "Hey, you know what? Wainwright's giving a big cookout next weekend at that place he has in the country. I heard about it in his office. All kinds of big people will be there. Big politicians. All that. I think I'll send twenty, thirty cases. He'd like it. Maybe he'll invite me."

Agnes turned to him as though she could not believe her ears. "Invite *you?*"

"Sure, why not?"

"Oh, Richie," she said, "when are you going to come to your senses? Can't you see he's just using you? He doesn't care anything about you." She hid her face in her hands and began to weep.

Rage welled up in him. "Listen," he said, "you got it wrong. He needs me. Without me, he's got nothing."

"For God's sake, he's got everything. This isn't the Giants, Richie. You're not scoring a touchdown. He is."

"You just love to put me down, don't you? You really get a kick out of it."

"Stop!" she cried. "I can't stand this anymore."

"Maybe we should wait downstairs," one of the marshals said.

"Yeah," Flynn said, his voice thick, "I'll see you guys later," and stepped toward her, an arm up.

"Go ahead," she said, "hit me, you big, important man."

Flynn glanced at Sean. "Go to your room."

The boy stationed himself in front of Agnes. "No," he said, fists balled up at his sides.

"It's all right, sweetheart," she said. "He won't do anything."

After Sean had left, Flynn sneered, "You're right. I won't. You'd like me to hit you. Then you could run around telling everybody how I beat you. Look at you. Didn't you ever want anything in your life? Didn't you ever want to score? Look at the way you've let yourself go. The truth is you'd be afraid to go to Wainwright's."

The tears slid down her cheeks. "You know," she said, "you're crazy. It's all your drinking."

"Good. Have it your way." He walked out of the apartment, slamming the door behind him. The marshals were waiting in the lobby. *"Jesus!"* he said to them. "Well, what can you do? Come on, I'm going to show you some real New York."

He took them to the Liffey Bar & Grill. When they went in, Flynn pointed to his old high school football picture, still in place above a row of bottles. "How does that grab you?" he said. "Richie Flynn. The early years!"

He laughed and moved exuberantly along the bar, greeting the regulars. "What's doing, Richie?" they said. "How's it going?" and he replied, "Never better."

Flynn beckoned the marshals to follow him to a rear table. He passed the retired carnival man, Cornelius J. MacShane, sitting with his jigger of Jack Daniel's. "Richie," he said, "I haven't seen you since that night you were with Scanlon."

"I haven't had the time," Flynn said. "I'm into big things, really big things. You'll be reading about it in the papers."

"Oh, that's grand, Richie," the old man said, peering at him sharply.

Flynn ordered a round of scotch. When the marshals hesitated, he insisted. "Nothing's going to happen to me here. These are all my friends."

He returned home after midnight. There was a scribbled message on the night table by his bed from Agnes saying that she and Sean had moved to her mother's and please not to bother them. Fuck her, Flynn thought, and only in the morning did he realize that he was truly alone.

━━━☆━━━

23

Wainwright personally announced the indictments at a crowded, televised press conference. Named as defendants were Frank Donato, Vincente D'Angelo, Anthony Valente, Albert Karpstein and Thomas Biondo. The indictments charged that they had "unlawfully and willfully conspired and agreed together to violate interstate commerce laws of traveling to commit racketeering" and that in furtherance of the conspiracy, they had also made use of "interstate facilities of communication, to wit, the telephone."

The intent of the defendants, Wainwright declared, was "to extort money and other things in violation of the laws of New York and New Jersey," and Richie Flynn, in borrowing first from Karpstein and then from Valente, had been "caught between two rival gangs." Karpstein and Biondo both were singled out as having threatened Flynn with "bodily injury."

To protect Valente's loan, he continued, Frank Donato, invoking his powers as a Mafia boss, had ruled that Flynn "did not have to pay any more money to Karpstein until he paid Valente" and had caused another defendant, Vincente D'Angelo, to meet with unknown allies of Karpstein to ensure that Flynn "would be free of intimidation, assaults and death" from Karpstein. Then Wainwright paused dramatically and said, "When it became evident that Flynn could not pay Valente, Donato lifted his protection of Flynn and informed Karpstein through D'Angelo that he could do whatever he wanted about collecting the money."

After he had finished the formal reading of the indictments, Wainwright raised his eyes to the television cameras and said, "This case marks the beginning of the end for the national crime syndicate. For too long the rulers of organized crime have considered themselves invincible, beyond the reach of the law. That myth of invincibility has now been exploded."

A reporter asked if there were not in fact two separate

extortions, and Wainwright replied, "No, it was a criminal partnership. Only the techniques were different. Karpstein used a mailed fist, and Donato the silken glove."

"I don't see what Donato got out of it," another reporter persisted. "Was some of the money supposed to go to him?"

"It doesn't matter," Wainwright said. "What was at stake for Frank Donato was his authority as a Mafia don. Without a constant demonstration of power, no don can operate. That's why this case is so important. For once we have hit the syndicate's top leadership instead of just the underlings."

The media had been tipped off as to the time and place of the arraignments, and as the indictments were being revealed, photographs and film were taken of D'Angelo and Valente, their faces concealed behind hats, of Biondo grinning vacantly toward the cameras and of Karpstein, manacled and under heavy guard, being brought into court from the county jail.

Wainwright ended his press conference on a startling note that sent all the reporters dashing to telephones. Although Donato had been under surveillance for several days and Wainwright knew that he was on a fishing boat off eastern Long Island, the special prosecutor said, "We have been unable to locate Frank Donato. He has not been seen in his usual haunts for several days. A warrant has been issued for his arrest, and he has been declared a fugitive from justice. I have called upon the Department of State to revoke his passport, effective immediately."

The local evening television news showed footage of Flynn's run for the Giants. Donato's mysterious disappearance guaranteed extensive network coverage, which featured film clips of his writhing hands during his Senate testimony. In the morning the *Daily News* gave over its entire front page to "Mob Kingpin Charged in Grid Star Extort," and the lead story in the New York *Times* was headlined "Donato, Four Others Indicted by Grand Jury Here," with a subhead that said, "Worldwide Search Conducted for Alleged Organized Crime Chief." The *Times* also profiled Wainwright as its "Man in the News," the wire services transmitted lengthy interviews with him and the news-magazines began to research him as a cover-story candidate.

Flynn's current employment at Goldblatt was prominently mentioned in all the stories, and the day after the indictments were announced, the brewery's president, unhappy with the publicity, called Wainwright and said, "You never told me this would happen. We're going to have to let him go."

"You do that," Wainwright said, "and you'll find out what bad publicity really is. How would you like some headlines saying, 'Company Fires Key Government Witness' or 'Brewery Dumps Crime Fighter'?"

"You can't be serious."

"Try me."

"All right. But how long is this going to go on?"

"Until the trial's over."

"Then what?"

"Then," Wainwright said, "you can do whatever you like."

☆

Donato's possible whereabouts kept the case alive in the press and on television and radio, and among the cities in which he was reportedly sighted were Rome and Naples, Miami Beach and San Francisco. On the same day different newscasts had him in the Bahamas and Brazil.

Donato had learned about his indictment, and all the places he was supposed to be in, the same way everyone else had—in the media. And sitting now in the cockpit of his boat, the *Caroline*, squinting into a spectacular sunset, sipping a glass of white wine, he thought again about Hamilton Wainwright. Two days earlier, when Donato had left New York for a marina near Montauk Point on Long Island, his driver, Enzo, had said as they passed through the Hamptons, "Boss, there's a car been on our ass. It's one of them green Chevies the feds use." Later Enzo reported that the car was parked off the highway near the side road leading to the marina. "It's the feds, all right," he had said. "I could tell by their suits and haircuts."

Until he found out about the indictment, Donato had been unconcerned about the surveillance. It had occurred periodically over the years, and he would wonder each time what had prompted it and marvel at the wasted expense to the nation's taxpayers. So Wainwright knew perfectly well where he was, and the great search for him was nothing more than a publicity stunt, But Donato decided to play along, for a while anyway, to ponder his situation.

He was fairly sure that his presence at the marina would not be known unless Wainwright elected to make it public. The marina had yet to be completed, and the *Caroline* was the only boat docked there. Moreover, both the marina and a big companion hotel were being built by the contracting firm Donato secretly owned. The hotel would be too large for normal resort business, but its spacious halls had been designed for easy conversion to gambling in anticipation of legalized casinos. Donato had no intention of risking exposure by opening up a casino himself. Instead, he planned to sell it at a considerable profit to some eminently respectable group while quietly retaining control of its various service aspects—liquor franchise, linen supply, vending machines and so on—and bids had already been made by an international hotel chain and a Wall Street investment house.

The last sliver of the sun disappeared below the horizon. Rose-colored streaks shot across the western sky. Minute waves slapped against the *Caroline*'s hull. The mooring lines creaked. The captain and mate had gone into the village to eat, and Donato was alone on the boat. He took another sip of wine. It should have been a moment to savor, but now it was etched with a certain sadness and regret.

An hour before, Enzo had driven Isidore Goldberg back to the city. Goldberg had been Donato's lawyer for nearly fifty years, and he had come out with the indictment papers to discuss the case. They shared a bond that went far beyond the usual ties of lawyer and client. If he had not been Isidore Goldberg with a ghetto accent that he could never quite rid of, he would have been snapped up by any one of a dozen prestigious partnerships when he graduated from law school. But he was. And so Goldberg, whose marriage in his early twenties quickly produced twin boys to support, had started representing racketeers. He had been retained by Donato during Prohibition, and one evening the two men, after a few too many glasses of Donato's bootleg scotch, spoke of themselves and their might-have-beens and how the shape of their lives had been almost predetermined. The subject never came up again between them, but after that night their friendship was sealed.

Although they were approximately the same age, Goldberg had started to decline markedly. For a time Donato had ignored it, but now he no longer could. When he had asked Goldberg his opinion of the indictment, the attorney, with his dewlaps and fingers quivering in tandem, snorted, "Ah, it's nothing to worry about, Frank. We'll win on appeal. Wainwright is serving up a juicy hunk of beef named Karpstein, and so what's better than throwing in a nice Italian salad called Donato?"

"No, Goldie, you're wrong," Donato had said, studying Goldberg carefully. *"I'm* the main course. This Wainwright isn't kidding around."

There had been an awkward silence. Then Donato made a decision. "Listen, we're both getting too old for this. I'm bringing in a younger guy to handle it."

"You're saying you don't want me?"

"I want your counsel."

"But not me?"

"Hey, Goldie."

"Like always, Frank, it's whatever you want." Goldberg's hands fluttered aimlessly. He bent to pick up his briefcase. "Anyway," he had said in a tight voice, almost as though it were a question, "you weren't ever in dope."

"No, I never was," Donato said.

"That's what I used to tell my sons," Goldberg said. "Well, Frank, I'll be seeing you."

"Sure, Goldie," Donato had said.

Donato watched the cloud of dust rise as the car carrying Goldberg out of his life wound along the bulrush-lined marina road. You do what you have to do, he thought, and that's the end of it.

Then Donato went to a pay telephone on the dock and called William J. McNulty in Washington, D.C. McNulty had been chief of the Justice Department's Organized Crime and Racketeering Section when Robert F. Kennedy was the attorney general and had since become one of the country's elite defense lawyers. Donato had noticed that most of the attorneys either representing or prosecuting the major figures in the Watergate scandal had once worked under Kennedy. It revealed, he had reflected, a great deal about lawyers. It also meant that Kennedy had recruited a very smart bunch of them, and none had more savvy than McNulty.

"Counselor," he said, "this is Frank Donato. Maybe you been reading about me."

"And seeing you on television. At least your hands."

"I been lucky. I missed that part. What would you say if I said I was being set up?"

"With Ham Wainwright involved, it wouldn't give me a coronary."

"You know him, huh? He was with you people?"

"No, he came later. Let's say I know *of* him."

"When could we get together, Counselor?"

"Where are you?"

"Montauk, on Long Island. I come out to relax, do some fishing for broadbills, you know, swordfish. There was a tournament I can forget about. It looks like somebody else is doing the fishing."

"That works out fine," McNulty said. "I have a new toy, a little executive jet. I was going to fly up to Nantucket in the morning for the weekend. I can drop in at Montauk on the way."

"Good. The two clowns that got me in this mess will be out here, and you can see them, too."

☆

"How come I can't go with you?" Tony Valente had said to D'Angelo.

"Because I can't stand the fucking sight of you any more than I have to. Here's the directions to the marina when you get there."

Valente's nerves were at the breaking point. While he had seen Donato once or twice in person at a distance, the fact was that in all the years he had been a member of the family, Valente had never actually met him. He wondered what he should wear. It was vital that Donato recognize at once that he was a man worthy of respect, and after much debate he selected a beige silk suit, white shirt, black tie and shoes and a tan fedora.

Then, when he reached the marina, and Enzo, the driver, had led him along the dock and left him standing there, perhaps ten feet from the *Caroline*, Valente never felt more foolish. He had picked all the wrong clothes. Donato was dressed in a blue and white striped jersey, white shorts and a white billed cap. There was a man with a round, freckled Irish face sitting next to Donato, wearing one of those short-sleeved shirts with an alligator on it. Even D'Angelo wore a sports shirt.

Valente did not know what to do. Nobody on the boat seemed to be aware of him. He shifted his feet uncomfortably. Finally he took off his fedora and placed it over his heart, as if saluting a passing flag. And waited, the sun beating down on him.

On the boat D'Angelo was saying to Donato, "I was just bluffing Joe Hobo. What the hell, I didn't want to get you involved."

Donato grunted. Then he nodded to D'Angelo, and D'Angelo said to Valente, "All right, get up here."

Valente tried to scramble on board, still clasping the fedora to his heart. He lost his footing. His hands flailed in the air to maintain his balance, and the fedora fell into the water. Valente watched helplessly as it floated under the dock.

"Jesus," D'Angelo said, "can't you do anything right?"

Valente, his face flushed, managed at last to climb into the boat. He stood in front of Donato and bowed deferentially.

Donato surveyed him for a moment and said, "You say anything about me to Flynn? *Anything?*"

"No, boss, I swear it. I just told him, that fucking Jew gives you any trouble, tell him to call me or Vinnie. I mean, Vinnie said it was all set."

"What do you think, Counselor?" Donato said to McNulty.

"They must have had a bug in the club and fed the information to Flynn. We used to do that all the time."

"Check it out," Donato said to D'Angelo.

"It's too late," McNulty said. "I'm sure they've yanked it."

"So this Flynn's the key."

"And Karpstein," McNulty said. "Don't forget, he's Wainwright's insurance policy. He's your co-defendant and co-conspirator, and he's going to be there in court right next to you, and by the time Wainwright is through with him, he's going to make Attila the Hun look like the kind of guy you'd want your sister to marry."

"Hey, boss," Valente suddenly said, "you want I should whack out Flynn?"

"You know what?" Donato said. "You're in the wrong business. You should be on television doing comedy routines."

Then he nodded to D'Angelo again, and D'Angelo said to Valente, "OK. Beat it, Tony."

Donato turned to McNulty. "After I go in, what happens? I haven't been locked up since 1925. I don't want my luck to change, even for ten minutes."

"That's no problem. I'll call the magistrate and find out what bail he's got in mind, and you can have your bondsman put it up in advance. Wainwright won't be able to do anything. There are plenty of precedents."

Donato shook McNulty's hand. "Good. I'll see you in court." When D'Angelo started to follow the attorney off the boat, Donato said, "You stay. I want to talk to you."

☆

Reporters thronged around Donato as he arrived for his arraignment, and to the shouted questions of where he had been, he replied, "I was out fishing. The newspaper deliveries ain't so good in the ocean. Soon as I heard what was going on, I contacted my lawyer and came in. I don't have anything to hide."

"What do you think about the indictment?" a reporter asked, and Donato drew a laugh from everyone when he said, "They pay you to ask questions like that? Listen, I'm no saint maybe, but they're charging me with extortion." His voice rose indignantly. "Let me tell you something. I never lent money at interest. The only money I ever lent was to my friends, and I don't charge my friends interest."

"Is there a Mafia, Mr. Donato?"

"That's what all those movie people say," Donato said. "And to tell you the truth, I wish I had the idea myself. Look at the dough they're making out of it."

"Do you think you can get a fair trial?"

"Sure, why not? This is America, isn't it?"

The arraignment proceedings lasted less than half an hour. Donato pleaded not guilty and was released on bail of fifty thousand dollars. If convicted, he would face five years in prison and a ten-thousand-dollar fine.

☆

In the Bourbon Street Club Diane Drahomanov had just finished a turn above the bar when the two men came in to take her to Vincente D'Angelo.

"Throw on a coat," one of them said. "He wants to see you right away."

"I've got to get dressed," she said.

"Why bother?" he said, staring at her body. "Everybody knows what you got."

And then D'Angelo was staring at her through gold-framed glasses from across his desk, his lips parted in his version of a smile. "How you doing, doll?"

"Fine, Mr. D'Angelo," she said.

"Well, you look fine, that's for sure. Say, listen, how's that little girl you got in Toledo?"

"My little girl?" she said uncertainly.

"Yeah, ain't this her?" D'Angelo said, holding up the photograph of her daughter in a white party dress that Diane kept by her bed.

Although she had insisted on getting dressed, she had never felt more naked in her life. "Yes," she whispered. "How did you get that?"

"Don't worry, it's OK. Here, take it. I just wanted to make sure it was her." D'Angelo leaned back in his chair. "Tell me," he said, "you still seeing that guy Flynn?"

"Oh, Mr. D'Angelo, I was," she said, speaking as rapidly as she could, "but I didn't know about any of this. I mean, Richie told me he was in some big investment, and I almost died when I saw on TV about you and him and everything. Honestly, I won't see him ever again."

"Yes, you will."

"No, I swear I won't."

"Does he come regular, or what?"

"Usually he calls first to see if I'm dancing at the club."

"Is he alone?"

"No, there's always some men with him. Richie said they were, uh, security."

"OK. Now listen to me. You know how to get in touch with him?"

"Yes, he gave me a number."

"Good. As of right this minute, forget about the club. And don't worry. You still get paid. What I want is for you to see him as much as you can. He don't call, you call him. Try and get him to talk about the case all you can. You got that?"

"Yes," she said. "Please, Mr. D'Angelo, don't hurt my baby."

"Just do what I told you, and you got nothing to worry about." D'Angelo took off his glasses and wiped them. "And," he said, leaning forward, "this is strictly between us. Understand?"

"Yes."

Then, after she had left, D'Angelo lit a cigar and puffed on it thoughtfully for a few minutes before he left to have another chat with Joe Hobo. This time, however, it would not be in the Ravens Club.

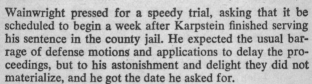

24

Wainwright pressed for a speedy trial, asking that it be scheduled to begin a week after Karpstein finished serving his sentence in the county jail. He expected the usual barrage of defense motions and applications to delay the proceedings, but to his astonishment and delight they did not materialize, and he got the date he asked for.

"What do you think McNulty's up to?" Simonetta said.

"I don't know, and I don't care," the special prosecutor replied. "It's good for us, and that's what counts. It keeps everything hot."

The fact was that McNulty had been just as surprised. When he had sketched out the available courses of legal action, Donato told him, "Counselor, everything is in your hands, like we agreed. Except I want this over with. I don't want it hanging over my head."

McNulty scrutinized his client for a moment and then said, "Fine."

D'Angelo, Valente and Bionde, once informed of Donato's wishes, promptly followed his lead.

Only Karpstein insisted on filing a novel motion for dismissal of his indictment, claiming that "to merely seek money legitimately owed, even if it was accompanied by threats and even if it was the result of a usurious loan, is not extortion."

"There's no way we'll get by with it," his lawyer had advised, but Karpstein snarled, "It don't matter. That's how I feel and I want it on the record."

The day before Karpstein was to be let out of jail, a detainer was issued to place him in federal custody upon his release, and that evening Joe Hobo could no longer put off executing a contract he had concluded with D'Angelo. "This time I'm not bullshitting," D'Angelo had said in the back of a car that cruised through Little Italy. "This is how F.D. wants it, and this is how it's got to be."

So Joe Hobo called Herman Mueller and said, "How's Milky, Warden?"

"Milky? Oh, you mean Albert."

"Yeah, Milky. How's he doing?"

"It's hard to say. The last few days he's been acting strange. He stays in his pajamas, and he doesn't shave or wash, and he mumbles a lot to himself. He's in these striped pajamas all the time, and he says he's going to wear them in court. He showed me a book he has full of concentration-camp pictures and he said, 'See, this is the uniform of the Jews.' Maybe he's setting up an insanity plea. Who knows what's in his head? But he hasn't caused any trouble, if that's what you mean."

"Yeah, well, I'm coming to see him tonight. Only don't tell him, so it'll be a surprise. And, Warden, I'll be asking for you. I don't want no signing-in crap or nothing."

Joe Hobo arrived at the jail with Sally Dimples, an exceptionally homely former wrestler who had been his bodyguard and driver for years. "Stick around, Warden," Joe Hobo told Mueller. "I might want to see you later."

Mueller led them to Karpstein's room, knocked on the door first, then opened it and said, "Albert, you have some visitors."

The room was about fifteen feet deep and eight wide. The walls were unpainted concrete. There was an unmade cot at the far end. Against one wall were a hot plate, a small refrigerator and a television set. Karpstein sat at a table in the middle of the room, facing the door. His pajama top was unbuttoned, and a gold Star of David dangled on his massive chest. He seemed not to have shaved for several days. Mueller was right, Joe Hobo thought, he's going nuts.

Karpstein looked at him with blank eyes. "So you finally showed up."

Joe Hobo picked some lint from a sleeve of his black mohair suit. "Come on, Milky, this is a nice setup you got. I knew you was all right. I checked with Mueller. Didn't he tell you?"

He stepped into the room, and Sally Dimples closed the door behind them. Joe Hobo took the chair across the table from Karpstein. Books were piled on the table. One was titled *The Federal Criminal Code;* another, *The U.S. Constitution;* a third, *Auschwitz.* Joe Hobo turned to Sally Dimples and pointed toward the cot and said, "Go sit there."

Sally Dimples went to the cot, although he remained standing.

"What's he here for?" Karpstein said. "You afraid I'll do something? I could break him in half, I wanted to."

"Hey, Sally's always with me," Joe Hobo said. "Don't go hurting his feelings. He's good people."

"Yeah, good people," Karpstein said. "I thought you was all good people. But I know better now. Now I know you got to stick with your own kind."

"What kind of talk is that?"

"The truth," Karpstein said, his tone strangely plaintive. "All I done for you, you don't do nothing for me. Flynn's the whole case. You finish Flynn, it's all finished." Suddenly his voice pitched higher. "I can't do nothing myself because of you, on account of trying to collect your fucking money."

"Listen to me," Joe Hobo said. "That's why I'm here. Everything is being taken care of. It took time, is all."

"It better be. Because if I go, you go, too."

Joe Hobo stared at Karpstein. "What's that mean?"

"It means I got it all written down, and it's in a safe place where you can't get at it. Everything I ever done for you. All them bodies I buried for you."

"Hey, Milky, that's not nice."

"That's too fucking bad!" Karpstein shouted.

At least he's making this easier, Joe Hobo thought, and with enormous effort, he kept his eyes fastened on Karpstein as Sally Dimples began drawing the piece of iron pipe out of his belt. Sally Dimples was left-handed, so when he swung the pipe, it caved in the left side of Karpstein's skull above the ear.

Karpstein's eyes bulged. His mouth opened. But instead of falling, he rose dazedly from the chair, his hands clawing the air across the table. His lips tried to work, but the only sound that came through them was a guttural moan. Joe Hobo shrank back.

"No, Milky!" he screamed.

Then, all at once, Karpstein toppled sideways, knocking over his chair. His head thudded against the concrete wall. It left a bloody smear matted with hair. He lay on the floor, inert. Sally Dimples bent over him, the pipe poised for another blow.

"No, that's perfect the way it is," Joe Hobo yelled, pointing at the blood on the wall. Originally he had planned to have the assault on Karpstein attributed to one of those unsolvable acts of violence that are always happening in jails. But this was much better. "It looks like he fell off the chair. Is he alive?"

"I can't tell," Sally Dimples said.

"Well, it don't matter. He can't last. Let's get out of here," he said.

Joe Hobo went directly to Mueller's office. "Warden, Milky's had an accident."

Mueller looked alarmed. "What happened?"

Joe Hobo pulled out a roll of bills. "Here're five Gs for your trouble and all."

Mueller looked less alarmed. "An accident, huh?"

"Yeah," Joe Hobo said. "It was terrible. He must of got dizzy or whatever and fell and hit his head against the wall. There's blood all over the wall where he hit it. You could see for yourself."

"Is that so?" Mueller said, pocketing the money. "I suppose I should call the infirmary."

"I was you, I wouldn't," Joe Hobo said. "A man in Milky's condition, it could be dangerous moving him too quick, you know what I mean. Maybe he should just rest where he is till morning."

"Perhaps you're right," Mueller said.

As soon as Joe Hobo left the jail through a side door, he had Sally Dimples drive him to Karpstein's home and took a final deep breath to calm himself before ringing the bell.

Angelina was in a bathrobe when she let him in. "Oh, Mr. Iacovelli," she said, "I'm so honored, but I had no idea you were coming. Excuse how I look."

"Please," Joe Hobo said. "You look wonderful. How are the children, your mother?"

"They're fine. My mother's asleep. She won't believe it when I tell her you were here. Sit down. Can I get you something? Some coffee. A drink."

"Thank you, no." He gazed at her solemnly. "Listen, my dear, you know who I am and how I care for you and your family."

"Yes, of course. Albert and I talk about it all the time. What you've done for us. Is something wrong?"

His eyes remained fixed on her. "Angelina, I got some bad news. Milky, ah, Albert had an accident. He fell in his room in the jail and hurt his head. I was just there. It don't look good."

She instinctively made the sign of the cross. "I'll get dressed right away."

"No," he said. "That's why I came instead of calling. It won't do no good. I mean, he's out of it. I'll go with you myself in the morning."

"Oh, my God!"

"Angelina!" he said sharply.

"Yes, Mr. Iacovelli?"

"I know what you're feeling. You been a wonderful wife, a wonderful mother. But a time like this you got to be practical, too. You listening to me?"

"Yes."

"I just want you should know, whatever happens to Albert, you and your family got nothing to worry about. People like us, we got to take care of each other, and you'll be taken care of. You understand?"

"Yes. Thank you."

"Don't mention it," Joe Hobo said. "Now let me ask you, did Albert ever say he had anything put away somewhere safe, like in a safe-deposit box or something? Maybe some papers and whatnot."

"Yes, in a safe-deposit box. How did you know that?"

"Well, he told me, too. Did he tell you what was in them papers?"

"He just said that it was his protection, and he would let me know if I should ever open the box."

"That's what he told me. Listen, you go get that key and give it to me, and we'll go to the bank in the morning, and then we'll go see Albert."

She looked at him and knew she had no choice.

☆

During a routine morning inspection a jail guard discovered Karpstein crumpled on the floor. He was rushed to the county hospital, where he underwent emergency surgery to remove bone fragments that had penetrated the temporal lobe in the left hemisphere of his brain. He survived that as well, thereby confounding the attending physicians, and after forty-eight hours regained a consciousness of sorts.

"He has some eye movement, but that's about it," Simonetta told Wainwright. "So it's hard to say what comprehension he has. Unfortunately it's the left side of his brain, which controls articulation. Besides not being able to talk, the entire right side of his body is paralyzed."

"In a word, he's a goddamn vegetable."

"Practically speaking, yes. For the time being anyhow."

Wainwright picked up a pencil from his desk and broke it in half. "What's the prognosis?"

"They say there could be a gradual improvement over the next two or three months. Or he could get worse. He could start to hemorrhage and go into a coma and punch out. In any event, there's no way he's going to be Exhibit A in front of a jury next week. Maybe we should try for an adjournment."

Wainwright snapped the half of the pencil he was still holding. "That's out of the question, Nick, and you know it. We're the ones who pushed for trial. McNulty would be in like a shot with a motion to dismiss. I can hear him now. 'The government's had adequate time to prepare its case! Any delay would prejudice my client's rights!' And he'd get it."

Wainwright's voice, which went to a falsetto as he mimicked McNulty, dropped to its normal tone. He stared into space. Then he tried to break the last bit of the pencil and, failing, flung it angrily across his office. "That goddamn warden," he said. "He's sticking to his story?"

"Yes. He says their investigation indicated that Karpstein fell off his chair and struck his head against the wall. He says that Karpstein had been acting queer recently, and maybe he had a fit. The doctors say that it's unlikely he could have suffered such an injury that way. On the other hand, the doctors say anything is possible. So much for the doctors."

"OK. Donato stuck it to us," Wainwright said, "but now it's our turn. And I guarantee you one thing. That jury may not get to see Karpstein, but it's going to hear plenty about him."

☆

As a precautionary measure, Richie Flynn was moved from his apartment to a U.S. Coast Guard installation on Governors Island off the southern end of Manhattan. The sole access to the island was by ferry, and in addition to the normal security forces, marshals were stationed nightly outside the small ground-floor apartment he was assigned to in a building reserved for bachelor officers.

After his initial rush of relief that the loan shark was apparently out of his life forever, Flynn found that he had a strange reaction to the news about Karpstein. What he constantly imagined was a titanic struggle going on inside Karpstein, Karpstein in a volcanic rage, straining to escape from himself, unable to talk, to act. Simonetta had told him that Karpstein's eyes suggested the possibility that he could understand what was being said to him even if he could not respond, and he pictured Karpstein lying mute and immobile on his bed while somebody leaned over him and urged, "Come on, Albert, tell us what happened," and Karpstein's face turning purple with futile effort. He wondered what Karpstein's fearsome eyes looked like now, and he saw them darting, beseeching, helpless. The thought awed him and disturbed him, although he could not understand why until he blurted it out in a telephone conversation with Agnes.

"Did you read about Karpstein?" he had said.

"Yes," she said.

There was a silence. She had obtained work as a bookkeeper just as his mother had after his father died, only it was in a pharmacy instead of a saloon.

"How's the job going?"

"Fine."

Since she had moved out, he had spoken to her only on the phone. Three times he had the marshals take him to Inwood to pick up Sean at her mother's. The visits had been unbearably awkward. Once when they were walking through Inwood Park together, Flynn had pointed to a refuse-strewn field and said, "That's where I first started playing ball. It was really nice then." His son surveyed the field without comment. A soft-drink vendor came by. "Hey, what about some soda?" Flynn had urged, but the boy said, "No, thanks."

And now, talking to Agnes, after another pause, he said, "How's Sean?"

"Fine."

"Uh, he'd love it here. There're bowling alleys and game rooms and stuff like that. I should have joined up."

She did not say anything.

"It's funny about me and Karpstein," he said.

"What's so funny?" she said tonelessly.

"I don't know. I guess it's that we're both trapped. He has Donato, and I have Wainwright." Then, suddenly, he said, "And in the end we both wind up alone. Isn't that funny?"

"No, it isn't. But you're right. You're both alone," she said, and hung up.

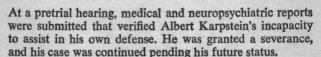

25

At a pretrial hearing, medical and neuropsychiatric reports were submitted that verified Albert Karpstein's incapacity to assist in his own defense. He was granted a severance, and his case was continued pending his future status.

Tommy Biondo's lawyer, a burly Sicilian sporting a violet suit with matching suede shoes, who had been mistaken by a young television reporter for one of the defendants, then stepped forward to move that Biondo be severed from the trial as well.

"On what grounds?" the federal district judge, Matthew X. Cody, asked.

"Because my client's main defense witness is Mr. Karptein."

The silver-maned jurist usually sat sideways while presiding in court so as to best display his resemblance to his illustrious ancestor Buffalo Bill Cody, but now he swiveled around and peered straight down from the bench in some amazement. "Where," he said, "did you get that suit?"

"Nunzio Tailors," Biondo's lawyer replied. "I'll be glad to introduce you."

"Motion denied," the judge said.

Cody was quite pleased with himself. He was a law-and-order judge who yearned mightily to be elevated to the appeals level. In theory, federal judges are selected on a random basis to preside over trials, but if a judge wants a particular case, he can drop a note to the clerk of the court requesting it. The judge has nothing to worry about, since the communication is not part of the case record. So as soon as Cody heard about Donato's indictment, he recognized the trial as a plum assignment and quickly bid for it, pointing out that he had recently handled another organized crime case prosecuted by Wainwright's office.

Over breakfast on the morning the case was to be heard, Judge Cody was gratified to find his picture prominently displayed in the New York *Times*. And upon arriving in his chambers, the first thing he did was instruct his secretary to secure five more copies to be clipped for posterity. Cody's good humor was further improved when he saw how crowded the courtroom was. Most trials are attended by a desultory sprinkling of onlookers, the same sort of blank faces that while away the day watching the ticker tape in branch brokerage offices. But today Cody's courtroom was packed with attorneys, law students and the media, drawn by the notoriety of the chief defendant and the prospect of seeing Wainwright and McNulty in action against each other.

They did not have to wait long for a clash. After seven jurors had been picked, Wainwright had yet to accept one of Italian descent, and William J. McNulty jumped up and angrily accused him of a deliberate pattern of discrimination. "This isn't a court of law as far as the special prosecutor is concerned," he stormed. "It's a street fight, and he'll use any means to win, no matter how foul. He's striking Italians from the jury because the defendants are Italian. And he's striking blacks as well."

Before Wainwright could respond, Cody said, "I don't see what blacks have to do with this."

"If a black was a defendant and blacks were excluded from the jury," McNulty retorted, "there'd be hell to pay, and Your Honor knows it. Besides, as the special prosecutor is well aware, blacks have a far more realistic view of life than the nice lily-white jury he wants."

"You're not going to influence this court by losing your temper," Judge Cody said in sternly resonant tones. But then, to be on the safe side, the judge interjected himself into the selection process, and the last two jurors turned out to be Italian women, and one of the two alternates was a black man.

"Hey, that was good, Counselor," Donato whispered.

"I hope so," McNulty said, "but don't be surprised if they're the ones who hang you." McNulty's wisecracking candor was as famous as his courtroom expertise. He and Wainwright had once addressed the same law school seminar during which they discussed their adversary roles in the judicial system. "They say," Wainwright had noted, "that man's sweetest pleasure is an orgasm. I submit that a foreman of a jury declaring, 'We find the defendant guilty,' is every bit as sweet," and McNulty had laughed and said, "For me, the thing is not to get too involved personally. The worst defense lawyers I know believe their clients are innocent."

Catchall federal conspiracy statutes formed the legal umbrella for Wainwright's prosecution, and in his opening statement to the jurors he stressed that the case was one not of simple extortion but of "conspiracy" to extort. "The defendants," he said, "criminally banded together in a grand design of evil purpose. And it is a matter of law, as the judge will tell you, that each defendant is equally liable for the acts of his co-conspirators, even though he did not know about or participate in any one or more of them."

"The learned prosecutor is correct," McNulty said in his response. "Except that he has forgotten one thing. He must also demonstrate the existence of his alleged conspiracy."

☆

Harry Fowler was the first government witness. Questioned by Simonetta, he explained in halting tones how he had conceived the day-care center deal and how he had approached Flynn to finance it. Fowler, Simonetta was careful to bring out, was a broken man who had nothing to gain by testifying. He had lost his job, his civil service standing and his pension.

Wainwright then questioned Donny Scanlon, who recalled the evening Flynn had met him in the Liffey Bar and had asked him to arrange a meeting with a loan shark.

"Was any particular loan shark mentioned?"

"Yes," Scanlon said. "He wanted to meet with King Kong Karpstein, and I tried to talk him out of it."

"*King Kong?*"

"Yes," Scanlon said. "That's the name he goes by. Because he's like an animal. He hopes you don't pay, so he can hurt you."

McNulty was on his feet at once. "Your Honor, this is totally unfair. At the very outset the government is painting a picture of a monster, trying to associate my client with a monster, who isn't a defendant in this trial, who isn't even in the courtroom."

"He's still a co-conspirator," Wainwright broke in.

"*If* there was a conspiracy. *If* it is shown that my client was involved as a partner, agent or co-conspirator, that's one thing, but from the prosecutor's opening statement, it's clear that he intends to go all over the lot to convict my client."

"We are merely trying," Wainwright said, "to show how certain declarations and acts pertain to a defendant or co-conspirator. The cumulative effect of these declarations and acts will prove the conspiracy the government has charged. We only ask the court to permit us to proceed in chronological order. We will tie everything in with the conspiracy at a later date. Our position is that it is within the sound discretion of the trial judge to determine what order of proof will be allowed."

"If Your Honor pleases," McNulty insisted, "the prosecutor can't have it both ways. He says he's going to prove the existence of a conspiracy by these acts and declarations, but they can't prove anything because the existence of a conspiracy must precede their admission."

"All right, the jury will consider what counsel said," Judge Cody announced, with an acid glance at Wainwright for putting him in this position. "Testimony heard about a party alleged to be co-conspirator or defendant concerns only that party until the participation of each individual is tied in and established in the case. Is that satisfactory, Mr. McNulty?"

"Thank you, Your Honor."

Wainwright could not have been more pleased. McNulty had no choice except to lodge these protests, and the jurors already appeared bored by them. "Let him make all the technical points he wants," Wainwright had said to Simonetta, "so long as they get a clear idea of Karpstein."

Wainwright continued to hammer at this theme when Richie Flynn took the stand. "What did Karpstein look like?"

"Well, he was very big, and his eyes were, uh, beady."

"Objection!" McNulty shouted.

"Overruled," the judge said. "The jury has been cautioned."

On the witness stand, Flynn felt strangely disembodied, as if he were perched twenty or thirty feet above the courtroom. Even the sound of his voice seemed to be coming from somewhere else. Wainwright had instructed him to look at the jury when he spoke, but when he did, their faces swam and became distorted, like reflections in a fun-house mirror, and he locked his eyes on the prosecutor to fight off the vertigo that assailed him, to keep from falling.

"And after Albert Karpstein gave you the money," Wainwright was saying, "what did he do?"

"He took out a gun and a piece of cable. He said that while he could use the gun, he preferred the cable, and he hit his desk with the cable." Flynn's eyes shut at the memory. His voice was barely audible.

"I know this is difficult, Mr. Flynn, but would you please speak up so the jury can hear you?"

"He hit the desk with the cable, to show what he would do to me if I didn't pay."

Wainwright led Flynn step by step through his subsequent meetings with Karpstein. "And then, you say, he made you hold out your hand and stabbed it, and blood spurted, and he said that made the two of you blood brothers. What did that mean?"

"I don't know," Flynn said. "All I know is that it made me afraid."

"And when problems developed with the day-care center and you no longer could meet your payments, what did you do?"

"I went to Tony Valente to borrow some more money to pay Mr. Karpstein."

"Do you see Mr. Valente in the courtroom?"

Flynn was momentarily confused. Valente? In the courtroom? When he had first taken the stand, he had purposely avoided looking at the defendants, and then, after Wainwright began to question him, in concentrating completely on Wainwright he had forgotten that they were even there.

Now, reluctantly, Flynn acknowledged their presence. On the left Biondo mouthed a silent curse. Valente and D'Angelo, in the middle, looked stonily at him. Donato was on the far right, removed from the others. Flynn recognized him from his pictures. He was nattily dressed in an Oxford-gray suit with a blue shirt and darker blue tie, a touch of white handkerchief peeking above his breast pocket. Unlike the others, he did not emanate any malevolence. Instead, he seemed to be studying Flynn, his head cocked slightly to one side, as if he were a connoisseur appraising an especially interesting objet d'art. It left Flynn unnerved.

"Mr. Flynn!" Wainwright said impatiently. "Will you please point out Valente?"

"Uh, yes. He's the second man on the left behind the table there. In the brown suit."

"Let the record indicate that the witness has identified Mr. Anthony Valente."

Then Wainwright said, "Did going to Valente settle the problem?"

"No, Karpstein kept after me for the money."

"What did you do?"

"I told Tony Valente."

"And what did Valente say?"

"He said I didn't have to worry. He said that he had gone to Vinnie D'Angelo, and Vinnie D'Angelo had spoken to their boss, Mr. F.D. And Mr. F.D. had made an edict that Mr. Karpstein couldn't do anything until Tony Valente got his money first."

"Who is Mr. F.D.?"

"Objection!" McNulty said. "It's leading and calls for a conclusion."

Wainwright glowered at McNulty. "I'll rephrase the question. Mr. Flynn, did Valente say who Mr. F.D. was?"

"Yes, and everyone knows it. He's Valente's boss, Frank Donato." Flynn prayed that Wainwright would not ask him to identify Donato, and then realized, of course, that he would not, that Donato's role in the case was the all-powerful, unseen mastermind.

"Did Mr. Valente say anything else?"

"Yes, he said that if I was bothered again, I should tell Karpstein to call him or D'Angelo."

"And after this conversation with Mr. Valente, did Albert Karpstein in fact leave you alone?"

"Yes, for a while."

"For a while?"

"Yes. But there were more problems with the day-care center, and when I asked Valente for more time, he said he was sorry. The matter was out of his hands now, and they couldn't hold off Karpstein anymore."

"Did another event then occur?"

"Karpstein came to my apartment in the middle of the

night and pounded on the door and yelled for me to open it."

"In the middle of the night?"

"Yes, around one A.M."

"Who was in the apartment with you?"

"Well, my wife and my son."

"How old is your son, Mr. Flynn?"

"He's eleven."

"Then what happened?"

"I remained quiet and didn't open the door, and finally he left."

"Why didn't you let Albert Karpstein in?"

"I was afraid to. He had already told me he was going to collect the money one way or another. Either I was going to pay him or he was going to cash in my life insurance policy."

There was not a sound in the courtroom. Wainwright looked at the jury. Three of the women on it, including one of the Italian women, seemed transfixed, hands covering their mouths.

"Unless the special prosecutor has an objection, we'll recess until ten o'clock tomorrow morning," Judge Cody said.

"None whatsoever," Wainwright replied, happy to end the day like this.

"What do you think?" Donato whispered to McNulty.

"Flynn's killing us," McNulty said.

☆

Following his testimony, Flynn returned to his quarters on Governors Island. There was an athletic field across the street, and he sat morosely watching a touch football game through the window while he worked on his fourth scotch.

The phone call from Diane came a little after seven P.M. "Oh, honey," she said in her breathless baby voice, "did you see the news on TV?"

"No, I forgot."

"Well, it was all about you and what a fantastic witness you were. They showed pictures of you coming out of court, and you really looked cute." She paused and then said, "Honey?"

"Yeah?"

"What are you doing?"

"Nothing. Just having a drink."

"Can you come up? Oh, I want you so much."

Several of the off-duty Coast Guardsmen playing football collided. One of them got up limping badly, and Flynn winced as he held the phone. "I'll be there in about an hour," he said.

The marshal riding with Flynn in the back of the car was from Casper, Wyoming, and sported a cowboy Stetson. The first time he had seen Diane, he had blushed shamelessly and called her "ma'am."

And now when she opened the apartment door, dressed in nothing but a transparent light green chemise, he gazed openmouthed at her and blushed again. She embraced Flynn and then slipped away and looked coldly at the marshal and said, "Do *they* always have to be here?"

New, deeper splotches of scarlet appeared on the marshal's face. "Uh, Mr. Flynn," he said, "maybe I could just look around and see if everything's OK and wait outside."

The television set was on in the living room. "No, it's all right. Just turn up the TV." Flynn looked at Diane and said, "Come on, baby, he's only doing his job."

She shrugged and led him into the bedroom. As Flynn closed the door, he felt the gun barrel against his neck right under his jawbone. "You make a sound," Tony Valente said, "and it's good-bye."

Flynn stood stock-still. His eyes sought Diane.

"I'm sorry, Richie," she whispered. "They were going to hurt my little girl."

Flynn could hear the television in the living room. Vincente D'Angelo came out of the bathroom and said in a low voice, "Take your clothes off."

After Flynn had stripped, D'Angelo said, "Open the door and stand so that dummy out there can see you ain't got nothing on, and get rid of him."

When Flynn opened the door, the marshal looked quizzically at him and started to rise from his chair. Flynn waved him back. "Everything's fine," he said. "But she's a little uptight. I don't know why. Do me a favor. Leave us alone. I'll see you later."

Flynn winked at the marshal, who nodded sympathetically. "You want me to turn off the TV?"

"No, just beat it."

As soon as the marshal left, D'Angelo turned to Diane. "Get in the other room. Me and Richie got some things to talk about."

"Could I put my shorts back on?" Flynn asked.

"Sure, Richie," D'Angelo said. "Anything you want."

☆

The next day in court Donato told McNulty, "That Flynn could help us, you ask the right questions."

"Really?"

"Really," Donato said.

McNulty looked at Donato, who was not smiling.

"I'll remember," McNulty said.

In his cross-examination of Flynn, McNulty retraced the day-care center deal and how the twelve thousand five hundred dollars had been borrowed from Karpstein.

"Why did you go to someone with his reputation?"

"Well, I knew he had the money, and I had the hope that the deal would go through right away and I would pay him."

"Now, Mr. Flynn, you have told us the circumstances under which you obtained the money, and you have also told us that there came a time when you were afraid you would be treated violently in an effort to collect the money you owed."

"Yes, sir."

"Up to that time did you ever hear Mr. Donato's name mentioned in connection with any of this?"

"No, sir."

"Did you ever hear Mr. D'Angelo's name mentioned?"

"No, sir."

"How about Mr. Valente?"

"No, sir."

"Mr. Flynn, have you ever met Frank Donato?"

"No, sir."

"Have you ever spoken to him?"

"No, sir."

"Did you ever receive any threat, directly or indirectly, from Mr. Donato during this entire transaction?"

"No, sir."

"Did Mr. D'Angelo threaten you?"

"No, sir."

"How about Mr. Valente? He must have been pretty upset when he found out what happened to his ten thousand dollars. Did he threaten you with a piece of cable? Or stab your hand? Or come to your home in the middle of the night? Anything like that?"

"No, sir."

"Mr. Flynn, you're under the protection of federal marshals, are you not?"

"Yes, sir."

"Is this because you had anything to fear from Mr. Donato?"

"No, it was because of Mr. Karpstein."

Wainwright could no longer contain himself. "Your Honor," he said, "may we have a brief recess?"

"Objection," McNulty said. He smiled at the jury. "I'm conducting an orderly examination of the witness. Could it be that the prosecutor doesn't like what he's hearing?"

"Mr. Wainwright?" Judge Cody said.

"Your Honor, it's that I, ah, have been informed of an urgent call from the attorney general. I don't see how a delay of a few minutes will stop the world from spinning."

"Well, I see now that one of the jurors is signaling that he wouldn't mind a recess, so we'll take five minutes." The judge cleared his throat officiously. "But don't make a habit of this. The court's time is valuable, too, you know."

A marshal took Flynn to a small office off the courtroom. Then Wainwright stormed in, Simonetta behind him. "What the hell do you think you're doing out there?" Wainwright demanded. "Testifying for Donato?"

"I'm trying to tell the truth."

"The truth, is it? You better take another look at that statement you signed. I'll have you up for perjury so fast you won't know what hit you. The truth is that they were all in this together, and you better start remembering it. You're supposed to be just as afraid of Donato as you were of Karpstein."

You don't know the half of it, Flynn thought.

In Diane's bedroom the night before, D'Angelo had said to him, "We know you been spoon-fed all this bullshit about the old man doing this and doing that."

Flynn had said nothing, his eyes riveted on the revolver Valente was pointing at him, and D'Angelo had said to Valente, "Jesus, will you put that fucking cannon away?"

and then he had looked at Flynn and said, "Listen, we was in your spot with that gorilla loose, we'd do the same, but he's out of the picture now, and I'll tell you who put him out. *We* did. So you don't have to worry about him anymore. And the dough Tony here gave you is a wash. You can forget about it. You understand my meaning? You getting this, Richie?"

"Yes," Flynn had said, and D'Angelo said, "OK. Let's get on with it. That fucking prosecutor has promised you a new name, a new identity and a job somewhere and whatever, and you think you're home free, right?" and Flynn had wondered what D'Angelo would say if he told him that Wainwright had not promised anything like that, that he had gone to Wainwright so terrorized that the subject never came up, and all anybody would have to do to find Richie Flynn was to ask around for him.

"But we'll find you," D'Angelo had continued. "You put the old man away on a bum rap like this, he'll reach out for you wherever you are and you're dead. Believe me, there's no way you could get away. So the smart thing is to forgive and forget and start over. I'm speaking for the old man, and he's a man of his word. You need something, you got it. Be smart, Richie. Think. You want to spend the rest of your life looking over your shoulder, waiting for something to happen?"

A court attendant knocked on the door and said, "The judge is coming in."

"You just remember," Wainwright warned.

"Yeah," Flynn said, "I will."

☆

"And so there came a time, did it not, Mr. Flynn," McNulty was now asking him in court, "when you went to Mr. Valente and he gave you the ten thousand dollars?"

"Yes, sir."

"Was that money a loan or was it actually an investment in the day-care center?"

"I don't know, sir."

"Well, isn't it clear, from what you've already told us, that Mr. Valente did not expect the return of the principal until the day-care center went through and that he would subsequently receive twenty percent of the profits?"

"That's right."

"When Mr. Valente gave you the money, did he know that you were going to turn it over to Albert Karpstein?"

"No, sir."

"Whose money was it that Mr. Valente gave you?"

"As far as I know, it was his own."

"And what specifically was his reaction when he learned where the money had gone?"

"He couldn't believe it."

"What did he say after you told him of Karpstein's threats?"

"He said he would see what he could do."

"As any close friend might? As a father, for instance, might do for his son?"

"Objection, Your Honor," Wainwright said. "It's argumentative."

"Sustained. Counsel will restrain himself."

"All right, Mr. Flynn," McNulty said, "was there a period after you spoke to Mr. Valente when Karpstein left you alone?"

"Yes, sir."

"And then Valente finally informed you that there wasn't anything more he could do about Karpstein?"

"Yes, sir."

"What did Mr. Valente say?"

"That he was sorry."

"He said he was sorry, is that right?"

"Yes, sir."

"Mr. Flynn, you have testified that in trying to help you with Karpstein, Mr. Valente approached Mr. D'Angelo about this matter and that Mr. D'Angelo went to a Mr. F.D. and this Mr. F.D. decreed that Albert Karpstein had to get off your back?"

"Yes, sir."

"You also testified that Mr. Valente identified Mr. F.D. as Frank Donato?"

"I believe he did."

"You *believe* it. You're not sure?"

"Well, I'm pretty sure. I was under a lot of pressure."

"But any reference or connection between Mr. F.D. and this case was only because of what somebody might have told you and not from your own personal knowledge. Is that correct?"

"Yes, sir."

"And when Albert Karpstein continued to harass you, did Mr. Valente instruct you to tell Karpstein to call either him or Mr. D'Angelo?"

"Yes, sir."

"Did Mr. Valente instruct you to tell Karpstein to call Frank Donato?"

"No, he didn't."

"Did you ever consider Frank Donato as being involved in a conspiracy against you?"

"No, sir."

"Objection!" Wainwright shouted. "That calls for a conclusion of law."

"Nonsense," McNulty said. "I have a right to inquire as to his mental state at the time, and that's all I'm doing."

The judge hesitated and finally said, "Overruled. Go ahead, Counselor."

"Mr. Flynn, so far as you know, the first time you ever laid eyes on Mr. Donato was when you walked into this courtroom. Is that so?"

"Yes, sir."

"I have no further questions," McNulty said.

Before Wainwright began his redirect examination, he requested a conference in Judge Cody's robing room. To nobody's surprise he wanted Cody to declare Flynn a hostile witness not only for its psychological impact on the jury but also to enable him to treat Flynn as though he were a witness for the defense.

"On what basis?" the judge said.

"Information and belief that he has been spoken to and is tailoring his testimony to the defense's needs."

McNulty reddened. "Just a minute. Is the prosecutor accusing defense counsel of improper actions?"

"I'm not accusing defense counsel of anything," Wainwright snapped, "but there has clearly been some breach of security surrounding the witness."

"I'm not going along with this, Your Honor," McNulty said. "Having failed with his original conspiracy theory, the prosecutor wants to concoct a new one."

"Now hold on here!" Wainwright said.

"Don't interrupt me. Judge, he wants you to let him go out there and attack his own witness. And without a shred of evidence to back it up. He doesn't have the slightest proof that Flynn hasn't been telling the truth. All that's happened is that I asked different questions and the special prosecutor doesn't like the answers, and I don't blame him. I guess this time he's going to have to settle for an orgasm."

Matthew X. Cody could not help grinning despite his chagrin at the turn the case had taken. And while it was now all bollixed up, he told himself, at least he knew one thing. Committing a reversible error at this point was no way for a federal judge to get promoted, so he turned to Wainwright and said, "Denied."

Hamilton Wainwright tried one last sally in court. "Mr. Flynn," he said with as much sarcasm as he could muster, "your relation to one of the defendants, Tony Valente, has been likened to that of a father and son. Do you recall that?"

"Yes."

"Is your father living?"

"No, he isn't."

"Would he have turned you over to someone like Albert Karpstein?"

"Really, Your Honor," McNulty said, "I think that goes beyond the bounds."

None of the defendants took the stand. The jury deliberated for nearly six hours, devoting almost all its time to the guilt or innocence of Vincente D'Angelo and Anthony Valente, and eventually it could reach no decision. Within the first fifteen minutes of debate, however, Tommy Biondo was found guilty of conspiracy to extort, and Frank Donato was acquitted.

Once the verdicts were announced, Wainwright strode from the courtroom, pushing his way through a swarm of reporters, refusing any comment. Then he thought better of it and returned to face the television cameras. "Naturally I'm disappointed," he said in a strained voice. "But what we've lost is only a battle. I want the public to know that as far as I'm concerned, the war goes on."

Donato's departure was more leisurely. And as the reporters gathered around him, one of them asked, "What are your plans?"

"My plans? Well, when this thing started, I was out fishing, and it's too late to go back. But I think I'll relax. Maybe go to the track. Got any hot tips?"

After the laughter subsided, another reporter called out,

"Seriously, were you surprised by the verdict, Frank? Were you ever worried?"

"Hey, what can I tell you?" Donato said. "This is a great country. I always had faith in American justice, and this proves I was right."

26

━━━━━━ ☆ ━━━━━━

The day after the trial Flynn was fired by Goldblatt.

He was alone in his apartment when the bell rang. He opened the door, and Enzo, Donato's driver, handed him a large manila envelope. When he opened it, he found ten packets of ten one-hundred-dollar bills with a note enclosed. The note advised Flynn that there was a sales position available at a company that distributed Black Feather scotch. The note also said, "Remember something. When the elephants fight, it's the ants that get hurt."

The note, of course, was unsigned.

I would like to express my thanks to Sam Cohn and Arlene Donovan for their support, to Marc Jaffe and Elisabeth Sifton for their editorial guidance and to Joan Spano for her editing of the copy.

ABOUT THE AUTHOR

PETER MAAS is the author of the critically acclaimed nonfiction bestsellers *The Valachi Papers* and *Serpico*. This is his first novel.

Bantam Book Catalog

Here's your up-to-the-minute listing of over 1,400 titles by your favorite authors.

This illustrated, large format catalog gives a description of each title. For your convenience, it is divided into categories in fiction and non-fiction—gothics, science fiction, westerns, mysteries, cookbooks, mysticism and occult, biographies, history, family living, health, psychology, art.

So don't delay—take advantage of this special opportunity to increase your reading pleasure.

Just send us your name and address and 50¢ (to help defray postage and handling costs).